A GOAT'S SONG

Also by Dermot Healy

FICTION

Banished Misfortune
Fighting with Shadows

POETRY

The Ballyconnell Colours

Dermot Healy

A GOAT'S SONG

VIKING

VIKING
Published by the Penguin Group
Penguin Books USA Inc., 375 Hudson Street,
New York, New York 10014, U.S.A.
Penguin Books Ltd, 27 Wrights Lane,
London W8 5TZ, England
Penguin Books Australia Ltd, Ringwood,
Victoria, Australia
Penguin Books Canada Ltd, 10 Alcorn Avenue,
Toronto, Ontario, Canada M4V 3B2
Penguin Books (N.Z.) Ltd, 182–190 Wairau Road,
Auckland 10, New Zealand

Penguin Books Ltd, Registered Offices:
Harmondsworth, Middlesex, England

First American edition
Published in 1995 by Viking Penguin,
a division of Penguin Books USA Inc.

1 3 5 7 9 10 8 6 4 2

The author would like to thank his publishers in England, Harvill, and his editor, Bill
Swainson, for their support; the editors of *Ambit* and *The Picador Book of Contemporary Irish
Fiction*, in which extracts from this novel first appeared; The Society of Authors for their
Authors Foundation Award; and the Tyrone Guthrie Centre where some of this novel
was written.

Grateful acknowledgment is made for permission to reprint excerpts from
"You Can't Get a Man with a Gun" by Irving Berlin on pages 125 and 126.© Copyright
1946 by Irving Berlin. Copyright renewed. International copyright secured. Used by permission. All rights reserved.

PUBLISHER'S NOTE
This is a work of fiction. Names, characters, places, and incidents either are the product
of the author's imagination or are used fictiously, and any resemblance to actual
persons, living or dead, events, or locales is entirely coincidental.

ISBN 0-670-86156-1
CIP data available

This book is printed on acid-free paper.

∞

Printed in the United States of America
Set in Linotron Bembo

CONTENTS

I

CHRISTMAS DAY IN THE WORKHOUSE

1

Waiting for Catherine

The bad times were over at last. He stood on the new bridge that opened onto the Mullet and waited for Catherine to appear. In the side pocket of his jacket, folded into a notebook, he had her letter. Just when he'd given up hope it had arrived. *I love you and want to be with you*, she had written. The last time he'd heard her speak, her voice was a crackle of disembodiment, a screech of static over the radio on the boat. Now her words were clear and purposeful. She was coming back to him.

If only he had known earlier he would never have been plunged into such despair, nor imagined such desperate revenges as those his wounded mind concocted in his dark cottage. But that was all finished with. When he'd lifted the letter off the floor of the wet hall in Corrloch he hadn't known what to expect. The words were blurred and damp. His own name on the envelope had faded into a wash of blue ink. And even as he'd read the letter he had not taken it in.

The truth was that his first reaction was one of disbelief. He was ready for the worst as he tore open the envelope. He had steeled himself against hope. Over the time they'd been together hundreds of love letters, notes, scribbles, cards had come from Catherine and he had put them by after one reading. Only when her anger was raised to fever pitch by some argument he had started would he take note of what she had written. Only when he had forced her to admit to some disloyalty would her words leap off the page. His hunger for hurt was insatiable. But now he had to find new reserves within himself to deal with her declaration of love.

This letter was different. It was not what he had imagined. The brave words of tenderness and trust she'd written confounded him. He had expected the worst and couldn't believe that it wasn't going to happen. He even resented the fact that they could be starting over.

The letter he had been expecting would have told him the relationship was really over. Instead this brief, tender missal of love had arrived. *I'm sorry I didn't get to see you. It was wonderful to hear you over the radio on the trawler. You sounded strange. We have a break this weekend and I'll be down to see you. There are other people and we could be with them. But we know we want to be with each other. Let's grow old and sober together. Meet me at the bridge some time Saturday afternoon.* It took a great effort to separate his perspective from hers. And yet he had to enter her mind completely to believe what she'd written. Which came first he wondered: the words into which she poured her heart unashamedly, or the emotion that in a panic selected the words? She was letting go the addiction to self. She had done what they say you shouldn't, she had given herself to another person.

I just want to be with you.

Behind him sheep smudged with blue walked a low field. Out beyond was a cold stretch of sea, and boats tied up for the winter. The storm of the night before had left the beach like a bed tossed in a nightmare. He walked through the town. The lads in Belmullet were kicking a football over the ESB wires on the square. It was a Saturday afternoon. A few women were sitting in The Appetizer eating cream buns. He watched a tractor pull a trailer-load of Christmas trees up Seán America Street in the eerie December light.

Jack Ferris had been up and down Belmullet town since early Saturday morning waiting for Catherine. His black hair was pinned to his head with salt. His boots were comic and sandy. He was talking to himself.

The previous night they had docked just before the storm started and he had strolled from the pier to her summer home in Corrloch, pushed in the heavy door and on the wet mat in the hall found the letter waiting for him.

He tore it open – certain that it contained some final words of bitterness. He read it and felt blessed. He lit fires in every

4

room, swept the floors and cooked a meal for her arrival. He was saved.

He sat in the Adams' house, read from the Bible and studied a line her father had underlined in red – *to give some form to that which cannot be uttered.* He tidied the rooms. He washed the dishes she'd left behind. He swept away mouse droppings and poured disinfectant along the ledges. He sat on the small bed in Jonathan Adams' old study and read a children's Irish Grammar – *tá me, tá tu.* I am, you are. At three in the morning he walked back across the fields to his cold cottage in Aghadoon. He fed the animals in a wind that blew the milk out of the cat's bowl. The roof groaned like the keel of a ship. The thump of waves went through the floor under his bed. He had not slept. He scribbled new lines onto the text of the play. He watched the sea, put on the tilley-lamp repeatedly, re-read the letter like you'd read a train timetable to find, yes, I still have time. Any bitterness that had accrued, he let it pass. Because the comfort of her commitment was there. Yes, she'd written, *we were just denying love to ourselves. What we had wasn't love, but nostalgia for love.*

He could hear her say that word *nostalgia.* When she'd say it, his senses would rear back in alarm, then relax, for her inflexion carried all the meanings of the word – her woman's past, her childhood, her jealousies, her other lovers, her private moments – everything that was herself. *Nostalgia. Nostalgia.* It was like breathing out after holding your breath for a long time.

Next morning, he turned at the new bridge that spanned a canal linking the two waters of Broad Haven and Blacksod Bay, then retraced his steps, his elderly dog, Daisy, awkwardly skelping elbow-high alongside him on the whitewashed wall. He looked at the scaffolding that had gone up round the water-tower at the hospital. He stopped, clasped his hands in front of his chest, then rubbed the heels of his palms vigorously together. He clapped his hands; his eyes closed, and his mouth veered into a grimace. He bent his head. He opened his eyes and stood with his arms straight down by his sides, shivering.

"Catherine," he said.

* * *

Well, whatever happens, I can never live through this day again. It was the light that accompanied November into December, sheer light; with the full moon of the night before the tide had gone far out; the white sands shimmered, then grew heavy. Further sands were torched. These were short days. The black was rolling in across the sky. He greeted Joe Love, the postman, who was standing in green tweeds on Main Street. He was holding a white shopping bag. Daisy immediately began barking.

"You're looking well," said Jack.

"Sacred Heart, what's the use of it now," Joe Love replied, "since my partner's dead and gone?" The man's face breathed health and security. The brown eyes spoke lively. His head was covered with a shoal of gleaming white hair. Yet, he was saying he was alone. That encounter stayed in Jack's mind throughout the day. It was the first time Joe Love had ever mentioned this bereavement. In the early morning he came to the Adams' house, dropped the post through the letterbox in the porch door and slipped away into the mist. Spent few words. Now, in a few banal moments, dressed in his Sunday suit on a Saturday afternoon, he had told the story of his life.

"I'm waiting on Catherine," explained Jack.

"That's the thing," Joe Love said. "It's best not to be caught alone at Christmas."

He lifted a massive brown hand and patted his forehead.

"Did you have some mail for me?" asked Jack.

"I had, but whenever I call you've not been at home. You should get yourself some kind of a postbox. You can't put letters under a stone in that wild place."

"I was off in the *Blue*."

"So I dropped them into Bernie Burke's," he said.

"Now I know what's wrong," said Jack. "Bernie's been in hospital."

"Is he still away, the poor fellow?"

"Never mind, I'll get them when he returns."

"I hope it was nothing important," said Joe Love.

"No," said Jack, "no."

They said goodbye. Daisy watched Joe's dog rise off its arse and follow his master. Jack turned into the paper shop.

"How are you, Jack?" the woman asked.

"Oh, I'm waiting on Catherine," he replied. "She's due down today."

"Give her my regards," the woman said.

He immediately turned the *Irish Times* to the arts page. He entered the Erris Hotel and ordered a coffee and rang Eddie who was directing the play.

"Could I speak to Eddie?"

"Certainly. Who will I say is calling?"

"Jack Ferris," he replied.

"Ha-ho," said Eddie.

"You've started rehearsals?"

"We have."

"And Catherine's OK?"

"As I told you she would be."

"That's great. I'd love to have a look."

"Ah, we're just going to try and get a few days in before the Christmas."

"I might go up for a day or two."

"Well, that's up to you." Eddie's hesitation unnerved Jack. "There's really no need. We have your notes. It's only a matter of running it through a few times."

"I might have some changes."

"Send them on then as soon as you can," he said, reluctantly.

"I'll give them to Catherine."

"Catherine?"

"Yes, Catherine," said Jack sharply. There was a long tantalizing silence. "She's coming down today,"

"Is she?" Eddie replied with a disconcerting change of tone. "I didn't know."

"That's the way. Good luck," Jack said in an empty voice, and for fear of hearing anything that might destroy the illusion of happiness, he replaced the phone and stepped out quickly onto the street to greet a Lada which was not hers.

He hitched out to Corrloch for she might have got home without him seeing her on the road, but she was not there. He relit the fires in the Adams' house and began sweeping out the rooms

7

again. In the kitchen the hot water cylinder creaked wildly. He sat sober and correct at the kitchen table.

"It's all right," someone told him once, "when the loved one enters the subconscious. That's fine. Let them stay there. It's when they are alive and kicking in your every thought, that's when it means trouble."

He tried to put her by but she would not have it. She was as stubborn in his recreation of her as she was in real life. In her absence he felt her physical presence even more profoundly than the moment when she would actually be there in front of him. Everywhere he went he caught hints of her imminent return. He saw her expression in certain women as they approached him from a distance. Overheard her laugh on a street.

He rushed forward towards each disappointment with manic haste. His panic increased the more his expectations were confounded. This was always the way it was.

He lay on her bed and looked at the ceiling. There was a sour indoor smell of vegetables on the turn. He searched the house for the source of the smell but couldn't find it. Presently he realized he was longing for a drink.

He walked the few miles through the falling dark to Belmullet and stood at the bridge. He ordered a coffee and sat in the sun lounge of the Erris Hotel. It looked out on the street where Catherine would arrive. A country couple and a brightly dressed, middle-aged American in check trousers entered. The countryman, who was wearing a baseball cap, disengaged himself from the others and sat down by Jack.

"You have any Yanks in your family?" he asked.

"No," replied Jack.

"That's a brother of mine gone in." He nodded towards the bar.

"I see."

"Are you staying here?"

"No."

"You must have a girl," he said after a while.

"I do," Jack smiled.

"Well, then, she must be very beautiful," the man nodded

sagely. "I live up the pass with my sister. That's her gone in with him. He's just in for the Christmas holidays, God bless us. We're going out for a bite tonight, but I'll sit here with you."

Jack turned to look at him, the schoolboy face, the simple hands, the brown eyes high in the sockets and the sockets high in the head, the marvelling forehead. Jack pointed at the baseball cap. "Have you been across the water?"

"Not at all." He leaned closer and looked into Jack's eyes.

"Where are you from?" he asked.

"Leitrim."

"Holy God," he said, "they have their problems there, too. Would you like a drink?"

"No thanks," said Jack.

"You're better off. They don't tell you everything when you're drunk," and he tapped his skull.

Now, both men looked at the street through the lace curtains waiting for Catherine. Soon the man's sister loomed in the lounge. She gestured over her shoulder sharply with her thumb in that condescending, familiar manner used with someone you consider touched. Her brother looked at her a long time. There was a mild rebellion in his failure to recognize her. Behind her, the American brother hovered uncertainly.

"I'll have to go now," he said, looking at his sister.

"Goodbye," said Jack.

"Good luck, Leitrim," he replied.

He saw her on the road to the west, foot to the ground in the Lada, African freedom songs playing on the car stereo. Or with her head firmly slanted as she held the car in first at some lights.

He did not want to think of the past; she had given herself to him – perhaps there was a note of hesitation, maybe it was not complete commitment, maybe some part of her was holding back – but there was hope.

What words he could conjure seemed trite and inconsequential. How extraordinary it was that he could describe what he saw – the contents of a sun lounge or what's afoot on a village street – and yet not be able to articulate the chaotic events that

9

had thrown their lives into turmoil. These, too, had a sequence. But where do you step into a life to say: *Here it begins!*?

Some part of him had stopped on the hour. A part of him was refusing to go forward till something terrible happened. He saw the gardener at the bar.

"I met your lady friend as she was leaving town last Sunday," sneered the gardener.

"Oh yeah?"

"Yes. She was asking if you were drinking."

"What did you say?"

"What could I say?" replied the gardener.

Everyone at the bar stopped talking. Just when everything seemed possible, the nightmare had started again.

"Well I'm sober now," declared Jack.

"Is that so?" said the gardener, and he laughed.

"I think I'll go a bit further," said Jack. At that moment his sobriety seemed a small price to pay for happiness. He always thought that the price would be more ephemeral, exotic, metaphysical. He felt humiliated and debased that her love demanded something as mundane as sobriety. A few weeks had passed and he'd been sober. She, too, wherever she was, was sober. *Let us grow old and sober together.* Yes, why not. She was coming to see him. But what did it all mean? Why did it feel so trivial? How do you build from within as your identity falters? He left the hotel.

Something was wrong.

Someone had been living through all of this on his behalf – a stranger. Now he had to create something from nothing. A man. He didn't know what expression he should wear. What politics he had. Or the architecture that surrounded him. Yet once, out of habit, he walked in his shoes.

For her he must remake himself. But she had all the materials which he needed to begin.

As he sat waiting in the darkened sun lounge in the early evening, a bus disgorged a gaggle of youths and six priests onto Main Street. It had begun raining and they were drenched in the downpour. "That's a shocking evening," a priest said to

Jack. The youngsters were sent into the eating house beyond the lounge for chips and sausages. Immediately they created an uproar. The sorry-looking priests, with brandies and gins, came into the lounge. A buxom woman brought them salmon sandwiches.

"Where are you from?" Jack asked the priest nearest to him.

"Castlebar," he replied. "We are giving the altar boys of the diocese a day out."

"You didn't, by any chance, pass a Lada on the road?"

"I'm sure we passed plenty," the priest laughed.

Jack looked into his eyes. "A blue Lada. Maybe it was broken down. And a woman. She'd be wearing a black scarf."

"Not that I can remember," said the priest.

The priests hunched over their drinks in a single-minded way. Some wore old childish ganseys, others black, loosely knit vests. Here the back of a neck bulged, there it was graceful and white and reeked of a fleshly morbid sensuality. They chewed the white bread and lettuce with relish. One man, back from the missions, tanned and feral, talked of Chile, the Shining Path and Christopher Columbus while he sipped a Baileys Irish Cream. Then their conversation dropped to whispers. Jack gagged a little, and stabbed a finger into his thigh to control his stomach. His eyes watered.

"Don't look so sad, me buck," the missioner called across, "it might never happen."

The nausea made Jack swoon. He gagged again and pressed his finger deep into his thigh till the nail punctured the skin. The smell of old drink seemed to erupt from the pores of his body.

He was standing in the rain down on the Shore Road looking out at the violent sea which made no sound. Turning, he saw two dogs watching him, also silently, through a blue galvanize gate. One stood, his snout resting on his forepaws in the hole behind which the bolt is shot home. The other was stretched flat out on the cobbles so he could see under the corner of the gate. They were brown-and-white sheepdogs. Daisy lay in the middle of the road with his snout cushioned on a handful of grass and watched them. The three dogs and the man regarded each other silently.

The hotel gardener, shaking his disconsolate head and fingers, as if he were feeding birds, foundered down the road.

"How are you?" shouted Jack.

The gardener did not answer, but stopped, looked and moved on with an ironic smile.

"Don't worry about it," mumbled Jack.

Dusk was falling. The surf rose silently. Outside a pub two tractors sat with their engines running. Local girls, high-cheeked, with jet-black Spanish hair, and dressed in virgin white, spilled out of a house speaking Irish. Dusk was falling quicker. The beach, when he reached it, was possessed of a low light. The sand was a quiet phosphorescent carpet. Suds lay the landward side of the wrack.

It was Saturday night, and all the Catholics were headed for evening Mass. The old sabbath was being rejuvenated. The roads on the peninsula were lit by a convoy of trundling cars. The town was deserted, except for the hotel where the priests sat drinking, and the eating house, where the altar boys were shooting pool. An old gambling machine blinked on and off. In the distance, on the mainland, limestone glittered as if the sun were shining.

He walked a street of ruined houses, then took a short cut across the lawns of the small industrial estate. The names were floodlit – Warners (Éire) Teo, Ionad Cloch Iorrais, Ruibéar Chomhlacht Atlantach Teo, Fás. He went along a road where old shopfronts stared back with blank faces. The light from Eagle Island lighthouse swept across the sky three times. Count eight. Three times again. He stood on the new bridge. A light came on in the golf club. Nurses stepped into cars at the hospital. Standing there he listened to the alarming silence. The black sky blinked again.

"Isn't it getting late terribly early," Mrs Moloney, the receptionist, said to him when he re-entered the hotel.

"Were there any calls for me?"

"No," she said. "There was none since you last asked."

"Are you sure?"

"Yes, Jack."

"Fair enough."

He stood by the desk wondering what to do.

He went into the bar.

"Hugh."

"Jack."

"Aye."

"No sign yet?" asked Hugh.

"No," answered Jack, "that's about it."

The wind thrashed against the glass windows in the roof.

"I think I'll have a brandy."

"Why wouldn't you?"

"A brandy and crème de menthe I think."

Hugh filled a double measure.

"Good luck," Hugh said.

It was only as he entered the sun lounge that Jack became aware of the glass in his hand. He stopped on the threshold and looked at the glass and thought, how did that happen? It was as if he had been transformed into someone else, someone he had once been. Someone he disliked entirely. In his sleep on the boat he'd often dream of drinking and wake with immense relief to find that it had not happened. The glass of whiskey he'd been swallowing in some unlit room of his consciousness he'd find did not exist. Now it did. It sat whole in his hand. After his two weeks of sobriety he'd ordered a drink without thinking. If she comes now what will I do? *I'll not drink it!* He found the carpet under his feet. *I have not drunk it yet!* Holding the drink away from him he made his way to a deserted corner of the room and put the glass down at a safe distance from himself.

"There's the buck back," said one of the priests. "Call me Peter," he added. "We hear you do a bit of writing."

"I'm afraid you have the wrong man," said Jack.

If she'd been coming today, she'd have been down by now.

"Sit down with us," said Father Peter, "and give us some of your crack."

He sat down with the priests. They all sat round waiting for Catherine.

13

2

Walking the Triangle

While he slept his body had ballooned out. A calf-hide receptacle of warm blood, he lay on his side. The panic that was his first reaction, could not be smoothed away. Everything was charged with static.

He got up and dressed. His clothes stank of damp heat. Fungus had bloomed overnight on the walls. As he entered the middle room Gay Byrne's voice suddenly boomed forth speaking to a woman of some distant sexual problem. "Jesus Christ," said Jack, and switched the radio off. He threw half a mackerel from a Donegal Catch packet to the wild cat who was screaming at the door. When Daisy ran under his feet, full of earnest early-morning enthusiasm, Jack roared at him. The dog, his tail curled up under his rump, backed away into a corner of the room. "And stay there!" shouted Jack. He saw the misshapen image of his own face in the dog's black eye as the animal circled the table.

"Stop looking at me," he said to the dog. Daisy immediately turned away.

Jack spat out a globule of sick. The white fluid turned dry as if he had spat on a hot pan.

Something had happened to his mind. His consciousness had always been protected by a sieve, but while he'd slept the holes had grown larger. Now the holes were as big as cherrystones. And they were growing bigger by the minute.

He put one hand on the mantelpiece and stayed that way a few minutes. Where did Sunday go? I must have slept through it all. Then, sitting by the radio, he saw a bottle of sherry standing, the cork still half in. And tenderly he thought with a smile: I saved that for myself.

The priests left that.

The bottle was half full. He watched the bottle. If I start on that I'll never telephone. I must do it while I'm sober. It's eleven-fifteen. The first train is into Ballina. The first train has left Castlebar. She has not come. That's the position. Maybe she's been and gone. Maybe she has driven straight to the Adams' house in Corrloch and is still there. I should walk up and see. Three and a half mile to Corrloch. Six miles to Belmullet. Is she in Dublin still? What did the fucking gardener tell her? Maybe she never left. Did she have an accident? Maybe I should go there. I can't make Dublin now unless I hitch. Sometimes if you get up and go and don't think about it, you can do it. If I have to hitch, I mustn't drink.

The room was cold. The wind fierce.

He lifted her letter out of his pocket and read it.

He stood reading it, then drank from the bottle.

He filled a glass and drank and thought: She was never coming, I've been fooling myself. Then, while the alcohol sang in his head, he remembered her love pledge. He read the letter again, then walked the few miles to Corrloch across the fields, saw that her car wasn't there but knocked on the door all the same; he entered the empty house and sat in the kitchen and saw it coming, whatever it was. I should ring. And yet he didn't want to ring because he didn't want to know. He walked the five and a half miles to Belmullet town. The dog appeared from nowhere by his side. "I'm sorry about this morning, Daisy," he explained to the animal.

In the Erris Hotel he asked Mrs Moloney to put a call through to the theatre in Dublin while he ordered a gin and tonic at the bar. Immediately he had put the call through he regretted it. He went out and cancelled it. He ordered another drink. The TV was on. He read the value of the punt in sterling. He watched the flickering digits of the day's stock market prices. The TV grew abnormally large. He must have been standing there for more than an hour staring at the screen before Hugh switched it off. Then Jack sat down. His limbs stirred of themselves. His feet felt stone cold.

He put the call through again. Mrs Moloney handed him the phone.

15

"I'm sorry, Mr Ferris, Miss Adams is in rehearsal right now," came the voice.

"Could I speak to Eddie?"

"*Mr* Brady?" she said correcting him.

"Mr Brady, yes," he agreed.

"I'll see."

Jack, as he waited, smiled at Mrs Moloney.

"Jack?" said Eddie.

"Is Catherine there?"

Pause. "Yes, she is."

"Can I speak to her?"

"Look, Jack, I don't know what's happening between you two, but she has refused to come to the phone."

"I was expecting her down here at the weekend."

"I know nothing about that. It's best to leave her alone, I'd think, at present. It'll sort itself out."

"She wrote to say she was coming, but she never came."

"I would know nothing about that."

"Tell her I'm still waiting."

"I will."

"Tell her I'm sober." Then he added, "Tell her I'm sorry."

"I will."

"Eddie," he said, hating the whinge in his voice. "Will you please ask her to speak to me?"

"Look, Jack, you are putting me in a terrible position. I don't want to interfere."

"Will you ask her?"

"I'll try. Will you hold?"

Jack pulled his stomach muscles taut to smother a wave of nausea. A long time passed.

"She's refused to come to the phone."

"Did she say why?"

"I shouldn't expect her to tell me."

"Tell her I need to talk to her."

"Look, Jack, we are in rehearsal."

There was silence for a few seconds.

"Jack, leave it for a few days. We've just begun. Wait till we've settled in a bit, OK?"

16

"I'm coming up."

Pause. "I can't stop you."

"Ask her to speak to me," came out of his mouth like a screech.

"I'm sorry, Jack."

The line went dead.

He put the receiver down. Mrs Moloney, who was wiping down tables in the foyer, looked at him. Embarrassed he paid her for the call. "I have no luck with phones," he explained cheerfully.

The minute he entered the bar a cold light came on in his head. Is this what it is like? Will it happen now?

The air was filled with dark threads of hair. He refocused his eyes.

Some local men, the gardener among them, came in and chatted jovially. They did not look in his direction. He wanted to speak to them but didn't. He could feel the hostility. He ordered a double sherry.

"And put it in a lemonade glass."

"Right," said Hugh. "Do you want to speak to anyone at sea?" he asked in a conspiratorial voice. As he twisted the knob on the illegal two-wave radio a jumble of German and Russian voices came in from the Atlantic. "There's none of us out there in this weather, anyway."

After a while he drank a brandy. A gin. Which one is it will bring us over the whatever-it-is? The what-do-you-call-it. Keep moving! By then a red wedding carpet had been thrown along the garden path and in through the front door. It led to a table where sherry glasses stood brimful, awaiting the bride and groom. On his way to the toilet Jack asked the lad for one.

"I'm a guest," Jack said.

"Is that so?"

"That's right. Just pour it in there," and Jack proffered the lemonade glass. But the lad gave him none through some misunderstanding that was beyond Jack. In the toilet he placed the lemonade glass on the pink-tiled window ledge and retched violently. I'm not getting any better, he thought.

The gardener came in and combed his hair.

"Vanity is lost on you, squire," said Jack, recovering himself.

"You don't look so good yourself, boss." The gardener skimmed a grey lock across his weatherbeaten skull, shook his member generously and spat into the urinal.

"Why," Jack asked, "are thoroughbreds put into horseboxes on their own?"

"I don't know," the man said, without looking at him.

"It's for the same reason," replied Jack, laughing hysterically, "that cardinals wear tall hats."

The gardener considered Jack and said: "I'd have a long rest if I was you."

A lot of people have sat like me, thought Jack, throughout the world, their hearts stopped on the half-hour, and soot falling.

He was overflying the place he was in. He filled a glass with vodka, and put it under his chair. He wrote into his notebook. Then he searched round for his glass. When he drank he was surprised to find it was vodka in the glass. He could've sworn it would be sherry. Then he was equally surprised to find he was back in the Adams' house. I should not be here, he thought. This is not home.

I'm in the wrong fucking house, for the wrong fucking reason. How the fuck did I get here? Where did Sunday go? He looked round him in alarm and the recollection of other days spent in those rooms flooded through him. Sitting there, well removed from her, he again felt her mind entering his. He jumped to his feet. I have to get out of here! As he walked up the street in Corrloch he found he still had a mouthful of vodka kept in a ball on his tongue. He stopped outside the prefab primary school with its red chairs, painted flowers and multicoloured maps of the world. Watched by the children inside, he stood hitching, but when the first vehicle that came did not stop he started walking.

Again he was on the road to Belmullet in an east wind. He passed the turning for Aghadoon and thought of going home. He passed the Church of the Holy Family – a ball-alley of red girders – and stood a moment thinking. He continued on. The wind howled through the shuttering on the new mushroom-shaped water towers. A plane from Knock airport flew over the town towards America as he entered the hotel. Guiltily he stood in the foyer and watched the gardener ascend a ladder to change a light bulb. Very uncertain of himself he searched through his pockets for change. He had none. He rang the theatre, reversing the charges. The call was refused.

"Try again," he told the operator. "My name is F–E–R–R–I–S, Jack," he said angrily spelling his name out.

"I can try."

Then he overheard the girl in the theatre say that she was not to allow any calls through to the rehearsal room.

"I'm sorry," said the operator.

"Tell her," said Jack, "that I'm the author of the bloody play." Another few seconds silence.

"I think," said the operator, "that she is aware of that."

"Jesus Christ," he said.

"Excuse me," said the operator, and she rang off. Jack smiled across at Mrs Moloney and carried on talking into the void. "Catherine," he said, "it's good to hear from you. How are things?" He listened with a false laugh to imagined replies. "Great! Great!" he said and chuckled cheerfully into the receiver. He spoke of spring, politics, and wished everyone well. And hoped – he was smiling up at the gardener – to see them all soon. "See you on opening night," he said expansively. "There you are now," he said to Mrs Moloney, as he replaced the phone. "It was as easy as that."

Each day he walked over the fields or took the road from his isolated cottage in Aghadoon to the Adams' house in the village of Corrloch and from there took the road back again to Belmullet town and the Erris Hotel. It was a bewildering triangle. Sometimes he was on the road for hours. And on the roads the people gave him that look that people give when they think they're safe. He has it – he has the disease!

Hypocrites, he'd murmur. And yet he knew there can be no more pitiful sight than those who are defeated in love. He was an object of pity and therefore to be avoided. He had become the very thing he despised – a man obsessed with his own misfortune. And yet each afternoon he found himself on the bridge looking with a beating heart towards the mainland.

He dreamed he was about some business in the yard with a torch, moving bags of bottles through a tentative dusk-light, when she beckoned him from the kitchen door. He found that he was standing in his pyjamas. Jack dropped the spanner, checked the sky and went in.

She sat and looked at him. "Have you come back to me?" he asked. She nodded. "It's very sensible here," she said. She looked with admiration round his small house. He knelt beside her and she began to look quite practical, the way women do when they know there's pleasure ahead. Her eyes had a bright, knowing light. Jack needed to rest his head in her lap. "I'm so glad to see you," he said, and he leaned forward to rest his head. Then the blur, increasing its soft outlines, troubled him again. "Catherine, Catherine," he said, but she kept silent, afraid maybe of argument, of saying the wrong things, of committing herself.

Then some part of his consciousness began, against his will, to stand aside.

He woke to find himself crying in a shocking free manner. Her visit had been so unbelievably real that for a long time he fought against returning to the waking world. The sheds were lit by a violet dawn light. Eagle Island sent out its three flashes. He tuned the radio to popular songs, and lay in the bed, his head upright, listening intently.

Someone shouted his name in the late afternoon, and hammered at the door. He heard the dog barking. Jack pulled on a pair of jeans. He opened the door. The dog raced into the room. The wind was screeching. He opened the door wider. There was no one there. He stepped round to the gable. There stood Hugh, the chef and barman from the Erris Hotel, and his wife Isobel.

"Yes?" said Jack.

"You asked me to call," said Hugh.

"Oh that's right," he mumbled.

"You have the place looking well."

"Inside is a mess."

He shook Isobel's hand. "I couldn't invite you in with the house the way it is."

"Let us give you a hand to clean it up," said Isobel.

They walked by him into the kitchen. He stood there uncertain of what to do. They had come in the midst of one of his reveries of despair to which he wanted badly to return. Isobel washed cups. Hugh fed the dog while Jack sat by the empty grate.

"You don't look well," said Isobel.

"What's wrong with me!"

She glanced at the red sore in the white of his eye that looked like a dash of Tabasco sauce, she took in the black matted hair, the dirty fingernails, the white cheeks. "Have you been eating?"

"I can't bring myself to eat." He indicated the bottles. "I was drinking with priests from Castlebar."

"That will happen," nodded Hugh. "I remember a few years ago I got off a boat in Killybegs and I ended up drinking with Russians."

"Russians?"

"Russians are serious."

"In the next few years we are going to have a lay church," said Jack, unexpectedly. "Did the Russians tell you that?"

"No," said Hugh.

"That's what the priests told me."

"That's a good thing to know," said Isobel uneasily.

They sat there in the cold watching the fire take.

"Are you all right?" she asked.

"I'd like to know," he explained, "why she didn't come. I'd like to know what kept her away."

"I'm sure she had her reasons," said Isobel.

"Then why did she write to me, hah?" he said angrily.

As they were getting into the car he said: "Don't go yet. Give me a few minutes and I'll take a lift with you."

They carried bags of bottles to the front wall. Then they took a bag of rubbish and burned it in a steel rain barrel at the end of the field. The smoke went flying across Gleann Thomáis.

The fire was still burning as they hurried in the car through the failing light to Belmullet. "The truth is," said Jack, "that I've been fooling myself. She was never coming."

"I'm sorry to hear that," said Hugh.

A Christmas tree had been erected in a corner of the hotel. Bells jingled on the toilet door. Hugh appeared behind the bar. Thady, full as a tick from drink, sauntered in. Jack ordered a drink and paid for it with money he had secreted in his top-right shirt pocket.

"Wild day," he said to the gardener.

A Derry couple, who had arrived to the Mullet Peninsula for Christmas, joined Jack. They sat down at his table after Thady left. Jack was glad they did because Northerners understood drunkenness. They seemed not to notice that Jack was very drunk. He found it hard to keep his eyes open. His throat was hot. The man began explaining to Jack how the Catholics of Derry had had enough of the Provisionals. If they ever get power, he was saying, he would be the first up the coast to kill him – the man at the top.

"Can we talk of something else?" asked Jack.

"There's Catholics hate him," he said. "We know who he is."

"I don't know that we should talk about it."

"We know who he is," the man continued. "We know the very house he stays in when he comes over to Donegal."

"I took you to be a peaceful man," said Jack.

"I never said I was against violence, did I, Sue?" he replied. "The Northerner is by nature a military man. We are reared to it. When you were playing with your dick I was learning how to use a –"

"That's nice," interrupted Sue. "That's really nice".

"I know him," he continued. "I know where the car turns, what gear the driver will be in on the hill. I know my Donegal. I may not know Mayo, but I know Donegal. At the end of the day someone has to take him." He drank. "The Donegals are soft. Fuck. And they make him welcome. They do not know the real man. I know him," he said. "I know what he stands for."

"So do I," said Jack. "I taught him Irish for a while."

The wife gave a scream of laughter.

"Oh, you're a laugh," she said.

"You think you know him," the man continued undeterred, "but you don't know us. When we drive over the border into the South something sacred happens. Something holy. We are safe for a while. But if he gets to power, we are not safe. If I have to go up to Belfast, I'll kill him," he said in a quiet obsessive voice, and both of them looked at his wife who had gone to the bar.

He lifted his gin and tonic. He was thirty, fresh-faced, and had lived a couple of lifetimes. His wife, small and dark and pertly over-dressed, came back from the bar smiling. She put a drink in front of Jack. He thanked her.

"The Provos have used our house twice to kill. So we've moved twice. Both houses were used, can you believe that? Now we're in a new place on the border with Derry. We are starting a new life. But I know a gun. The insides of a gun. And if I have to, I will. I won't walk around in fear. The Donegals think he's a great fellow. I know different. They just want to help us Northerners and they think he stands for justice. They're wrong. I'll take him the day he comes to power. Believe me, Mister. And I don't intend to wing him, no. The Catholics, never mind the Protestants, have had enough."

For a while the three of them sat facing forward, saying nothing as the bar filled up.

"I love this place," said Sue, turning to Jack.

"They say you grow used to it," replied Jack.

"Never!" she exclaimed and she shook her head. He found her eyes on his. "What do you do?" she asked.

"Years ago I went on to be a doctor."

She laughed in disbelief.

"Now I'm a fisherman," he admitted.

"That's more like it," she said and then the three of them resumed their watch.

"Of course, the Republic is soft like that," ruminated the husband. "They feel guilty. Who wouldn't."

"I have to go to the toilet," said Jack.

23

And when he returned he explained: "I'm having trouble, myself, with a woman."

"Is she a feminist?" asked Sue. "Because if she is I don't want to hear about her. Don't talk to me of women's rights. They'd have you believe a woman can't be violent. I've heard enough of that till I'm sick." She drank. "There's something greater wrong and no one will own up to it. Am I right?"

"You're right," said her husband.

"The Provos tied us up in the kitchen," she continued. "We were there for hours. There was only one gun – "

"The first time it was a Lee Enfield .303 mark 1 with sights," the husband interrupted. "The second time it was a Lee Enfield .303 mark 2 with sights and a light intensifier. Things had improved in the meantime. It had a calibrated barrel, I'd swear, and a stock made to measure." He thought back, "About sixteen inches."

"It was a Lee Enfield with sights and they'd settled for our bedroom. I could hear their every move above my head. The window must have given them a clear view. Hours went by. There wasn't a sound. We just waited."

"Same as them," said her husband.

"Then, when it came, it didn't sound like a shot."

"They never do."

"It was like someone had dropped an egg. I thought I'd only imagined it. Then the three lads went by us. They untied us. They even apologized. 'You can give us two hours,' they said. But within a half an hour came the policemen. A soldier had been killed in Rake's Avenue."

"Corporal Wilson," said the husband. "He took it in the head."

"Considering what had happened in our house," she continued, "they were not bad to us, the police."

"I saw his name in the papers. He was Manchester, wasn't he, Sue?"

"He was Manchester all right. Derek Wilson I think it was." She drank. She caught Jack's eye, then looked away. "I couldn't bear to sleep in our room after that," she added.

The bar was filling up with men in brightly coloured clothes and local women in white skirts and trousers and white shirts, and belts slipped at the waist so that they hung towards the groin. The gardener was drinking alone though surrounded by people. Once the gardener had turned and said to Jack: "You don't fool me!" Now he was pinned in by all the newcomers yet he took no notice of them. He was a constant man, round-shouldered, soft, and his legs were wrapped round the stool like a young boy's.

"Are you high?" she asked

"I am," Jack replied.

"He's high," Sue told her husband.

He nodded, went to the bar and called a round. He returned without the drinks. Jack went up to get them, and ordered another round. He searched in his pockets but found he had no money left.

"You wouldn't have the lend of a tenner?" he asked the gardener.

"You must be joking," he said.

"I didn't think so. Will you put it down to me, Hugh?"

"Your friend owes for one as well."

"It's getting confusing," said Jack. Then he found the money in the pocket of his shirt. He paid Hugh and returned to the couple. "This is your round, I think," he said, "and this is mine."

"Aren't they the same either way?" said the husband.

"Except that one is paid for and one is not."

"Which one is not paid for?"

"Yours."

"Right. I'll look after that. Then tomorrow we'll drive down round Blacksod Bay."

"I like it here," Sue told Jack. "I really do."

Jack asked him what trade he was in.

"Fireplaces," he replied.

"Fireplaces?" asked Jack.

"Have you heard of Grampian rock?"

"Jack would not understand you," his wife said.

"It looks good," explained the man.

"I can't believe it when I wake in the mornings and see the

sand dunes from my bed," she continued. "Then I hear the sea. I can actually feel the waves. It's beautiful. It's beautiful, isn't it?"

"Sure," agreed her husband.

"You'd want for nothing," she smiled as she imitated the Southern accent. "I know," she continued, "what it is like to feel disorientated. Most of the time I feel out of this world."

Jack passed the night being led cheerfully through all that had happened to her: who had died, what she'd seen; while her husband, on cue, filled in the facts, the concrete details. If Catherine was here, he thought, she'd despise him. A sense of how Catherine would hate him sitting here drinking and enjoying the random world swept through him. She'd have left long ago. Her negativity returned to him and it stirred in his consciousness like a malignant spirit. As the woman spoke, he thought of Catherine. His empathy for the couple felt sacrilegious, and his genial drunkenness profane.

"You can't sit on the stile," said Jack.

"What's he talking about?"

"Never mind him," she told her husband, "he's high."

Next morning he went outside to shout for the dog. Through the breeze came the stink of piss. He stood against the gable of the small cottage and tried to remember anything that might save him. A low mist was swirling along Gleann Thomáis. On the other side the white sea was floundering on Seagull's Rock. Salt fell in the garden. And his great wonder was – would Catherine, wherever she now was, think of him? Would she be able to look back without pointing the finger of blame?

He was standing at the gable, and someone brushed by him and entered the cottage. She was sitting there in judgment on his mind. As he might at this moment be sitting in hers. He walked directly to Belmullet and from the post office phoned the theatre.

"Could I speak to Catherine Adams?" he asked, businesslike.

There was silence a while, then a muffled conversation. He whistled tunelessly, then like a man making an obscene phone call he started whispering into the receiver.

3

A Taxi Through New York
at Midnight

Jack took the bus to Ballina, from where he intended to catch
the train to Dublin. His intention was to go to the theatre, stand
outside it for a while and hope to catch sight of her. There
would be no argument. No. If she spoke to him, then he'd
reply. If she didn't, he'd return to Mayo. It would be as simple
as that. It would be enough for her to see him standing there.

Yet the minute he stepped on the Ballina bus his scheme
foundered. He could not envisage himself ever reaching Dublin.
He thought he was living through a nightmare that would soon
end, like all the others did. But it didn't. With each day he was
being pushed deeper under until he'd make a decision to change
everything. What was the point? He was no longer able to
control the darkness. But *darkness* was too broad a word for
what was overwhelming him, as was *overwhelming* the wrong
word, as all words were the wrong words when they had not
been lived in. Everything, in fact, was happening in lurid techni-
color. The wall that separated him from everyone was growing
higher and more impenetrable. Reality had been a small window
at the end of a dark corridor. Now a wall had gone up in front
of the window. It was a skin-coloured wall.

He had lived in his body and now it was the wrong body.
His body, errant and sickly, was what controlled his mind, and
ultimately the language that mind expressed itself in.

For the first time, after all the sleepless nights, he considered
the word illness, which led to the word disease, which led to
the phrase *failure of the imagination*. For the first time in his life
he had a slight insight into what the word *imagination* might
mean. To live on in a different world, to transcend, to enter a

new story. As they passed through Crossmolina he realized that it was not going to happen.

I am diseased, he thought.

And he felt – my God – how vulnerable people are, how short their stay in consciousness really is, and how the self they think they know they take for granted. He was maddened by the other passengers, how their identities remained comfortable and intact while his careered around him. Everything he did seemed a betrayal of the truth, while they surveyed the world, uninhibited, sure of themselves, without a hint of the fact that consciousness was something visited on people.

This was going to be a bad day. He could feel it. He could end up anywhere. He should have stopped at home.

Suddenly, Jack was swept into the panic of non-being. He looked round at the vigilant passengers. He clamped his feet on the floor and made his hands into fists. The interior of the bus was a chute along which he would be swept if he did not hold on.

Passing a church, a few passengers in front crossed themselves. And though Jack did not, still he did, secretly, in a psychic mime where a finger touched the forehead, the two shoulders, the heart. He might even have raised a rosary to his lips.

I exist, mumbled Jack. I can pray.

We can't say we don't exist, for we do. Each stronger in the other's mind than in our own. But that was the mind on a good day. The distant cure, the harmony we seek as lost souls. But on the bad days? It was getting difficult for him to stay long in his body. To carry it around normally. To reach out for things. To know his body belonged to him. That when habit said sit, his body would sit. That if he looked to his left it would be for a reason. And when he'd look he must know the reason why. Yet there was always some perverse self-consciousness that made the simple command unreasonable. Every move he made he questioned. He was fighting against a lifetime's habits. Every thought he had was suspect. He felt all his actions were false, masks behind which he imitated and observed normality. That meant he was false, playing to an audience. But the chief member of the audience was missing – Catherine.

He himself it was – before he met Catherine – judged what

28

was right and what was wrong. He it was had accepted that these were his hands and these his knees. Now they looked like someone else's. Then the panic began again, for the mind, outside the body, did not wish to deny the body.

He looked through the bus window. He wiped away his breath, but what lay beyond could not be identified. Even the surface of the oncoming road was a great mystery. It was hard to believe that a few days ago he had been filled with happiness at the prospect of Catherine's return. His heart raced as they turned a corner. Fear made the mind settle into the body again, to protect its instrument; he held the seat in front of him; they swung out over the white line, they rose into the air over a bump on a small bridge, then the bus righted itself again.

The physical sickness was itself a reprieve. This will be soon over. It will soon end. And another voice said, Never. You will have to live with this. Forever! The doctrine of endless torments. The unseen world where his misgivings began. *And I will put enmity between thee and the woman, and between thy seed and her seed; it shall bruise thy head, and thou shalt bruise his heel.* He felt his face to see whether all his features were still in place. But touch would not reassure him. He needed to see. His eyes needed to see themselves. And yet he longed to rest from this ceaseless activity of naming the parts of the mind. He wanted to close his eyes and let his body be free of this constant surveillance.

They entered the last stretch of road before Ballina.

I'll never make Dublin if I feel like this! He looked out of the windows but found for a second that nothing he saw was familiar. They stopped for a flock of sheep, haphazardly dabbed with green, to pass. The sheep wandered one behind the other into a field of standing stones. Then, as if someone had reassembled the landscape, it ceased to be strange. I know this bit, he realized. I recognize here. He nodded at someone across the aisle.

"There's not far to go," Jack called in a strangely cheerful voice.

"And then, bless us," complained the woman, "we'll have to do the same journey all over again on the return."

He looked at her aghast.

"Are you under pressure?" she asked with a small curtsy of her eyes and mouth.

"It's severe, Ma'am," he smiled.

She nodded in reply, then nodded again, and her face filled with sympathy and quiet satisfaction.

In Ballina it was cold. At the entrance to the town a girl, half-dressed, was tied to a pole. A light drizzle, turning to sleet, was falling. Out of the pub opposite women came and began pelting the girl with plastic bags of soot.

"Christ!" said Jack.

"She's to be married," his neighbour explained. "She's a Mullarkey girl from Muinguingane."

"Oh."

The girl bent her head and jerked sharply at the ropes ,that held her. Her blouse in the fracas had been torn so now she had a breast full of soot. Her skirt rode up round her thighs. She was drenched. Quick as it happened it was over. All the women, laughing, returned to the pub.

She did not go with them, but seemed to disappear into some hole in Jack's memory. One minute she was being showered with soot, the next minute the ropes that held her swung in the wind, the wet soot lay round the pole, but she, who a second before had been distraught and hysterical with laughter, was gone.

The rain fell loudly.

As he walked the town, he was followed by the sound of coins tumbling, extraterrestrial sounds and muffled explosions. Unlit Christmas stars and coloured bulbs hung above the streets. A small, dark-skinned fat man, bowed over so that his chin was tucked into his chest, came towards him pulling a suitcase on wheels. The man stepped out of the rain into the doorway beside Jack. He had enormous old-fashioned glasses behind which his mischievous eyes were perked up in elaborate gaiety. He turned his head sideways and looked at Jack.

"The best film I see in a while was *Crocodile Dundee*," he said.

"You go to the pictures?" asked Jack.

"Oh the young women love me," he told Jack. "They like to gee-gee with me," he smiled. "The Irish women like the Jew."

He asked Jack to pull his suitcase for him. He was eighty years of age and had been selling parts for spectacles round Ireland since the Second World War. Jack walked ahead pulling the case while the old man, unabashed, followed behind describing his unbelievable sexual conquests. He held up a hand to stop the traffic. "The Irish," he told Jack in the middle of the street, "lack self-esteem," and the two of them trundled forward. They continued up another sidewalk through shoppers hurrying between showers. "Over there," said the old man, and they crossed the road again. They had reached a bed-and-breakfast. The Jew handed him a brown paper bag containing two ham sandwiches.

"Take these, please," he said.

Jack took the bag. The Jew entered the hallway. He stood on the battered lino talking to himself, then headed off down the corridor trailing his case. Jack stepped up onto a weighing scale that stood in the doorway of a chemist's shop. He dropped a five-pence piece into the slot and watched the hand swing to nine and a half stone. First he thought, I've lost a stone, and then he thought, as he looked at the hand quivering round the figures, that's me, that's the weight of a human body. That's who I am.

He was putting off the moment when he would go into the pub. It was the type of day when anything might happen. The warning signals were there. The distorted perspective, the disturbing thoughts, the loud voice of his consciousness. He went to a draper's and bought a shirt and a pair of trousers. I need shoes, thought Jack. "I've been wearing the same pair of boots for the last two years," he said. "Well, that's no good," replied the assistant. "Go across the street to Burke's. Here," he said, "you forgot your lunch." He handed Jack the sandwiches. Jack stood in a doorway again. More people hurried by.

The sleet turned to snow. Then sleet again. Then hail. The hail blew down the street bouncing like popcorn. Slush, thrown up by cars, followed. He counted his money. If I buy shoes I'll have nothing left for a drink. I can't go up looking like this. He stood in a doorway looking across at Burke's shoe shop. This morning I made a promise to myself. But what's the point? I'm going to die anyway. But who would I like to meet on resurrection day? *Who would I like to find by my side?* The thought unnerved him. The wind changed direction and blew frantically to and fro. When he was wet and cold enough he went into the nearest pub. But he didn't drink there. Nor in the pub after that. No, he was looking for someone. In the third pub he was looking for no one, but found instinctively that he was. This is what I'm doing here, he reminded himself – looking for someone. The men drinking there watched him for a second as if they, too, understood – that you keep searching till you find the right place to begin the day's drinking.

He sat down, thinking he had reached the place. He put his hand in his pocket to search for money. When he looked up each face had grown pale and ignorant and hostile. Then indifferent. Each was cocooned, not a human soul stirred among them. It was as if there was nobody there.

"I was looking for someone," he said to the barman and left, taking care as he did not to walk into anything.

He moved on with the drinker's ploy for fending off the first drink. The first drink that must be taken when all the signs are right. But none of the pubs was right. Loud TVs, piped music, strange glances. Eventually, in the fourth pub, he found that someone he was searching for. That someone who was no one. The person who didn't exist was an excuse to move on. But here, in the low light, that non-person was.

He stayed in the fourth pub because he recognized the girl who had been covered in soot and tied to the pole. Now she was sitting with three other women at the bar drinking hot whiskey.

Jack was glad to see her again.

"I'm in mourning," he said.

"Are you all right?" she asked.

"I've been pissing balls," he replied, "and I keep them back in my room. I keep them in little bags."

"We had a brother went like you," she said.

He ordered his first drink. "I like a Harvey's Bristol Cream for breakfast."

"Is that so?"

"I like the taste in the nose."

"Do you want to join us?"

"Nah," he said, "I'm getting the train to Dublin."

They drank. The old feeling of being a camera returned. He panned the bar. He focused on the women with their hair piled and blow-dried who sat around him. Cuff links gleamed. Men lifted drinks to their lips. It's a B-movie, that's what my subconscious is, and he laughed.

"Tell us the joke," said the bride-to-be. "You remind me of my da."

"He'd be a Mullarkey," said Jack, "from Muinguingane."

The camera closed in on her face. Unabashed, she stared back.

"How do you know?" she asked.

"That would be telling," he said.

"Go on," she said.

Little pods of soot stood like flecks of rain on her lashes and brows and in the corners of her eyes. The corners were inordinately exposed. What holds the eye in tension so that it can see? Her eyes closed as she waited for his reply. The darkness seemed to last a long time.

He sat into a taxi in New York. He was quite happy to find the warm upholstery against his back.

"How long have you been driving taxis?" he asked the figure behind the wheel.

"This is not a taxi," the man replied.

"I've always wanted to go in a taxi through New York," said Jack, looking at the city.

The man replied with words Jack could not understand. They passed beneath high buildings, and arcades lit up, and small ponds that were behind dark trees. A brilliant sign for GINGS, UNDERTAKERS, sped by. Jack continued to talk away about America. Kafka never went, you know, he said. Is that so? asked the chauffeur. No, said Jack. It just goes to show you, said the chauffeur. Yes, said Jack, but he got there still the same. For you see, explained Jack, time is not linear. It does not go in straight lines. Indeed it does not, agreed the driver as he

33

flicked a light on his wide and shining instrument panel. That's not to say it's cyclical either, continued Jack. No, the man nodded. It goes, said Jack, leaning forward, in stops and starts. That's right, said the chauffeur.

Eventually the taxi pulled in. The man came round, still wearing his light blue chauffeur's outfit, and opened the door. Thank you, said Jack grandly. He got out awkwardly. He was very tired. And must have slept a little. Because now he saw that the chauffeur was not a chauffeur at all. The policeman led him into the barracks.

"I found him sleeping out on the side of the road," said the guard to an orderly who was standing in a wide blue shirt.

"I wasn't sleeping," said Jack, "I was hitching home."

"He was lying stretched out on the side of the road and could have been run over," said the guard.

"I was hitching," said Jack. Then he added. "I might have sat down." He thought again. "No one was stopping."

"Where were you going?" asked the orderly.

"I was going to Belfast."

"Were you now?"

"Yes I was."

"Well, son," said the guard, "if you were going to Belfast, you were on the wrong road."

Jack reconsidered, then he remembered. "I'm sorry," he said, "I was actually going to Dublin."

"That's a horse of a different colour."

"I must have missed the train."

"I'd say you did. It's three in the morning."

"I'm charging him with being drunk in a public place," said the guard.

"Right." The orderly was taking out a clean sheet and about to write down the details of what happened when the sergeant appeared.

"That's Jack Ferris," declared the sergeant. "From Kilty."

"That's right," said Jack, gratefullly.

"That's the playwright," he said.

"That's right," said Jack.

"You live only two doors up from me. We're neighbours at home."

"That's right," said Jack, "Can I make a phone call?"

"Fire away."

"You see," explained Jack, "the woman might be worried."

So while the guard explained where Jack had been found, Jack dialled the theatre. In the far distance he heard a recorded voice repeating the times of various shows. "Catherine," he said, "can you pick me up?" – he swung round to look at the group of policemen – "I'm in the Garda station in Ballina." He listened a moment over the phone. "That's a pity."

"I'm afraid she can't come," he said, replacing the receiver.

"Never mind," said the sergeant. "We'll drive you home."

The guard who had wanted to arrest him sheepishly led him out to the squad car and Jack sat into the back. The sergeant got in behind the wheel. The guard sat silently in the passenger seat. Then the orderly closed the barracks and sat in beside Jack.

"I'll be glad of the spin," he said. "We're not expecting trouble tonight anyway."

"It's all for the sake of art," said the Leitrim man. "Where do you live?"

"Mullet."

"Fuck me," said the sergeant.

Dawn was breaking on the Atlantic when the squad car pulled in at the gate that opened onto the path that led to his bare back wall.

"You live here?" asked the sergeant.

"I do."

"Fuck me," said the sergeant.

"Here," said the guard, "you forgot these," and he handed Jack the two sandwiches in the sodden brown paper bag.

He lay on his bed for an hour. A storm had started. He got up, still drunk, and left three feeds for the dog alongside the gable. He sipped a cup of tea and imagined the first drink he would have. It might be a gin. It might be a tequila. It was eight in the morning when he set off for Dublin again. This time he arrived in the city near two in a newspaper van. He went

35

directly to the theatre through streets that were filled with reindeer and bells and Christmas music.

But he did not stand outside waiting for Catherine to make her appearance. Instead, he strode through the foyer past the girl at the desk, who followed behind calling him back. He fled up a deep-carpeted stairs, ran past walls of portraits of old actors and playwrights, and then on through the theatre itself. He found his way backstage by instinct to the rehearsal rooms. Through the door he could hear some actor intoning lines of dialogue that were his. He stood and listened and then flung open the door. Immediately everything stopped. The actors swung round to look at him and Eddie turned, irritated, script in hand, to banish whoever it was.

"I tried to stop him," exclaimed the girl.

A doorman, breathing heavily, ran in.

"Ha-ho!" said Jack shrilly and he took a seat.

"Come with me, son." said the doorman.

"It's all right," said Eddie. "This is Mr Ferris. This is our playwright."

The cast, bewildered by his appearance, turned to look at Jack Ferris. His eyes were nervous and exhausted, the black hair turning grey was swept back so tight to his head that the bones of his forehead gleamed like horns. The laces on his mud-caked army boots were hanging askew. The zip on the fork of his jeans came to half-way. He was wearing a bright-red jumper under a green oilskin coat that had one ripped pocket.

"Ha-ho!" he said. The girl nervously withdrew while the doorman held the door ajar for her.

"OK, everyone take a break," said Eddie.

He approached Jack warily.

"I brought you some more revised pages," said Jack pulling a bundle of sheets from under his jumper.

Eddie took them without comment.

Jack looked at the actors who had gathered embarrassed round a kettle and some paper cups.

"Would you like to go some place where we can talk in private?" Eddie asked.

"Here will do nicely, thank you." He watched the actors

36

regain their composure. They started to chat as if he wasn't there.

"Where's Catherine?" he asked.

"She's free today."

"That's a coincidence."

Eddie held the revised pages uneasily. "Look, Jack, I don't want an argument."

"There will be no argument. I wanted to see her, that's all – if she was here. If she's not here, fine. I just came to deliver the new text."

Relieved, Eddie skimmed through the handwritten notes.

"What do you think?" Jack asked.

"I'll need time. There's an awful lot of changes here."

"Don't you think it makes for a better script?"

"If you say so."

He continued to read the pages. "Lots of this we have already rehearsed. We've moved it, it's all nearly done." Then he placed the pages into his script. "I'll look at it later, OK?" They sat there a while in silence.

"I was thinking of sitting in on a few rehearsals."

"In the circumstances, I'd rather you didn't."

"Is Catherine of that opinion?"

"It's my choice. And I don't want you talking to the actors."

Again came the silence. "Would you like a cup of tea?"

"No," said Jack. "I think I'll go. I just wanted to make sure you got that stuff." He stood. "I'll send the others on."

"Thank you, Jack."

"Good luck," he shouted to the cast.

Embarrassed they mumbled greetings in reply. The girl followed him with her eyes as he walked through the foyer. The doorman opened the door but kept his eyes aloft. "Thank you," said Jack. He went into a bar down the street, and found a place where he had the theatre under view. He stayed there watching the front door and everyone that came and went, but Catherine did not appear.

At five Eddie and the rest of the cast came out. With a sick feeling he wondered what he should do. Then he saw that Eddie was heading straight for the pub he was in.

He heard the door swing open. Now what?

"Jack – you didn't go back," he said.

"Not yet."

"Can I get you a drink?"

"I'll have something small. A whiskey. I have a train to catch."

"Look," Eddie said, leaning towards him, "you're going through a bad time. I understand that."

"Did you read the new pages?"

"And you look dreadful." He laid the script on the bar. "No, I didn't read them."

"Why not?"

"I didn't have time."

"Tell her I just want one word with her."

"Sober up. Go home and rest a few days."

"I can't rest."

"You only think that. One day you'll look back on this and wonder why you acted so stupid."

"You think so?"

"Yes, I do." Eddie wearily handed back the handwritten notes to Jack. "You'd better take these with you."

"Why?"

"They belong to another play. They don't belong to this play."

Jack drank the whiskey.

"I thought you didn't read them?"

"I'd be grateful if you made no more phone calls to the theatre," Eddie continued, "and interrupted no more rehearsals."

"I'm out of my head with grief," said Jack.

They sat in silence.

"I thought you were my friend."

"I am. That's why I'm trying to keep you out of the way. Do you need some more money?" Jack looked at him. "How much do you need?"

"I need a hundred."

"Here's a cheque for two."

He wrote out the cheque and Jack put it in his shirt pocket and took a taxi to the railway station. From there he shared a table on the westbound train with a Westmeath nurse who worked in St John of God's hospital for the insane.

Some days later, after making a light meal in the cottage, Jack lay down on the bed, brought Catherine to mind and settled his member in the palm of his hand. He was feeling sexually wild. Just then the gardener's face appeared at the window. He was standing shading his forehead with his hand, the better to see into the unlit room. Then he moved on. Startled, Jack pulled his trousers up and swung his feet onto the floor. He went to the window.

By then the face had disappeared.

He went out through the kitchen and opened the front door to find an elderly Irish playwright of the absurd standing there with his wife. Jack looked askance at them.

"Good man, Jack," the playwright said turning, "that's a big lump of a sea out there."

"It's a big sea," agreed Jack. "For a minute there I took you to be the gardener."

"You have a gardener?" asked the playwright, astounded.

"No," said Jack, "but I have a dog."

"I don't doubt it. This is Manie. We've been searching for you for hours."

"This gardener is haunting me. I could not believe it when I saw him at the window."

"Well, it wasn't him, was it?"

"No. It wasn't, but it could have been."

"Do you take a drink in the middle of the day?"

They went to the Erris Hotel, where Jack was entertained lavishly. At one stage he asked the playwright for his jacket.

"You want my jacket?"

"I do. It looks fierce like one I used to have."

"And you want it?"

"I'll give you mine for it," said Jack.

"Right," said the playwright, and started to take off his sports jacket as Jack took off his blue shop-coat.

"Keep that on you," said Manie to her husband. "Can't you see, it won't fit?"

39

"Are you sure?"

"Of course I'm sure."

"That's a pity," said the playwright. They toasted each other. "You should be happy. I see they are saying nice things about you in the newspapers, Jack."

"I have to go to the toilet."

"He must have something against compliments," the playwright laughed at his wife.

"I have the runs."

"Oh dear," said Manie, and she closed her eyes.

"Can I tell you something in confidence?" Jack said when he returned.

"Yes?"

"I'm thinking of calling it off!" he confided. He came closer. "Did you know they won't allow me into rehearsals."

"I didn't know that."

"That's what's going on now," he whispered in a self-righteous voice.

"Why?" asked the woman.

"And they've refused to accept my changes to the script," he continued.

"You should tell them to fuck off," declared the playwright, "and get yourself a solicitor."

"Do you think so?"

"I do."

"But there must be some reason," Manie persevered.

"Say nothing," Jack suddenly whispered.

"What?"

"That's him now," Jack nodded secretively and winked.

"Who?" asked the playwright, looking round anxiously.

"That fucking gardener."

"And he is actually a little like you," said Manie in wonder.

"Could you excuse me a moment?" asked Jack.

"Are you off again?"

"I am."

He went to the public phone in the village, taking with him the correct change. When the girl answered he whispered in a strong Northern accent: "There's ah bomb in the theatre."

40

"What!" screamed the girl.

"A'm telling you nagh, and awl tell yee na more, there's a bomb set ta go off in five minutes."

"You must be joking."

"Fuck, lady, you'll fucking find out whether I'm joking or not," he said savagely. "Just say Shamey Coyle rang, OK?"

He replaced the phone. Then he returned and took his place beside the playwright and his wife in the restaurant. There was hilarity in the confidences exchanged. The night ended in confusion.

They drove him home. He found himself lying alone in bed and he thought of her and cursed her: *May she not have the memory of the good times.*

Jack answered a timid knock at the door of his cottage in his trousers. Daisy was leaping madly on the white road and barking.

"Hello, Jack," said Bernie Burke. He was pale and blue-lipped.

"You got back," said Jack.

"I did. Joe Love must have dropped these off for you while I was away," and he handed Jack a bunch of letters bound by an elastic band. The top one, he saw, was addressed to him in Catherine's handwriting.

"Someone is thinking of you," Bernie said.

"And how are you now, Bernie?"

"I'm not well, thank you. I lost a lung."

"I'm sorry to hear that."

"This is it," said Bernie. "You're doing a good job on the place. I came up a couple of times but you weren't about."

"I'm sorry. I was away."

"Well, you have them now. I hope they bring you luck."

"I'm sure they will."

"I'll go now, thank you."

"Good luck, Bernie."

The old fisherman steered his way up the path through the blinding wind. Stood a moment to look at the sea then turned into the valley towards his own house. Jack opened the first envelope and found a card inside. He put the card on the kitchen table. Then he opened the others. Each contained a letter and he laid them out one on top of the other.

He felt terrible shame. The full force of his curse was returning on himself. He looked at the envelopes, knowing that they would be dated weeks previous, before all this nightmare began. It would be better if he didn't know, if he threw them away altogether. They contained possibilities that were no longer available to him. Then he searched through the cottage for something he couldn't find. He was sick and shaking. With the usual distress of the drinker he fought to establish his physical terrain. He started to sweep out the kitchen. Today he was going to start again, right from the beginning. As he started each morning. He began at the back door. He cleaned every item in the kitchen, then he brushed out the bedroom. He settled his papers in the third room. He lit a fire and put on water to boil. He sat down before the fire and smoked a cigarette which brought on waves of nausea.

He lifted the envelopes and looked at them. He looked at the stamps. He looked at the Dublin postmarks. He looked at the handwriting on the letters without trying to understand what was written there. He lifted the postcard, and read the first line again – *Jack, I love you.* Then he replaced it on the table. Dizzy with anxiety, he made tea.

He boiled cloths in a saucepan, he fed Daisy, he fed the wild cat, he cleaned the gas stove again. Today, he said. It will happen today. He stood in a basin in the middle of the floor and washed himself.

He lifted the postcard up to the light of a window. *Dear Jack, I love you. Whatever bad things we've done should be forgotten. I am always yours. We have only each other. I've written to you over and over explaining everything. I'm sending you this card because of the picture on the front.* He turned it over. There was a picture of a corncrake. *Do you remember? We'll have good days again. Every day from now I will write to you. You are never out of my mind. I am sober,* she wrote, *you are sober and I love you. I love you dearly.*

It was what he had prayed she'd write to him and now he could not take it in. His eyes clouded over. I still have a chance, one part of his mind was saying. A few weeks ago she wrote this. He read the eight letters, but with each declaration of her love, the worse his despair became. *Each day I will write to you.* And he had been walking the peninsula, oblivious.

He cursed himself.

For days he had been tormented by despair while the letters awaited him in the sick man's house. While he was lying sleepless her love notes were sitting in Bernie's house down the road. And by the time he had read them the affair was over. She had never intended coming down. Not from the moment the gardener told her I was back drinking. All that waiting was in vain. Words for which he had waited day after day now arrived when it was too late, and yet, like the first letter, they bore the news he craved. He lay on the bed, his heart beating. Is this it now? The same flesh-coloured light shone down. He jumped up and sat on the chair. But it was not hard enough. He lay on the cement floor in front of the smouldering fire. Again he was down to the one second. The minute that contained it. And the hour that contained the minute. The minutes that contained the seconds. The half-second.

Once more he made the journey to a phone.

He rang the theatre, but there came only a reply from the answering machine: Leave a message after the beep! The tape turned, but he said nothing, only whispered: "Catherine". He did not know what to do. He went back to the cottage carrying a bottle of vodka. Terrible memories propelled him round the three rooms. But he could find no place where the reconciliation might begin.

"Jack!" Hugh cried from the kitchen. Hugh came into the bedroom. "Are you all right?"

"Of course I'm all right."

"You'd better get up."

"I am up!"

"No you're not. You're in bed."

"I can see that."

"Did you have anything to eat?"

"I've just had my breakfast, haven't I," he replied bad-temperedly. "Hugh?"

"Yeh."

"Go away."

"No."

"Jesus Christ!"

"The kettle is on."

"OK, OK. I'll be with you in a minute." He pulled on his yellow cape and green waterproof trousers.

"Jack," said Hugh, "we're not going out to sea."

Jack sat on a kitchen chair.

"Where are we going?"

"That's up to you."

"I think we'll go for a drink," Jack said eventually.

"I'd like that," said Hugh cheerfully.

Jack pulled off the oilskins.

"Will you drive me to Castlebar?"

"I will."

"Will you look after the livestock? I'll be a few days away."

"The children will like that."

"Take what it costs out of that."

"I don't need your money," but Jack pressed a twenty-pound note into his pocket. He packed a bag. Put the wild kitten in a cardboard box. Called Daisy, and the dog leapt into the back of the car.

They drove down to O'Malley's pub in Corrloch.

The bar was empty.

"Now I know what's happening," Jack declared.

"That's good."

"At last I have it all worked out." He threw what money he had on the bar. "Two pints," Jack said to the barman, "and one for yourself, and then do you know what I'm going to do?" – he looked at Hugh – "I'm going away for a while." The barman refused to accept any money.

"It's Christmas Eve," he said, "put your money away."

"Get something for the childer." Jack pressed a tenner down between the keys of the till. "And give me the price of a phone call to Dublin. There's one more job to be done before I have a drink."

He went out and lifted the phone in the small alcove. He felt light-headed and sad as he heard it ringing away. Then came a voice which wished him a Happy Christmas and told him to leave a message – after the beep.

He waited on the beep. He heard it, but seconds passed and he could not speak. Dull sounds came across the earpiece. Shrieks. Warbles. Screeches from demons in space. "This is Jack Ferris here," he said at last, looking up at the wall. "I want to wish everyone the best of luck." He considered what he should say next. "I'm sorry about the telephone calls." He searched for further words to say. Something for Catherine. A message for Catherine. "Goodbye," he said.

"That's it," said Jack.

They walked back to the car. The cat was pawing frantically at the cardboard box. Daisy leapt into Jack's lap. In Belmullet the animals got out and Isobel and the kids got in. "I haven't shopped in Castlebar in ages," she said. They drove through Bangor, Largan and Bellacorrick. Then Beltra. They walked round the town of Castlebar with Isobel as she stepped through the various shops. Laden down with bags they entered a pub for a farewell drink.

"Do you want me to drive you where you are going?"

"You could drive me as far as the hospital."

"Are you going to visit someone there?" Isobel asked, as she shepherded the children into the car.

He did not answer. They pulled out into a line of cars that moved slowly along Main Street under Christmas bulbs that were strung like bunting overhead. A Santa, his beard blowing wildly in the wind, walked out of a bar and sneezed.

"Jack is crying," said Sandra, their daughter.

They drove some way in silence.

"Why is Jack crying?" the girl asked.

"You could come and spend Christmas with us," said Hugh.

"No, no," said Jack.

The car pulled into the dark foreground of the hospital. He looked at the hospital windows with their familiar vertical blinds and horizontal fluorescent lights and felt inordinate relief, as if some tiring journey he had been on for years was at last coming to an end.

4

Shangrila

The first night he slept in a high bunk at sea facing the porthole. Through the porthole could be seen the city they were leaving at a steady, remorseless pace.

The ship was moving so slow that all night he could see the city through the round porthole.

They were moving painfully slow, and no matter how he turned in his bed he'd look up to see the city was still there.

They were making no headway.

The men in the other beds had made that journey many times. They slept easily and heavily while all night Jack looked at Catherine. Through a fall of light, left on lest anyone stumble in the dark, he had pinned her icon to the wall above bed No. 7.

All night the painful image stared unflinchingly back at him.

As it would sometimes in the future from a splinter of wood. A splinter of wood told her face. From blurred print on a page her features would one day emerge. For a long time her face would enter inanimate objects. Then her likeness began to haunt the living. And one day he would see a picture of Our Mother of Perpetual Succour on the TV before the evening news and even see Catherine's face there. This was what he had feared ever since he was a child, a fear that he would forever be followed by the face of one he loved and yet never be able to make contact.

Every second signified no change in the icon. The night-light was unerring. Her gaze, a distilled distance.

A man's heart clicked like a wristwatch in the dim ward.

"Take no notice," the man in the next bed said in his sleep.

*   *   *

"We're all neighbours here," the Leitrim man explained. "We're all in the shit. I lost two stone because my brain was moving too fast."

"Never listen to all the things that are said on both sides when your mind is astray," advised Leitrim. "Why do I wear galoshes? I wear them because I have poor hips."

The patients, Jack among them, sat around drinking in each other's thoughts. It was a glasshouse. A shudder ran through the roses when the wrong person entered. But today everything was perfectly normal. The nurses had their feet up.

Jack felt impure in there.

The rest were touched by a violet light.

It was raining. Jack was looking forward to his first sleep in days. He seemed to have spent days walking and walking. He put on the pyjamas he'd brought with him. They felt comfortable. It was raining. The rain will make you sleep, he was told.

Beat death!

Breathe in!

Breathe out!

That's what one of the women patients told him.

The rain will make you sleep.

First he watched the programmes on TV with mindless dread. The TV was a couple of fields away. The Christmas programmes were long and sluggish and no one laughed. It was impossible to follow the story of any film. Pill time came but they gave him nothing to take for sleep. Not till the drink was out of his system. Then he knew he would not sleep.

Pill time. A Catholic remedy for a Protestant problem. Or is it the other way round?

To sleep for a thousand years. And to wake up and find it's over.

His loneliness made him rigid. His loneliness was mistaken for aggression. So, as yet, the nurses did not sit by him.

But Jack had found a friend. A Bohola man paced up and down telling him he wouldn't run out of fags. "You won't run out of fags while I'm around, son," he said. It's eleven-fifteen. He has to go through with this. Possessed by all the bad memories and transfixed by the light above bed No. 7 on the wall opposite, his mind, becoming a persecutor, turned on him. On the hour, till dawn, the male nurse came. The few words he whispered to Jack brought a distant consolation. Then Jack returned to the icon. Her voice and her image merged with his mind.

Down the corridor on Christmas morning comes the sound of Perry Como and Dean Martin. In a little room a bald man is crouched over an old-fashioned gramophone. At meal times the same man does all the washing up. He is cheerful in the face of all that's wrong with him – a garden in Greece with a bottle of gin buried at the root of every tree.

When Mass came the place went quiet. Because of his sickness Jack missed all the Christmas dances down the wards. He sought solace thinking of Catherine. He shared his towel with the most sick man. As he towelled himself the sick man said: "They're all Mayo men in here except for you and me. We're the only Leitrim men that's left in this part of the world. The rest are Mayo. Poor Mayo. And Roscommon. Watch out for Roscommon. They come on your blind side." He towelled his jaw. "The madness started because of emigration. They only left the flawed behind."

"No," said Jack. "It's the cowards run, it's the warriors stay behind."

"And what about you?"

"I have to stop punishing myself. And I have to watch that I don't go religious."

"It's tricky, but then you're an intelligent man." They walked out onto the tarmac a little unsteady. They stood there in their pyjamas.

"Christmas Day in the workhouse," said Jack.

"I often pondered the meaning of that," the other replied.

* * *

48

Since she had the strength to stay away from him, he should have the strength to stay away from her.

The psychiatrist argues politics with Jack. The night Jack appeared on the doorstep of the hospital he had been about to turn him away. Then he relented. But now no matter how Jack tries to explain the quandary he's in, the doctor returns the conversation to Belfast. Jack tells him that doctors drive home to the safe parts of Belfast. The only blood they see is on the operating table. It's not spilt on their doorstep. The psychiatrist speaks of Wolfe Tone. Jack speaks of his fears.

"You've had a nervous breakdown," the psychiatrist says, "and you can find out for yourself if you're an alcoholic. The only one who can tell you that is yourself."

There is an awkward silence.

"Why did you go to live in Belfast?"

"To live with Catherine."

"You could have found a more congenial home."

"I had no illusions about the North," replies Jack, aware that he is answering a question that he has posed himself, "if that's what you are insinuating."

"No?"

"I thought maybe I could help."

The psychiatrist lets this go. "This play of yours," he asks, "is it about the North?"

"It used to be."

"And now?"

"I don't know," Jack answers painfully.

"And I suppose it was about the Catholic unemployed?"

"And the Protestant."

"Maybe that was your mistake. Trying to write 'the scripture of the poor', as Tom Kettle called it."

"I wasn't aware it was a mistake."

"Then why are you here?"

"Because I'm heartbroken."

"Let's leave that aside for a while, if you don't mind."

"I can't."

49

"I suppose you can't. It's always difficult with you arty types."

There's another silence.

"Do you object to the word 'arty'?" he asks.

"Yes," said Jack.

"Well what do you want me to call you? You're not a scientist, are you?"

"Hamlet was a psychiatric patient like us," said the Leitrim man. It was Sunday morning. "Where are you for now?"

"I'm going to an AA meeting."

"There's always an awkward silence," said Hamlet, "when a crowd of alcoholics are collected in one room." The stories in the room are lucid accounts of fear and death and discovery of God. On the steps of the hospital the sick man told Jack he was finest man in the place.

"One minute," he said, "you're the one thing, the next, the other thing. How do you explain that?"

He gave Jack an apple.

"How do you explain that?" he asked again. Then he offered a cigarette which Jack refused.

One of the AA men picked Jack up outside the hospital by chance. Jack said he was on his way to have a cup of coffee with a girl in the outside world. Instead, the man – slight, fair-haired, freckled – took Jack up roads he didn't know. He drove on, here and there, making phone calls.

Jack said: "Where are we going?"

"We are just driving," he replied.

He was kind and intelligent and he listened. Jack was ashamed of saying hurtful things about Catherine. "I don't want to blame anyone," said Jack. Then he'd over-compensate and praise her, then criticize her again. Or worse, criticize her to himself for being a hypocrite. "I distrusted her," said Jack, "since I first trusted her. I disbelieved her. She considered me her ballast. I loved her humour." The man drove on. They stopped a second for a view of Lough Conn from Pontoon Bridge. Then on again. Some time later, Jack was back sitting by Bohola in the waiting room of the hospital. Bohola broke wind violently, then suddenly jumped up, ran outside and started walking round and round the hospital while the others sat inside eating.

Love was when she let him take care of her. When she ran to him for comfort. When she fell asleep first. When she fell on the path and ran past her mother and sister into his arms. But most of all when they stepped through the countryside together, two human beings, glad to be together.

The day she did not come began the other life, the life without her. If he had stayed sober then they would be drunk together now. The argument emanates from his mind. She is not present. He cannot ask her to remain with him since she is not here. That is good. You are not present, whispered Jack.

Now she can never return because they have misrepresented each other. He can never again exist as a possibility in her mind. That is good. He is not present where she is.

The second love is different, but bearable, and sad, but bearable. The first love was stormy, astonishing and unfulfilled. It's as if life selects two people to go through all the experiences of love so that they will know it is denied them. But they had to live through all this sordidness. He tries to imagine a world where his self-respect would be restored. But his psyche is not capable of such a journey alone.

There are a few private moments of truth that can't be said. That stay outside the reach of language. Yet the words persist somewhere at the back of his mind, and a hope of reconciliation with her, more distant each time, returns – but returns somehow heightened, because it will pass out of his consciousness once again.

He once was merry and now cannot sleep. How many brain cells has he destroyed? He despises himself. The night nurse comes and goes. The light burns above the dreaming men.

5

The Nomads

"Every time I look at you I see my son."

"What are you in for?" asked Jack.

"Delusions," Bohola answers. A long time passes. "And anxieties," he adds.

They sit on a while longer, troubled and untroubled by these intimacies, each trying wildly to keep his mind in the one direction.

"You'd be fooling yourself," Bohola continued, "if you ever said you were really happy."

Jack agrees. The hairdresser sits down. "I can call no one," she complains. "The phone is closed down except for local calls. But I know no one here." She places her hands on her knees. "I should not be here. My husband took away my car keys and had me put in here. I should be elsewhere." She gives the men a quick sweep of her eyes so that they might understand she comes from another place altogether.

"Sligo," she says fretfully, aware that she should not be boasting, "Sligo is a superior hospital." She tut-tuts. "Have you been to Sligo Hospital?" she asks Jack in a deliberately kind manner.

"No," he replies.

"If I could have only got my sleep," she thinks out loud, wistfully, "I could have got home for Christmas Day. But do you think could I get any sleep here? Never. I've just had a baby," she explains. "She's over the road in the General Hospital and I'm here. But my husband is a good man. He is a good man!" She looks askance at Jack. "They've promised to bring me over to see my baby tomorrow. I want you there to help me."

"I'll be with you," said Jack.

"You are a good man too," said the hairdresser.

Over in the corner an argument starts about Val Doonican and Christmas and Christians. Like the wandering plots of the films, it cannot be unravelled. Jack suddenly wants something to do. To be useful. To be occupied. Like the sick man in pyjamas putting everything away – vases into vases, ashtrays into ashtrays.

"Is *Glenroe* on tonight?" he asked.

"I would not have taken you to be a fan," said the nurse.

Beside Jack the old fellow breathes sleep through his nostrils like a child humming in his cot.

Jack stares at the same space. But her face is going. Dawn is coming in. Dawn light is washing her features away. On the hour he awaits the male nurse's visit and his gentle enquiry. The rest wake into a world that he has not left. They sit in the ward on the side of their own beds, then moments later all move to one bed, and sit there smoking and talking in quiet voices. They are neighbours. Neighbours here, and neighbours at home. They might have just met on the street, crossed a field to the other fellow's house. Then they walk the corridors with an air of quiet expectancy like you'd come down the stairs on Christmas morning wondering what had been left for you below during the night.

They all gather together round the Christmas tree in the waiting room. They take their chairs. When the trolley comes they queue up like sleepwalkers. Instead of presents, they are given their pills. Jack is given his first measure of Librium. Then, with the others, he takes a chair. Everyone lights up.

The first heavy cheerfulness reaches him.

Jack was on the phone to wish everyone he knew a happy Christmas. The first person he rang was his mother.

"Happy Christmas," he said.

He heard her turn aside and whisper to his father: "It's Jack, he sounds quite sensible."

"Where are you?" his mother asked.

"Oh," he said, "in north Tipperary."

"Of all places," she said. "What took you there?"

"The want of wit," said Jack.

She handed him over to his father.

"So you won't be coming up to these parts?" asked his father.

"I'm in a hospital. I didn't want to tell her."

"Did someone put something into your drink?"

"Something like that."

"Well, it happens to us all. If you want anything let us know."

"I will, thanks."

He handed the phone on to the next patient, and thought – it's not so bad. It's not so bad being crazy.

"My woman said I had buried myself in drink," he tells the night nurse.

"You have to learn to love yourself first."

"How can I love someone who is not there?"

"Clint Eastwood is Laurel Hardy's son. Did you know that?" asked Leitrim.

"No," said Jack.

"There's not a word about it," said the nurse, as he palmed tobacco out of a pouch. He had his legs stretched out so that his feet rested on a chair in front of him. He recrossed his legs and jiggled his feet.

"Have you got UTV here?" asked Jack.

"We have indeed." He switched stations. Jack stared at the TV screen intently. The news was on. He watched every move and listened to every line with fascination.

Then the ad for lager came on.

"Jesus," said Jack.

"What's wrong with you?" asked the nurse.

"I know someone in it," answered Jack.

The nurse burst out laughing.

"Of course he does," said Leitrim. "Jack knows everyone."

With trepidation Jack watched Princess Diana walk up a snowy lane in Scotland. Africans, laden with bundles, trooped towards a food distribution centre. An American announcer ran footage of a plane crash. Survivors of some catastrophe sat on a hillside in blankets. Then the break for advertisements came. Still, when the lager advertisement appeared the next time Jack was not ready for it. He held his hand palm upward in front of the TV to block his view. His eyes watered.

"Do you want me to change the station?" asked a woman.

"No," he said, "it's all right."

"What ails you, Jack?" the nurse asked.

"It's the sight of the beer," the woman explained. "It's making him thirsty."

"I know someone in it," answered Jack.

"Sure you do."

The nurse sat with him till the same advertisement appeared once more. Immediately Jack stiffened. He leaned forward with a demented look on his face. The swirl of familiar guitar music started.

"Which one of them do you know?" asked the nurse.

Jack pointed towards the blond girl who now entered the bar on the arm of a cowboy. With a demure look she laid a playful hand on the cowboy's hand.

"She's very beautiful all right," said the nurse helpfully.

"That's right," said Jack.

"That's right," agreed the woman. "Some have it."

Jack, as a correction against over-exposure to his self, read a book on Republican prisoners by Republican prisoners. Hugh brought him the book and also a bedside lamp. What were his thoughts as he read it? None could be read from his face or his general demeanour. What he was looking for was evidence that the prisoners were at odds with those Republicans living outside of jail. This, at the time, appeared to him to be an important theme. The book was a re-reading of Irish history. He read avidly their account of Wolfe Tone. Next morning he is prepared for the psychiatrist. But he cannot sustain another man's argument.

The psychiatrist presses him on his political ideology. Jack tries to be objective. He wants to speak of his broken heart. But the psychiatrist presses on, praising the much-maligned bourgeoisie of Ireland. Jack misses both supper and medication.

"Why did you not marry this woman?" the psychiatrist asks. He is smoking a pipe.

"She would view marriage as a situation where a woman can be raped legally."

The psychiatrist condemns feminists. Jack defends them. He hears himself present a very ordered defence of Catherine's ideas. The argument continues. Jack tells him that he drinks only the same amount as other people. Then he admits to telling lies. He drinks, he confesses, sometimes maybe too much.

"I could not see my contribution, he tells the psychiatrist."

Immediately they are back talking of Wolfe Tone.

At last, the two of them stand facing each other across the table. He is dismissed. Leitrim has kept him a plate of hot supper. The night nurse has his pills, and a few extras. "You must have him puzzled," he grins. And then he adds: "You want to watch the news?" Again he leans forward in his chair to follow the programmes and sits white-faced as the break for advertisements comes on.

Each man in the hospital sets up house for the night, and breaks camp the following morning. Next begins the arduous task of walking.

Walking, along the same path if necessary, walking with eyes down and intent, walking without sympathy, walking in the scent of another creature with the head held arrogantly back, stalking feverishly, stopping to listen, stopping as if there was another following you as you followed someone who wasn't there, walking, sometimes in slippers but mostly going back to the boots you wore the first day you came into the hospital. Then the walking stops. The motor has sensed the uselessness. The drugs have made the instinct paper-thin.

Collapsed into a chair, the mind is frightened and tired. The sense of illusion makes the men and the women sorry. Though some, more highly charged than others, keep on. And others will never start out physically at all.

Instead of their bodies, they've sent their minds out to roam. Going, if necessary, along the same path.

At night time all collect tired by their beds. For the newcomers this is always the moment of dread. For the old-timers

56

from Mayo, who have been walking like Job through the Land of Nod, this is the moment of heart's desire. They pull back the sheets with perfect care. Then begins the little industry of going to bed. Now they prepare for the moment when sleep takes them off during the night.

Sleep is the perfect wanderer – he carries nothing at all. All he needs is a mind to journey in and to rest in. They lie preparing for him.

And when they close their eyes they cross this familiar pasture. They feel purged as Jack did the first time he thought he would go into the asylum. They are asleep within seconds. And next morning they know they can leave once more without the burden of ties.

Each night they return to a different bed. Or sometimes to the same bed after a day of intense walking. And now as they lie down, their minds, too, return to rest. They tell the body where they have been. They exhaust themselves with stories of the world. And they forget the moment they knew it was only an illusion, and put it by. Then, when all the patients are asleep, the nurse who last year had his own trouble turns into a nomad. He starts his patrol on the outer reaches of consciousness. Under the cloak of responsibility, he starts his walk. And the sleepers have made room for his step in their dreams. The hospital becomes a great walking space for those who are active and those who are still.

In their boots the Mayo men walk to the end of the corridor, turn and tramp back; neighbouring men, fags burning next the little finger, butterflies in their stomachs, dogs at their heels and animals looking over hedges at them. When you've found someone to walk with you're happy, even when that someone is yourself.

They need this enclosed space to remember in. They do not walk with purpose at the beginning. But soon they see new prospects away in the distance, and sometimes a person who may be a stranger or a friend.

Jack often saw a man trundling along who he was sure he knew.

At breakfast time he caught his eye. The brows were broad

and black as if pencilled on. He saw him disappear into a room at the end of a corridor. He saw him leap up out of a chair in the TV room just as Jack entered. *The face*, where had he seen that face before? He carried the face in his head until one day it materialized before him as the man approached him in the small lobby that led to the phone. Neither could escape the other.

"Excuse me," said Jack, "Don't I know you?"

"I'm afraid not," the man replied with a pathetic frown, and headed off at a sharp gait. For a moment Jack stood bewildered, then ran after him and fell into step with him. The two marched quickly by the reception area, down the corridor, then, reaching the room where he would often disappear from view the man turned, looked into Jack's eye and said: "I must leave you here." The door closed behind him.

He knocked on the man's door and opened it.

"I have to speak to you," said Jack. "You wouldn't have a relation that's a gardener out in Mullet?"

The man turned and as he did so a phial of pills fell from his hands and burst asunder on the tiled floor. He went to his knees and began gathering them. Embarrassed, Jack withdrew. The following morning he saw the old man climb into a blue Mini and drive away furtively, like someone who had left midway through a wedding celebration.

6

Christmas Morning

"Mr Ferris is a writer," the hairdresser informed the nurse in the maternity ward. "At present he is writing my story."

"Oh?" said the nurse.

"Certainly." She smiled at Jack. "And I have some interesting things to tell."

She took her child out of the cot and held her on her knee as if she was holding a stranger. "Isn't she sweet, Mr Ferris?" she said.

"Yes," agreed Jack.

After an hour the two of them returned from the hospital to the asylum. Arrangements were made for them to return the following day at the same hour.

"If that's all right with you," said the nurse ironically.

"Of course," said Jack.

The hairdresser was pleased. Back in the asylum again, she asked Jack to begin her story that very day. The male nurse gave them a room, and a notebook for Jack to write in.

Later, after she was gone, he looked through some of his copybooks into which, when he woke at night, he had been writing notes. It was nearly impossible to read them. Now in the office with the desk and the swivel chair he started to write again, but his hand refused to move. He could write down the hairdresser's words but not his own. The struggle was enormous to pen one word. And one word seemed to contain such a myriad of meanings that it was impossible to complete even a sentence.

He sat immobile in front of the desk. His mind was trying to make a leap into the dark but his hands would not comply. His thumb and forefinger were numb. If he tried to write they froze. And inside his head language no longer arrived grammatically, but surfaced as a series of bizarre signs. He walked out into the lounge. A nurse was standing by the window. He told her what had happened.

"I'll write it down for you," she said.

He was overwhelmed with gratitude.

And so his day began with a visit to the maternity ward, followed by a session with the hairdresser when she would tell him her story, and then for an hour he would dictate his confession to the nurse. At first all that emerged was a mix of blame, distress and hurt. The nurse quietly wrote down what he had to say. Sometimes the door opened and one of the patients would look in, glance around slowly at the two of them and then go away.

She'd ask him to spell certain words, she'd wait, he'd keep his eyes away from her, he'd turn and start again.

The hour with the nurse became for Jack a spiritual reprieve. As he spoke to her he fell in love with her. And he knew that this was an old medical cliché, but he didn't care. He let his love for the nurse wash over him. The nurse told him that she trusted him. Why she said this to him he could not remember. That was when he fell in love with her. And when she was gone, the hairdresser would step in again. Then Jack would begin on her story. Word for word. From her birth in Ballyhooley on Clare Island until the moment she was apprenticed to a hairdresser in Sligo town. That was when the trouble began. Then would come the dark gaps, the single words, the silences. Silences to questions you ask yourself. He would sit pen in hand as the nurse had sat before him. And the hairdresser, brimful of love, would look away from him. And after the hairdresser left, Bohola would walk in, direct him to a clean sheet and recall his days in Finsbury Park in London, "It being somewhere near autumn and me having emerged from a locked ward in the north of England. Have you got that?" he'd ask Jack. "Me and London town. The Paddy in London in February of '62. Me down at Beachy Head in Eastbourne. Have you got that? I like to hear it ring along like Shakespeare," said Bohola.

*　　*　　*

As Rita the nurse listened to his confession, he had a great urge to put his arms round her. She said: "It must be a struggle for you to say these things."

"Because you are here it makes it easier," he told her.

"Is there self-pity in it?" he asked. She said not. He knew there was, but didn't care. He thought Rita looked very beautiful. For a while they'd sit together saying nothing. Across from him she smelt very human. They'd start again.

"You have to live with evil. It will not go away. It will steal your energy. It must be faced. It's serious," the hairdresser said. "It's a serious business. Let no one tell you otherwise."

A man says: "It's a wonderful Christmas day." It is. The sun is shining. "It has shone for the past seven Christmas Days," says Jack. It is wonderful. It is wonderful to him who says it. Wonderful to him who hears it. Any words that surface now are the real thing. In the other world they were meaningless. Now they are vital and amazing. The soul seated across from Jack who said the day was wonderful exudes wonder himself – that life should have accompanied him this far, given him mild weather, pills that balance him for a moment; he hears no children crying but knows they do, he knows people are dying on the upper floors of Castlebar General Hospital which sits across the grass verge; he may not like his own selfishness, his rancour, his innocence, but here in the clinic that runs along a lawn, much like an American chalet, he has got the far side of the moment when his consciousness seized up.

"It's a wonderful day, Jack," he says. "Anything might happen."

That is why the man has declined to walk outside. He is alive by that window. He is the first man to say it: It's a wonderful day. It is wonderful weather. Yes, and it was wonderful to have the words to say it, it was wonderful that the effort was made. A new planet is named. And the greatest wonder of that day was that the soul of the man beside you agreed and saw it as you did.

Then you knew it was no addiction. No high. Nor a search

for a high that prompted this wonder. It was a blessing. It was enough. In Jack, the moment passed. But you could tell that for the man commanding the window what he'd seen would remain with him for some time. Some day, unbeknownst to him, it would return. In Bellagarvaun, the land flooded, fingers burnt from hot tobacco, a child sitting abstracted, a woman askew, a light would strike a cushion and the man would be visited by that wonder. On that day he might conceal it thoroughly as a sane man would, but for a second it would be there. Till the day be robbed of its wonder, the cliché regain the senses, language fail him, the respite go.

Jack sat there, considering the window and all the alternatives, and sadness stirred in him like an aphrodisiac. Not far off was desperation, the climax. He savoured the panic, the mild otherworld of absence, the beached self, the love blunted by nostalgia, and his sadness was increased by the self-conscious cheerfulness of Christmas Day visitors as they alighted from their cars.

"Does the west wind," asked Jack, "blow to the west or from the west?"

"To its grief," the Bellagarvaun man answered like a sage, "the west wind is known by where it comes from."

It is night. It has never happened. He tries to plug the gaps through which the nightmare enters. Mostly those gaps open onto nothingness. Then an argument begins in a flash. *You're so sorry for yourself,* he'd hear her say. *I think you are despicable.* This is sanity returning like a type of revenge. I'll show those fuckers outside! Is there anyone will come part of the road with me? The man from Bohola will. So will the man from Bellagarvaun. And the man from Buleenaun. The man from Balla. His friend from Manulla. The girl from Dereen. And the woman out of Pontoon who wears football socks.

Then we'll begin to wear each other down.

Each man has a fellow who gives him counsel.

If they take away the drugs they fear the loss of their soul. They need their souls. The soul does not fear isolation. It has no time for bitterness. It has unhinged bitterness. The nurse

62

talks to him, taking down his words in her own hand. He can't write. They sit in the Male Admissions office trying to spell certain words. When he hears his first name on her lips he feels weak.

He would like to sit in a room with nurse Rita forever dictating his confession. What he says to Rita is believed by her. Rita is sloe-black and tender. She takes up her pen. He recommences. Each man's story must be written down. He writes theirs. She writes his. As he hesitates, she looks away desiring something back there, something else. She looks bruised; remembering passes the thing on.

"God stands beside me like a bedside lamp," said the hairdresser, and she formed an O with her lips.

Jack dreamt that Catherine's clitoris came away in his hands though it still remained part of her. He did not realize immediately what it was. She observed him closely as he moved around with her pleasure-centre in his hand. To him for a while it looked like a goanna, but presently it became a frog. When the goanna became a frog the room smelled of mushrooms and wet grass.

With that, he realized with a shock what he was carrying. He asked her if he took it behind the wall and rubbed it would she still feel pleasure? But Catherine said: No, you must be where I can see you. Then she closed her eyes. The fact that she closed her eyes could be interpreted as meaning that she trusted him completely, or that she had complete power over him as she lay there passively. Or, indeed, that she was entering a fantasy in which he had no part, all because of her propensity, as she would call it, for the stranger.

When Jack awoke he was disturbed by all these contradictions, but more so because now he found that not only his own loins, but her loins, floated free in his dreams. Always in the dream of the severed penis, which had afflicted him for years, was the fear that overcame him as he tried hurriedly to fit his cut cock back into place only to find it coming away again in his hands. No matter what he did, his prick would not take. He interpreted this as his desire to be a woman, and the man in him bemoaning the fact. The cry of the buck wailing always brought him awake, and with a sense of relief he'd find himself intact, though the sense of loss still remained.

Now the clitoris had freed itself from her dressed groin and the quest in the dream was how to tickle it that it might jump in ecstasy, but this, even though she had her eyes closed, could not be done outside of Catherine's perspective. Yet despite his delicate nudging of the frog's wet rump, it sat in the palm of his hand eyeing him and remained unmoved by all his coaxing. Nor could he bring it elsewhere because it still remained part of her.

He was sad that he had no control over her pleasure even though he carried its source around in his hand. And if he took his eye away – even for an instant – from the eye of the frog, it was gone. Then began the search to find it again, sometimes here, sometimes there, sometimes gone altogether. Then back again giving him that long, infinite gaze from the cup of his hand.

He realized that he had no control over the mystery.

Then, with a tightening of the knuckle of the spine, he considered the prospect of having a mind in which, while it slept, parts of the body disengaged themselves and floated free, and then he considered why the penis and the clitoris of his dreaming self and his dream-figure Catherine should so wander. And he wondered why, in the case of the male member, its painless severance brought not so much terror as the overwhelming urge that it be replaced immediately. "Some men," Catherine once said, "are afraid to put it in lest they might never get it back again." "Did you ever meet anyone like that?" he had enquired nonchalantly. "Only once," she answered. They were walking at the time through a wood, and she laughed. He considered this implication now and knew it did not apply in his case, instead he became intensely aware of the fact that when the intimacy of two people ends, the secrets of their experience are handed on as tensions to the new lover.

Now he felt for the plight of this other man who feared entry into a woman, and that it was not a laughing matter. Then he went on to consider why, in the case of the clitoris, its position in the cup of his hand had brought both wonder and responsibility for its well-being. He was glad that the frog had remained moist and oiled, for that was a good sign. Yet he felt guilty that the sexual parts should have been chosen by his subconscious mind to be severed from their fellows, but there was relief in the fact (after all those repeated dreams in which the penis had come away in his hand) that now in some sort of sympathy the clitoris had followed his sad appendage into the unknown to keep it company.

He was happy about this, even though he knew that the companionship was emanating from his mind only, and not from Catherine's. And even though no dream was occupied by the two free-floating loins at the same time (although that too might come in time, he thought) he was glad of the dream, for its sense of fellowship and exotica. Intoxicated, he remembered fondly eyeing the frog as it sat crouched in his hand, moist, ready to spring.

He knew it – the sexual parts were trying to break through the prejudice of the mind.

But in the world of the real and normal the place beside him in the bed was empty. He struggled up from sleep still carrying the clitoris in his hand, like a diver striking to the surface of the sea with a pearl.

He looked around bewildered. The ward was filled with the smell of may-blossom. The stench of lust. What was happening? Then the dream returned to him from another dream. He'd been dreaming about her again. And he felt a deep nostalgia for Catherine, for that sick feeling of wondering: Would Catherine be there, would she turn up, would she be beside him? It was a mystery. He felt there was some awful truth about himself he had to tell before she would return to him, but what it was he could not say.

For hours Jack walked the corridor, perplexed and delighted by the scandalous dream. The other patients, knowing the by-laws of another's obsession, kept out of his way. He relived the dream to find its meaning.

All he could think was that a false author dwelt within him.

In his dreams the true author existed, unhampered by reality. He re-entered his office and immediately thought of Catherine learning to play the trumpet.

She is aged nine. Sunday school is just over. There is something strikingly true, he finds, in this portrait of her. She holds the trumpet between her tiny hands on a Sunday afternoon in the Protestant North. She is wearing the uniform of the Salvation Army band. She is in her own room and in that room she weaves no fantasies, but concentrates totally on blowing a recognizable air.

The image brings him great satisfaction. His spirit returns.

He finds his spirit safe at his side and is content. His spirit has a laughing, gangling form. "You've been away some time," Jack says to his spirit. But the mind-spirit, like some stranger, just nods. The nod could be benign, the nod could be dangerous.

"I grieved over your absence," says Jack.

"Maybe you should stay quiet for a while," says Leitrim, who is sitting across from him.

Hugh arrived. He brought with him an invitation to the first night of the play. It was opening the following night.

"Did you get one?"

"No," said Jack.

"Why send one to me?" asked Hugh.

"It's a way of telling me not to come," replied Jack. He studied the invitation.

"You take it," said Hugh. "You should go."

Jack thought of the train journey from Castlebar to Dublin. The curtain going up. The shouts of *Author! Author!* Liar! Liar! When Hugh was gone he showed the invitation to the Leitrim man.

"Is that you?" he asked, pointing at Jack's name.

"Yes."

"It's a nice card," he said.

It was a long delirious day. He let the hours pass. High on Librium and Mogadon, he lay peacefully that night among the sleeping men. With love he watched the Madonna on the wall. The next morning he again imagined making the journey to the east. Hugh rang. A journalist was on the phone from Dublin looking for his telephone number. "I'm not here," said Jack. It was a true statement. It was a long day, tantalizing, full of the fantasy of journeying, of arriving, moving through the theatre-goers. Seeing her above on the lighted stage.

A few times he strolled as far as the road, then turned back and paced the corridor. He stood and studied the hospital clock. Sat in the empty dining room and watched the cooks make the dinner. He listened to the clash of cutlery, and smoked. Other patients came and sat at the empty tables and watched those working in the kitchen with a quiet, transfixed curiosity. He returned to watch them make the evening meal. It did not seem possible that he could last out the day. That it would pass like others did. But it did. And he was still there in that place when it was too late to have gone. As the hour came for the curtain to go up he fought the desire to lift the phone and ring the theatre. As the minutes dwindled he grew euphoric. He imagined the crowd sitting in the dark and he not among them, and was filled with wonder. The minute passed. Relief flooded through him. *I've stayed away.*

I didn't go.

It has started.

He stood in the corridor outside the room of the man who had buried his bottles of gin in a Greek garden. Out came the Cole Porter song "Every Time We Say Goodbye". Jack grew to love those words. Especially the refrain – *the change from major to minor.*

He wished Catherine well.

Then he began pacing the corridors like a popular song.

Corrloch. Belmullet. Aghadoon.

7

The Love Object

"So, you've lost your love object," said the psychiatrist.

To hear Catherine reduced to such a crude nonentity was a comic blow to Jack's pride. He stared at the man defensively.

"I'm thinking of letting you go," the psychiatrist continued. "Stay off the drink for a while, and then, if you want, begin again. Start with a couple of pints. You are the only one will know if you are an alcoholic."

Jack, in a panic, asked: "When do I have to go?"

"In a few days. It's up to you. The main thing is there's nothing chemically wrong with you."

Jack walked the hospital pondering the words *love object*. Then he pondered the words *letting you go*. And after that *chemically wrong*. But, as yet, he did not begin to ponder the word *alcoholic*. From it grew all the strands of unreason and fanaticism and hopelessness that terrified him.

He sat among the friendly alcoholics on a Sunday morning in a small wooden room in the basement of the asylum. They shook his hand and he sat down and waited. A ray of cold sunlight came though the single window onto clouds of cigarette smoke.

"I can see you've suffered," said the man beside him.

The door opened slightly and a head appeared. "Have you a cigarette, mister?" came the faraway familiar voice of a small farmer. The alcoholics handed over cigarettes to the chemically mad. Then, as if they were under the power of some medium, the drinkers, like austere feminists, began to bare their souls.

Jack was welcomed to the meeting.

"My name is Jack," he said when his turn to speak came

round. He could not bring himself to say he was an alcoholic. Instead he said: "I hope in time to have the courage to say I am an alcoholic." The little group shook their heads knowingly. He reminded them of themselves. They all knew that defence, that dependence on self which was an even stronger addiction than drink. The self, which was governed by the will, would not negate its own existence.

"It's a life sentence," said the final speaker. "You don't cease to be an alcoholic. Never. It's in the genes. The same flawed cell will burn brightly again the next time you take a drink, if there ever is a next time."

They stood with heads bowed for the serenity prayer. Someone opened a window. Fag smoke blew outwards like incense from a ritual.

The nurses moved lightly in their own sure personalities between people lost in spasms of loneliness.

An identity was affirmed. The nurse moved on. The patient, feeling pure because of the sympathy, looked after the disappearing nurse, or irked by the return of some reality, didn't.

Jack was happy on Librium.

Then came another responsibility. That all that happened in the hospital, even as it happened, had to be written down. Now his time there was running out Jack was visited by an obsession that he must become the chronicler of those who were his companions.

It was a time that must be remembered. Because of this obsession, he sat in the unused office for Male Admissions those last few days feverishly writing. He answered the telephone, gave precise directions to those in the outside world, then resumed his task. From now on, everything was going to happen for a first time.

It was present times he was addicted to. The notebook stayed with him throughout the day. It was there beside him while he slept, it was there first thing in the morning.

He wrote down immediately what he saw. The villagers collecting. The nomads heading off. The icon, still and perfect.

69

But sometimes, for what he saw or felt, there were no words. No words would come. The writing stopped. His hand could not form a word. And the word he might have written down disappeared into the void. He no longer had any language in which he might contemplate the world, but only stinging asides from his past with Catherine. His memory was impaired, and since memory depended on words, no words would come except those which had already been defiled. So he listened intently to the others, as he had once listened to popular songs. He'd write down a sentence spoken by the villagers as they unrolled their bedclothes and greeted each other, as they shuffled towards breakfast, as they fasted before their pills.

It's a dirty old morning, a voice sang out.

You're a trickster – like a weather pot, came the reply.

What's a weather pot?

A weather-gauge. A class of thermometer. Like yourself, it's got two readings.

Oh.

I'll give you £2 for the woollen cap.

How about £2.50?

Are you a bit of a farmer?

Yes, and I worked in a factory in Killalla, God bless us. But it's dear honey that's licked off the whins. I've already lost two of these woollen hats. But they're great, they are. You can roll them up and put them in your pocket.

Like a sheep. You can roll them up and put *them* in your pocket.

This will be all yours one day, my uncle told me. Oh, but if I had only got it in writing.

If I could only see her again, said Jack.

You'd be well, but sick again.

Where there's two in it, the guilt is halved, said a listener.

People worry something wicked about themselves.

It's a pity about them.

Each man has his savings, said an old trim voice.

I broke the rule to find out the right way, explained Bohola. I'm told the right way, but when you are used to your own way you can't correct it.

God help us, Kiltimagh!

What is the name for a lady's frustration?

Oh, sacred!

There is an earth outside the Shangrila, and its purpose is misguided, spoke the hippy. Could you help Jack to put it back on the path to Heaven?

We all have people somewhere, said Jack to the hairdresser.

Yes, and we're not with them, she replied.

As time passed, he found one day was not long enough to contain all that happened in it. Each moment had at its centre a hint of eternity. Some day, he knew, he would lift these papers and hate them, yet it had to be done.

The men and women came, tapped on the door of his office, and impatiently began to tell their stories. He fought to sustain the inflexion, the pause, the backward look. He wrote, they spoke. And there was some sanity in this. As he wrote their stories down, it was as if his imagination had been granted time to see their lives in another light.

For each detail of their lives, though it had already happened, had to be tortuously reinvented. He wrote down their lives because every time he thought of his own he thought of Catherine and their togetherness, and then began the turmoil. His spirit would vanish. The hospital was no longer home. Only when the patients spoke did he know peace.

When I was fourteen I used an ass for pleasure.

Was it any good? asked Jack.

It was perfect, the man replied.

The story went on. He was glad for the man that it had been perfect. When one speaker went, another sat in the chair. He turned the page, wrote the date, the time, the place, then they began telling him terrible things. When the stories stopped, he felt drained but satisfied. The hospital induced in him a warm satisfaction that he had not felt in years. The first minutes of the day and the last minutes of the night a holy breeze blew down the corridor.

The nurses sent him patients who wanted to tell their tale. The doctor he had not become he now was, one that cured others that he might himself be preserved. It was a great time of not knowing, of being whoever the patients judged he was. Contrary waters met. They subsided. His notebooks filled with stories that had once made perfect sense.

One clear day will come, he thought, when I will find what I am addicted to. He sat in his office, happy at his pad. The hospital was the free world. Never again would he be able to walk happily through the unnatural world outside. So, on the morning he was to leave he woke with a heavy heart. He was frightened and anxious. The nurse gave him extra pills to help him through the coming weeks.

"I had so much more work to do here," Jack said.

"You were great," said the night nurse, "but I'm worried about you returning to be alone. Is there no one you can ask to stop with you?"

"I won't be alone," said Jack. "I will have you all with me."

He searched the wards to find Nurse Rita, only to discover it was her day off. He crossed the lawns carrying his bag and stepped through the gates of the General Hospital and was shocked to see a sculpture of the Virgin holding Christ on the far side of the road. The flesh-coloured plaster arms and leg made him stop in his tracks. He turned towards town.

He felt a holiday sense of dread. He should be enjoying this moment, instead he felt disloyal. He had formed mental associations inside the hospital that would be considered improper in the outside world.

No one outside the hospital where he now stood would admit to such an appalling lack of intimacy. Nor would they try to overcome it in that same genial way. *I have been cured by the Mayo men.* But the minute he stepped through the gates he was suddenly afflicted with his need of Catherine in a terrible new way. For he had gone through this alone. She had not been with him. It was his first independent act in years, and he had an overpowering wish to tell Catherine about all that had impressed him.

Already, as he walked through Castlebar, he was preparing

72

for his encounter with her. He felt strange on the streets. He had been happy with the hospital order of sleeping, waking, strolling, sitting, without the burden of guilt. Now, as he went down the road, another self stepped out and accompanied him. Then another. And another. The old crew, acrimonious, scolding, shouting, were back. By the time he reached the bus, they had all returned. He had a gathering of many selves, each wrapped up in their own condition and each demanding his attention by their gesticulations, their silence, their bitter talk, and their dreadful insecurity.

Each of these would be with him on the bus to Ballina, on the bus to Belmullet. They would be about the house when he got there. They would arrive ahead of him wherever he went. They would be with him – these ghosts – for the rest of his life, until, by some act of faith, he could incorporate them into himself. He tried to put them by. And to keep self-pity at bay. But that was to induce a worse sentiment – nothingness – in its place.

In a pub he sat down. He had entered it with habitual familiarity only to find that here his ghosts grew abusive and hurried. Each drinker there betrayed the same quiet mindless absorption that Jack knew of old, but now it had lost its centre. The smell of the alcohol threw him off-balance. Each face was brightly discoloured and dry. Jack nodded to them as he ordered his coffee. When someone ordered a whiskey his senses were filled with furious memories. He could feel the alcohol as it flowed down the tubes and pipes to the drinker's stomach.

He turned his back and swallowed a Librium. God, I've shamed myself. He asked the time. He ordered another cup of coffee. Turned, swallowed another Librium. By the time the Ballina bus arrived, he was beginning to feel that it was possible. That he would have the strength to hide away from everyone, even her.

8

The Cockatiel

He reared up that night in the cold cottage and yelled at the thought of his loss and the stupidity of his thinking. He knew finally that the only intoxication he could live with would be himself and yet he wanted more than ever to meet Catherine. He needed to make peace. He needed forgiveness. It had happened in the past – he thought it might happen again.

He took out what remained of her letters and began reading them. He found his heart raging. He swallowed a few Librium. Then read the letters over and over again. Soon the tone, the sound, the hesitations, the acrimony, the exaggerations, the humour, the sensuousness of her voice was pouring through his consciousness. In these letters were references to people he had long forgotten, to old arguments that seemed futile now. Places, words of love, encouragements, erotic endearments. Where was all that love now? Had it drifted into the upper air?

Sleep eventually came amidst a letter of love and reconciliation he was dreaming up in his head to reply to hers.

The skipper he fished with visited him the following day.

"You're welcome back, Jack," the skipper said. "Hugh told me you've been having a bit of bother."

"It's over now," said Jack and he sought for the skipper's name.

One night, in his drunkenness, Jack had forgotten it. And now, without the excuse of drunkenness he found in a panic that he again could not remember the man's name. The nameless figure sat before him stirring a cup of tea and eating a sweet biscuit with uncouth relish. Jack looked at this strange face – windswept, with a garish swollen nose and huge ravaged teeth – and tried to restore an identity to it that he had once known.

But the man's identity remained a mystery. He wondered was this the beginning of cynicism and distortion in himself. Would he begin to lose everyone he'd known?

"I think you should stay," the skipper continued. "You shouldn't run."

"You'll always have a berth with me," he said, "out on the *Blue*."

He walked with him down the white path. The skipper got up on his Honda 50.

"Be seeing you, Jack."

"Good luck," said Jack, and he waved and watched him till he was gone from view, but still the name did not return.

At noon Joe Love appeared in his green post van. While the van rocked in the wind and Daisy barked wildly, Joe handed Jack his mail. Jack looked at Joe Love's face with its huge forehead, snow-white hair and full whorish lips as if he were seeing him for the first time.

"How are you, Jack?" he asked.

"I'm grand."

"I saw your picture in the paper," said the postman. "You looked mighty."

He slit open the envelope. It was a bunch of reviews sent on by Eddie. Jack read them, but the only words that registered in his mind were those that referred to Catherine. "Catherine Adams delivers a stunning performance." "Miss Adams is impeccable. She was born for the part." "An actress new to the Dublin stage, Miss Catherine Adams, turns in a rare and moving performance." He felt a painful twinge of bitterness, of jealousy and sadness. The two of them should have been sharing this moment together. He would have liked to have been called onto the stage, and to take her hand and bow. It would not happen. It would never happen.

He stuffed the newspaper cuttings in the pocket of his oilskins and sauntered fearfully round the peninsula. The sea roads were creamy yellow in the cold January sun. Each person he met tumbled by, full of their own life, at home in their own consciousness while he was trapped in an alien perspective from which there was no relief.

75

He sat in the cottage for two days without stirring. Then Hugh the chef arrived with Daisy and the cat. He was glad that he remembered Hugh's name but distraught to find that he had forgotten the dog. Daisy went frantic with joy at seeing him, then lay down in his accustomed place. This is how it will be, thought Jack. Who do we have to talk to when we are alone? He looked at the holy pictures that he had kept on the wall and wondered should he remove them. If he left them there what magnificent madness, he wondered, might home in on his deranged mind? He took down the Madonna, the Crucified Christ and yet could not bring himself to remove a small plaster cast of Joseph holding his son, for the shadow the statue threw on the wall of the mantle he found comforting.

The banal and the ordinary things began to count. Through them he would re-enter the world, for he had not the strength to begin listening to God. He tried to imagine her in her new life. Would she be able to trade in ceaseless affection with some other again? Would the evil energy be dissipated now? They had lived together thinking they knew everything about each other, but they had forgotten the strange world that would be there after they parted.

Who would take care of them now?

For a long time their life had been full of forgiveness. How serene the world was after they'd argued! Then the forgiveness stopped. The moment that had actually happened he could not remember. It had passed him by.

For hours he'd be filled with unrelenting hurt and resentment. He culled old notebooks written in Belfast and found there no record of their day-to-day life. He had always, out of a naïve sense of loyalty, wanted to live there and yet his time in Belfast had barely registered in his mind. What was I doing, he thought, during those years?

A link had snapped between him and the past. There was no use looking for it. He stopped mourning his forthcoming death. The drunk, Jack realized, is the chief mourner at his own funeral. The drinker would like it all to happen in the one day: his birth, his lovemaking, his death. So he speeds up the process.

Scarves, he thought joyfully, she had an inordinate number of scarves. Some that were large as the capes west of Ireland women wore; scarves that were black, made of crepe, black satin, green woollen scarves, red cotton scarves. The memory of the scarves filled him with tenderness. As he used to be filled with sentiment at the sight of her washing hanging up in the back yard of their house in Belfast, or in the sea-fog in the back garden of the dwellings in Corrloch – the line of black skirts, jumpers, blouses.

Scarves, he thought.

When the bad days came he'd grow frantic and nervous. His heart would beat like an oncoming train. He'd wait. His body would shudder. I'm being punished. Let it pass. His daily life became a battle between resignation and the will to change. He began to find comfort in his bed, in the Tilley lamp beside it, the candles burning, in Hugh who had visited him. The male nurse who gave him the extra pills. The Leitrim man. Nurse Rita. The hairdresser. The woman from Pontoon. The dining room where he'd waited all that long day and listened to the raucous chatter of the kitchen staff.

At last he walked the peninsula, but the insults he expected never came. Life was going on without him. Then one day, with an overpowering sense of guilt as if he had recommenced secretly drinking, he began again walking like a disturbed soul past the Adams' house. The next evening he was back and the gardener, whistling softly, slipped by him into the dusk.

At last, he completed the triangle and ventured as far as the Erris Hotel for coffee. Mrs Moloney stepped out from behind the counter.

She leaned forward and took his hand.

"You're welcome home, Jack Ferris," she said. "We could all do with a break."

"Thank you," said Jack.

"Do you know what's wrong with us?" she confided. "We're far too passive. There should be a band out on the street to welcome you back."

"Do you think so?" he asked incredulously.

"I do. We never look after our own. My daughter saw your play and thought it was wonderful."

"I'm glad."

"You must have had a great time up above on opening night."

"Yes," he answered smiling, "we did."

"It was my dream," she said, "that something like that might happen to me."

"It might yet."

"Never," she declared.

He sauntered the streets. And then again walked the road to Corrloch. With dread he entered the door of Lavell's shop.

"You've been away, Jack," Mrs Lavell said.

"I have," he said.

"Can you hear the cockatiel?"

Jack was startled.

"What?"

"Since you've been away I have a cockatiel. Her boyfriend bought my daughter Marie one in Dublin. The bird was driving the aunt mad. Marie was out at work all day and then out with the boyfriend at night and the bird was jabbering away. So, her aunt – my sister – said the bird must go."

"I'll have half a dozen eggs."

"So my daughter asked me to take him in."

"And half a pound of sausages."

"Now he has me awake at the crack of dawn."

"He'll be a companion," said Jack.

"It's a long winter," nodded Mrs Lavell.

Next morning he crossed the fields and went up to the shop to buy bread. The old fisherman, Bernie Burke, was seated on a sack of spuds getting his breath.

"Morning," said Jack.

"It's good to see you," said Bernie. "I saw your name in the papers, I did. And I saw Catherine's."

"Has the bird talked yet?" asked Jack.

"All he says is in another language," replied Mrs Lavell.

"You should leave him listening to the radio," said Bernie. "That's how they learn."

"The radio," said Mrs Lavell, "would only sicken him."

Jack laughed.

"Isn't that right, Jack?"

All three laughed together. Jack took a newspaper, and laid the change on the counter. He stepped out. He was home. It was blowing hail. He read that night an *Irish Independent* dated 1933 from cover to cover. Next morning Daisy fell in behind him and prepared for the walk to the Adams' house. "Not today," said Jack.

And so it was. If he loved her in the body once, let his imagination seek her out as best it could. He arranged himself at the kitchen table. He waited. As he had waited in the hospital. But as long as he loved her he could not begin writing again.

The minute he put a word on the page he would stop loving her. Once it became a story it was over. Some other person would materialize.

Still his imagination would not comply. He was not ready yet to consign the real living Catherine to the world of imagination. He wanted to stay in life, to continue with the adventure.

There was one more trial of nerves that had to be gone through. He would not be free till he had spoken to her. He visualized the street he would meet her on. What coat she might be wearing. What she would say. What he would say. And how he'd keep his distance and his dignity. He would not hang on to her. This was how he would behave – with respect. He would not persist. He would be regretful and not argue.

He caught a bus to Ballina. He had been sober some time but he took his phial of Librium with him. He hurried through the wet streets that were rampant with hallucinations. He caught the afternoon train. He went round Dublin terrified of walking into her, and yet craving to see her. He turned into the street where the theatre was.

He stood in an alleyway watching his name and hers emblazoned across the entrance. The role he had written for her had released her from him. Just like that the emphasis shifted. *Catherine*, he'd say, *I just came up to wish you the best of luck.*

79

Footage of their previous encounters passed swiftly through his mind while he imagined some final heroic encounter. Fearful of being seen he slipped along the outside walls of the theatre and looked at the strange black-and-white stills from the play. He looked at them and tried to place them within the context of the script but couldn't. He fled across to a side-street. At first it seemed a colossal joke that he should be standing there opposite a theatre in which his play was being performed while he had not the authority to enter it. Then came the sense of déjà-vu. When was it he had stood here before? He could not remember, and yet he saw himself in his mind's enlarged cyclopic eye standing there in that very place waiting for Catherine. Every aspect – sound, light, taste – was exactly as he expected, and yet the scene contained an extra dimension he had not previously encountered. And with a shock he realized that this was the street where for so long he had imagined he would meet her. This was the time. She suddenly came walking towards him and stepped into a telephone booth. He felt his heart pounding. His hands shook. He watched her talk, gesticulate, frown, smile. This familiar mute performance made his heart beat giddily.

When she stepped out he approached her from behind and said: "Catherine."

She turned and froze. For a second, just as she heard his voice, she had been about to smile in greeting. Then despair descended over her face. She stood there fighting to control herself, then she walked off.

"Please," he pleaded, following her, "can we remain friends?"

"No," she said coldly, striding on. "You let me down."

"I was sick," he replied.

"You can say that again. What about the phone calls?" she said, turning on him.

"I'm sorry."

"Do you understand half of the terror you caused?"

"I should have been let attend rehearsals of my own play."

"They didn't want you. No one wants to see you again. *No one!* You're a joke, do you know that? Do you realize what people think of you?"

80

"I can imagine," he replied. And before he could stop himself he caught her arm: "I was in hospital."

"You were only there," she answered, looking angrily at his hand, "collecting notes for your next play."

"Christ! How can you say that?"

She looked away from him. "Take your hand off my arm, please."

"Let me go, please," she said.

He stood back. She walked off towards the theatre, proud and convinced, as if she had won some final argument. Already he had lost control. Everything he had meant to say he had forgotten. He turned away, ashamed of himself. Yet when he looked back after her she glanced towards him with wild agitated eyes. He ran after her again. When he caught up with her, she raced ahead of him.

"I waited for you."

"You told me lies," she said. "You were drinking all the time."

"I'm sober now."

"It's too late."

"Don't say that."

"Go away," she shrilly whispered.

"What do you want me to do?" he asked, as he trotted alongside her.

"I want you to go away." She walked faster.

"OK," he mumbled.

He stopped. Humiliation and defeat made the air in the street curve before his eyes.

He walked through Dublin, drinking coffee, in cafés and bars filled with the European tourists of early spring. The coffee drinking continued all that evening. He knew that he should leave, go home, be elsewhere, but he moved from pub to pub like a sick dog because there was always the chance he might run into friends who might speak on his behalf to her. Who these friends were he didn't know. He didn't drink. Not because he had chosen not to, not because of any great sense of discipline, but because he had forgotten about drink. He had forgotten that drink might ease the pain. And yet all those mad laps of the city had the hallmarks of a binge. The coffee was making him insane.

The trek from pub to pub, trying to talk to the odd person that congratulated him while his nervous consciousness chattered away; the foolish expectancy as he turned a corner, the comic inevitability, the talking to himself; the seeking out the eyes of sympathetic women, crying dry-eyed, saying his serenity prayer; all this had to be gone through even though the irreversible moment had passed.

He was opposite the theatre again as the crowds emerged when the play finished sometime after ten. They passed by him chatting, laughing, hailing taxis. He watched the doors, the lights go off, the poster boards taken indoors. A couple of men he took to be technicians strolled by him to the pub. An actress, still dabbing make-up from her face with a tissue, stood on the sidewalk and sneezed.

"Bless you," said Jack.

"My God," she said, "it's you."

"I was just wondering was Catherine about?"

"She's gone."

"Oh."

She rushed away. Then the street went quiet. He began to search the nearby pubs.

That search ended as the pubs closed. Then he set off towards the last address that Catherine had given him. He did not want to go there as that seemed like a breach of trust. To meet her by chance was acceptable, to go to her home was wrong. Yet he could not stop himself. By now he had perfected the walk he had established in hospital. The intent gait that bore the impatience of a relentless search. The obsessive drive through psychological terrain. The disturbed soul was on the move again.

His fingers working themselves in his pockets. His socks sliding in his shoes. The manic breathing. The lights from cars and traffic lights blinding him.

When suddenly he came to a stop he found that he had long ago walked past the house. He stopped, bewildered by the fact that he had gone so far out of his way. He turned and went back again. When he eventually reached the red-brick two-storey house in a side street off the South Circular Road he stood for a moment unsure of himself. He knocked on the door. A curtain was drawn overhead and a face came to the window. Then the curtain quickly fell into place again. "Catherine," he called out. He heard voices in the hallway. Steps, whispers. All the quiet insignificant sounds that paranoia feeds upon. "Catherine," he called again. He listened for as long as he could bear then he walked off down Camden Street, feeling that he had at least discharged a psychic duty that was expected of him.

The long drunkenness was nearly over. Now began the long insane journey into sobriety. For what, he wondered, had he survived?

He made it back to his house out on Mullet two days later. The papers were still set out on the table. The starving animals scraped the door. Daisy went beserk when Jack threw him some bones. The wild cat meowed round his feet, her tail stiff with hunger. He fed her milk gone off and porridge oats. The house felt unlived in. It smelled of old distemper and stale potatoes. He passed by the kitchen where his papers were and moved on into the bedroom. He lay down and lifted one of her letters onto his chest. The hopelessness was intense. The badness started. The veins on the back of his hands began to pulsate. He was back among the enemy. Future realities were being measured out in woeful doses. Jesus Christ! He got up and put her letters away. And he said the only way I can free myself is to imagine her, not as herself, but as someone else, someone different, for then I can think of her without resenting her.

And then he realized with a start what she had done; she had saved them from each other. He saw the smile that had partly formed on her lips as she heard his familiar voice behind her. For an instant it was there, her old longing. Then he cringed as he heard the sound of his loathsome plea. He saw her turn, with wild eyes, towards him on the street. Her sadness, her loveliness. For a moment it could have begun all over, but it

83

didn't. She had struggled against the disillusionment. She had seen what was coming.

Now he had to live on in a different world. To transcend. To enter a new story. She must be imagined. He opened a spiral-bound notebook and thought, Here it begins.

II

THE SALMON OF KNOWLEDGE

9

The Death of Matti Bonner

Catherine was thirteen the day that Matti hanged himself from a tree midway between the Catholic chapel and the Presbyterian church. She was first down the steps of the church to face his contorted visage.

At the beginning she did not realize what had happened.

He was like a climber reaching out for the next branch, or someone hiding up a tree, but then she saw that his two boots were resting on nothing. She had left the church because religious gatherings often made her sick. Now, filling her lungs with air, she saw Matti Bonner's face. She came forward a bit. The right hand, that lacked a middle finger, seemed to stir imperceptibly. Behind her an organ played and a choir was singing a hymn.

"Daddy!" she screamed.

In convulsions she ran back to the church.

"Daddy! Daddy!" she screamed, and men, embarrassed, stood up to let Jonathan Adams through to his daughter.

Jonathan Adams ordered everyone to remain where they were. Then, knowing Matti Bonner to have been a parishioner of St Mary's, he stepped quietly into the sour-cream smell of the Catholic chapel to tell those standing at the back what had happened. As the communicants were coming down the aisle a labourer cut the dead man down, Jonathan Adams received him and an on-duty RUC man laid him out on the ground.

By then the congregations of both churches had been released, though each Sunday, morning service began in one when Mass in the other was nearly over. The two were timed so that the congregations would not meet, either going or returning. But this morning the service had ended abruptly when Catherine ran in, and the Mass had faltered after communion. The parishioners gathered round the dead man, they studied the tree, the cut of the knot, and fended off certain political thoughts. The Presbyterians looked on remotely as the priest whispered into Matti's ear.

The Catholics appeared awed.

But for all there this death was uninspiring. It did not lead to awesome thoughts about the hereafter. It disputed grief. It seemed the work of a man intent on turning his face away from God.

It was the third suicide in two years. A young reservist had been washed up at Dernish Island on the Erne, a girl had cut her wrists in a shed. Both of these were Protestant deaths. The first brought on by manic depression, the second by domestic trouble. But this was the first time in recent history that a Catholic had taken his own life in that territory.

Matti Bonner's death gave the Loyalist village an insight into how vulnerable the enemy was.

The Presbyterian elders who were standing under the birch tree felt both alienated and aggrieved. His death had somehow exposed them. Even though this suicide should have been a reproach to the Catholics, they felt it was directed at them. It involved them all. There was a curse in what he'd done. It was a sign. He wanted to remain forever in their minds.

And as for the Catholics, who moved round his death with an easy familiarity, they, at a further remove, felt let down. By his suicide he had gone over to the other side. He had smashed the idol of life itself. By his death he had turned informer. They were embarrassed by the obvious grief of Jonathan Adams, while they themselves were not so moved. Matti Bonner had even robbed them of their right to mourn. That he should have hanged himself facing the Catholic chapel meant he was pointing the finger at them.

He was saying: In the chapel there is no peace.

And there were some who privately understood Matti Bonner's despair.

He had picked that spot and that time and those two churches, and said: *I've had enough – one day you go out alone and marry death.* Matti Bonner was not saying he died because of politics, or economics, or because of a broken heart. He was saying that God had failed him in his despair. And so he risked the concept of everlasting mercy. *I am not staying around,* said Matti Bonner from the tree, *I've had enough.*

So, because of neighbourliness, or secret approval of his sense of courage and drama, or out of plain curiosity to see would the Catholics bury him in consecrated ground since it was rumoured that his church might not, Matti Bonner had a big funeral. People of most beliefs appeared, at least to walk the short distance behind the hearse. It was a time when all sects could attend each others' funerals. Ecumenism was in the air, and the war had only just begun. Some of the more severe Presbyterians did disappear at some point on the street. They were still, for the moment, survivors. Others, the apologists, stood in the doorway of the chapel till the funeral Mass was over. Over the heads of the congregation they watched with fascination all that their forebears had forsworn take place on the altar. Lighted candles. Chalices. Beads in prayer. Instead of a supper that was a memorial, here was a feast that was a sacrifice. The ecumenical men looked on bemused at all the trappings, while others, like Jonathan Adams, watched with distaste the red gorge of the priest billow out like a frog's as he drank the wine. His fingers fumble with the wafer. How he dusted his hands and knelt with a rustle and turned and blessed the congregation.

The just shall live by faith alone, Jonathan Adams said to himself.

The congregation could feel the priest's embarrassment as he sprinkled holy water over the suicide and invited the soul to enter heaven. *An eternity of the tabor.* Four labouring men shouldered Matti high, and as the mourners walked behind, they looked at each other to see who was weakening. His death modified the Protestant strut, the Catholic lurch. The mourners did not grieve. Decency made it proper that they attend, not to grieve but to observe each other about their rituals. The warp of superstition attending this lone man into the grave. But then they were shocked to find that they were following the coffin of a man who by his death had belittled their existence. His suicide was preying on their minds.

And when they buried him, it was into a deep compartment of the mind that they put Matti Bonner, a place where the existence of God has never been fully resolved, nor their own lives really authenticated. His death triggered off in their psyches questions about the meaning of the word *everlasting*, the meaning of *despair*, and the meaning of the concept of *redemption*. There could be no uplift of the spirit in burying a man who had died by his own hand opposite two churches on Thanksgiving Day. Even the earth that was thrown on his coffin was somehow transparent, made of nothing. And the prayers for the dead seemed the final blasphemy.

Matti Bonner hanged himself from a birch that to the north commanded a view of a field where the Reverend Ian Paisley had come at midnight with torches and flares and flute bands to summon up votes for his entry into Stormont. Under it, Catholics usually stood smoking after Mass and watched the other sects file past. To the west was a small soccer pitch.

From a distance the tree looked like a man taking off his feathered hat with a flourish.

Some names had been cut into the bark with a penknife. The most famous of them now was Matti Bonner's own, undated, dark and deep.

The Irish for the townland was *Cul Fada*. The English was Cullada. In the fields behind the birch Matti Bonner used to turn hay for his Protestant neighbours when they went off to celebrate the twelfth of July. He would have known the birch from all sides. Now, when the Catholics passed the tree they made the sign of the cross, and when the Adams girls talked in their rooms they talked of Matti Bonner the bachelor, who used walk the back garden of his house with his flies undone. They'd saunter up the road to stare at the tree where the bit of a rope without its noose still hung; they'd pick their way down to the untidy house and peer into the rooms with dizzy stomachs, see the porringers and cups, the milk pail by the door. They'd see the old black Ford tipped into a ditch, the red, upturned cart, the TV aerial cocked back at an angle after a severe gust in a storm, the Christmas cards still on the mantel, and, despite the hostile Catholic spirit, they'd feel a twinge of sentiment. Then they came across the skull of a dead cow under the apple trees and thought it was his; they stood petrified in his galvanize shed in a fall of hail and knew God existed, and yet whispered hard, uncaring things.

They were trying to outwit their fear.

They could see his house from theirs, for theirs was next along, just a field away, and the house since his death seemed to have grown enormous. For now that he had died, his consciousness seemed to inhabit the place more fully. At night they could hear Matti whistling to his dog. From their upstairs bedroom they looked over towards his house and swore they saw a Scared Heart lamp burning. Congealed blood began to drip from the heart of Christ in his kitchen. His house grew more barbaric and profane than when he'd been alive.

Because now, added to their disdain, came pity that turned to revulsion at the Catholic appetite for suffering.

And because of what she had seen – this Catholic nightmare – and for fear the face of the dead man would haunt her, Catherine was allowed to sleep next to Sara, and from Sara's window the girls now watched his house till the edge of the buildings gave off a blue haze. His sudden whistling could be heard through the trees. The poor man's scandalous image of Christ burned through the night like a Christmas fairy. The hair stood on their heads. He was in Hell.

"Is he there forever?" Catherine, terrified, ran in and asked her father.

Jonathan Adams considered the word that gave rise to that concept of everlasting, αἰώνιος, meaning eternal, age-long. Was the absolute eternity of evil affirmed? Was there a difference between everlasting and eternal? He sought a psalm that might alleviate Matti Bonner's suffering and calm his daughters' fears.

"For his anger endureth but a moment: in his favour is life:

weeping may endure for a night, but joy cometh in the morning," their father read from the book of Psalms.

And then he considered the words for hell. *Sheol*: the world beyond the grave. *Tartarus*: an intermediate state prior to judgment. *Hades*: the unseen world. And *Gehenna*, the word the Lord had used: the common sewer of a Jewish city where the corpses of the worst criminals were flung and fires lit to purify the contaminated air.

That was where Matti Bonner was, the girls decided as they stood by their window looking out into the darkness. And it was everlasting. Matti Bonner was in the Valley of Hinnom; his unburied corpse had been cast forth amid the worms and fires of the polluted valley. The stench of the dead reached them, and their cries, and then the yelps of a barking dog.

In time Matti Bonner's animals crossed the fields to the Adams' house.

His hens came. His white nanny goat, langled as she was, came over the walls on her knees. Finally came his dog. But the dog only came for food. Always he returned to his old house to wait for his master. Lights would go on, and lights would go off. Catholic relations trooped through the rooms like grave robbers. At midnight the dog would whine till all hours. He startled the geese who began honking and screeching. Cocks were crowing the night through. Reilly tore away with his claws at Matti Bonner's kitchen door. "Let me in!" he yelled, "Let me in!" Then the seagulls chasing seed in the fields began barking like dogs. Reilly turned cross. The night was full of barking, followed by long mournful whining, till it felt as if only an animal could really mourn a human's passing.

If the girls went near the house during the day Reilly would turn on them, though he knew them both. He was cross, possessed, his spine drawn back like a bow. Yet when he came across to the Adams' he would immediately roll on his back for them, baring his loins and smiling. By night the dog became the curse of the village. The girls would call him from their window. "Reilly," they'd call. He'd stop a minute then carry on whining. The geese would screech. All manner of birds would wake. The night air filled with disturbance.

The girls would lie in Sara's bed listening to the dog and wondering at the nerve of a man who could hang himself opposite the two churches. They wondered how he felt as he walked to make his protest. The Protestant boys in the village said that when a man hangs himself his cock stands. They said that Matti Bonner, the Taig, had his trousers open at the flies the day he died facing the Catholic chapel.

That was what Sara wanted to know. Was it true? Had Catherine seen his mickey standing? Catherine said she thought she had seen something white like his belly. She could not be sure. But in time she came to believe she had. Yes, it was a stiff white cock. Not a married, fatherly cock, nestling quiet and brown on her father, but something foreign, something even independent of Matti Bonner. His cock took on a life of its own. In the dark she'd see it, the male penis that only stood when a man was hanged. First she'd see his face scowling and then his frail white member hanging, not standing, but child-like. Then, as the rope stiffened, so did his penis.

"Could you see any hair? He had red hair," said Sara seriously.

"Yes," she'd seen hair where his trousers had been torn by barbed wire. She saw the scratch marks on his skin. Their scandalous whispers grew enthralled by fear. *Outside were dogs.* Catherine's lies and Sara's imagination kept them hallucinating tiredly while they grew acquainted with Matti Bonner, the first real person they'd known to die. They grew to like their fear of this man as night fell. He had been such a man that if you looked away you would not remember him. He was a small house with poor walls, a name, a Catholic yard, a white bleating goat, a way of walking, a way of talking with bothered outbursts, a bachelor with a missing digit on the right hand. Someone they could look down upon. Now he was an immense frightening figure in a state of eerie erection whose pathetic dog, night after night, whinged on the step of his house.

*   *   *

93

One night, the girls not only saw lights in Matti Bonner's house, but furniture being hurled through the windows. The dog was frantic. Then, there was the sudden discharge of a shotgun, a terrifying shriek from Reilly, another shot and then silence. The countryside at last went quiet. The torment of his soul had suddenly ended.

The next day Jonathan Adams said: "That's it. Tonight, Catherine, go back to your own room."

"Daddy, I'm afeared."

"And what's there to be afeared of?"

"Matti Bonner."

"Go long."

"I am."

"That's enough out of ye, once is enough, Catherine, for me to tell ye. Matti is in heaven."

"He's in hell."

"Stop it, Catherine. Tonight you'll hike yourself back to your room."

"But Daddy, he'll folly me."

"Foll-ow!" the Sergeant said correcting her.

"Follow," said Catherine, "he'll *follow* me."

"There's no one going to folly ye, daughter." He took her by the hand and the two stepped briskly along. "Once you start that kinda talk, you're asking for it. People should learn when young to be alone."

So Catherine went back to her room and strangely enough Matti Bonner did not visit her that night. It was the ghost of the dog haunted her and Sara, till eventually the dog backed off, as a dog will in terror from the unknown. Reilly was forgotten. Matti's house housed animals, his furniture sat in his nephew's garage. The gap leading to the subconscious was filled in, and finally the land was sold to a Free Presbyterian from Tyrone who scoured the walls and the floors clean of all signs of Catholic possession and painted on the gable RIGHTEOUSNESS IS OF THE LORD.

Across the fields Matti Bonner now lay in consecrated ground.

But Catherine knew he was out there somewhere trying to get back in.

The first time she lay tight against Jack Ferris she remembered the Catholic bachelor silently hanging from the tree and again imagined his member standing softly up out of his navy-blue trousers. It was not true, it had never happened in reality. But it did happen in her dreams. The erect penis meant death by hanging. Often in years to come she would jump awake covered in sweat to recall that a second before she had been making love to a disembodied penis. It was the penis of someone who wasn't there. Only this male member jammed into her. She'd reach out to hold the person only to find him missing. The shock would bring her awake.

Then she'd realize with a terrible sense of unease that there had been no man there a few seconds before, only this disembodied penis making love to her. And her unease would be greater when she'd remember that the penis belonged to Matti Bonner. He, she'd realize in terror, had been the strange elusive man she had been reaching out to embrace and comfort. But in her dreams there was never anyone there but a nameless spirit in a state of arousal. In panic she'd flail out either side of her to touch him, and wake terrified to find no one, only this distant sexual joy receding fast from her scalded thighs. A phantom penis had been sent to pleasure her in her sleep from the world of the dead.

10

The Fenian Ledger

The chestnut trees blossomed. The Fermanagh village forgot Matti Bonner. But Sergeant Adams did not. Shocked by the death, he searched through his memory for the moment when Matti Bonner had betrayed by any word or gesture that he intended to take his own life. In the RUC station his fellow policemen had other things on their minds. But they said it was well known that he had threatened suicide.

"Did he never, ah, say nothing tee ye?" asked the desk officer.

"He did not mention this obsession," replied Sergeant Adams, with a hint of regret.

"And ye that drove by his door most every day," the desk officer said in wonder. Then he laughed. "It goes to show ye can never trust a Roman Catholic."

But in Jonathan Adams' mind the issue was one of *delusion*. For the past twenty years they had probably spoken to each other every day. And never once had Matti Bonner been anything but genial and offhand. They had an understanding. Now it made the Sergeant think he had imagined a friendship that did not exist. Matti Bonner had no confidence in him, the man's tribal distrust had prevented him from asking for help.

He had taken his secret to the grave.

"The poor man must not have been well," replied Maisie.

"And why didn't he tell us?"

Sergeant Adams would often conjure up moments in the past. An image of Matti would materialize, an unprincipled and menial man in one sense, in another, dangerously subversive. When he touched the corpse he remembered the long drive they'd made together to Rathkeale. Two men in a car hurtling South without a word. The warmth of Matti Bonner's voice

96

behind him in the church the morning of his wedding – "Good luck, Boss. They're good auld stock." Now the dead man was a complete stranger.

Jonathan Adams was stunned by grief. And so, despite being a policeman, he had braved the Catholic graveside to say his goodbyes to his best man. The men and women who stood in the graveyard were all enemies of Jonathan Adams. There was a cursory nod from the priest, a handshake from the nephew, a fatalistic silence, then they stood aside to give him a view of the naked coffin. Look what you've done, their movement said. I knew him better than any of you, he wanted to shout. But he acted his part. Submissive. Holier than thou. Yet somehow the sense of being at a funeral by-passed Jonathan Adams. For, throughout it, he was disputing with the living man.

Why did you not speak to me? Why did you hold back? Where are you now? Well, one thing, there was no Roman Catholic priest to guide you into the hereafter when you died. Thinking this, Jonathan Adams felt blasphemous. "That's what they do to us," he recalled Matti saying, "slip an arm around you just when you're gone senile. It's the priest talking, not you at all. You're not there. It's the infant you once were is being blessed. Aye. I don't want it. Never."

Thinking on these words, the Sergeant remembered how delighted he had been to hear a Catholic deriding the priests. But now the words, enriched by Matti's death, returned to him from a different, dangerous perspective. For, though Matti had seen no priest and had died by his own hand, yet he had died a Catholic. It didn't matter that there was no priest present. Now Jonathan Adams wished that the priest had been there to attend to Matti as he climbed the tree.

For there was something offensive in such a staunch death.

Something that drove him to ask Matti, Are there balconies up there? Are there trees? Are there stars?

Matti Bonner had harvested for both sides, and was known by none. Yet he died a Catholic. His religion could accommodate his despair.

Now, about a hundred people stood round his grave, bound

to him by mended fences, by the milking of cows, the shovelling of gravel, the spreading of manure. Thinking this, Jonathan Adams was struck by a sudden insight into the decency of Matti Bonner's life. Many of the graves each side of the one he was being put into, Matti himself had dug. He would have cleaned his shovel with the heel of his boot onto the plot in which he now was laid.

This togetherness of things, this stubborn harmony, this realization of how for years Matti Bonner had been separating himself from others so that he might have the strength to carry out his quest, struck the old Presbyterian with a fine high feeling of prophecy mixed with anger.

He looked out onto the road at his car. He looked back at the chapel. What am I doing here? Then he stepped through the creaking turn-gate. He felt under the passenger seat for his rifle. He drove back towards the village. Some of those in the graveyard who had moved on to visit the plots of their relations watched him go.

Jonathan Adams had white hair with black roots, salmon cheeks, walnut eyes and, in his latter years, a nervous shaking of the head and chin which he always feared might lead to the same Parkinson's disease that killed his father.

He had been a member of the Royal Ulster Constabulary for thirty years, yet he had never managed to develop a policeman's bearing. The uniform sat ill on him. The figure itself was apparently straight and manly, but was somehow not correct. Slouches hung around the buttocks and the armpits. And he never shook off the hump that learning had given him. Despite cultivating the rough accent of his youth and refining his knowledge, he had a habit of speaking above the other policemen. The other learned phrasing still haunted his words. Once upon a time his belief lay in the simple statement: *Conscience demands knowledge.* As a policeman he had to relinquish the higher ground, yet his scholar's demeanour persisted in the hesitant tone of voice.

For three years prior to joining the police he had studied at small Presbyterian seminaries. The first in Belfast, which dealt with theology alone, then for a while in Edinburgh. Those few years had given him a scholar's mien, and a dislike for what he called in a letter home to his father *the mocking hypocrisy, defined scepticism, reeking impiety and shameless revelry* of life beyond the new, emergent Northern Ireland State.

It's people that matter, the doctors told him. Be popular with the congregation. Keep up the home visits. You need peace of mind to find God's will.

His family helped the young student get his first living at Cullybackey in Co. Antrim. The apprentice minister was introduced to the elders in a low wooden church with a red galvanize roof. Only one masonic banner hung from the wall. He had chosen as his homily the powerful line – *to give some form to that which cannot be uttered*. It proved an unfortunate choice. For the minute he started to preach that which he had feared happened – he was possessed of such a feeling of disorientation that his chin and wrists shook uncontrollably. The joy the congregation did not see stirred in his soul, but elation did not reach his lips.

Words refused to come to him. Meaning departed.

"I would like to begin . . ." he hesitated, and then became trapped in a set of thoughts which were denoted by the pronoun "I". "I," he said again and stopped. To say "I" implied a thinking subject, and yet he suddenly realized: I know nothing of myself. To whom does this "I" refer? He tried desperately to get hold of some valid point of principle for his assertions, but a void opened. A tremor ran through him.

"Abraham," he said, "stands at the head of one dispensation; Moses at . . ." He steadied his hands. "David at the head of a third. John the Baptist . . ." He had seen it coming, this failure to preach, throughout all the weeks – the years – of preparation, and yet could do nothing about it. The sermon was a disaster. The arrangement of his thoughts spilled over into foolishness once he was confronted with that one word, that super-confident assumption of experience – "I". And although he was greeted with sympathy, the young Jonathan Adams could not believe that joy would come in the morning.

They had tried to teach him to read distinctly, but, in the eyes of the doctors he proved "a mean reader". No matter how much he perused beforehand the chapters and homilies to be read in public, the words came out disjointed and led only to misunderstandings among the listeners. The pause they had instilled in him as a prerequisite for delivering sermons turned into a long embarrassing silence. If he lifted his head for a moment from the text, he found himself unable to find his place again. He'd stand transfixed before the eyes of the doctors and students and hear this remote foolish monotone issuing uncontrollably from his lips.

"Perhaps you might consider scholastic teaching," he was advised.

"Never."

And so it came to happen in Cullybackey: his powerlessness was carried from the finite to the infinite. He looked up after the first line and saw his father out there being taken by a muscular spasm, and replied with one of his own. He found the next line, and then it happened again. The old RIC man was urging his son on with his eyes, but the shame of being an evangelical preacher who could not preach overtook Jonathan Adams. *Look at the text, hear it in your head, it will reveal itself. Commence!* These orders from the past issued more strongly through his mind than the words he intended to say.

He had dreamed of this moment – the first sermon he would give – and now it was here. He had sought to prepare a text that would be lofty, indignant, mournful, eloquent; but when he looked at his father his sermon turned into a sorry performance bereft of definite views and strong convictions. His learning had turned to blather. "*To give some form to that which cannot be uttered,*" he repeated, blushing, in a false dramatic climax. At that moment he would not have minded being borne away to the great audit. The kirk greeted his finale with embarrassed silence. And afterwards the same nervousness afflicted him as he supped tea with his family and the congregation.

After that first terrifying experience his heart quailed at the thought of having to perform at another public service.

If he could only enter their interior without words! If even words could be swept away!

His dreams of becoming another Wycliffe, Huss or Patrick

Hamilton were shattered. Instead of his first sermon bringing him peace it had seemed as if he had returned to Cullybackey to answer an indictment. He felt like Knox before Queen Mary in the palace of Holyrood. But unlike Knox, he had acquitted himself badly. He had earned his family's shame, his father's rancour. As the doctors had foreseen, Jonathan Adams proved a poor preacher, unlike his brother Willy who was established in a living as a successful Evangelical minister in Tyrone. The mortification Jonathan Adams felt at the money wasted on him by his parents was increased when Willy left after the service without speaking to him. Over the following months he attended Synods, Presbyteries, Assemblies, but could offer no discourse.

The elders who accompanied him tried steering him towards a clear strong delivery but his words on behalf of his congregation never rose above a whisper. Soon his stipend would come under question. He worked at becoming approachable, friendly, but only succeeded in creating greater distances between himself and those who wished him well; he tried to throw off his learning, but only succeeded in sounding condescending. Eventually the chore of being a churchman proved too much.

He went to his father.

"I think I must leave the Church," he said.

"Per-sev-ere!" his father replied staunchly.

"I hear it in my head but it will not come onto my lips."

"It will in time."

But it did not. Still in a suit of grey Jonathan Adams stepped into a sunless office off the Crumlin Road in Belfast and signed on with the Royal Ulster Constabulary, which had replaced the old RIC, disbanded after the new Northern Ireland state was founded.

It was one final attempt to appease his father who had been a policeman before him. Old Adams had seen his son George established as an engineer in Toronto, his daughter as a librarian at All Souls in Oxford. Willy in a ministry in Tyrone. All his family had done well. But somehow Jonathan had let him down. He had not persevered. Like the Jonathan of old he had disobeyed his father. He had tasted food before evening had come.

He did but taste a little honey with the end of the rod that was in his hand, and lo, he must die.

If he could not spread the word of God throughout the new state, then at least, thought Jonathan Adams, he could guard its laws.

His father's words – *if you leave the ministry of the Church you'll be cursed* – remained a challenge that Jonathan Adams had to contend with all his life. His first few years in the RUC were even more humiliating for him than his period as a Presbyterian minister. Those who joined in the twenties were old RIC veterans from the South as well as the North, and all, including ex-servicemen, were sure of preferment. They had quickly taken all available positions of authority so that the young Presbyterian men like Jonathan Adams who joined in the late thirties had little hope of improvement. They remained at the level of Southern Catholic RIC men who were reaccepted into the force only on sufferance. None had the chance of rising above the rank of sergeant until political experience showed that Catholic inspectors stopped the cries of sectarianism.

He was assigned to a village in County Fermanagh. His ignorance of farming and farming communities was profound. He despised the uncouth RUC men who surrounded him, their corruption, their garrulousness, their ill-fed consciences, their sham, Church of Ireland pieties which seemed devoid of the principle that underlay true Protestantism. In his first station, his manners, temper, education and celibacy were a constant source of merriment for his fellow policemen.

He lived in the barracks and slept in a small bed placed in an office off the day-room. It fell to him to do the last round of the village at night. The step was quick, faultless, unerring. He wrung the handle of every shop-door. Stood a second or two in the alleys off the pubs and listened acutely. Shone his torch into vehicles left overnight on the street. He read nightly to the sergeant's children from the scriptures. Sat by their bedside during their fevers. Stoked the fires. Retired to his room to sit and read. Oil his revolver. Shine his buckles, his leather belt, his hat's insignia. He did it without a soldier's conviction, slowly, and then slept without dreaming. Drunks found porridge in their cell at first light. And morning found coals blazing in the blue-and-yellow tiled fireplace in the day-room. Jonathan Adams was already abroad on his bike, calling on people in remote areas to collect the unpaid licences for dogs, radios, bulls, guns, cars. He came only once to collect the fee. If it was not paid, then despite protests, the summons invariably arrived soon after, in that unyielding script the whole area recognized as stemming from the unforgiving, scholarly hand of Jonathan Adams.

And when he entered the court with his victims, no first names passed his lips. Every man was *Mister*, even his neighbours. Jonathan Adams brooked no familiarity till the case was over. Civilians to him were criminals once they had charges to answer.

"I'm afeared ye can't address me now, Mr Pratt, if you please."

"Right, Constable."

In silence, like strangers, he and Pratt would sit on a bench outside the court, policeman and farmer, each eating from their own sandwich bag and drinking from identical blue bottles of milk. As they waited they studied the other offenders. The sheepstealers. The brawlers. The whispering doe-eyed Catholics who always lived in the vicinity of guilt. Avid with the assumption of contrition. Sly. The barristers. The brass nameplates of the famous above where they sat in the cold air of the outside chamber.

"Now," breathed Jonathan Adams, as Pratt's name was called. He dropped a hand on Pratt's shoulder and led him in. He stood by the accused throughout the proceedings, grim, unsmiling. Out came the notebook. *On the 22nd of June I had reason* . . . The business of the court took place in a formal language which pleased the constable. Then, when it was over, Pratt and himself climbed on their bikes and cycled home, shoulder to shoulder, through the tree-lined roads of Fermanagh.

The Second World War came to his village. Americans moved through the fields in camouflage. Black men appeared in the choirs at church and sang lustily. And in the same way as he treated locals, Jonathan Adams arrested the soldiers for being drunk and disorderly. He brought charges of theft when he discovered goods sold between soldiers and civilians. With resentment he saw summonses dropped. He checked cars to see had the petrol originated in the camps. He checked food in shops to see whether it was of American origin. He hounded the by-roads where soldiers courted local women.

The neutrality of the Southern Republic in the war only confirmed what he already believed – that this was a war begun by Hitler to reinstate Catholicism throughout Europe. This was why Spain remained neutral, this was why Mussolini entered the war on Hitler's side. Rome, while the rest of Europe was devastated, sat out the war. Hitler, Mussolini, Franco, De Valera, the Catholic warlords, and the Jesuits – these were the enemies of the Allies. But, at home, in Fermanagh, the law must take its course. He charged Yankee soldiers with indecent exposure when he found them urinating in the local graveyard. Jonathan Adams became the scourge of the military, and his activities led to a rift between the barracks and the American authorities.

"I have a request here, Constable Adams, from the Americans," said his sergeant.

"Yes, sir."

"They would like you to allow them to get on with the war."

"Yes sir."

"You think you can do that?"

"If they'll refrain from drunken excesses and sexual debauchery in the village."

"It's a small price to pay, Constable, don't you think?"

After the war he was occupied with the black market, with smuggling and customs abuse between the Republic and the North of Ireland. One night, the only time he had done so, he discharged a shot over a boat on the Erne, then another, until the Bardwells came ashore with a cargo of butter. Then in the fifties came an IRA Nationalist campaign that soon petered out, but not as far as Jonathan Adams was concerned. Throughout it, and long after, he kept a list of Fenians from his district who were involved. Alongside each name was noted the date of birth, the background of the father and mother. Various relations who had possible Republican interests were added. In red he wrote under each *Roman Catholic*. Then went on to other headings: prison record, employment, local disturbances.

On a scale of one to three he estimated their potential treason. *Possible, definite, committed.* It was on his word council houses were given, the few times they were given, to Catholics.

If any Catholics applied for gun licences he took his Fenian ledger out and checked their credentials. And that same Fenian ledger was to dictate who would be arrested the night Internment began years later. Even after Jonathan Adams was long dead the list of names he had prepared was still running through the British Army computers at check-points and border posts throughout the North. It sat on the desk of intelligence agents in London.

Each night during the fifties campaign he opened the ledger and added new names:

Flynn, Nevill. Roman Catholic.

B. 1932. Farmer. 14 head. Mixed marriage. Roman Catholic father, John. Mother, Church of Ireland, Dorothy. No prison record. Uncle, Robert Flynn, arrested after IRA raid on Beleek barracks. Eventually released without charge. Nevill Flynn suspected of storing arms. House searched four times in January, 1st, 22nd, 23rd, 31st. Nothing found, but library stocked with Nationalist literature. Refused to co-operate. Complained of ill-treatment by Special Officer Thompson. No basis. Sometimes drives a car registered in the South – ID 510. 42 acres. Lives at home. Neighbours convinced he is heavily involved. Stands while drunk provoking neighbours singing Republican songs out on the roadway. Believed to have torn down the Union Jack off a neighbour's tree. Check with Special Officer Thompson about threat of "tearing his tonsils out".

Description: A drunkard. High complexion. 5 foot 11 inches. Eyes blue. Mousey hair. Inclined to stammer. No special distinguishing marks. Perhaps easily led.

Possible.

Throughout those years the barracks were turned into sleeping quarters for B-specials, who came in drenched in the middle of the night and lay exhausted in cells next door to the men they'd arrested, interrogated, and beaten. The B-Specials were supposed to be part-time policemen, but were in fact a private army over which the police had little control. Many were Southern Protestants who came from over the border and were bereft of all the austere religious convictions of their Northern Brethren. They were green Orangemen. They drank wildly, used crude language and created mayhem, then left it to the ordinary police to clean up after them when they went back to their safe lives in the South.

When he let the Catholics out of their cells in the morning they complained in whispers about ill-treatment. Jonathan Adams neither spoke to them nor looked at them nor wrote anything down. They sought his attention, speaking to him in that beseeching tone of false innocence he so abhorred.

"What have ye to say about this?" he'd turn and ask the Special when the barrage had finished.

"It's all lies," came the reply.

"Do ye want me," he asked the prisoner, again without looking at him, "to take your complaint in writing?"

"And be haunted?" The Nationalist would shake his head. "Away outa that." Then Jonathan Adams would ask his name, address, age. This later, along with his observations, he'd add to the Fenian ledger. Next he took down the B-Specials' reports.

Mostly no charges accrued. A complaint from one side meant a summons from the other. He kept a neutral stance between the two. Then both parties waited while he went through the paperwork. Those days it seemed the stations were always damp. He could smell the wet from the bodies of the Cavan Specials as they sat puffy-faced and small-eyed for want of sleep. Back across the border their animals were waiting to be fed. Beside them the Fenians looked into their hands. They waited. Then after a while he let them go.

The B-Specials and the Republicans stepped onto the street and went their separate ways. This fighting too would end. And soon it did. Peaceful times returned to the province. Money intended for new council homes was instead spent on roads. The smell of tar crossed the province. Ulster began preparing to become an industrial miracle. Jonathan Adams became sergeant. Moved in alone to the married quarters. And here on winter nights he gave tuition in all manner of subjects to young scholars from the village, wrote out their job applications and filled in forms that their fathers could not understand.

He drew up schedules, entered his observations in the daybook and placed each policeman's wage in a brown envelope in the desk in the day-room. On each he wrote in pen the policeman's name, the overall figure, tax reductions, special charges, certain fees.

It was because of his fluency in the world of figures – exact figures – that Jonathan Adams eventually got preferment. The other policemen might consider him an oddity, an outsider, but he earned the rank of sergeant because his paperwork was always fastidious. The reports he drew up in the barracks were minutely detailed, dated correctly and coolly observed. His initials on a piece of paper meant all contained therein was exact. He was a man the judges liked to see in court. He may have been a poor preacher, but explaining facts came easily to him. His evidence was trustworthy. They understood each other, the judges and Jonathan Adams. The judges appreciated the discreet scholarly aside. The evangelical turn of phrase.

For years he kept the same quiet profile. A reserved man, a church-goer who seldom went to church, a reader of odd doctrines, a man who lived by himself in the barracks, a man whose prejudices were hidden from the world. And perhaps he would have remained like that, if, in the same year that both his parents died, he had not met Maisie Ruttle, a gangly, fair-haired woman who was a Methodist, born and bred in the Free State. She had come North to work as a cook for Lord Brookborough. Jonathan met her on the tarmacadam path that was being laid through the estate. A roadworker had a finger severed by a winch that was hauling stone, and the police had been called. She was holding the man's hand in a bloodied towel by the edge of the path under a spreading elm. Very gently she got the labourer seated next to her in the back of the police car. All the way to Enniskillen hospital she talked to the man as she held his wounded hand – you'll be all right, don't fret, easy now – and only let him go when the doctor came.

"The poor fellow," she said.

The Sergeant nodded.

Then she stopped talking. They sat facing a blank wall in the hospital for more than two hours without speaking. Then, again without speaking, they sat another hour each side of the labourer's bed. Then there was the silent drive home. Hay was being tossed in the fields.

"I spent my childhood playing in haylofts," she said.

"Mine," he replied, "was spent in police barracks around the North."

A few nights later she climbed out of the pantry window and met him on the edge of the private lake. He stood skimming stones across the surface of the moon in the water. She sat with her back to the trunk of a tree.

"Would you like," he asked her, "to be buried with my people?"

She was eighteen when she married Jonathan Adams. He was forty-three. The day before the marriage he drove down to her home place in the townland of Ballindan, just outside Rathkeale, Co. Limerick. Accompanying him was Matti Bonner, the Catholic labourer Maisie had taken to the hospital that day.

Some time after he proposed Jonathan bought a small house a few miles outside the village. Their nearest neighbour they discovered was Matti Bonner. Since he'd lost his finger in the winch certain types of work were denied him. Maisie hired him to decorate the old house. Having been born in the Republic, she had no religious qualms about knowing Catholics. But the first thing Jonathan Adams did was lift his Fenian ledger to check to see if his new neighbour's name was in it. It wasn't.

Matti Bonner arrived in his blue overalls and with his toolbox. Maisie came out each evening she could get away and gave him instructions. A timber porch was erected round the back. Trellises were raised. Rooms were painted a mint green. He followed her plans exactly. She supervised the plumbing of the kitchen. He ploughed the garden. Set apples trees. Then one night as she and Jonathan sat in the police car surveying the house she said: "I think Matti should be your best man."

"You must be out of your mind."

"He brought us together," she said, "and it was a costly experience for him."

"It's not our fault he lost a finger."

"If he hadn't we would not be here."

"If that man is to be my best man," said Jonathan horrified, "there is not one of my family will attend the wedding."

"It's only right that he be our witness."

"They won't come, I tell you."

"Maybe they didn't intend to from the beginning. I don't think your brother Willy approves of me."

"Matti is Catholic."

"I know that. But remember you'll be miles from here. It will all be happening in another part of the world."

"I dare say."

"Now go up there to his house and ask him."

"Now?"

"Yes, right now."

Jonathan pulled back the gate and tapped on Matti's door. The labourer stepped out into the twilight in his vest.

"Sergeant," he said.

"Matti," said Jonathan.

They stood there a few moments. "Will you come in?"

"Oh, no, no, no," said the Sergeant. "I have a question to put to you."

"Aye?"

"It entails a certain amount of travelling."

"I see."

"Well, I can bring you down, but you might have to come home on your own."

"From where, pray?"

"The county Limerick. You see, I have never been down there," he said with embarrassment.

"I'd be glad to, Sergeant."

"Well that's that then. I should add that the woman out there in the car wants you as my best man."

"She does?" asked Matti in amazement.

They left together the day before the wedding. It was the Sergeant's first time south of the border that he had so astutely protected all those years and suddenly he found himself on collapsing roads that grew narrow, and then narrower. "Aisy, Sergeant," said Matti Bonner. Each town was announced by a handball alley and a dance hall. Catholic spires and cathedrals, treeless, flush with Roman excess, sat on the hills while the grey Protestant churches, behind beeches, stood at the end of old-world streets. Gypsy camps, with piles of lead, galavanize sheets and batteries, were scattered on the side of roads. The two men stopped for weak tea, rashers, sausages and eggs in Galway town.

"What do you think, Sergeant?" asked Matti Bonner.

"It's not as bad as I thought."

Then as they approached Limerick bunting flew overhead.

"They must have been expecting us," said Matti.

In the centre of the city itself a guard waved them into a parking space. They saw that in every doorway the Holy Family stood.

"You'll have to stop there for a bit, I'm afraid," he said.

"Is there something wrong?"

"Not a thing."

Jonathan Adams took stock of the guard's over-sized trousers and dull shoes, the whiskey glint in the eyes.

"Up North," said Jonathan, "I might have had that man taken in for questioning."

"I'll just hop over the road for a minute," said Matti as they waited. "I have to relieve myself."

He disappeared into a pub. Then suddenly a gigantic crowd came round the corner celebrating what a banner called the Solemn Novena. Women, praying in blue, passed in marching lines. The Virgin, also in blue, under a white canopy, was steered down the street. Behind her came a priest flanked by altar boys swishing clouds of incense from thuribles. The priest was reading out the rosary through a microphone, and behind him the others answered, heads back, while thousands of beads moved through their fingers.

When the procession had passed, Matti Bonner climbed back in.

"I took the chance, if you don't mind, to get myself a whiskey," explained the labourer.

"You can go now," said the guard, "just cut across through there and you'll be right as rain for Rathkeale."

"Thank you, Constable," said the Sergeant.

"Well, lo and behold you," the guard replied, "that's the first time I was ever called that."

They arrived to Maisie's farm in the late evening. Old Ruttle greeted them on the doorstep. His daughter, he said, would be down in a few moments. A sloe-coloured sky lay behind the house. Dark-nosed swifts were darting round a snug Dutch barn at the back. A timbered porch, like the one Matti had built in Fermanagh, opened onto a garden of beehives. In the distance was another farm, just like Ruttle's, and beyond that another, and another, each similar and each with an orchard. And from everywhere came the honk of geese as they roamed the orchards looking for fallen fruit.

In the kitchen they drank cold lemonade with a ham salad and homemade bread. Maisie shyly made her appearance.

She took them across the fields to meet her neighbours. Matti Bonner was installed with Walter Bovinger. Jonathan Adams in Arthur Teskey's. They met Pamela Gilliard, Gareth Shier, Walter Sparling. Hazel Gardener handed the groom a bouquet of freshly picked flowers. They walked up the disused railway that used to take the American emigrants on to Foyle when the seaplanes were in operation. In the cool dark they sat in a handball-alley and kissed.

The morning of his wedding the geese woke him. An argument had broken out among the birds. He watched the males, with necks lowered, begin battle then he went below. The Teskeys were squeezing blackberries into white pails in the kitchen. He washed, and Arthur Teskey drove him to the church.

He sat on his empty side one seat ahead of Matti Bonner. The church was bare and dark. The grain in the wooden seats shone. He could smell the Brilliantine from his neighbour's hair. He heard the steps of the Methodists and the Palatines entering the church. "Good luck, Boss. They're good auld stock," whispered Matti. Then, from among the other steps, he picked out hers.

Afterwards, if she had let him, he would have driven straight back to Northern Ireland. Instead, she had him drive her through the Ring of Kerry. On to Kinsale, to Wexford, all the places he had never been. She had him promise that he would take her South each year. They drove to Westmeath, then Monaghan, then home.

As her family had done in the South, Maisie set apple trees and fed the apples to the geese she bought at Enniskillen market. Now it was the sound of geese that started Jonathan Adams' days in the North. She set a herb garden. Cherry trees. Placed flower-sprigged pillows and peach sheets in the visitors bedrooms. And in their own – white and navy reversible bed linen. In quick succession, when Jonathan Adams was in his late forties, she had two daughters, Catherine, named after Maisie's mother, and Sara.

"They were both conceived in Rathkeale," she told him.

"It accounts," he replied, "for their reluctance to be specific."

From the beginning he expected a policeman's daughters to be beyond reproach. He took them to school, to Sunday school, to services. One on either hand, he descended the barracks steps. He washed them in the bath together. He was an old man graced by the miracle of young daughters. And the first thing their father did when they had learned to speak was to send them to elocution and drama classes. They learned to balance the sound of a word on their palate before they spoke it. He did not want any child of his to find themselves before a congregation or audience stumbling over the meaning of that word "I".

They were taught the trumpet and the violin. Maisie made them velvet pouches to place over the chin rests. Their small heads fell sideways behind the bow. A moment's silence while they fretted and grimaced and tried to remember the tune. He brought them to the spring agricultural shows in Enniskillen. Huge brown bulls with white loins stared at them through the railings. Each side of him they stood on Remembrance Days by the monument. They watched the Salvation Army Band and clapped when he clapped.

Each night he read to them from the scriptures. His daughters and his wife became the congregation he had lost that fateful day in Cullybackey. From her father Catherine first heard warnings against the sins of the flesh through the words *lust, carnal, licentious*. The words swooped from her father's tongue onto hers, words that years later used to send dizzy tremors of desire through Jack Ferris.

"Lust," Jonathan Adams would say, and the girls could feel it – a surge of feeling that started in the body and entered the spirit like a black wind.

11

The News at Six

Along with geese and apples and Catholics, Maisie Ruttle brought fiction into Jonathan Adams' life. On the mantelpiece, leaning against a clock shaped like a windmill, were copies of Dickens, Thackeray, Balzac – novels belonging to an earlier generation on Maisie's side. Jonathan Adams was a widely read man, but unlike his wife or daughters he did not read fiction. Fiction contained inaccuracies, untruths, generalizations, assumptions. The real world was a poor metaphor for what might happen in the hereafter, but at least it was more true than fiction.

The language of the imagination offered licentious freedom. It acquired trappings, idols, delusions, false promises, too much madness. Not till Matti Bonner died did Jonathan Adams rediscover fiction. And this was his attempt at trying to recall Matti Bonner's life. That life, which he had presumed he was familiar with, now grew strange.

He could not place his hand on the facts. Yet throughout his life Jonathan Adams at heart was a reader. The real world, with its physical discomforts, could not accommodate the shocking facts that remained to the fore in his brain. He wanted knowledge of God, and though he baulked at attributing to Him human qualities, this he did, in the full awareness of the fragility of human knowledge when faced with the *Uncognoscibility of the Absolute*, as John Stuart Mill called it.

For Jonathan Adams reality was scripture. It was the sacred history of a people finding their God. So, though Jonathan might wish to transcend history, he grew to love its bare inviolable physicality. As a reader, like many of his age, he had turned to autobiographies, to biography, to see how others had succeeded in dealing with their demons. He had entered again that boyish period of life when the mind selects figures: the numbers on opposing sides in the siege of Derry; the numbers on opposing sides in the Battle of the Boyne; the number of languages spoken when we were given the gift of tongues. Is life not tuned more to the ear than to the eye? How many royals died of choking on fish bones? How many royals were afflicted by small gullets? How many Napoleons existed? How many Jews? How many gypsies? How many Ulstermen died at the Somme? What was the number of Presbyterians that travelled in the Famine ships to America? He traced Carson's lineage and counted the number of homosexual politicians in Britain. He estimated the number of Catholics in the world. How many Protestants died at the hands of the Godfathers of the Roman Church in the Inquisition? How many Ulster Protestants died, were tortured, had their breasts sheared off by blood-thirsty Catholics on 23 October 1641, the feast of Ignatius Loyola, founder of the Jesuits? 30,000? 40,000? 50,000? Who was Roger Casement? What are Rome's finances? How war-worthy were Russian tanks? Did the Russians actually try to send messages through space by means of brain waves? Was it true that Communism only flourished in Catholic countries? How many Jews died so that their blood could be shipped to the front to keep the German Army going? He read magazines on American rifles, on wild pheasants in Ireland. Articles on Paisley. Biographies of American presidents, histories of the Boer War, the Second World War. Geese. Peel and the Law and Order Bill of 1852.

"You must read *Pride and Prejudice*," said Maisie, "that at least."

"No," replied the Sergeant.

He gave her no moral or high-minded reason. Sometimes he might counter with the weak excuse that *fiction was the outcome of idleness*, that it was *fantasy rather than fiction*, but the real reason was that he had a fine memory which could not be induced to recall an imagined narrative. He read fiction as a child, but in the aftermath it remained a blur. Fiction was the shameful stories prisoners made up to escape prison. It was created to obscure guilt. Fiction for him was irreligious, the act of imagination itself was a door opening onto the void. His mind baulked at characters who entered the first line of a novel but did not reside in the real world. In truth, what did not come from the Bible was fiction.

Yet, he was addicted to mythology. Here there was no author, the author had been erased through time. And so the characters thrived, they became real. The New Testament, though it was told through Matthew, Mark, Luke and John, presented no problem. The author was Jesus, and he was not of this world.

The Old Testament was the history of memory itself.

At school, Jonathan Adams had been an outstanding Biblical scholar. The story of the Bible was for him like a roll call of everything that existed in nature and in himself.

The name Abraham sounded like an Indian gong that called the people to morning prayer. It was a wide primal landscape. It was a name given by simple men to a simple man. Abraham was one of the first words breathed by men. As men were naming the colours and the plants and the animals, they were naming each other. In the word Abraham were deserts, famine, emigration ships. In his private world, as he drove or walked, here and there, when he lay down before sleep, lines from the Book of Job would stir in Jonathan Adams' mind and haunt his subconscious.

It was the people's book. They had named the flowers and the rain. They had recreated the world being made before their very eyes in a language given them by God. The movements of the tribes were poems. The translations of the Bible by Wycliffe into English, Luther into German, Calvin into French had extended and enriched all those languages more than ever poetry or drama or fiction had. And yet the story was intended for simple men. *Their ears did not sleep*. They were simple exact words.

At Pentecost, the gift of first fruits, he could actually hear that sound from heaven fill the room they were in. He imagined the eleven tongues of fire leaping over the heads of the 120 members of the congregation. The words the Holy Spirit gave them were words of law. As the Spirit gave utterance, the people named the world.

And when the world was created the angels shouted for joy!

The people had named the oak and the ash. The parts of the body, the brain. And they named the places where they had stood. They had named the ancient places of Ireland. Places were not a statistic. They were where language stood still, where people had settled before they moved on. But Jonathan Adams, and his people, had come to stay. And he himself, though he did not know it then, was to become one of his most uncherished statistics. Already fate was preparing that path for him.

Meanwhile, he read, he wrote out summonses, he cycled to his barracks through Ulster's quiet years, he felt safe as a policeman.

It was being a policeman saved Jonathan Adams from continuing as an evangelist. Sometimes when he listened to Willy he was shocked and enthralled by his brother's lack of intellectualism, the lack of humility. His shameless oratory made the Sergeant wince. Jonathan Adams did not want to hear the words read out. The policeman in him did not want to hear raised voices. And it was being a policeman brought Jonathan Adams face to face with an element in himself he would rather never have encountered.

When the Civil Rights march on 5 October 1968 passed through the city of Derry it was met by a police baton-charge. Jonathan Adams, along with other elder policemen, had been called up from various counties in the North for the day. Not only because of a shortfall in numbers but also because outsiders would not be recognized. The air was rank with bigotry and acrimonious shouts like "In the name of God let us through". The whole affair, the police thought, would be restricted to a small side street, and here it was proposed that Law and Order would make its stand on a genuine footing. The police had been told beforehand that the march had not been properly endorsed by the Civil Rights movement, that it was directly Republican, directly IRA. This was the perfect chance to settle old grievances.

First the Catholics parleyed, then became adamant. But the route they wished to take was closed to them. Then it started. It was a hectic violent day.

Jonathan Adams clouted with euphoria to the right and left of him.

That was the night, in the aftermath of the march that did not take place, that the riots started in the Catholic Bogside area of the city. But by then the old timers had been removed from the scene, the young local police took over, and Jonathan Adams, battle-worn and fiercely satisfied, had returned home to Fermanagh. The following morning he began three days' leave with his wife and daughters.

They drove at break of day into the west through Bally-shannon. With a sense of pride Jonathan Adams flashed his identity card as they entered the Republic. The guard, with a knowing nod, leaned in and said: "That was a bad doing, yesterday." "What did he mean?" asked Maisie as they drove through the uplifted barrier. "I don't know. Every last man of them is a Republican," said the Sergeant, "but they don't frighten me." Then the family was undecided as to what to do. Because the girls wanted to see Yeats' grave they turned south and drove along the coast to Sligo. From Sligo, they drove out west to Achill Island. They stopped there for the night in the Valley House Hotel.

"What's thon island I can see from here?" Sergeant Adams asked.

"What's that you're saying?" asked the man.

"What is that island over there?"

"That's Mullet peninsula," the manager told him. "It's where the Playboy of the Western World came from."

The intention was to spend the next night somewhere in Galway, but Jonathan Adams was drawn to explore the isolated peninsula to the north, and so at noon the following day they entered Belmullet town after a long drive through the unpopulated bogland of Erris. The Nephin Beg range of mountains, which had been shrouded the day before in mist, now rose clear and pure.

An old Fair Day was in progress in the town. Cattle and

sheep and chickens were being bartered. Gypsies sold socks, gates and radios. A man swallowed lit cigarettes and brought them back up again still burning. Dogs fought. Goats butted the sideboards of carts. Men sat on steps eating sandwiches. Cows shat on pavements. Men sat on tractors licking ice-cream cones. It was like watching some medieval pageant. They drove from Erris Head in Broad Haven Bay down to Blacksod in the south, amazed at the isolation, the white sandy roads that ran by the sea; the Inishkea Islands, holy, absolute; the wind-glazed violent cliffs; the meteorological station; the endless bogs, the rips and cracks through the huge dunes; the black curraghs; the lighthouse that sat perched on Eagle Island like a castle in a fairy story; the piers, the harbour, the sea.

"What's the island beyant?" asked Jonathan Adams of a man who was oiling his Honda 50. He straightened up with a grimace.

"They are a great bike," said the man, "if you look after them." He wiped his hands on his trousers, looked at the Honda and then looked at the island. "That'd be Inishglora," he said, and felt his wet nose with his thumb and forefinger. "The Isle of Purity."

"Oh."

"That's right. Yes indeed." He grimaced again. "It's where Brendan landed."

He saw that this remark did not signify anything to the Adams family.

"Brendan the navigator," he explained, "the lad who discovered America – like the rest of us. Except that he was the first. Though of course that may not be true." The family and himself stood looking out, with the Honda up on its stand, and the car engine running. "And it's where the Children of Lir are buried, God bless them." He felt his nose again. "And there you have it."

"Thanking you," said the Sergeant, humbly.

"And what part of the world do ye hail from?"

"Fermanagh," said Jonathan.

"Oh, but they're giving you a hard time," said the man, and he shook his head sadly. "The sooner you drive them to feck out of there the better."

Sheepishly, they got into the car, the man slapped the roof and they drove on. And the man stood there, his hands on the grips of the Honda, looking out on Inishglora as if he were seeing it for the first time.

They booked into a bed-and-breakfast a few mile out the road in Corrloch. From her window there Maisie Adams saw that a large cut-stone house opposite was for sale. She was intrigued to hear from their landlady that the price of the property was only £1,200. Next morning, despite her husband's entreaties, Maisie arranged a viewing of the house with the auctioneer.

"The lighthouse men lived here," he explained, "They're known locally as The Dwellings."

"Such huge rooms," said Maisie.

"This one is mine," said Sara.

But Jonathan Adams, treating the whole affair as foolishness, kept up only a desultory conversation with the auctioneer. And as the man pointed out what came with the property the Sergeant merely nodded, not wanting to enter into any false dealings. Yes, it was a fine house, he agreed, indeed it had a wonderful view. This being as far as manners and prudence would allow.

Afterwards, Jonathan Adams went down to the hotel in Belmullet for a coffee. They served him in the bar where he sat uncomfortably among the drinkers. First the Angelus rang out, then came the news from RTE on the black-and-white TV. The Sergeant took no notice till he heard sounds and names that gradually grew familiar. He looked up with terror and saw they were re-running an account of the march. This came as a shock to Jonathan Adams. He had seen no TV men there, nor was he used to them. It showed the Catholics gathering in Duke Street. Then the chaotic start of the march. The shouts for the police to give way were raised. With great religious zeal the Catholics called to the policemen. Within seconds a protester was being batoned. What happened next was seen by Jonathan Adams with blinding clarity. To the left of the picture could be seen a grey-haired policeman, hatless, chasing after a youth. When he lost him among the other marchers, he turned and batoned a middle-aged man who was already pouring blood.

The crowd in the bar shouted "bastards".

On the TV the old policeman had found his hat. As he put it on, he looked round for someone else to hit. Seeing no one he turned back and hit the screaming man again. A woman crouched low as she pulled her man away. The old policeman charged past the camera. Then, wild-eyed and wielding a baton, he stared remorselessly straight at the lens. Jonathan Adams had become a witness to himself. He saw the mad look of fury in his own eye. He looked round the bar but no one was taking any notice of him. His chin began shaking. Then he shook uncontrollably.

"Bastards," said someone.

Jonathan Adams slipped away.

Next morning at six they left Mayo without breakfast. They were on the road in the dark. He brooked no complaints. And this time he kept his head down as they crossed the border lest anyone might recognize him. Everywhere this RTE film of the confrontation was being viewed. He was terrified. He could not wait to get back to the safety of his own home. He drove furiously, in his mind's eye watching himself right his hat and turn back to strike the man who was down and screaming.

Jonathan Adams had become a part of history. Whenever a documentary of those troubled years in Ireland was made, that clip from the Telefís Éireann file would be shown. Word went out through the police that the cameraman responsible should be dealt with. But by now, TV men were coming from all over the world.

That evening on Ulster Television, as his family sat round after dinner, the news turned to the riots in Derry. Again, in slow motion, the Catholics collected in Duke Street. Again they began to move forward. Again they implored, hysterically, in the name of God, to be let through. Jonathan Adams stood up and switched off the TV. He said nothing. He left the room. Catherine switched the TV back on. In his kitchen, Jonathan Adams heard the eerie voices call out again. He thought it was fiction, but it was reality. He could envisage the whole scene, the heads, the hatred, the jerky movements. He came in shaking with wrath. The TV was switched off again.

"I don't want ye to look at that," he roared.

He unplugged the TV and put it into his car.

By the following day it was obvious that everyone in the village, including Matti Bonner, had seen Jonathan Adams on the news the night before. He sent the TV back to the company he had hired it from. He phoned his superiors to see if they could bring forward his retirement. In the barracks, young Saunderson joked: "Ye still have it in ye, Sergeant."

"Mind your own business, sonny," said Sergeant Adams.

He was terrified. Terrified and angry. The seal on his privacy had been broken. Sleepless nights followed. Each night the same set of images swam again before his mind, and he succumbed to such fear that he spent the night at the foot of the stairs, a loaded revolver in his hand, facing the door.

Then the girls learned at school how their father had been teaching manners to the popeheads.

"Everyone saw you on television," Catherine said, when she came in from school.

He was sitting in his uniform in the kitchen. He looked at Maisie and then at Catherine, and then he went up to his room and prayed. He called on God to give him peace. They were calling him a bigot, but he was a patriot. He was not by nature a violent man. The camera could not tell the history that led to that moment when he had become one of those statistics he despised.

The camera did not hear orders. The camera did not hear the chants of hate. It did not remember that wherever the Mass was said soon men were burning upon the stake. It selected its own branch of history. But why had he retaliated like that? And why had the young policemen held back? Had they seen the camera? Had the Fenians known the whole time that this would appear on TV and so deliberately driven the police to it? It was the old fogies like himself who had struck out, not knowing that they were being filmed. The young fellows had known.

It was them that went up under cover of darkness to the Bogside.

In the light of day he had become the author of his own misfortune. Jonathan Adams cursed the cameraman. He cursed the police that had used him and his stupidity. He remembered going up together with other policemen in the minibus from Fermanagh on the fatal day. They had stopped off at a seaside town for dinner at a hotel. All the talk that day was of how they would put a stop to Rome. We'll show them! Hey! Now he felt that the same policemen had thrown him to the lions. After he turned on Saunderson for mentioning that escapade, his appearance on the TV was never mentioned. But sometimes, out of the corner of his eye, he caught them smiling. There was no escape.

The whole of the world had seen him.

Because someone had knocked off his hat, Jonathan Adams had started a war.

12

The Summer Home

After this, and because of the accelerating war in the years that followed, Jonathan Adams became estranged from his daughters. He no longer collected them from school. He did not walk the roads with them. He did not go shopping in town with them. He no longer went to public occasions. Each time they came home with him in the car he approached the house from a different direction, through tree-lined back roads, along laneways. All the ground-floor windows of the house were barred, new safety glass was installed, the doors bolted. The girls could invite few friends home.

He sat in the house like a trapped animal. Nervousness distorted his features. His chin began to twitch. Before he stepped out in the mornings he stood a while behind a slit in the closed curtains searching the garden and the road with his eyes. A knock on the door once night fell was never answered.

It was during this period of isolation that Catherine made her first appearance on stage. She joined the chorus in the school production of *Annie Get Your Gun* and was soon drafted into the lead. Sara played her leading man. The teachers were amazed at how seriously the Adams girls took the business of learning their lines. From the first day they'd attended the auditions and read out the parts chosen for them, the script had never left their hands. They went into swoons of exaggerated pathos. Each rivalled the other's cowboy drawl. Maisie made the small red tight-fitting dress that Catherine would wear for the finale from bed-sheets soaked in raspberry dye. She corrected the bodice a number of times to suit her daughter's taste. For Sara an old school blouse was transformed with gold-stitch embroidery into a Western dandy's shirt. A cowboy hat was bought in

Woolworth's. In the world of make believe the women suddenly found themselves at home. The living room, with its bullet-proof glass and bars, was turned into a Wild West wardrobe.

Annie Oakley's hillbilly costume was made from bald velvet dyed brown. Old riding boots were found that went back to Jonathan's father's time and into them he inserted cardboard insoles cut from ammunition boxes. The toes he stuffed with newspaper. One night Jonathan Adams came home to find his daughter, in leather boots to her thighs, standing in front of the mirror practising her draw with a silver six-gun he had carved in the long afternoons at the station.

"This is too much," he told Maisie.

"They want you to come," she replied, "on opening night."

"I can't."

"They will be very disappointed."

"It's too risky," he said. "We'll see."

Catherine started gargling. She practised voice exercises. She changed her walk. She stopped eating chocolate when she heard it prevented proper delivery. She began dreaming unashamedly of fame. She perfected a male stance by opening her knees wide as men do. She hunched her shoulders and took large comical strides. Then, when she donned the dress, she made two cute false breasts from rolls of tissue. She perfected a small maidenly walk for her forthcoming wedding to Frank Butler, her sister. Before the mirror in the drawing room she tried out her various roles as man and woman, and then, with her knees far apart, sang:

> You can't get a man,
> Oh, you can't get a man . . .

On opening night, Maisie sat in the second row beside an empty seat. She put her handbag on it and waited. Every so often she looked over her shoulder to see if he had come. The hall filled with the murmur of voices and the crackling of chocolate papers. From behind the curtain came the boom of a micro-phone, or the clatter of dance steps. The lights were lowered. In the dark Jonathan Adams slipped in beside Maisie. She reached over and took his hand. He heard the opening chorus as if it were coming from a different planet. Then his eyes watered as Catherine, nervous and covered in shiny red make-up, threw her arms dramatically wide, and stamped to the centre of the small stage in her riding boots and buckskin trousers. She pulled out a gun and fired overhead with a quiet click. Offstage, the sound of the shot came seconds later. Then Annie Oakley, with a wild whorish fling, sat on her sister's shining-trousered knee and, swaying her legs like a trollop, began singing a song whose refrain was taken up by fifty girls dressed as cowboys. And it was a refrain that Jonathan Adams despite himself could not get out of his head that night as he drove through the black lanes of the border country:

> Oh, you can't get a man
>   with a gun
> Oh, you can't get a man
>   with a gun
> With a gu-un, with a gu-un
> No, you can't get a man
>   with a gun

Jonathan Adams had learned his lesson.

Now, when he had to accompany Major Bunting and the Reverend Paisley, he always stood at the furthest remove. When the Apprentice Boys marched, he stood in any available laneway away from the action. He heard the shots in Derry that were fired supposedly by the IRA before the British Army shot thirteen dead. A month later, he was standing at the start of a march that set off to commemorate the deaths of the thirteen. He saw assembled there faces he knew from posters, faces of Catholic revolutionaries, Marxists, students. He had got to know them all over the years since that terrible day in Duke Street. He might even have seen Jack Ferris there. He was helpful and tactful. And it was not cowardice, but cunning, that drove him into the background.

He was only waiting to get out. *A man of understanding holdeth his peace. The merciful man doeth good to his own soul; but he that is cruel troubleth his own flesh.* He learned to hold his peace. To

126

let the law protect him. He must not be one who *soweth discord among his brethren.*

Not that these Republicans were his brothers.

They were not his brothers. They walked in the imagination of their evil hearts and *went backward and not forward.* Catholics were not of the people. The God of the Bible was the people's God, but they were afraid of Him. They held fast to deceit. They spoke peacefully to their neighbours with their mouths, but in their hearts they lay in wait. They were filled with delusions and assumptions. All the Catholics of the North were on the move. They had fooled themselves into thinking they were in the right. But the Protestants were marching to meet them.

And out of sight, accompanying them, went Jonathan Adams, his eye raised like a hawk for the telling angle of the hand-held camera. But he did not despise those Catholics he watched burying their dead, carrying Civil Rights banners or marching to confront the Housing Authority. He pitied them, and he was afraid of them. He pitied them because they were corrupt, he was afraid of them because they were the mercenaries of Rome. The year after Duke Street, a British report called for the disarming of the RUC. Then in October the first policeman was killed. It did not matter that he died by a Protestant hand, though some took vain refuge in that. The liberals always liked telling that story – how the first policeman died through Protestant terrorism. Or how there would have been no terrorism only for Protestant sectarianism and hatred. Jonathan knew that the enemy was always lying in wait. With the death of the policeman in Belfast Jonathan Adams knew it had begun. Soon policemen would die by guns fired by Catholics.

And not too long afterwards it happened. A cold tremor ran through all the RUC barracks of the North of Ireland. The disarming of the police was forgotten. It was too late. They had become the targets. And now the young policemen felt as Jonathan Adams did. The cry went out for revenge. And orders came through for them to hold their anger.

It was their turn to walk in fear.

For years the Church of Ireland had jeered at the Presbyterian's unrelenting nature, their extremes of evangelism, their tribal fear of change. The lowly Presbyterian that had been the cohort of the Fenian in '98. In some quarters they were even seen as a radical sect who had again stirred up revolution among the more conservative Roman Catholics. But now the Church of Ireland, too, was a tribe cast out of the land. Death chased them through the shadows. Vodka could not stop it. The minute he entered the station he would find the whiff in the air. The male smell of fear. The smell was there before you reached the door. A yard from the door the stench began. And mixed with it were other odours: the metallic smell from the clips of bullets, magazine oil, poster paint, shoe polish, sweat, and then the scent of male flesh exposed to overpowering heat that came from hundreds of lights. It was always dark in there. There were few windows. And as the day dragged on, even while rain fell, the station would at its core remain intolerably dry. The long hours of dryness were debilitating.

Feet, tonsils and the upper arms would grow heavy.

But fear kept the policemen agile. When they lifted their SRN rifles their arms would grow light.

Still the dryness stayed in the air. Everyone was afraid to leave the station. Even the godless new recruits, joining now in huge numbers because of the pay, crowded round their seniors in friendly banter. They felt trapped within a province that had grown small as a townland. Over short distances they always went by car. The smell went with them. No policeman sat on a bicycle in the province anymore. In four years their wages practically doubled. Tall fences went up outside the existing walls that surrounded each police station. This had been one of Matti Bonner's last jobs. And even he must have felt it – the sensation of something burning, the sensation of something that was eating up all the oxygen in the air. And perhaps, since he had only a few weeks to live, Matti Bonner may have felt some empathy between himself and these men in olive green – Protestant Zionists some, successful terrorists others; gentlemen who hallucinated, labourers, holy crusaders, farmers' sons. It was Matti Bonner, the Sergeant's best man, who, working for a contractor from Enniskillen, helped fence them in.

*   *   *

Jonathan Adams loved his village. It was neat like the interior of his house. It was ordered, civic, with houses of cut stone, with fine mill walls, a clear stream, fields of potatoes, window boxes with wild flowers in bloom, with the same wild flowers in bloom under the mill walls. Sheep grazed in an orderly fashion and were daubed neatly at the same precise spot, great Charolais cattle grazed, antiques sat on shelves, in gardens, on floors where they had stood for over a hundred years. Eagles from a stonemason's yard in Enniskillen sat on all the piers.

Everywhere was the same healthy tradition and yet now Jonathan Adams found himself removed from it all.

He did not walk the village any more, only took the few steps from his car that led to the new barrier at the station. In time he drove out of the garage adjoining his house and entered the station through a gate that closed automatically behind him. So, in fact, he never had to encounter the public at all. And the first thing he heard, the first thing the new shift heard as they approached the station, was Matti Bonner whistling. He was whistling "Mary from Dunloe". In time, as the policemen sat into their cars to drive to some new crisis area, they stole his tune. They were whistling a tune about love in the Republic they despised. And when Matti Bonner went home he had taken away something from them. The dryness came with him. The smell of fear.

It was Sergeant Adams had arranged for the Catholic labourer to find work there. He was his neighbour. It did not strike him as ironic that a Catholic should put up defences that other Catholics would tear down, defences against which other Catholics would hurl stones, petrol bombs, and then, as the war progressed, mortar bombs. He was not to know that the American and Russian rifles he had read about, and which appeared so far away and exotic, would one day be homing in on men who wore his uniform. Or that in a few years workmen like Matti Bonner would have been murdered for collaborating with the enemy. He did not foresee the day when the IRA would get that well organized. For him, Matti Bonner was a man who provoked care and curiosity, who had a knack with machines, who caused no trouble, who spoke contemptuously of priests, who had witnessed his nuptials, who would listen sheepishly to Sergeant Adams' speculations about the hereafter. We can talk about things, Sergeant Adams would say, we are ordinary men.

Nevertheless, when Matti Bonner died, he would have wished a priest was with him.

It is said the spirit of the suicide lingers near the body of the dead person for a very short time. It could well be reasoned that the man who commits suicide has, long before he dies, begun to mourn his own death. When a person dies in an accident, you would expect their spirit to hover around for days, for years. When sickness claims someone, you would expect their spirit to be reluctant to leave, for that person wanted to live. The spirit would long to caress fondly the body in which it once existed, would spread itself round the aged corpse of the cancer-ridden young woman that stood in her prime some months before. But you would expect the spirit of the suicide to part quickly from the physical body which had rejected it. That was Jonathan Adams' conjecture. He had seen many that died sudden physical deaths, or had endured long drawn out agonies. And their spirit seemed assured of a long stay in the minds and presences of those that had known them. But now, with Matti Bonner's death, he found the dead man's spirit would not leave his consciousness. Not because it could not find peace, but out of perversity against the physical world that had rejected it.

The village seemed to harbour a vengeful spirit. The death of Matti Bonner and the melée in Duke Street became linked in a fatal manner in the Sergeant's mind.

Often, in the old days, he used call down to his neighbour. And he'd witness some extraordinary things. The act of life itself was a miracle in Jonathan Adams' eyes. It seemed at its most fruitful in Matti Bonner. He had a small, cramped, natural face, thin, muscled arms, long legs, and farmer's hands. He seemed always a satisfied soul, satisfied with his bare routine, his tuneful language, his pathos. That anything even faintly like despair could have occupied his neighbour's mind was beyond

Jonathan Adams. He found Matti the job at the station, but it was with a heavy heart that the Sergeant watched the wire grids go up. That country stations should be fenced in was to declare to the world: *This is not only a war, it is going to be a long war.*

For a while the police took shelter there and the British Army took to the streets. And it bred in the police a hopelessness, for they had been trained as an army. There was cowardice in handing over the fighting to another battalion. But because they had always been armed, they had never been real policemen – not as in Britain or the Republic where policemen went unarmed. They had prided themselves on their guns, but now, like a crowd of unruly and cowardly deserters, they had been withdrawn to barracks.

It was a demoralizing blow to the RUC.

The province had been taken out of their hands, all for the sake of propaganda.

Except for their families, they saw no one. They holidayed far from home. In the Canaries, in South Africa, in Greece. Some began moving their homes into protected areas. The thought of leaving the house that Maisie had designed to enter some estate of identical dwellings seemed a travesty. They talked about it, but didn't move. They were in a Protestant village. It was safe for a while. The place would protect them. But in other parts the cars belonging to policemen became vehicles that careered into eternity. The police, like the rest of the province, began to watch the war from a chair in front of the TV.

Jonathan Adams would call down to his neighbour's house to find the dark kitchen filled with gunfire and galloping horses. In his own house he never watched television yet that was where Jonathan Adams sometimes sat in Matti Bonner's house – before the television, his legs crossed and a look of frustrated revenge in his eye.

There are two things dear to Northern Ireland Protestant hearts: the royal family in England and the Catholic mind. Especially the Catholic mind of the South. Matti Bonner had been his guide to the South, Maisie his route to the Queen. And Matti was very curious about Ian Paisley. Ian Paisley is very dear to the Catholic mind – he is the most successful Protestant of them all. He had his own religion, and one day he'd have his own political party. The two men, Jonathan and Matti, would sit in the back kitchen over mugs of tea talking about British royalty and the South of Ireland.

And when silence descended on them, Matti Bonner would talk to Reilly the dog. Then he'd check the back fields when Jonathan Adams was ready to leave.

"It's all right, Sergeant," Matti would say, "you can go."

One winter, when Maisie was suffering from weak lungs, Matti gave the Sergeant a blessed piece of felt to spread over his wife's chest. And to the amazement of the Presbyterian household it brought relief to Maisie. He carried up goat's milk every second day, for goat's milk, he claimed, was alive with wild herbs that would cure all ailments of the lung. In return Jonathan Adams took Matti cauliflowers, peas and spring onions. He brought him homemade jam, Maisie's pear wine and always, at Christmas, a Guinness cake. Matti learned to love Maisie's cooking.

"I'll say this for you," Matti would say, "the Northern Protestant knows how to ate. The Prod keeps a good table." It was true. While Matti hurled the heels of his loaves to his dog, or let them go blue with mould, in the Adams house they became bread pudding laced with raisins.

Any labouring job at the home of the Adamses was sure to go to Matti Bonner.

"It must be your conscience," Matti would joke.

"Indeed," Maisie'd reply, "we have you to thank for introducing us."

"It was dear bought, Missus," Matti would laugh, and raise his right hand to display the small worsted piece of flesh that did him as a middle finger.

"I don't know what we'd do without you."

Thus they treated each other as neighbours. At the RUC station, though, for the few weeks he worked there, the two men never spoke. And they never spoke at all of sex, except in jest. So, at a deeper level, where a man might contemplate death, they remained complete strangers to each other. Instead, they spoke of the backwardness of the Catholic South. They made jokes about the huge families of Catholic Northerners.

"I'm past it now," Matti would say. "You'll have no threat from me in that quarter."

They spoke of how classless the North was. Homes would be built for everyone, it would all be sorted out. He could recall Matti agreeing, nodding, then he'd look away. But two things that were never mentioned were suicide and Sergeant Adams' part in the doings on Duke Street. For a few weeks after the news programme that made him such a figure of scorn, Jonathan Adams did not visit Matti Bonner. In fact he feared that Matti might set him up. Meanwhile an enquiry into the televised account of Duke Street took place in Enniskillen. The old policemen from throughout the province gathered. Like criminals they waited to be called in. There was talk of losing seniority, of sackings, of loss of pensions.

Jonathan Adams, distraught and angry, was led into an office where a young English officer and his Northern Ireland superior from the Police Authority awaited him. They shook hands.

"I'm sure you have your own reasons for what took place, Sergeant Adams," the Englishman began.

"I have."

"I shan't bother going into them now."

"We were led to believe we were dealing with the IRA."

"IRA or not, Sergeant Adams, we can't afford to have displays of police violence on the television screens of these islands. I'm sure you are aware of that."

"I was not aware of the television's presence there, sir."

"They were there, and they will be there from now on. They have been given by you a veritable feast of police violence." He felt the back of his neck. "Things will be different from now on, Sergeant Adams. You may have enjoyed years of isolation to assert your prejudices, but those days are over."

"I take great exception to your suggestion."

"You are not only representing the police, may I remind you, Sergeant, you are representing the Protestant people as well."

Jonathan Adams lifted a humiliated eye towards his superior.

"I take it this was an isolated incident."

"Yes, sir."

"I would like you to read this carefully."

"Thank you."

He was ushered out. He read the new code of conduct for police on duty at demonstrations as he sat in his living room and knew it was all a façade. Public relations was replacing justice. The war had taken a fresh turn. In the new propaganda the Catholic was the victim. He read it and placed it under a pot of jam. Then from his window he saw Matti Bonner. With an enormous sense of relief he saw him moving through the Adams' orchard collecting apples in a basket while the geese followed behind, yelling. He had returned of his own volition. It was one of the happiest sights Jonathan had ever seen. It meant he was forgiven.

That night in the labourer's cottage he watched *Coronation Street*, followed by a film about mountaineers climbing the sheer rock face of some precipice in Scotland. Matti Bonner, he knew, would have heard or seen the item about Duke Street on the news in a bar, as everyone in Ireland had. But Matti Bonner said nothing. A few times that night Jonathan Adams tried to refer to it in an oblique way, but the Catholic labourer would not be drawn.

As he sat in the labourer's kitchen the Sergeant tried to imagine what Matti Bonner felt as he saw his neighbour baton so-called peaceful Catholics. The Sergeant wanted to scream out his innocence, to have Matti Bonner see it all from his perspective. What did Matti Bonner do when he saw it on the TV? Did he shout out in rage? Did he scream out obscenities like the others did in the bar in Belmullet? But to imagine the labyrinths of the Catholic mind was beyond Sergeant Adams. Matti Bonner's silence he took for blame. As he sat there in his neighbour's kitchen the feeling he got was of being afloat on the high seas far from land. While he sat making small talk what occupied him was that image of himself on the screen – old, bitter, crazy-eyed. In certain cultures he knew that peasants refused to be photographed for fear the camera would steal their soul away. Now Sergeant Adams understood that superstition perfectly. The RTE man who had filmed him in Duke Street had stolen his soul.

And the one man – Matti Bonner – who knew of the Sergeant's distress refused ever to discuss it. Now Jonathan Adams was forever fixed in the mind of the world as a bigot dressed in the uniform of the Queen. He would have done anything to have that image removed from the viewer's mind. "I saw you on the TV," old knowing Protestants would say, and he'd wince, and feel an inordinate wish to cease to exist. And yet in Matti Bonner's kitchen it was as if it had never happened. The labourer made tea, looked into the fire, stirred the burning coals and shook his head at the mystery of the mundane.

The sound or sight of the TV in those days used to make Jonathan Adams unsure of his own sanity. In it was stored a horrific blasphemy, a soul-destroying accusation. There was nothing worse than to see your own self-image transposed, violated, dehumanized. In Matti Bonner's kitchen Jonathan Adams sat perplexed as he watched wild dogs roam the plains of South Africa or mountaineers whispering to each other over walkie-talkies while they hung suspended in the high crackling air. And each time the labourer looked at him the Sergeant wondered, yet no word of condemnation was uttered. Matti Bonner kept his silence.

He kept his silence right up until the last night when Matti stepped out into the dark night, looked around and said: "All right, Sergeant. It's safe, you can go."

"Thank you, Matti."

He stepped into the dark and turned back once to see Matti still standing at the lit kitchen door. He stood there, framed in the small doorway, till the Sergeant had regained the safety of his house, then Matti went in. Not till the following day when the Sergeant saw him hanging from the birch, did the silence of the labourer turn into one long note of defiance.

Now, along with the image of himself in Duke Street, came another image that would accompany Jonathan Adams for the rest of his life – that of Matti Bonner, hanging in his Sunday trousers and vest, shoeless, from a tree. As he had been dressing himself some demon had gripped him and he'd fled barefoot across the fields to the spot he'd chosen, where all the villagers as they stepped out of church would find him. They would see the tears the barbed wire had made in his trousers and the bloody welts across his thighs. He'd run uncaring through fences. What torment had driven him forward in such haste? Jonathan Adams did not know. When Matti died, Jonathan Adams was shocked at how quickly all signs of the labourer disappeared from the world. What work he had done in the village was quickly absorbed. New and more elaborate defences went up. And Jonathan Adams could no longer holiday in the Catholic dimension. The only kind witness to his other nature had departed this world.

When he began to live in a world of fear, Jonathan Adams felt an outsider in Northern Ireland. He began to look for an escape. He was too old for Australia. He was too old for South Africa. He thought of Canada. Then one day Maisie brought up the question of the house she'd fallen in love with in Belmullet. The Sergeant was taken aback. "I miss the Republic," said Maisie.

"It's . . . it's inconceivable," he replied, "that you should even consider it. You must be out of your mind."

"We could live there during the summers," she continued wistfully. "Lord Mountbatten does. Judges do. Why shouldn't we?"

"I don't believe you're sensible."

"We owe it to the girls." She indicated by pursing her lips that the matter would not end at that. She stood. "And we owe it to ourselves."

"This is blackmail," said the Sergeant stoutly.

"Homes are going there for a song," she answered.

"Indeed." He gave her a stern glance. "Ye have, a'course, established this beyond doubt."

"Yes."

"I see." He looked out the window above the sink. "I'm sure I'll be med very welcome in the Free State."

"No one will know who you are down there."

"They'll know soon enough."

"By then it will be forgotten."

136

"Ye underrate the Catholic mind," replied the Sergeant. "They never forget."

"The South has forgotten."

"Has it?" His voice rose angrily. "Is that so!"

"We can't go on living like this."

"What would you have me do?"

"I'd have you take us elsewhere." Though it never struck the Sergeant that he would ever live in the Republic, he found himself the following weekend taking the shortest route to the west, via Blacklion, Manorhamilton, Sligo, Ballina. On the road between Easkey and Ballina they ran out of petrol. Now, he said, Easkey, this is where the madness will end. But before the Sergeant had time to raise a lament a friendly man stepped out of a cottage with a can of petrol to help them on their way. Nor would he take any money.

That afternoon they entered Belmullet. The sky was a vast blue. Even nature was conniving with the women against the Sergeant. The FOR SALE sign was still there on the pier of the gate. With a neighbour who had the key the family toured the light-keepers' house. But while the others grew excited, Jonathan Adams remained negative and condescending. He found damp where there was no damp. He pointed out that no one had lived in the house since the days of the light-keeper. But the neighbour corrected him there. A local family had lived there till the late sixties. Jonathan Adams said the stonework collected damp. It's quite the opposite, the neighbour corrected him, these houses are built to withstand the weather. Water does not come through these stones. A new coat of plaster and you'll be flying. Jonathan Adams found fault with the roof, with the porch. The wood in the windows was destroyed, he said. A few days' work, said the neighbour, and you won't know the place. What Jonathan Adams was really afraid of he did not say. But Sara and Catherine were all agog with the idea of having a house a stone's throw from the sea.

"And there's a *gaeltacht* down the road," added the neighbour.

The Adamses went quiet.

Eventually Catherine said: "I'm sure they won't mind us."

"Why should they? They don't mind people that speak

English. As a matter of fact they speak a little English themselves."

"They do?" said Jonathan Adams, astounded.

"They only speak the Irish among themselves." The neighbour smiled. "And in time you might pick up a word or two."

"Say something in Irish," asked Catherine.

"*Taim go maith*," said the woman.

"*Taw im guh my*," repeated Catherine, "What does it mean?"

"I am good," she replied.

"Not an appropriate beginning in a new language for you, Miss," said her father.

Jonathan Adams marched round the house, then set off for home. But in Ballina they stopped and while Maisie and the girls went off shopping he entered a nearby bookshop. He was about to buy a local history of West Mayo when he discovered it was really a listing of local Catholic churches and the saints who had visited the area. Every history book he looked at concerned itself with Craoch Patrick, known as The Reek, a small mountain that stood in the distance on a clear day like a child's sandcastle on a beach. Each year troops of stalwart pilgrims climbed to its summit. He studied their faces closely in the book as if he were viewing evidence of a New Guinea tribe that had stepped suddenly out of a forest. He took down from the shelves small ecclesiastical books on the story of Knock, a tiny village in Mayo where the Virgin Mary had appeared. He looked furtively through the photographs as if he were reading pornography.

He had entered Mayo – a county of graven images; pilgrimages with bagpipes, fiddles and whiskey; apparitions. The wanton songs of men and women. Images that should nowise be worshipped. There shall be no making of images, nor bowing down to them, nor to idolaters, Augustine cried.

"Can I help you?" the male assistant asked.

"Aye. Just looking," said Jonathan Adams.

And everywhere he looked Catholicism was rampant. Davitt and the Land League. Parnell in Crossmolina. *A Book of Ancient Superstitions and Cures*. The Famine. 1916.

He was about to make a hasty retreat, when he found the

wary eye of the shop assistant on him. He turned towards the shelves of fiction.

Eventually, out of panic and embarrassment at standing around in the shop so long, he bought a school edition of *A Tale of Two Cities*. It was nigh on fifty years since he'd read it, in a bedroom he shared with his brother in another older barracks under the old RIC where his father had been Sergeant. That barracks had been blown sky high in the 1920s and *A Tale of Two Cities*, its print small as porridge meal, went with it. Now, out of confusion, he had bought the book again. This time in very large print. He heard the opening sentence echo faintly in his head: "It was the spring of hope, it was the winter of despair." To give his purchase some credibility he also bought a map.

"Are you going far?" asked the shop assistant without looking at him.

"Cork," lied the Sergeant.

"You have some distance ahead of you then." He slipped the books into a paper bag. "We have some people from home, from Bonniconlon, down there. Are you in the city?"

"That's right."

"A man by the name of Gillan, Paddy Gillan?"

"Well, we've moved recently. Further out. Kinsale, in fact."

"I see." The shop assistant rose his eyebrows. "You wouldn't have come across him by any chance before that?"

"No, I'm sorry."

"I suppose it's not likely." The shop assistant broke out into a horrendous laugh. "Of course you wouldn't be from there originally," he said counting out his change coin by coin onto the counter, "not with your accent." He smiled wickedly. "I can understand you. But it's hard to understand the Cork man." He stepped out from behind the small counter and accompanied the Sergeant to the door. "When I land down there and step off the train, and hear them talking. Oh Lord. To tell you the truth, I often think they are trying to fool me."

"Oh, aye," said Jonathan Adams.

"You'll get that," agreed the man as he opened the door.

Jonathan Adams escaped onto the street. What now? Where

to? For a moment he could not get his bearings, so he headed off confidently in the wrong direction. It was typical of the Republic, he realized, that he should get lost in a small town, that he should be driven out of despair into telling a useless lie, and then be forced by embarrassment into buying the first work of fiction he had bought in years. He walked around Ballina and found a place to sit by the river Moy. He watched fishermen standing thigh-high in foaming waders casting flies downstream. What's the name of the river? He opened the map of Erris. He looked at it a long time, and yet he could discover no place that would tell him he would be safe if he lived there.

"The only Protestant church on Mullet," he said to Maisie as they drove back, "is closed."

"You're not thinking of opening one, are you?" she asked.

The peninsula, joined to the mainland only by the old bridge at Belmullet, was so isolated that it made him feel secure. It was a small, safe enclave, surrounded by huge seas. And one other extra feature made him optimistic: he heard tell there were as yet few televisions on the peninsula.

But he would not make up his mind.

Even on the long journey home he remained undecided. As they entered Leitrim and left the West behind, he began to try out the image of the house in his mind. Is it a house I would like to die in? he asked himself. They arrived back at their fortress in the North feeling disorientated, but still he would not say yes or no. That night the house in Belmullet visited him. In one dream he entered the porch and passed by a group of light-keepers playing cards in the tall kitchen. "Where's the joker?" a clear-eyed man called out. Jonathan Adams climbed the stairs that instead of going up were going down. He found he was at a window on the second floor of the house and Matti Bonner was about to fall out, but luckily Jonathan caught him. "Keep smiling," said Jonathan. "Don't let on you were falling. Think what the neighbours might say."

"You can go now, Sergeant," said Matti. "It's safe."

He woke distressed, as if he had been visited by his own

death. But Maisie Adams had already begun to decorate the light-keepers' house.

"I'd carpet that living room in green. The girls could have the attic." She would clear it of Catholic bad taste, the seamen's Madonnas would go. She'd open up the earth – she had begun to hang curtains.

"It will be our summer home," she said. "You'll be able to relax there."

The girls pleaded. That his family should seek to go South to the Republic was a situation the Sergeant was not prepared for. The house grew on him. One day he agreed. Just like that. "I want no Catholics calling – agreed?" he told Maisie. She nodded. Yet it would be him that would later invite them in. They drove down to Belmullet and handed over a deposit of five hundred pounds to the auctioneer. They signed the contract. When they reached The Dwellings that night a wind had turned the peninsula into a tornado of stinging sand and hail. They fought to open the huge door. Once inside, Jonathan Adams was surprised to find that the table in the tall kitchen was exactly as it had been in his dream, and that in its drawer was a deck of old playing cards.

13

The Outsiders

His last year as a policeman was a long one for Jonathan Adams. In Fermanagh, the occupants of every Protestant farmhouse along the border lived in dread. Once night fell, the phone calls started. They rang the barracks to say someone was seen in the barn, lights were seen back of the soilage pit. The dog was barking. The Catholics next door were moving guns. There were boats on the lake. A strange car had revved up on the lane. Pamela was not back. George had been to a dance across the border and his empty car had been seen near Melvin. Then the police would ring back to check the authenticity of the call. And even when they knew that there was a crisis out there, the police did not leave the barracks.

"You'll have to hold on till morning," the orderly would say.

They rang again and again, their voices filled with terror. "Come over now!" they begged. But who was to know what was waiting out there. Who was to know that the voice over the phone was who it claimed to be. Hysterical wives waiting the return of their husbands. UDR recruits sitting out the night by the bedroom window with a shotgun in their hand. They could have been the IRA setting up an ambush.

Shootings occurred within miles of the barracks and still the police did not venture out.

"Wait till the morning," they said over the phone. And when morning came they did not know what awaited them. "You're dead," voices said over the phone. "You're a dead man, Adams," a whinnying voice said into his ear. "You hear me?" He swallowed and shivered. The threat was recorded and put with the other menacing voices that named names, named members of families. Under the fluorescent bulbs in the barracks those on duty sat idle as they awaited first light. Already marriages among the young men were coming under strain. Sick leave depleted the barracks staff. They returned white-faced and hung-over. And sometimes the Sergeant didn't get home till morning as patrol groups, British Army Units, SAS undercover teams used his station as a central control unit.

The police had no say in what happened. They watched their authority eroded, and their relations with the people systematically destroyed. Whatever happened, happened in their name. They were blamed for leaving the people defenceless. Their informers turned to British Intelligence for higher rewards. Typewriters that no one could work were installed. Jonathan Adams lost touch. As Northern Ireland started to collapse, he began travelling around Fermanagh on school buses.

Fights had broken out in the buses that brought students into Enniskillen. He waited with his daughters at their stop, and got on. For weeks he travelled to and fro, a rifle in his hand, keeping the law between Catholic students on one side, and Protestants on the other, till eventually separate buses for each religious tribe were provided. Returning, he began to dread the moment he had to enter the barracks. What had been his Fenian ledger was now a classified document, as large as a dictionary, filled with photos, intimate descriptions of persons in frazzled print, and bizarre psychological data.

He'd turn aside. Into the hot barracks in Fermanagh came a cool breeze from the Atlantic. He dreamed of retirement, that his face might disappear from public consciousness. He saw himself digging potato drills. Setting daffodil bulbs. Going out with the fishermen. Naming birds. Naming wild flowers. Re-reading the lives of obscure martyrs in the wars of the Reformation in Scotland. He would renew his knowledge of Geneva and Berne and Bohemia.

He asked the few Catholics in the force whether they knew Belmullet.

"Belmullet? That's the end of the earth," Constable Morris told him. He wore an even more haunted look than did Adams himself. That year an ultimatum had gone out from the IRA that all Catholic members of the RUC should leave the force, or else should consider themselves legitimate targets. "You're not thinking of going down there?"

"I was considering it – temporarily."

Morris shook his head. He knew the stories of Adams' other-worldliness but could not believe that the Sergeant had convinced himself of the possibility of some romantic nook in the South.

"I don't know the area, Sergeant. Perhaps you should speak to some of the local Protestants down there."

"I doubt there are any."

"Oh," said Morris, "In that case, you might be safer down there than you are here. In fact, you might be safer there than I would be."

And there was some truth in that. Within the year Morris had resigned though he had four years to go till he received a full pension. But not only Catholics left the force. Protestants went, too, on half-pensions, for they saw no way they could be protected from the assassins. And Jonathan Adams began to see how lucky he was. His retirement was coming just in time. Like the rest of the old-timers he sat out his remaining term without inviting attention to himself, knowing he must not put a foot wrong. At IRA funerals he kept a discreet distance, and yet once, as the cortege of a man killed in a shoot-out passed the place where he stood behind a group of soldiers, it was said that Sergeant Adams came sharply to attention and raised a formal salute to the dead IRA man.

The mourners saw this and were astounded. They looked again to find that his hand had dropped to his side. The heels of his boots now stood apart. The face remained distant, disinterested. It was as if it had never happened. When the story was told later, it was not believed. He was only raising his hand to his head, some said. He was righting his cap. And yet the chief mourners swore they'd seen it – the last salute an RUC officer of the old guard would give to the passing coffin of an IRA man.

This image of Jonathan Adams, along with the moving pictures of him batoning defenceless Catholics, went on into the traditions. The one image was fixed forever in visual history by television. The other was hardly ever mentioned. It could never be verified. It existed only in folk memory. It could only be recalled by a few of those who were there on the day.

He did it surely, the brave fucker. He did. I saw it, wi' me own two eyes.

Like fuck he did.

That particular day was Jonathan Adams' last in the RUC. Next morning he would be saying goodbye to nigh on forty years as a policeman. It appeared that his last act as a policeman was to salute the traditional enemy as he was borne past from this life to the other. A few days later, towing a trailer filled with yelling geese, he headed South.

The Mullet peninsula gave Jonathan Adams and his family a foothold in a new reality.

During the whole of that spring and summer, the family journeyed down to The Dwellings every third weekend. A neighbour fed the birds when they were away. It was in Corrloch that the Sergeant at last relented and allowed his daughters to wear miniskirts, something he would not have permitted in Fermanagh. They were now free to inhabit a world he and Maisie had renounced. He got the names of some families in Newport and Westport, where he called to probe the psyche of the Southern Protestant so that he might find an entrance into the sandy Gaelic-speaking catacombs of Mullet. But the members of the Erris Church of Ireland proved to be even more ambiguous and elusive than the Southern Catholics were.

That was his only contact with the outside world in the west. They moved furniture from Fermanagh to Mayo in a trailer. He replastered and painted walls. With Maisie and Catherine he set pines, fuchsia, holly. Then Sara came behind them with a watering can. They set camelias, roses, flame creepers and a single laburnum. Only to find the following spring that not one plant or tree had survived the winds. The next year, after taking advice, they set escallonia, but only two out of six plants remained alive. Lilies did not appear; crocuses put their heads above ground and died. No snowdrops came. Then they knew they were in an elementary world, of winds and weather.

Nothing survived the winters in Belmullet it seemed. To set a shelter belt became an obsession for the Adamses, as it was for all the people of Mullet.

But these revelations were all in the future. Those first weekends they spent there they set whatever came to hand. Cuttings from their garden in Fermanagh. Cuttings from the old Presbyterian Church. Good weather saw roses blossoming. Jonathan Adams carried the seamen's Madonnas into a back shed. Then Maisie began to saw logs. The girls searched the beaches for stones to make a rockery. And he sat in a maple rocking chair, with a long sloping Boston back, that he'd bought in Sligo town, and in the long evening he rocked to and fro in the room he had chosen as his study, high in the north gable, with a view to Scotchport, and beyond that, the great dunes, where blown sand reached heights of near three hundred feet.

It was enough for him to know that it was out there waiting. All he had to do was to give it time. For years he had lain awake listening for the crash of glass as the window came in. Now it was the constant wind from the Atlantic he heard, walloping the rocks and scattering stinging sand. He watched the lines of tractors bearing turf home, and bought a trailer load. The farmer heeled it up against the side of the house and the family in the evenings tried building the sods into pyramid-shaped stacks like those of their neighbours.

Attacked by midges, they persevered haphazardly throughout the weekend, but only succeeded in leaving behind them a crumbling, half-finished stack of sods, all awry and proud and shapeless, when they left for home. Three weeks later they returned to find that some nameless neighbour had finished it in their absence. It stood beside the gable wall, tidy and perfect as a hermit's beehive hut. This was a miracle in Jonathan Adams' eyes. He tried to imagine from the look in the eye of neighbours passing who it was had built his turf house for him, but no one owned up.

He imagined that someone would call, and refer to it, this favour they had done the Adamses, but no one did.

"It was a very Christian act," said Jonathan Adams.

"I wonder," laughed Maisie, "should I leave my dirty washing out?"

"Sometimes woman, I despair of you."

They invited local carpenters in to pull out the cupboards. They paid their bills in Irish pound notes. Sometimes of an evening, Jonathan Adams accompanied Maisie for a walk on the beach. People called out to them and they called back. It was a new experience. To find they could befriend Catholics without appearing Fenian-lovers. It was a great release that first summer. A night sky illuminated every ten seconds by three sweeping flashes of light from Eagle Island. When they woke in the middle of the night, they waited for them: the Three Horsemen of the Apocalypse.

In the year of his retirement Sergeant Adams and his wife became dependent, like many other Northerners, Catholic and Protestant, on their hideaway in the South. By locals they were seen as romanticists. They were the preservers of old Romantic Ireland.

They were delighted that complete strangers on country roads waved at their car. The finger of a Southerner would rise peasant-like to the forehead in a gesture that was individual, submissive and comic. The girls were taken by these greetings, and tried to mime the movements in the car. A single finger to the temple, a raised palm, a small sweep of the hand, an index finger pointed to the sky. A single, solitary thumb. A nod. A downward nod of the chin. A huge wink.

It could be simple-minded, it could be tradition, it could be habit, but somehow it soothed them. Yet, it never struck them that when they were walking on a country road they, too, should salute the strange car approaching them. Only when it had gone by would they remember. They were conscious of this restraint. And the gesture, when they tried it, appeared contrived.

The South was a museum in which Jonathan Adams, at least, wandered as a stranger. It stored quaint phrasing, soft vowels, superstitions, unpunctual tradesmen, maddening longueurs, stray donkeys. Shouts at midday, cheers at midnight. And no violence. Goats strolled the village. Turf went over and back. Swans flew. And the price of goods changed every day. They bought old crockery. Had a second-hand range from an old estate cottage installed. They queried the cost of everything and drove miles for bargains.

Like everyone else who came there to visit, they deplored the new bungalows, the stone houses ruined by pebble-dash, the absence of flowers, the untidiness. They considered the prices of certain goods horrendous. They considered it contemptible that the Southern farmers had abandoned husbandry. They wanted to see the old style of thatched cottage remain.

They walked the beach. Sergeant Adams had found a home from home, and carefully ignorant of the politics of the South, he walked the unending bogs thinking of the politics of the North. Evenings, he drove with Maisie and sat in his car to watch the salmon boats coming in to Ballyglass pier.

Here again he might by chance have seen Jack Ferris. For Jack, that year, had left college and come to Mullet to work the fishing boats for the summer. Perhaps one day it might have been Jack Ferris' turn to toss the rope onto the pier, and the old Sergeant might have held it till the boat was secured. The fishermen got to know him and sold him plastic bags of herring, or pollack. Sometimes they refused his money, but he would have none of that.

"We'd be throwing them away anyway," they'd say.

"I'm sorry, I can't have that," he'd reply and try to press the money upon them.

He admired the dour unspeaking presence of the fishermen when they returned after a long haul in the Atlantic. They'd step off the boat onto the pier like zombies. Their eyes would have a glazed, exhausted look, a mindlessness. Yet they'd carry out what duties remained. Jonathan Adams would have admired that, tired men finishing what they'd begun.

On days like that he did not approach them but sat in the car watching while Maisie sewed. From the safety and privacy of their car they watched events and people all over the peninsula.

Guilt and strangeness had fixed Jonathan Adams in the role

of observer of a culture that satisfied some tortured need in him. It was a culture to which he could not belong, but felt he once had when that same culture had existed in its purest form, as it had once on Inishglora, Island of Purity.

The mechanics of everyday political life in the Irish Republic were a source of constant amusement to the Adamses. Like many Northerners, Catholic and Protestant, they felt superior to the Southern Irish in education, in manners, in politics, in commerce. The war in Northern Ireland had made them very sophisticated political creatures.

The civil war in the South and the insurrection of 1916 were trivial affairs compared to the Somme, to the cruel undertow the Loyalists felt dragging at them.

Yet when the summer ended, and they returned with their wailing geese to the stricter regime in Northern Ireland, their lives were racked by the pervasive sentiment of their summer home. Names of neighbours and their doings in Belmullet and the rest of the peninsula were more commonplace topics of conversation among the Adamses than were their neighbours in Fermanagh or the increasing violence in the North. Soon they began going down every weekend, though the drive took more than three hours. They installed an old fashioned, balloon-like leather suite. Desk lamps. Set sea-holly. The girls hung Chinese bells. Did their home work for the college in Fermanagh while looking out on the wild seas of the Atlantic. Bit by bit they were trying to banish from the house the temporary air.

Jonathan Adams would hear of all that was happening on the peninsula through his daughters and his wife. Maisie read the Southern papers to him as they sat close to the range in the draughty kitchen. The kitchen was always cold. They never succeeded in getting the range going at full heat because of the spartan amounts of coal and turf they added. They were divided between two houses. In the North, heat sped through the house. They had an electric cooker, a fridge. In Mullet, in a house twice the size of the other, they cooked on a picnic stove for more than a year, kept food in plastic boxes, added single sods of turf to a miserable fire.

It was in these conditions that Jonathan Adams heard how Mr Blaney, who had been involved in the arms trial that toppled the Irish government a few years before, was now running as a Euro-MP; that Mr Haughey, thrown from a horse and out of his party, was now installed in power again; Gay Byrne was opening boutiques; a Mayo bishop was calling for an International Airport in Knock. The Adamses gossiped scandalously and bitterly in low whispers about Irish hypocrisy, and took hot water bottles to bed.

It was a temporary sojourn, or so it appeared at first.

Soon their summer journeys to the South spread into the autumn, into the early spring. One year, they spent Christmas there with the girls. A wind of a ferocity they had never before experienced kept them indoors for the entire festival. Instead of news about Northern Ireland they began to listen to weather reports from Radio Éireann, something they had never done before.

They waited as the voice ran through all the meteorological stations round Ireland, then at last it came: *And now Belmullet.* For the two weeks they were there, the wind averaged 12.3 knots with gusts of over 90 mph. The Atlantic gales from the west never ceased. Maisie watched, with a sense of sadness, the few plants that still remained being driven parallel with the ground. The wind whipped the breath out of the bodies of the girls when they ran outside for turf. Sheets of black plastic flew by.

Now they understood for the first time the sheer strength of the house they'd bought. They grew grateful to the Irish Lights Commission who had built these two-storey dwellings for families on leave from the lighthouses of north-west Mayo. The slate roofs remained intact. Rain burst from the gutters and spilled in a wind-frenzy across the yard, but stone drains took it away.

During their first storm there the Adamses sat in the draughty kitchen reading, or else remained in bed while the demonic elements raged. Jonathan Adams, wrapped in a blanket, could be found every day somewhere to the back of the left window on the first floor seated by the desk in his study. Draughts blew from every aperture. The windows shook. The third night,

the lights gave. A pole was down somewhere. The neighbours offered Maisie candles. In the kitchen at night the girls
read extracts from the classics, and acted out little maidenly
parts.

"I used to act too," suddenly Maisie declared.

Under pressure, she agreed to perform. She disappeared for
a while. The candles were blown out. Then she entered, bowed
low, a candle flaring in one hand, a key shaped from the *Irish
Times* in the other. Her head was crowned by the Sergeant's
panama hat draped with a black veil.

She turned to the audience, and genuflected demurely.

"Ladies and gentlemen, the task of time goes on and on without our knowing. With my key I keep the hands turning. With
my oil can I keep the parts oiled. Oh, the clock says, when she
hears me coming, he is coming at last."

Slowly, burdened down with age, she took a chair across the
room, stood on it, and began to wind the air in front of her,
while she sang a demure rendition of what had once put her
name on the Scripture Cup in Rathkeale – *Maisie Ruttle 1st Prize:
The German Clock Winder.*

> The old clockwinder
> He did it by night
>> He did it by night
> And he did it by day
>
>> With my turaluma luma luma
> Turaluma luma luma
>> Tura liay,
> Tura liura liura liay,
>
>> Turaluma luma luma
> Turaluma luma luma
>> Tura liay

Then they all joined in

> Tura li-ura li-ura liay

And she blew the candle out. The girls began to stamp the floor
for more.

"Dooo! Dooo!" Maisie hollered, imitating the hoot of a railway train, "The train from Ballingrane is leaving for the seaplanes in Foynes. Dooo! Dooo! Last change for Askeaton, Foynes and America. Dooo! Doooooo!"

"Dooo! Dooo!" hollered Catherine.

"Dooo! Dooo! Dooo! Dooo!," shouted Sara.

The kitchen filled up with whistling trains.

On their second night without electricity they were playing patience with the light-keepers' deck of cards in the wavering flame from the butts of candles. Then the postman who lived across the road came with an oil lamp and a small drum of oil, and pounded on their door.

Joe Love trimmed the wick and set it on the table.

"That'll keep you going," he said.

"Will you have tea?"

"Ah no, no, no." He looked at the cards spread out. "Have ya heard of 25? That's the boy to set you thinking."

"I never learned," said Maisie.

"It's never too late, Ma'am."

Over the next few hours, he taught them the meaning of the five of trumps; the ace of hearts; the highest in the red, the lowest in black. He said: "That's a very poor fire you have on there." Dismayed they watched him pile on turf and coal. "You wouldn't want to be holding back on the hate in this weather," he advised.

"Now," he said, "that you have the 25, the next thing you should do is learn the Irish."

"The language?" Jonathan Adams asked.

"What else is there? You have two bright daughters there."

"Is it hard?" asked Catherine.

"Hard? Indeed there's nothing aisy. It would while away the hours for you."

After he was gone, the game of 25 and talk of learning Irish became the major pastime throughout the rest of the storm. Otherwise they read. Jonathan Adams fled biography for Irish history in a volume going back to his grandfather's time, till eventually, as a buttress against idiocy, he began reading early

Irish mythology. To his knowledge of Moses and King Henry, in the year after his retirement, he added the trials of Cuchulainn and Ferdia on the ford, and stayed his hand momentarily, with a shiver of anticipation, over *The Salmon of Knowledge*, thinking, I'll leave that for again.

Life in the South was the beginning of freedom for the girls. To curtail them as he'd done at home would only draw attention to Jonathan Adams. He disapproved and yet consented when they asked to attend dances in the Barber's Hall. Discos in Belmullet. The Chieftains in Castlebar. The Dubliners in Pontoon.

They dropped the girls off at the door of the hall, and while they danced the Sergeant and Maisie drove round the various towns, or walked along a beach. At twelve they were back at the door of the dance to escort their daughters home. Soon, they relented and let them go by bus. Then eventually, they saw them off in a neighbour's car.

The beach was where the girls spent their days. Being within earshot of the waves was not enough. They'd walk up against the waves and climb the rocks, and sit there talking on summer evenings. Once, they found a tunnel formed by fallen rocks that led to an undisturbed pool. Because there was no place to stand or hang on to, they didn't stay in the pool too long. They'd swim there a little, then go back through the tunnel, flick themselves across the stones then, surfacing, kick on their backs for the shore, step out, sit up on the rocks and talk.

It would be too easy to imagine that they were talking of men. But the girls never talked about men directly. Their experiences were told as if they had happened to some other. They laughed at how men, in their excitement, would wet their trousers with semen.

"If a girl had a wee fellow knocking up against her," Catherine might say, "and she knocks back, do you think she might hurt him?"

Or Sara might say: "What would it be like for a girl to take one man after another into her?"

"Oh, can you do that? Wouldn't one of them mind?" asks Catherine.

"It must be strange to have something hanging off you like that," says Sara.

Catherine tucks her elbows in against her ribs and blows out as if she has the shivers.

Each remembers how coitus is described in a medical tome of their father's. How the organs are drawn in quick blue-and-white sketches. Their imaginations make certain words leap off the page. Words go beyond what they mean. They slacken, stand, grow moist. They mushroom at first light. They steal your breath away. For Catherine it is the word *intercourse*. For Sara, who has lately begun to masturbate vigorously, it is two phrases: *the penis at rest, the penis erect*. It has a Biblical sound – the penis. When Catherine touches herself she thinks of her body opening like a moist flower. Their heads are filled with dangerous diagrams and words that all arrow towards men. Each word points to the loins. None points towards the heart, the lungs, the brain.

They brave guilt and condemnation. They are glad their bodies contain the evil they do.

Humming of sex, the girls walk Corrloch. The Mullet boys lower their eyes. This is very enticing for the girls. The boys follow the thrust of the girls' calves, each slip of the heel, then, dry-mouthed, begin shouldering each other. The cry is issuing from someone else's throat. Someone else is having what they can only dream of.

Summers belong to the Adams girls.

"I don't want to go," said Catherine.

"I don't want to go back there," she said. She found her mother at her again. The room was still dark. She could not tell where she had been. Her mother swung her feet on to the floor and, shivering, Catherine hurried from her nightgown into her dress in one blind movement, then immediately into her coat. Sara was already in the kitchen. Both school briefcases were packed. No fire was lit. "Do we have to go?" Catherine asks. "Yes," Maisie says. Cold, disorientated, like sleepwalkers, the girls follow their parents to the car. Dawn is just breaking on the Atlantic and the sea is wild. Everything is blowing. There is hardly a word said as they drive through the salty light. Even the geese are quiet. The girls prop their chins on their palms and look far beyond what they see. Leaving Mullet again for Fermanagh, an intense nostalgia overcomes them. A fondness.

Jonathan asked his daughters: "What are the three laughing stocks of the world?"

"An angry man," answered Sara, "a jealous man, and I can't remember the other."

"A niggard," added Catherine.

"Good," he said. "And what are the three angry sisters?"

"Blasphemy," recalled Catherine. "Blasphemy, strife, cursing."

"I'm sure they sound better in Irish," explained Jonathan Adams. "Now, what are the three excellences of dress?"

But the girls did not know.

"You are wallowing," he said, "in the cesspool of your own ignorance. You've come no speed at all."

Catherine, one summer, lay with a man much older than herself in a desolate field above the cliffs in Glenlara. He was a bird watcher who had hitched from Wicklow over to Mullet to see a bird unique in Europe. He was searching, he said, for a sight of the phalarope, a tiny rare red-necked wader on its way from the Arctic to Africa.

"Here, take a look," he said.

She followed a tern going one way, then a shag going the other. He guided her eyes out to the islands. As she lay on her stomach looking through his binoculars, his hand rested lightly on her buttocks.

She continued to look out to sea as his hand moved. She lay perfectly still as his courtship began. She did not move to stop him as he touched her. She thought it would all happen as it had back home. He'd lie on her a moment, moan, and turn away with his trousers wet. This man's slowness she took for tenderness. His softness for concern. He was touching her all

155

over. She left down the binoculars and lay there on her stomach letting it happen. And she lost herself for a while, until, just casually, she opened her eyes and saw a hand.

With terror she wondered who owned the hand.

When she found the hand led to a stranger, she suddenly sat bolt upright.

She had got so carried away that she had forgotten all about the birdwatcher's existence. That he was even there. That he existed at all. He had become a mere extension of her pleasure. She kissed his face intending to go. Her dress lay against his leg.

"I'm too old for you," he said.

There was a brief silence.

Then she looked down and saw the size of his penis, so swollen she wondered how it would fit into her.

She asked: "Are you all right?"

She curled her hand round it, then he lay her back again. She said no, but he searched and found the place. Ever afterwards, even before her most passionate love-making, there was an argument in her mind, the argument that began when this man continued on after she said no.

Yet always also remained her sexual propensity for the stranger.

He shouted after her as she ran off. She cycled home without stopping. She ran through the house and tried the handle of Sara's door. But it was locked. She knocked but Sara would not answer. "I know you are in there," Catherine called. She sat with her back to the door. She waited for ages, but Sara did not come out. So, she told no one about that first love-making, which when she was older she called rape, when she opened her eyes and saw the hand that belonged to a stranger, when she'd lain with a birdwatcher in Glenlara and forgotten that he existed.

In his room, Jonathan Adams was engulfed in the history of fear. If he died, right now, he wondered, where would he be in his next moment of consciousness?

If someone shot him now, would he suddenly dart awake

after the resurrection? Would all that confused him now have been put to rights? Would Nimrod be there? Would Semiramis be there? Would Maisie? *So Abraham departed*, the Bible said, simply.

14

As Gaelige

The study of local history took Jonathan Adams out of doors again. He went in search of news of the Godstone. He was directed by Joe Love to go to P. Noone's public house in Belmullet town to hear the story of what the locals called the Naomhog – the small saint. He ordered a lemonade from the son of the house, who was behind the bar. Everyone stayed quiet for a time.

"Do you think will it rain?" young Noone asked.

"I don't know," someone replied.

"Will it blow?"

Then the old lady seated against the wall, proprietor of the pub, put the question to a Cork meteorologist who worked at the weather station.

"You should know," she said.

The man looked into his glass.

"What," she persisted, "is the weather going to be like?"

The weatherman went back on his stool, clutching the counter. He looked over, his small teeth bared with amusement, at Jonathan Adams.

"Ask me tomorrow," laughed the weatherman.

"Damn your soul!" she replied. "Won't I know myself what it'll be like by then."

"What is the Naomhog?" asked Jonathan Adams, trying to curb his natural caution.

"There's the very woman will tell you," smiled the meteorologist.

"Yes," the old lady said. "It was a stone statue kept on the Inishkea Islands that the people in another century, and for ever and ever before that, used to adore."

"What was it like?" asked Jonathan.

"Well, it wasn't like you or me, it was just a stone. That's what the Godstone was."

"A round stone maybe," said the son helpfully behind the bar.

"They kept him," said the old lady, "in a tweed jacket and trousers."

"In what?" Jonathan asked, marvelling.

"In tweed I was told," she continued. "And they prayed to him to keep the seas calm when they went fishing."

"And he did, no doubt," interrupted the weatherman.

"He was more reliable than you are," she jibed. "They prayed to him that their fishing might be successful. That he bring them luck. Then a group of visitors to the island saw the locals praying to the Naomhog, and they brought the story back with them to Dublin."

"Of course," said the Corkman drily.

"And an item appeared in a daily newspaper about the idolators on Inishkea Island."

"Trust them," the Corkman said to Jonathan.

"I don't know about that," she said. "And this item infuriated the local curate – one Father Pat O'Reilly – so much that nothing would do him but that he hire a boat to take him out to the island. Oh, he was mad. It was a pity there was a vessel to be had. They should never have brought him."

"They should not," said the son.

"What harm were they doing? None."

"That's right," said the son.

"And he went out to the Inishkeas, took the Naomhog and threw it into the sea."

"After he smashed it," nodded young Noone.

"Tell him the kernel of it," said the Corkman knowingly.

"Well, that same Father Pat was my great grand-uncle. Upstairs I have his memorial card, and his breviary." The old woman shook her head. "It travelled down to us. And there it is up above!" She looked upward in amused dismay. "He never should have done it. It brought bad luck on him. He took an ailment of the face and died six months after. As a matter of fact, all that had anything to do with the destruction of the Naomhog died soon after. And eventually the drownings came on the people of Inishkea. They left. And the government put them into Glash."

"And Glenlara," added the son.

"There's not a soul out there now," she said. "Oh, they were superstitious people then, God bless us. But he should never have done it.

And she shook her head mournfully in Jonathan Adams' direction. That night the Sergeant wrote down the story of the Naomhog exactly as he'd heard it. He tried to imagine a stone god in a tweed suit that could calm the sea. He stood on the pier and looked out at the Inishkeas with the same wonder he had once looked at the Isle of Purity. A man on the pier hailed him.

"I hear you're interested in the islands?"

"I am."

"Well Bernie Burke is the man to take you out there. Aren't you, Bernie?"

"I will, surely."

"Someday," said Jonathan.

"They know we're Protestant," complained Adams to his wife.

"Why wouldn't they. We don't go to Mass."

"I hope you're not suggesting that we should."

They were plied with questions in Lavell's shop. While Maisie filled a shopping bag, the old policeman stood uneasily inside the glass door, nodding fretfully at each further invasion of his privacy.

"Aren't you the great man," said Mrs Lavell, "for your age."

"He's quick on his feet, right enough," said Maisie.

"You must have had an active life," queried the shopkeeper, "before you retired?"

"Oh, he was always on the go," said Maisie.

"And what will he find to do out here, God bless us?"

"He's writing."

"Ah."

"I'm writing," he explained to Mrs Lavell, "a short religious history of the Mullet."

160

"And would a book like that sell?" she asked, astounded.

"Won't it pass the time for him?"

"I'm sure it will, the poor cratur."

Word got round that Adams was a deeply religious man who was penning an ecclesiastical account of Protestantism in Erris. On the road, people stopped to tell him names of long departed landlords, of churches gone into ruin. The Mullet folk told him stories of proselytizers of whom many, in years gone by, had come to the west.

"Are you sure you're not one yourself, Reverend?"

"You can rest easy there."

"Well, even if you were you're too late. The Irish Church Mission was here before you to teach the orphaned girls. They were housed for their pains just over there. Then a Father Nangle went to Achill to teach and feed the Famine victims. He did well, but his crowd are gone too. Oh, the Protestants came and went and here we are, Catholics still, for our sins."

And they laughed: "Now if you could build us a new bridge! Or give us jobs – who knows."

He wanted to hear everything. And each night he wrote up all he heard – who had returned from abroad, who'd gone away. He began recording what the gravestones told of that departed world of Protestantism, he wrote down speculations about stone-age settlements up at Aghadoon; he heard variations on the population of Belmullet and the population of Binghamstown; he was told stories of the old workhouse that became the fever hospital, of potato gathering in Scotland, of the disappearance of the barley and rye; he wrote short pieces on certain Saxon words still in use; he got a book from the travelling library that told him of findings from the Spanish Armada in Erris; he heard tales of the disappearance of the salmon, and the return of the salmon; he saw photographs from the good fishing days when Spanish and Welsh boats sheltered in Blind Harbour; he read of the daily trips to Sligo by sea. He wrote down tales of extraordinary and multiple animal births.

His book he called: The Mullet Ledger.

The people, learning the knack of his mind, ironically told Jonathan Adams extraordinary tales which he faithfully recorded. George Bernard Shaw going by Elly's Bay on a white ass during the Second World War. Synge, in 1904, taking notes for *The Playboy of the Western World* in the Royal Hotel. John McCormack, the tenor, breaking into song in the Seaview. A phrenologist from Cork who came and measured the old people's heads in the thirties to see was the head of a Catholic any different in size than the head of a Protestant.

"Did they arrive at any conclusion?" asked Jonathan.

"If they did, they didn't tell us, Reverend," laughed the woman.

"Bingham was the last Protestant to live on the Mullet," said Bernie Burke. "The last Bingham married a Catholic in the thirties. And he and the wife had an arrangement. If boys were born they'd be Protestant like yourself, excuse me, and if girls, well then they'd be Catholic. The last Bingham must have been an honest man. In one way. And a sorry one at that. For it was girls the poor woman had and I mind my father saying he saw them when he was young. Auld Bingham did not care to cross his wife. The daughters grew up Catholic and so auld Bingham lived to see himself as the last Protestant on Mullet."

"He was hard, you see," said old Mrs Noone. "He brought bad luck on himself."

"Oh, the Protestants are gone," said Bernie. "I can't think of one now. As a matter of fact, I don't think there are any." He thought for a moment. "Yes, Bingham was the last." Then he shook his head and smiled benevolently at Jonathan. "Until you came, Reverend."

They had chosen a peninsula where not one non-Catholic lived. The Carters, the Binghams were gone. The Protestants of Rossport, Rinroe, Portacloy, Laughmurray and Gorteadilla – all gone. Or if they were out there he could not find them. The Adamses were alone. He wrote down the stories and yet contended with his own life in a logical and legal way, as if fairies existed only in the minds of the people and not in his. His own mind, he believed, was an exact apolitical place guarded by sanity.

Disreputable locals who found their way into the house threw bleary looks at the girls. With the help of intoxicating liquor the Sergeant coaxed from them scandalous verse on local landlords. The wording of curses, old cures, songs of losses at sea, historical verse *as Gaelige*. He bought books in Irish for his daughters which no one could read, even with the help of a dictionary. Then he began a history of the place names of the area where the old evangelists and missionaries had lived. In America Street himself and Maisie visited the ruins of the Wesleyan Methodist Chapel. Inside not a whit remained, only stacked benches against the wall. The light from the shuttered windows fell onto a pool of water beneath a leak in the roof.

Maisie stood in the middle of the floor and said: "My father would die if he saw this."

"America Street?" asked Jonathan Adams of Joe Love.

"Oh, a fellow called Seán Reilly from Muings bought up the entire street. It was then Ballyglass Street. And he named it America Street. He'd made a mint in the States. They called him locally, wouldn't you know, Seán America."

Through Joe Love he was given sight of a bundle of letters in a local house that had been written by Presbyterian emigrants who'd left for America in one of the Famine ships. The list of deaths and trials at sea read to him like poetry. For the first time in his life he felt that literature might open the door that politics had closed on him.

Jonathan Adams stomped round the townlands drawing maps and marking in the boundaries of the old landlord's houses while Maisie sat in the car reading gardening books. Each place name had a different resonance and sound depending on who was talking. He wrote down the different versions and then tried them out on his neighbour Joe Love, who would guess their meaning. He watched Bernie Burke heading past the house with plastic bags of fish. A greeting in Irish was called. His lack of Irish began to infuriate him. Every door to the peninsula's past was closed to him. The Irish language was denying him entrance.

"I need books," he told Maisie, "and I need maps that are not Catholic maps."

He decided he must go down to consult the authorities in the Customs House or wherever a body went. But first he wrote to all the Presbyterian, Protestant and Methodist Church bodies for information on their former congregations in the Erris area. Then he sent all his findings off to the National Museum and waited to hear from them. No reply came. He could wait no longer. He took his Mullet Ledger and prepared for a trip to Dublin.

It was an extraordinary embarrassment for Jonathan Adams that he had never stood in Dublin. Money, a train schedule and a change of clothes were sorted out. He took the car to Castlebar. The scholar was to be gone a week. In fact, he was back in three days. Furious, he stepped in through the door, gave a savage shriek when spoken to, and retired to his room black-faced. For days not a word was spoken at meal times.

His daughters feared that he was back to being a Loyalist again.

At last, he brought himself to say: "My whole findings are seemingly of no scientific interest. And what I've learned has already been published." He looked at Maisie. "Do you think I am too old to learn a new language?"

"Are we going to France?"

"Be sensible, woman!"

The women had never seen him so upset.

"They took me for a crank!" he shouted. "They took me for a figure of fun! I've picked my own out of their blood in a heap on the road and these Nationalists have the temerity to laugh at me!" The blood ran to the exasperated old policeman's head.

His pride was gone. His chin at odd moments shook in a manner that made his daughters look away. From having developed a silent convivial nature since his retirement, he returned to his old austere self. "Take off those shameless garments!" he screamed. He became for a while a dispirited, aimless soul, as he'd been after Duke Street. "I shall die in this god-forsaken hamlet," he complained to Maisie. "And worse, without knowing its nature." He now dreaded going from one room to another. But the women would not let him be. They carried on as before.

"Do you know that we are the only Protestant family on this peninsula, are you aware of that?" he shouted at Maisie. "And you! You brought us here! And what I would like to know is what we are doing here? Have you any answer to that?"

"No, Jonathan. If you want us to return we can do so."

"I do want to return!" he exclaimed fiercely.

His rages were sudden and exhausting.

They were back in earlier times, when racked by fear and wrath, he'd shut himself away in his room in Fermanagh. He threatened to leave. To sell the light-keepers' house. He complained of an irritation of the bowel which the girls did not believe he had. It was an excuse for Maisie to take him away from Mullet. They drove to Castlebar hospital for tests but nothing was found. His anger increased. The girls and Maisie dreaded his sudden explosive outbursts at the kitchen table.

"I never want to see this place again," he'd say savagely. "I've been taken for a fool."

"Have ye been talking about me?" he shouted at the girls. "I told you not to breathe a word about the RUC!"

"I didn't!" answered Catherine.

"Someone has."

"No one knows, Jonathan," said Maisie gently.

"We'll have to leave here. Tomorrow!"

Age overnight harried his features. The cheeks sagged. Then one day the girls found him waiting for them at the boathouse at Scotchport beach, something he had never done before. The old fear and the new fear combined to make him distraught, yet he remained silent. The possession was over. He accompanied them to the house in a forgiving way. Then, come the afternoon, he made a fire of his papers in the back garden. "Watch," called Maisie, "that you don't burn the privy." Ash from the history he had attempted floated over the leafless escallonia. Scraps of dialect went over the roof of the house.

"Why are you destroying all that you've done?" she asked.

"Because," he said, "it's all been done before." He looked at Maisie. "You should have told me," he said sadly. "Someone should have told me when to stop."

165

Next morning there were wild flowers on the pillows of each of the three women.

By the time they came downstairs they knew the persecution was over. He was installed in his study reading. He had passed on into the role of elder from which the word Presbyter takes its name. They heard him, as they passed his door, reading out loud what they first took to be ancient Greek. *Vee shay, vee may, vee tu; vee shiv, vee ameed, vee adder. Cod taw harlaw? Cod ay sin? Kay will asti?*

All day it went on. Questions. Exclamations. Entreaties.

In 1710 the first Presbyterian preachers, hounded by the High Church, began translating the Bible into Irish. True to that ecclesiastical republicanism which let the individual form his own government, Jonathan Adams had set up his own private republic.

In The Dwellings he began his first translations into Irish with the help of schoolbooks loaned by Joe Love's children. He began at the beginning. *He was, I was, you were. We were. They were. We all were. What happened? What is that? Who is within?*

One summer's morning Jonathan Adams decreed that an extra place be set for dinner. There was a visitor arriving. Then the family went through the house with a fine-tooth comb to make sure there was no evidence of his previous life on show. He and the girls drove to Belmullet town.

Mr Thomas MacDonagh, who had arrived early, was standing where the bus had left him.

"Mr MacDonagh?" asked Jonathan Adams.

"*Sin ceart,*" said the Kerryman. He was stout with thin fair hair, rimless glasses and sensual lips. The daughters were introduced. He gave Catherine one damp, limp hand and looked at Sara as if he was seeing two of her.

"Come, Sara," said her father, "what have you been told about staring?"

MacDonagh shook his finger disapprovingly. "*As Gaelige, maith se do thoil,*" he said. In Irish, please.

Sara blushed and felt mortified.

It was not a good beginning. *As Gaelige* became a phrase that rang constantly, like some dread commandment from the Old Testament, throughout the house. They grew to hate that sound. Thomas MacDonagh soon learned that the use of the vernacular was at a low ebb in Adams' of Corrloch. And though he had been hired to teach young girls, his main student was in fact the father. Old Adams had no vocabulary and a reading accent which bordered on Arabic. When MacDonagh greeted her, as was customary, with a short nasal *Dia guit*, Maisie Adams returned a mindless response.

"I didn't catch that."

"Oh, I'm sorry, Mr MacDonagh," she'd reply and skip away.

The Sergeant, out of irony, he called *A mhaister*. Master, he exclaimed with rueful satisfaction. His early attempts to conduct all conversation at meal times in Irish ended with his finely modulated questions turning aggressive and abrupt. He'd start again. No reply ensued. Instead, he was met with a timorous, well-mannered silence. Their restraint perplexed the Irish teacher, while dinner time taxed the Sergeant. He'd speed through an English-Irish dictionary on his lap and with a word start a train of talk which had nothing to do with what had gone before.

"It surprises me that you did not get an Irish teacher from the locality," said MacDonagh.

"I did not want to be drawing attention to ourselves," said the Master.

"Is that so?" The inquisitive face broke into an alarming sneer. And in reply, Jonathan Adams' cold superiority: "I would watch my facial expressions, if I was you, Mr MacDonagh."

"What?"

MacDonagh tried to lord it over the girls, but from the beginning they were not given to submission in any language, and seemed to have entered into a conspiracy against him. They had a code of gesture and laughter which used to raise his hackles. They were too old to be precocious, too young to be sophisticated. The sexual tang of their presence shocked him deeply. Often during his first few days there he felt like shaking them. But he got on with it.

The girls' lesson took place in the kitchen between ten and twelve in the July mornings. Sometimes, to torment him, the girls would speak to each other in lewd French so that he was left as hopeless as they were when he'd break into a tirade of Irish.

"What did your father do above?" he asked casually.

"He was a traveller for chocolates," said Sara.

"Was he now?" replied MacDonagh.

The afternoon and much of the early evening the teacher spent above in the Master's room, from which, crestfallen and appalled, he'd make his way around nine to O'Malley's pub. Both the Sergeant and the girls found MacDonagh a very stern customer. A Hail Mary in Irish began each lesson. A strange, untranslatable plea to the Lord ended it. It often appeared that nothing had happened in the Irish language except worship of God. Should the girls turn noisy he was out the door complaining. He held a special spite against Catherine because she would have her lessons prepared, answer him with sarcasm and throughout the class preserve a hostile female air. He tried everything to win her over, and failing that, to humiliate her by humiliating himself. His voice would break at the end of a love poem. He'd look up to find her looking away. His treatment of Sara was at first matter of fact, and then he tried by praise to turn her into a collaborator. But his attempts to separate the girls brought them closer together. He remained outside, a figment of their father's imagination.

His inadequacy with the girls made him a stranger. But worse was to come. He made no bones of expressing his horror to Maisie Adams that a picture of Queen Victoria and other royal memorabilia took pride of place on the parlour mantelpiece. It was only mock horror, yet the woman of the house took it seriously. Now he began to realize why they had invited no local in. The Adamses had old-fashioned Royalist leanings. They were hiding a secret. Maisie remonstrated with her husband, who remonstrated with MacDonagh that the Queen was his wife's hobby.

"Hobby!" said MacDonagh astounded and looked with amusement at the Queen.

He would not let the argument be. He treated them at tea time to an account of how the Prince Regent had sped through Ireland two generations before. "In my village, the people laid out flowers for him. The tenants were made to line the platform like idiots. There was a brass band assembled to break into a colonial air. All were trained to wave in unison. They waved and the Prince, the bastard, shot by without losing speed."

"You are lucky," said Maisie. "He never made it to Rathkeale, where I came from."

"Most likely," he said jokingly, "living in a huge house where you lorded it over the natives."

"My father was a labourer. And his father before him, Mr MacDonagh," said Maisie Adams. "Before I met that man there I had no life." She turned to the girls. "Not until I met your father. He was a Northerner. I thought the Northerners had something about them. They were handsome creatures." Then she turned to the Irish teacher. "If I keep the Queen on my chest of drawers or on my mantelpiece or wherever I so choose it's because I was envious of a princess."

"Not every woman is," MacDonagh ventured.

"Every woman," said Maisie derisorily, "unless she would be king."

MacDonagh's laugh was a loud howl. Then, disbelievingly, he followed old Adams upstairs to continue with the Irish lessons.

What MacDonagh had found was a conservative household the like of which he had never encountered before. It was beyond him that such a family could have succeeded in living in such ignorance in Ireland with all that was happening not a hundred miles up the road. Yet, though he felt superior to the Adamses, their quaint domestic life and lack of bitterness would somehow entice him in. But not for long. When he found out in O'Malley's that, besides being a Protestant, it was rumoured that Jonathan Adams had also held some important government job, the penny dropped.

"Do you tell me that?" he said. "I thought he didn't look like a Cadbury's man."

"He was high up, too."

"I might have known," he said. "He has the head of one."

"Oh, they're decent, good-living people," replied O'Malley.

But now the inclination of Master Adams towards Irish and Irishness became contemptible in MacDonagh's eyes. What was driving the old bollacks? It derived from guilt over violence done. He had probably taken part in some vile deed in the past. His wish was not reconciliation, but to disguise himself in another culture. There was no other explanation.

"Are you aware there is a war going on in this country?" he asked over dinner.

"Yes," said Jonathan Adams quietly. "Thank you." Then he looked at MacDonagh with bitter, implacable scorn.

The teacher smiled uneasily.

"Yes," Jonathan Adams repeated, "we are aware, thank you, Mister MacDonagh."

There was such an air of finality about these words, of restrained tribal rage, of suppressed wrath, that MacDonagh wanted to let the matter be.

But the Sergeant, growing angrier, stood and said: "I would remind you that you are a paid guest in this house. You would delude yourself, Mr MacDonagh, if you think you understand my people."

MacDonagh lifted a piece of buttered potato to his mouth.

"I would not claim to understand you," he said quietly, and began to chew.

After this confrontation he turned his attention towards the girls. He grew to despise the slight tan on their skins, their infantile conversations, their sly fey world, their use of words like *swoon, sensual, dire, awry, dour, provocative, sensible, assured, emphatic, lonesomeness*. It was a language MacDonagh treated with polite condescension. His Irish grew evangelical. He alluded to historical knowledge they did not have.

He'd let go with reams of Gaelic names. Resurrected all the sexual words he could think of in Irish to shame them into subservience. Read entire pages of prose without stopping. He started making empty-headed talk about boys with a whingeing slur in his voice – that lad Noone, young Love, the *gasur* from Lavells – then laughed evilly. His gaze, his tone, imputing to the girls some moral discrepancies.

His intrusion into their lives became a sexual one.

And then, when he heard veiled stories of the Adams girls, even he was ashamed of the salacious thrill it gave him as he slept in Sara's bed, to think how close to him the girls were. Beyond the wall that divided his room from theirs he imagined them sleeping in their skin. They'd hear him moving round his room at all hours. The soft pop of a bottle. The roll of the mattress. Sara's sheets hauled aside. And such was his fantasy about the Protestant girls that his member would collapse into his hand without even standing. They'd see it in him the next morning with that sense of indignant sadness girls feel for unfortunate men. The sleepless round eyes, the pale twitching cheeks, the scarf round his neck fallen like an extra skin down from his pale head. Then, the quick unsatisfactory breath, and the constant slur. He said things, gave hints that told them he knew of their doings, yet he stopped from telling them all. That was left to their imaginings. Their rejection drove him to insurmountable peaks of self-abuse in Sara's bed. Sometimes he'd expend himself and stare listless and open-mouthed at the ceiling like a doll. For a moment he'd know peace, he'd hear his breath coming and going, then, first one woman would come into the Irish teacher's head, then the other, but hard as he tried he could not stop their personalities – their real selves – from intruding. His fantasy could not keep them under lock and key. Only as he approached his coming orgasm would they lie down obediently for him. From next door they'd hear his sigh. But his mind could not hold them in submission. He'd find one of their faces in his mind, then the other, looking away from him. His cock would collapse wet in his hand. It would be over.

In the morning Mr MacDonagh would descend the stairs very ashamed of himself and fearful that these orgies he conducted nightly with his person might have been heard throughout the house. He was afraid that they might see it in his eyes. He would start the lesson with the girls in a distracted manner.

"*As Gaelige,*" he'd whisper.

His guilt made him likeable. To see the girls he had dreamed of so licentiously now attend to his lessons made his voice break on such words as *pog, sneachta, taithneamh.* Kiss, snow, shining. He wondered where his antagonism used to come from. Now it seemed that Catherine had lost her loathing of him. That Sara had lost her distrust. Yet his cheerfulness did not last long. Embryos, swathed in green light, bathed in his hangover. He could not stand the protection the girls' manners gave them. Only through pitting himself against the enemy could he normalize himself. Beyond that hovered a space his spirit could not fill. He was a man who makes a language stand still, and so he stuck resolutely to the constraints of Irish grammar, for to venture beyond that was to invite period blood, the smell of the silk worm, the mushroom smell. As the day progressed his old prejudices would reassert themselves, his sexual guilt would give way to a puritanism that drove even Jonathan Adams, himself inclined to an excess of religious zeal, to remonstrate.

The Master one afternoon made the claim, when once again his language class had dissolved into political argument, that it was the Presbyterian had sided with the Catholic against the Protestant.

"For their own reasons," said MacDonagh, smiling.

"I see you know no difference between the history of the Presbyterian and the Church of Ireland."

"If there is one it escapes me."

But the old policeman was not to be stopped. He argued that the first Presbyterians of Ireland – to the North they came, he said – brought the concept of the Republic with them. Ha, ha, ha, went MacDonagh. They came not as colonists, but settlers. What's the difference? asked the teacher. The Presbyterians wanted to put England behind them. "The Presbyterian wished to begin again," concluded Adams, "in new, in more congenial surroundings."

"Am I to take it that you believe Catholicism to be corrupt?"

"No," said Mr Adams, correcting himself, yet not knowing where such an implication was issuing from.

"Well, go on."

But the old man carefully held his silence as if the matter was finished. Then MacDonagh rose and said: "I'm afraid, Master Adams, that you have the wrong end of the stick. You take great leeway." The Master warily waved him on. "I think you hold some spirited views, which I respect," MacDonagh opened the palm of his hand, "but I know which side I would be on."

"You are free to hold that view, Mr MacDonagh."

"I gather that your weakness for authority is based upon how quickly you can forfeit that authority for another."

"Could I have that again?" asked Mr Adams smiling. "The subordinate clause, please?"

Mr MacDonagh laid down his cigarette.

"You jest, *a mhaistir*."

"I am a bit too old," said Adams, "to be starting Dostoevsky. I have always taken my orders from above."

"And I suppose you believe in the law and order of the British Army and the RUC."

"I do, Mr MacDonagh."

"Hah!" said the teacher triumphantly.

They stared at each other a while.

"Perhaps we could take a break?"

"Suit yourself," said MacDonagh, then he strode to the door. "You are all at sea." Behind his glasses anger opened the white of his eyes as he descended the stairs. He was chuckling to himself in the manner of a man remembering violence done to him. He stepped into the kitchen, put his coat on the back of a chair, and stood there working his hands.

"Are ye at it again?" asked Mrs Adams.

"Your good man," he pouted, "has no sense of history."

"He is," said Maisie, "a demanding man."

"He drives me to say things I don't mean." The teacher sat and looked at the upper air. And just as he had the cup in his hand they heard the door open above.

"*Tarraing anseo, Mac an Du*," came the Sergeant's voice.

"Agh!" said the befuddled teacher. "The pain of it." He shook his head as if to clear his ears, made a gargling sound that had Maisie reaching a cloth to her lips to cover up her merriment, then he returned to his penance above. But at tea time Mac-Donagh would have his revenge. He returned to his favourite topic – a hatred of prostitutes. This was certain to make the Sergeant wince. Then, instead of ancient Ireland, more recent events were discussed. MacDonagh would have the Sergeant know that the Irish language begins in the soul, like all passions for beautiful things. And this the old scholar could not deny.

It soon became obvious to Jonathan Adams that his pleasurable search among the early Irish myths and antiquities had led him back inexorably, even contemptuously, to events in contemporary Ireland, a place where he did not want to be at all, having had his fair share of it in previous lives. He must listen to his daughter Sara ask after syphilis; his daughter Catherine after Republican jails. If they had not decided to speak Irish over tea none of this would have happened, all could, perhaps, have passed pleasantly in an English well used to censoring such prejudiced memories. For at table, even among themselves, the North was never discussed.

Papers were not bought. No radio played. Television was barred from the house. The North was silenced. Only at night in their bed did Maisie and Jonathan remember. Then they put it by till their return to Fermanagh in autumn. That would be soon enough. And when they'd return, with great swiftness it all came back.

It took ages before they could settle down once they went home. Then in Fermanagh he'd remember what they had learned in Mullet from MacDonagh. And it all appeared unreal. The verse of Dail Ó Higgins, the verse of Eogan Ó Rathaille. A smattering of Ó Raifteirí and Brian Merriman's *"Cuirt an Mhean Oiche"*, whose obscenity and vulgar feminism was of a physical variety the girls had deeply appreciated, while the Sergeant, expecting the usual lyrical soft-heartedness, was dumbfounded. And MacDonagh learned from them that Northern Presbyterians were a dangerous tribe. And all breathed a sigh of relief when, followed by a charge of angry geese, MacDonagh, after two weeks instead of three, took himself away. Sara moved back to her room and sprayed it with deodorant to kill the smell of the Irish teacher. The sheets from his bed were boiled, and the empty bottles of stout stored in the wardrobe were returned to O'Malley's.

"I wonder what the next fellow will be like?" said the Sergeant pensively, one afternoon the following summer. And the three women looked at each other in trepidation at what lay ahead for them in Jonathan Adams' search for some marvellous reconciliation.

15

O'Muichin and the *Cléirseach*

Catherine was standing on the step of the house weeding the fishnet globes of earth and flowers that hung each side of the porch when he alighted. Thomas O'Muichin was covered in sweat and still awed by all he had seen on the bicycle ride from Castlebar to Westport, and Westport to Belmullet. He had cycled to Corrloch on a trim blue three-speed bicycle that had accompanied him, rocking on a chain in the guard's van at the rear of the Castlebar train, from Dublin. He beat his knee with his cap, tossed the bike against the pier of the gate and saluted Catherine with the tip of the index finger to the eyebrow. "Hallo, Miss." This was followed by a stoic study of the inside of his cap, and a shy look back the way he had come.

"Am I at the right place?" he asked.

"Yes, but my father's not here at present. He is off having tests done in hospital."

"I'm sorry to hear that. My name is Thomas O'Muichin."

"I know. I hope you are nothing like the fellow we had last summer."

"Why?" he asked. "Who was he?"

"He was called MacDonagh." Then she added as a reproach, "And he was called Thomas, too."

"Oh." O'Muichin shook his head and whistled soundlessly. "Isn't that something."

The new teacher was a small retiring fellow, possessed of an incredible sense of gentleness, or lightness. A Dublin teacher had been chosen this time because Dublin Irish, although impure, was supposedly easier to learn.

But again Jonathan Adams was trying to save himself from too much familiarity with the natives. His rejection at the hands of the powers-that-be in Dublin still rankled. Then the editor of the *Western People* returned some interviews with local people he had supplied, with a note to the effect that the material *was not relevant. Would be slightly obscure for local readers.* In fact, he was trying to imply, the worship of graven images on the west coast of Ireland was a tall story. Well, Jonathan Adams would rectify that. What he intended to do was to immerse himself so completely in the old language that he might emerge one day from his home able to talk to all on an equal footing.

Maisie and Jonathan arrived back from the hospital to find O'Muichin finishing a dry-stone wall that had collapsed at the back of the house. They were taken aback at the stature of the cheerful teacher. The Adams had not expected an imp to arrive from Dublin. O'Muichin's feet barely touched the ground and his movements were those of a man treading water. He was forever on his bike, visiting Irish speakers in the area, head erect, buoyant and somehow soulless, or maybe all soul; his was a condition where body and soul were always on the move. He was domiciled in Catherine's room this time. "For variety's sake," Jonathan Adams pronounced. So Catherine's wardrobe was moved into Sara's room, and a coin tossed each night to see who would sleep on the outside of the bed.

The Sergeant did not advance straight away to meet O'Muichin, feeling, perhaps, that things had got out of control, that he should have called a halt to this procession of Irish teachers through his house, men set on turning myth into reality, and by virtue of their crude and unstable natures ruining his repose. But then O'Muichin presented himself at the study door and said: "I hate these particulars, but I have never done the likes of this before." For the new teacher to admit such ignorance was a consolation to Jonathan Adams. Now he foresaw fruitful hours ahead, when he, after regaining his rightful place as master of the house, might probe the genial Irish spirit, rather than be afflicted by the troublesome psyche MacDonagh had presented.

He felt O'Muichin was a man in whom the grudge was spent. No bitterness remained. So he took to O'Muichin. And O'Muichin found a further ally in Maisie Adams when, after supper, he rose and carried the dishes into the scullery in the manner of a man who lived alone.

"It's a matter of habit," he explained, then becoming distant, he took himself to his room.

For such a small man his snores that night carried throughout the house. But unlike his predecessor, he did not spend an age in the outdoor toilet reading from the squares of torn newspapers and inserting bizarre political comments in the margins of books, nor did he distress the girls by betraying the male weakness for innuendo and domination. His shyness was a bonus all round. He was a man, they all agreed, frightened of familiarity. Yet, especially for Mr Adams, a man whose words were both reassuring and intelligent.

And like all men who think in two languages, he was given to the odd discourse on this condition.

A language is for thinking in, O'Muichin had explained over supper. He grew verbose and animated. The original images are sometimes in Irish, he said, and the English occurs only by way of explanation. Sometimes, with concepts, the opposite is true. The new language is merely the learning of an old and well-tried discipline, he said, for which our senses – tired of the language we usually express ourselves in – cry out. A language will return to its source, even in a stranger's head. The great joy is selecting from various languages what best expresses the content of the mind. "I'm lost," said Catherine. Immediately the new teacher entertained the vapours, as if someone had just tightened his bodice, and a nervous ennui ensued. This malodorous silence continued until Sara said something to Catherine, then struck by an obscure thought, O'Muichin shot a notebook out of his pocket and scribbled some comment down. He looked up, found where he was and resumed his vacant air.

"We consider shapes, we do," he said out of the blue, "not colours. And another thing, you can't say 'I love you' in Irish. Don't let them tell you otherwise. In Irish the love is on you. It's not yours to command. Yes," he added thoughtfully.

*   *   *

178

O'Muichin hailed from the inner city, he was a working-class Gaelgoir, and he was glad to be away from Dublin for a time. The wages he earned as a schoolteacher he spent publishing his own books. "Yeats did it, so why shouldn't I?" he explained. *Fantasies* was his first publication.

"Fantasies?" asked the Sergeant.

"Yes, and I'm presently preparing Part II."

"These, I take it, are not of a ribald nature."

"The Fianna tales, Mr Adams. *The Táin*. I use these as my stepping off point."

"You might point out your sources to me," said the Sergeant, in scholarly vein, "if you have the time."

"Delighted," replied O'Muichin.

But for a man occupied in such a sphere as fantasy, he was immensely practical. The summer before this he had cycled from Malin Head in the North to Mizzen Head in the South. The sights he'd seen along the way he explained in graphic detail. When he went out on his bike, as was his wont each day, he carried materials for mending a puncture not in the carrier as a countryman might, but in a blue khaki bag over his shoulder. In the bag he also kept a bottle of ink, a pen, two notebooks and something to drink. Puffing and blowing hard, so that sometimes he took them into the air on his knees, he brought the girls in turn up and down the beach on the bar of his bike. Then Sara, and next Catherine, would attempt to ride the bike with one leg inserted under the crossbar to reach the far peddle, and so, sideways, they flew across the hard sand. It was considered unwomanly to throw your leg over the bar of the bike. A man's bike needed trousers. In his trousers it was O'Muichin's habit to ride each day to some nearby village and take, he said, particulars. He was also an early riser. The first morning of his stay, Maisie Adams came down to find he already had the fire lit from the embers of the night before, a cup of tea made, and yesterday's papers spread across his knees.

Not that anyone could ever rise before the father of the girls.

It was Jonathan Adams' habit to be up and out to the garden before anyone, and then he'd wake the girls and his wife out of their sleep to sniff the wild flowers he'd brought them. They'd sway gingerly up from the depths to find a flower, a dog rose, perhaps, on their pillow. Many's the morning Catherine found her final dream fill with an exquisite sense of another world, the room of her dream would suddenly fill with a vague blue, a delicate mist hanging tentatively out of reach. Then slowly it would move towards her, enveloping the dreamer; she'd swoon and wake to find a primrose pressed to her nostril.

"You haven't lived," Jonathan Adams believed, "if you haven't smelt the primrose."

The morning after O'Muichin's arrival it was single sprigs of lilac the women found. Descending in his socks, the teacher met the Sergeant ascending with the clump of lilac in his hand. Adams hung his head to be found about such a sentimental journey so early in the morning.

"*Is fior,*" said O'Muichin, nodding towards the flower, "*nach bhfuil blath nios cumhra na i.*"

"Pray?"

"There's nothing sweeter," said O'Muichin, "than the lilac."

For both men that first day had begun generously.

O'Muichin lit the fire, left a cup of tea at the door of the Sergeant's study, and leafed through various books – *Stray Thoughts on Reading* by L. H. M. Soulsby, Maisie's *Sea Gardening* and Catherine's *The Liverpool Poets* in the Penguin Modern Poets series – till the girls came down. When they did not appear he went out to weed in the garden and throw grain to the geese. The girls were slow in coming because they were talking in that languorous manner of people privileged to be alive without knowing it.

Theirs was a world of sensation only.

It was Catherine's turn to tickle her sister. This always took ages, for Sara was a great pleasure-seeker, and she would make promises way and beyond what she could carry out just for a few extra moments of leaving her body for that other body where the senses raised their perceptions like deer. First she lay on her stomach, then Catherine touched her neck, tiptoed down her spine with her fingertips, flattened her palms at the sudden curve of her sister's rump, then halted in the curved hollow at the bottom of Sara's spine. Sara turned over on to her back.

"Just a little more," she said. "You're very demanding," said Catherine. Now Catherine, thinking of something far removed from what she was at, traced her sister's breasts and upper arms. Then she'd consider a woman's body, knowing where each pleasurable stress lay. With a selfish edge of narcissism, she'd frustrate her sister. Hurrying, she sifted at the edge of places then flitted away, and looking out of the window, with one hand she tipped her sister's temples lightly while with the other she teased across her thighs, and with both hands, lastly, she felt the roots of the hair on her head.

"That's enough," said Catherine. "I'm getting up."

Sara came on to her elbow. "Could you pass me my socks?" she said, and then, as she pulled them on her beneath the sheets in the bed, she ventured idly: "I met a man raking seaweed into clumps below at low tide. He was very handsome. 'Are you local?' I asked him. 'No, Leitrim,' he replied. 'We're all mad in Leitrim.' Then he broke into a merciless laugh."

"Leitrim?" said Catherine. "I doubt that he's attractive."

"He is," Sara said confidently, "in a way."

"The Leitrim man always gives me the same feeling as the single red bloom of the geranium down in the porch," replied Catherine. "I can't bear to look at it without feeling sad and wanting to run away at one and the same time."

"I like him."

"You do?"

"Yes," said Sara.

Catherine looked at her sister, as she often did, with trepidation, because she felt Sara had crossed some invisible line that made them both wholly independent of each other, which in itself, though scaring, was ennobling. Sara led the way, Catherine followed.

"Good morning, ladies," O'Muichin said. From this out they were to be known as ladies it seemed. When, after breakfast, they sat down at the table with their notebooks and pens as they were accustomed, O'Muichin suggested a walk round the countryside instead. He took with him a bird book and a flower book, but he did not need them, for the girls – long encouraged by their father – recognized everything, recalled spring flowers, autumn flowers, told him in English, and he translated.

The meadowsweet was *airgead luadra*, the silver rushes. The primrose was *bainne bo bleachta*, the milk of the milch cow. The daffodil, the flower that hangs its head, *lus an chron chinn*. The ditches were filled with herb Robert and he became *lus coille*, flower of the wood, though there was not a tree in sight. And then came the daisy, *noinin*, little noon or midday.

The girls could not believe the soft nature of this man, with his upturned shoes, consoling eyes and frayed shirt collar, that could give the flowers they knew a different stance in another language. They walked from field to field accounting for the lesser celandine, the purple loosestrife, the purple head of the thistle, the grip of the leaf round the phallic head of the blossoming hemlock, and back again to the cluster of mauve lights from brave herb Robert in a ditch. Some plants he could translate by colour alone, for the Irish had no name for them. Then they passed on to birds: Robin, *spideog*, a snot or the little perky one; the scald crow, *preachan na gearcha*, crow of the hens or the chicken crow; *londubh*, blackbird, the black spout of music. The lady thrush, and the lady blackbird had the same name, he said.

"And what's that?" asked Sara.

Here O'Muichin hesitated.

"Some words for birds," he said, "are lost in meaning. If you take the male it's *smollach*, and that could be translated as a lighted coal. But if you take the *cléirseach* that could mean something else."

"And what's that?" asked Catherine.

"Oh, that's a hard one."

O'Muichin considered his book of birds where the female thrush was drawn in flight, and at rest, in quick dabs of faded watercolour; he looked at her coat of spots and wondered how the ancient Irish had found there what the word described.

"Cunt," he said. And before they had time to take this in he immediately turned and pointed at a magpie. "*Snag breac*," he said quickly. "*An snag breac*," he said again while they mulled over the wild consonants and soft vowels of the *cléirseach*. He spelt out the letters of the *snag breac*, smiling to himself.

"Meaning the piebald thief," he explained. They looked at the magpie while they thought of the thrush. "Isn't that good?" he asked. He went on to the chough, the corncrake, and the peregrine.

"There's one," said Catherine. "I don't suppose you have in Irish – what of the phalarope?"

"I'm afraid I never heard of him."

"He is," she said, holding his gaze, "perhaps the opposite of the *cléirseach*."

"Indeed?"

"A tiny wader, in fact."

"Oh," said their teacher, shyly. "Is that so?"

Across the sky a bank of threatening clouds gathered. A sharp wind, tough as hail, blew in. Within seconds, rain was falling on the islands. The girls took their teacher into a dried-up drain that ran under a dense wind-beaten arch of shrubbery. With sudden drops of rain tumbling through, they walked stooped for ages along the passage with its gold roof of crystals of rain and sun. Shafts of light struck their faces. O'Muichin was mesmerized. Sara whistled as she walked ahead, looking behind her now and then to make sure that the others were following. When they emerged from the tunnel the sun had given the mountains and sea a quality for which there are no words. The new hallucinatory light that precedes the rainbow covered everything, killing all colours except the simple green that cannot be defined as colour only, but is a state of being that follows on the heels of summer rain.

And, as always in such a light, Catherine, as she walked with the others, felt the uncanny sensation of being in the company of an illusion. She was part of a film being made. Sara's face loomed and blurred. As for O'Muichin, he became faceless and strange. The two were talking to each other in a familiar way that Catherine could not understand. I'm burning inside, she thought, for someone to tell me how beautiful I am. From the wet grass came the sound of birds like shook dice. As Catherine made a great effort to catch up with the others, she stumbled and her hand inadvertently touched O'Muichin's bottom, and she withdrew it in shock, not because her touch was accidentally rude, but because she was amazed to find his trousers were so cold.

You would have expected, she told Jack Ferris years later, an Irish teacher's bum to be warm.

"I'll put a cup of tea on," O'Muichin said to Jonathan Adams.

It was seven in the morning. The day outside was sandy-coloured and wet.

"Thank you," said the old Presbyterian.

He came in from the garden with a clump of yellow gazanias. His hair and face were damp. He placed the flowers very carefully on the sink. Turned and put an outstretched hand upon the table. "Oh," he said as if remembering something. Then O'Muichin saw that Jonathan Adams had turned wretchedly pale. "Mr Adams!" said O'Muichin. The old man shook his head. Another seizure of pain passed through him. He placed both hands on the table, leaned his head forward and down and stayed there like a man in the starting blocks.

After a while he lifted his eyes and looked at the teacher.

"Excuse me," he said. "I get these touches of indigestion. I'll go upstairs to my study now."

"Can I get you anything?"

"No, thank you," said Jonathan Adams, "I'll just go above."

He stopped at the foot of the stairs again. Another cramp pinned him to the bottom step. It passed.

O'Muichin's only bad points were flicking cigarette ash over the kitchen table, singing songs in Gaelic to himself at all hours of the night, suddenly cursing in a sharp Dublin aside, and shying away from all intimacy with the girls, beyond what his teaching called for. In the morning, Maisie would find the bed made, the hearth in his room littered with the stubs of cigarettes, and the candles he had brought with him burnt to a spit on the mantel.

"Why the candles?" she asked him.

"For the same reason that I love to listen to the rain," he explained.

Religion was another matter. Each Sunday he attended

a different church. And yet if he was asked, as he was by Catherine once, did he believe in God, he answered: "We have been alone for such a long time and then one day, one man comes along. Yes, Christ. I suppose it must mean something." Then he considered her question. "But God? Well, I love the man who made the world, but I don't believe in him." For a while it appeared he might continue, but then he winked and smiled, and Sara bared her bottom teeth to keep herself from laughing, for he seemed a very timorous man to be taking on the whole world. But he did not enter into such matters while he instructed the Master in his study of Sweeney, or the pursuit of Diarmuid and Grainne, or the Children of Lir.

"Have you been to the Island of Purity?" asked the Sergeant.

"What's that?" asked the teacher.

"Inishglora."

"I'm afraid not."

"You should go, for that's where those swans ended their days."

"I didn't know. One has to assume certain things."

"That is your error. You can assume nothing. Nothing at all."

These mythological tales, though they were known to the Sergeant in English, gained a vexing physical presence in the vernacular, so that in his dreams some strange man – perhaps O'Muichin – drove a herd of sheep, with the heads of men, before him; humans with whom he was somewhat familiar adopted the forms of animals he could not recognize; Mac-Donagh returned as a goose; and in one striking dream he saw his daughter Catherine ride a goat along the edge of a cliff while he called and called after her in vain. O'Muichin, besides reading hands, was also an interpreter of dreams, and on hearing the father's dream of the goat he said that the dream went back to Jonathan Adams' reading of Greek mythology. He said that the dream was one of two things, as all dreams are.

"And what are they, may I ask?" enquired the Master.

"I would have to know first," smiled O'Muichin, "whether the goat was a nanny or a buck."

Jonathan Adams for a long while considered the unruffled

mien of the man who was telling him his dreams were prompted not by classical tales but by the gender of animals.

"Would you not consider that interpretation a bit far-fetched?" he asked.

"Next time you see the goat," whispered O'Muichin, and he came closer to the Sergeant, "next time, now, that you see the goat – excuse me – check to see if it has its equipment."

"I see," said the Sergeant.

O'Muichin winked, and turned the talk to Oisin.

"It's hard to credit him, sometimes," said Sara, elsewhere.

"He's not afraid, anyway," said Catherine in a tone of voice that intimated she was standing up for him.

It was a Sunday, and later on that afternoon the Irish speaker turned despondent. It was the same boredom as before. There were no lessons that day. Not a word after dinner could be got out of him, and even leaning on the pier of the gate considering the village going about its business could not raise his spirits.

"Are you not speaking to the poor?" Sara asked him.

"I feel like I am expecting someone," he explained.

"There's a dance next Friday night in Bangor-Erris, if you'd care to venture there."

"*B'fheidir*," he muttered. "I like the western ladies. I never heard the word lady used except in a derisory fashion till I came here. I like the western ladies, I must admit. They are very open."

"Do you think so?"

"I do indeed."

He remained preoccupied, and just nodded at everything she said. Sara sat up on the gate and kicked against the pier. Catherine passed between them and went up to the village thinking: "Where is the rotten fucker who will love me?" The other pair stayed on silent by the gate.

"When someone gets like you I always feel to blame," Sara said.

Coming out of his reverie, O'Muichin thought aloud: "I have a feeling that I went this way once before."

O'Muichin, precursor of other lovers to come in the life of the girls, looked up at the starched white sky across which he could feel the sea moving. A cloud crossed like an exhausted wave. He studied an abandoned lobster pot on the windowsill of a deserted shed without a roof, and beyond that, a yard of collapsed and grinning galvanize. Gulls wheeled by, then scald crows started up, and for one brief inconclusive second he realized that birds never look at each other while they fly, nor when they sit on telegraph wires, not even when they perch in a cage. This he thought was something to ponder on.

He told this to Sara.

She said: "I never like to see someone who cannot look you in the eye."

The window of the study came down. "Teehaw," said the Sergeant using Sara's pet name, "leave Mr O'Muichin alone, and be off with you."

"She's all right, Mr Adams," said the Irish speaker, and then in a nervous fashion – some creature had tightened his bodice again – he took a walk up the peninsula.

In Belmullet the Dublin Jackeen was an object of great curiosity, as was the man before him, but O'Muichin even more so, since he did not fraternize. Nor did he relish at all the interest taken in him. He was a man constantly looking for an escape. To disappear. Become transparent. The people had a name for that, which translated means "head of straw". On his toes he leaned over to look at the water. He felt the rim of the old bridge with his hands and stood there for a while.

"When they build the new one they should make it so it opens to let boats through," said an old fellow beside him. "Then you'd be able to travel right round the peninsula by water."

O'Muichin snapped the notebook out of his pocket and jotted something down. He took another step towards the house, then stopped again to write. The spell was broken. He felt benign. The notebook came out, the thought was dismissed, he walked on. Catherine appeared. His walk eventually took them to a beach and Catherine accompanied him. First at a distance, then alongside.

There was an infinitesimal seam in her black stockings. She was a tall young woman in a grey, shapeless jumper. Lean, athletic, sure-footed. Black skirt, black slippers. The blond hair that fell into her eyes was kicked out behind. "God is good," said O'Muichin. "He sent me you." Catherine was glad that O'Muichin had cheered up. They talked of the disparity between different places, of things happening in different places simultaneously. Stepping over a stream there was the sensation of one hand letting the other hand go. Pure-wool clouds floated in a crevice of the mountains on Achill. Then a sudden squall.

"County Mayo," said Catherine.

"That's right," said O'Muichin. "And what are you going to be?"

"An actress," said Catherine.

"Well," said he, "you have a beautiful speaking voice."

"Thank you," she said. She reached over and kissed her teacher's cheek. A furious barking began. The two of them had to stand on a stone wall to avoid a cross dog until a boy, who appeared out of a nearby house, called him away.

"C'mon away you fucker, you," shouted the boy. "And the fucker isn't even ours. Ga lang out-a-that. Look at the head on him," he shouted. "Come up out of there. Go on!" Still shouting at the dog, the boy passed out of sight. And again O'Muichin took his notebook out of his pocket and jotted down in a terse style all he had seen and heard.

The following week O'Muichin passed on to the Irish for trees, but it was obvious that he was learning more from the girls than they were from him. He was learning a Northern language that was archaic. Like Jack Ferris long after him, he listened in awe to their succinct vocabulary that had about it an eroticism, a seduction, a wry humour, and a strange undertone of despair. And he was aware all the time that he must not succumb. As the days passed he became a strange bird. The notebook was never out of his hand, then he'd break out into long, abstract speeches, the gist being that the girls should keep diaries of their lives, for he felt that they had a gift greater than his, and he did not mind admitting it.

But he could not get them to be serious.

"We're not that foolish," replied Sara, "to write down what we really think."

"We're only passing through," said Catherine, though his would be the first name that would go into her book.

"My trouble is I wrote a book in Irish. In Irish it was spare and true. Now they want it in English, and in English I've added things I've never seen."

"I don't understand," said Catherine.

"It's this," explained O'Muichin. "You pair have entered my story. I'll be stuck with you for ever." Then he quoted Kafka: " 'You see – left to my own resources I should have long ago been lost.' "

Then their minds and bodies wandered apart so that he could make nothing of the girls. And because his own life felt like a fiction, these real people, real women, recalled O'Muichin to a physical and mental state of wellbeing he had rarely experienced. He watched a cow asleep, that was not asleep, for a moment later she flicked her tail, rose her head and looked over a wall topped with sweet broom. The wind gave a number of highly fraught hums. There were dogs asleep on a doorstep, not asleep. He looked into the worried, querying eyes of an ass, eyes affected with self-pity, as if the ass were approaching a fairly aggressive customer that she would fain be nervous of, but secretly despised. The despising was in the ass's bone-shattering roar; and in the aftermath was the journey back into subservience again.

"Did you ever," asked Catherine, "when you were half-way through writing a book find that you'd taken a wrong direction?"

"Touch wood," he replied.

So ended the lessons on trees. And in such a state of mind O'Muichin approached his final evening in the Adams' house.

The Sergeant wished to pay him, after supper was over, his two weeks' wages.

"Half of that will do," said O'Muichin. "I've been having a holiday."

But Mr Adams pressed the money upon him. It was the first time he had touched the old man and he found to his surprise a sort of elegant strength travel down Jonathan Adams' arm into his hand.

189

"I hope your fantasies do well," he said.

"Thank you," the teacher said.

At the dance that night all reticence left O'Muichin. He danced with one of the sisters, and then the other, with practised steps learned in a hall in Parnell Square. "You should go there. I go there every Thursday night," he said, while he avoided as best he could the wilder antics of the lads, for O'Muichin was a resourceful and patient man and knew that a stranger there was an object of male contempt. He slipped away before the dance was over, skimmed through a version of the tale of Maire Rua and was already in bed with his candle burning and his personal sense of euphoria established, before the girls, set on a long conversation, got home. The next morning he was sad to be leaving. He hung about the house. He let the morning bus go. Then it was too late to bike it down to Castlebar in time for the train. He was up and down from his room finding things he had left behind. His voice was heavy and he was shaking somewhat in the manner of a man possessed of a religious hangover. The girls were entranced by his romantic needs. He drank innumerable cups of tea. And then, when they were left alone in the kitchen, he let his hands rest lightly on the back of Catherine's head.

"Let me see now," he said, "if we have any fleas."

He sifted and nit-picked her hair with his fingers.

"Well, well," he said, sucking in in mock surprise.

"Did you find some?" she asked.

"Hold on now," he answered, "I think they've gone down the back of your dress."

"Do you think so?" said Catherine looking at Sara, and then she threw up her eyes in the joy of conspiracy.

"A bad case, I'm afraid." He shook his head.

The next thing he was tickling her under the arms and she fell to the floor laughing and screaming, and O'Muichin flailing after her. Then Sara jumped on top of him. Maisie Adams came in. Uncomfortably, the Irish speaker picked himself off the floor. "Sara Adams," her mother ordered, "get up." O'Muichin tried to speak and the girls laughed. Maisie Adams turned her back, her shoulders shaking with mirth.

"Are you respectable, Mr O'Muichin?" she asked.

"Yes, Ma'am," he meekly whispered.

"Still here, O'Muichin?" the Sergeant called as he entered the kitchen. The teacher reluctantly said goodbye, took his blue bag by the strap, put it on his back, and turned towards Belmullet. He stopped once to wave, then cycled on till he reached Maumaratta, the Mountain Pass of the Young Hares. There he passed the night in a sleeping bag among the airy stones.

16

The Salmon of Knowledge

Sergeant Adams succumbed to an illness in Fermanagh the following spring. The results of the tests were not good. He was removed to hospital, and three weeks later when he knew he was not going to get any better he asked to be moved to the light-keepers' house in Mullet. Maisie phoned Willy his brother to drive them down. The geese were farmed out to a neighbour. The girls were given leave from school. Willy, who they had not seen in years, thought the decision to go South was disastrous. But Jonathan was adamant.

Willy drove them to the west of Ireland, where he had never been, in the Adams' car, then immediately returned by public transport. It was a hard and treacherous spring, with gales hammering against the coastline. The dunes blew. Wrack was piled up in the fields. Foam from a blowhole rose over Aghadoon. The women stocked up with food. Joe Love and Bernie Burke came with coal and turf. They lit huge fires. A local nurse was employed. Jonathan Adams was scandalized to find a Catholic attending him. He asked to have her removed. But next morning she was there again. She walked him to the toilet and stood outside.

"All right, Mr Adams?" she'd call.

"Yes, yes," he'd reply angrily.

She injected him morning and evening with morphine. He'd wake up cold in the bed and see her, a human object in the coldness, wishing him good morning from midway across the room.

"Are you still here?"

"Yes. And so are you."

"What time is it?"

"Time to wash."

"I don't want to wash."

"You must wash. We don't want the infection spreading, do we now, Mr Adams?"

Reluctantly he'd offer one limp hand then the other. As she wiped his face he shivered with frustration. She had a habit of hugging him to her that he found distasteful. To do the back of his neck she pressed his face into her shoulder. He sat on the edge of the bed, his chin on her shoulder, looking helplessly towards the door of the bedroom as she towelled his back.

"All right, Mr Adams?"

"Yes," he hissed.

"It will all be over in a moment." She sprayed the room. Polished his bedside table. Ran the hoover round his bed. Emptied disinfectant into the toilet.

"Now, Mr Adams. Your daughters are here to see you."

The girls came and sat by his bed.

"Ask in the travelling library for something on water. Something with tall print," he asked.

Laid out in his sick bed, while the Atlantic winds howled from the northwest, Jonathan Adams read of the beginning of the great rivers of Ireland from a schoolbook propped on his chest. Knocking sounds came from all sides. The house shook underwater. He got so bad that a doctor was sent for. None from the locality could be found. Then Nurse Noone appeared with a Doctor Ferris who was visiting relations on the peninsula. When he sat down by the bed the stench of whiskey overwhelmed Jonathan Adams.

"Dear God," he said.

The doctor lifted the old policeman's hand and checked his pulse. "Dreadful weather," he said. He dropped the thin wrist and opened his bag. "We better increase the dose," he said. He handed the small bottles of morphine to the nurse. He leaned over the dying man and looked into his eyes.

"I wish you luck," he said.

"Maisie," called Jonathan Adams. "Is he gone?"

"Yes."

"Don't move so fast around the room," he told the girls.

Up till the last he attended to his own toilet, even after the nurse tried getting him to pee into a steel bedpan. He'd slide out of bed, feel his way along the iron railing, the armchair, the bannisters. "Yes, yes," he'd say through the closed door of the new bathroom to Nurse Noone. Then he'd stand a moment on the stairs like a sleepwalker. Enter the room and bow his head while the nurse, chatting the whole time, tidied his bed. With great distress he heard the bag, that had been attached to his stomach after the operation in Enniskillen, make loud farting noises. He closed his eyes in embarrassment. As he grew sicker, his skin took on a deep tan as if he had been abroad on holiday, and the whites of his eyes grew remarkably white. Red weals, like a whiskey drinker's, appeared on his cheeks. He lifted the schoolbook again, but since the doctor increased the morphine, he found he was unable to read. So Nurse Eitne Noone read to him, and after her, Sara, Catherine, and then Maisie.

There were many variants of the Salmon of Knowledge, Jonathan Adams found, as he began to search for the definitive version among the prose poems.

Some told of the beginning of great rivers. Of waters breaking down from the side of a mountain to make a sea. Others, of the reaching of enlightenment. Just as the halibut has the thumb mark of Christ upon it, so the salmon, he heard, bears the print of some long forgotten pagan who invested there under its fin a knowledge that concerns itself with the duality of things, the eternal going away and the eternal return.

The salmon carries this knowledge to and fro through the great seas of the world, and it can be released by the merest touch.

All knowledge, says the salmon, is a journey.

Such a salmon had eluded the fishermen for days by pretending to be a sun-shadow on the floor of the river. Eventually it was trapped on the banks of the Boyne after an arduous seven-year search of the waters; the fire was built up and the hero Aengus was ready for enlightenment. His slave Fionn dragged in wood for burning. Aengus prepared himself assiduously, he cleared his head of all material pleasure. He accepted that whatever

194

would happen that day was the fate intended for him. Then as the fire took he awaited the knowledge. But such knowledge does not come so easily to the one who craves it. Aengus was lying back basking in the smell of the fish, and thinking of the great wonders within reach when he heard a sharp yell. It was the hero's helper who had found enlightenment. For when Fionn touched the fish to see was it done, the scales of the cooked salmon adhered to his thumb. With a screech he reared back in fright, licked his fingers and the knowledge, as he leapt madly about, entered his soul.

So Fionn outwitted Aengus, though not deliberately.

Neither man was ever the same after. Aengus could not be consoled. This is the way it is with such knowledge – it comes to those who least expect it, and the first lesson such knowledge teaches is to console those who have not got it. Aengus was ready to do murder. Fionn had immediately, with humour and tact, to mollify him. Amelioration was necessary.

Fionn turned into a girl.

But this was no help. For Aengus fell in love with Fionn. Every step of the road she took, there was Aengus behind her. When she lay down to sleep Aengus was there beside her. When she went behind the bush Aengus was there before her. Aengus' tone, that was once manly, became a long ingratiating whinge. It struck Fionn that the knowledge given her by the salmon was not knowledge at all if it be used only to console. She thought hard on this as she lay in her woman's form by a small fire lit convenient to a salmon pool. And Aengus' beady eye on her in the dark. She realized that such knowledge could only be gained by a long and dangerous trek into the world alone.

She must leave her master, though the master barred her every escape. She must learn to control her passion and her vulnerability. She tossed and turned, and sighed. Putting one responsibility against another, she was saddened by the fact that such knowledge meant the end of friendship. They were then on the side of a highland in Knockbride. She made her decision. The sun was rolling across Meath county when Fionn turned into a bird, flew straight up, and braked a minute overhead. Aengus rose to his feet. The walls of his stomach shook like

195

the walls of a tent in a high wind. Then, with a neat jig of its arched shoulders, the swift fell into a low skim and went out of sight.

Aengus, greatly troubled, searched the sky for the place where the black-nosed swift, a moment before, had been.

"Take her away," said Jonathan when he saw the nurse at the end of his bed.

It can happen anywhere, so Aengus tried to explain. But no one would believe him. Ever since he'd returned alone, the people believed he'd killed his servant Fionn. In trying to tell the truth Aengus aged considerably.

Every man he met he told his story to, over and over, and it benefited him nothing. Who wants to hear one man's side of the story? What enlightenment is there in that? So, Aengus, perplexed and giddy, returned to the banks of the Boyne and counted the sun-shadows and noted the odour of his stools. It was here that he heard another version of the Salmon of Knowledge. A stranger came. He was from Dromohair. Aengus, glad of a listener, immediately began to tell his tale, how he had caught a fish after five years fishing the shadows, cooked him and then his manservant had stolen the knowledge. The cur, the Leitrim man said with a generous curse, may lightning strike the high hole of his arse! Amen, said Aengus. And worse still, the man Fionn had turned into a girl so that he fell in love with her, not knowing if he loved her because she was a woman, or because she possessed the knowledge he craved. And worst of all, before he could assimilate all this knowledge, the girl had gone and turned into a bird.

Now, here I lie, said Aengus, heartbroken.

It all depends, said the Leitrim man, whether the salmon is coming or going. He pondered the waters. You might well have encountered the dying salmon. The stranger considered the woe of that concept. He continued: To the man who interrupts the passage of the dying salmon, the knowledge will be of a sad variety. It explains the curse of what can never be attained.

Aengus clicked his tongue.

If you chance to encounter the dying salmon nothing further can be added to your learning, the sage from Leitrim continued. You will have arrived without journeying.

Poor Fionn, said Aengus, relieved.

For, you see, such a fish is tired and is about to shed his skin.

He appeared about to moult, said Aengus, now that I mind it.

Far better, nodded the stranger, that you find a salmon setting out on its journey so that your quest may concur with his.

Aye.

Then, instead of the fish, it is you turns out of the mouth of the river into the sea.

Oh wonders.

The Atlantic lies ahead of you.

I see it.

And the sure knowledge that the journey through the unknown leads to the known.

Good night! Aengus exclaimed.

So the sojourn in the familiar leads back to the strange.

It does. Certainly, Aengus extolled joyfully.

The journeying is the quest.

Aha! Well, now! And Fionn?

He shall never know human shape again. He may turn into what he is not. That, the knowledge will allow. He can be a girl today, a bird tomorrow. A fir tree the day after. He can exhaust all possible shapes but can never return to be a man again.

Aengus whistled. Poor Fionn, he said, thinking how easily it might have been him.

But Fionn, contrary to what was being said of him, discovered that his journey, in fact, was an attempt to find the size and the range of his consciousness.

Then came the day that he understood what language was – a bridge between the flesh and the spirit.

At the beginning, he'd thought the range of meaning extended to the supple body of the woman he'd been given to escape Aengus' wrath. Then in turn, he found it only covered the little black-nosed shape of the bird he'd taken to escape Aengus' fumbling in the dark and the burden of his love. Now, having on successive days become a doe, a fir and a blackguardly dog, he found that the memory of others contributed to what he now was, a horse quietly steeped in a manmade field on Aran. Around him goats were singing. Each mouthful of grass he knew meant a day's work by someone in the past. The very earth his hooves stood on would have come here by boat from the mainland. The seeds of the grass he now ate would have been carefully fed into the new seaweed-nourished soil one at a time. This, the man he had once been knew. Not only that but all he looked on he considered first as Fionn would, then as the woman did, as the bird, the tree, the doe, the dog and lastly the horse. It was the horse ate the grass but it was Fionn himself had sown it. His consciousness now extended through all he had seen. But there was loneliness in this condition. And that was when Fionn considered Fionn.

He wanted to talk to someone. And that is why the farmer who saw the strange beast nosing round the spring meadow found himself impelled to approach. With each step forward the farmer took, the more he found himself grow elongated. The spell of the animal was one of the obliteration of self. Still the islander was driven forward. At last the horse lifted a keen sad eye, brown as a turf bank. The man stood there, quite alone, reflected in a deep pool. A ripple of anticipation went across the flanks of the horse. But, try as he might, Fionn could not enter the farmer. There were two things at odds – Fionn could not return to another man's shape, only his own.

He whinnied his despair.

Nor could he really abandon the physical presence of the horse. He had become an animal for all time. He farted loudly.

Ya bould crature, said the farmer, I thought you had me.

The night was white and warm as milk just squeezed fresh from the udder. The Leitrim man had been entertaining Aengus for days with tales of the salmon, but Aengus grew tired of his company and wished the fellow would move on now that he had learnt from him all he needed to know.

In his heart, Aengus was set on capturing a further salmon, but wanted to carry out the act alone, seeing what had happened the last time. Every time a fish broke the waters of the river he'd turn the conversation to anything but what was uppermost in his mind. And invariably what he chose to speak of was intended to go against the grain of his companion. And so they argued over the concept of possession.

As dawn broke, a cow, staring impassive and steadfast ahead, floated past on a raft. A man, the island farmer, equally wrapped up in what lay beyond, sat at its front legs. This vision, in the mist of dawn, silenced the two men.

What was that? asked Aengus.

It was the cow, replied the Leitrim man.

The raft moved out of sight, the mist lifted and in the river the last of the Milky Way hovered. I never thought to see the cow here, the Leitrim man observed. Aengus, chided by such knowledge, let the new information filter through, but he was deeply troubled by the sight of that majestic creature, camouflaged to pass unseen on pastureland, float by. He was not to know that he had espied Fionn in a different role, and what plagued him was the cow's refusal to turn and admit, even by a quiet lowing, to his existence.

He stood up, unsure and afflicted by some grave loss.

This is the water on which the cow first appeared, nodded the Leitrim man.

So it was to be. The river became known as the Boyne, taking its name from Bo, meaning cow, and the Milky Way, known as *Bru an Boinne*, the path of the cow.

We should have killed the man, said Aengus, and eaten the cow.

There'll be more, replied the Leitrim man.

Aengus lay down heartened by the prospect of sleep, his need of argument sated. In some stories, said the Leitrim man, the salmon turns into a young woman who instructs the traveller in the nature of his quest, and sets him a series of tests concerning the logic of the mind and the magic of the senses. Because the traveller is usually a man and the salmon a woman, he is enthralled by her. He thinks of her as *cara m'anam*, friend of my soul.

The Leitrim man put his hand to his head and continued talking as he lightly stroked his forehead. He thinks from her he will learn all the secrets of knowledge, said Leitrim, especially the secrets of womanhood which have always been denied him since time eternal.

Her secret wish is to have her youth returned to her. But he has no knowledge of this. Or pretends he has not. He accepts the nature of the journey she sets him without question, for this is all part of a quest he must undergo.

A wave of nostalgia overcame Aengus. He listened as one does to a voice reaching across from a further shore.

As did Jonathan Adams. In the version that was being read to him by Catherine, the hero has completed two of the burdens laid on him by the curse of the woman, and, disconsolate and dejected, he sets out on the third. The world through which he wanders is a world where nothing is as it appears. All the ancient stones have crosses chipped onto the spirals to announce that Christ is in the land. All have been exorcized. Writing, which threatens memory, has made its appearance. Animals and humans in one last pagan frenzy are constantly interchanging shapes – *I become you, and you become me.* And the greatest mistake is to treat any man as a man only, or any woman as a woman only, for each has access to many roles, so many of the traveller's trials have concerned the humiliations he has undergone because of his prejudices.

Everyone is jealously succumbing to each wound made. It struck the traveller that he was re-journeying through the life of the young woman. She must have been through all this, he thought. Then, to keep himself going he recreated her in his own mind as he had first seen her. When she had changed from fish into woman, and now flitted to and fro in a sacred place in his consciousness. It was a long journey. Then he came to a place which reminded him of home. It felt like Ireland. He was not sure that this was a pleasant thing. He was afraid to be seen. It struck him that while he was seeking knowledge, other people were expending theirs. He had not been listening. He'd been off in the sensual world. The last thing the traveller was conscious of was his intelligence. It was a thing you did not admit.

These are all fine thoughts, he said to himself, no mention of the madness lurking in the heart. Sadly there, but rightly there.

Yes, thought Jonathan, and he dallied on a word that carried within it another word, and then another, so that the old scholar had to start all over again from the very beginning, making as he did a further version while sharp rain slanted over the Mullet.

All of a sudden, the traveller found himself outside the Tower of Babel, which, by virtue of that quest, was home. The red roof and timber walls of Cullybackey were instantly familiar. Each person he overheard talking was making sense, perfect sense, as he stood outside listening. He was astounded by the understanding and intelligence of the speakers within. Things must have changed while I was away, he said to himself.

It was for him a religious experience.

Jonathan Adams felt long-lost Presbyterian genes begin to surface in his consciousness. Now I will know whether the body is the source of evil! Into his eyes passed the distant lights of Dissenter, Calvin and Jesus Christ, then the brightly-featured faces of his daughters. He wished the traveller through the door.

I have found home at last, said the traveller.

But on entering the Tower he encountered nothing but chaos and pandemonium and total indifference. The speech he intended to make to the scholars within froze on his lips. His heart beat wildly as he strayed into the eye of the hallucination. In fright he thought he would never get out. First he tried in vain to talk to the people there collected in Irish. But all were busy in various languages of distress. Out of a sense of duty he continued to seek their attention. He saw the open door, but thought he would never make it. Yet, with perfect ease, he saw himself walk through the wall that only existed in his own mind. He emerged to find that the chaos made perfect sense again. This made him re-enter the Tower once more, even though some part of him screamed no. Again he strove to preach the word that could not be uttered. To give some form to that which cannot be said. But now the confusion was even more intense. His chin shook uncontrollably. His bowels pounded. This drove him outside, where again he overheard reasonable arguments in Latin, Greek and Hebrew from those within.

They spoke of the sanctity of life, of everlasting life, of violence and peace.

He entered again, like a swimmer going down for the third time. And he would have remained like this forever, going to and fro, if, when he emerged humiliated the next time, another man – a traveller also – had not come and stood enthralled by the perfect sense the babblers made within the Tower.

For a few minutes the two strangers stood together listening to the sensible thoughts, arrayed in the finest language, concerning each speaker's argument for continued occupation of the island.

Like the traveller before him, the newcomer became hypnotized by the pure disparity and common sense of the voices. Inside the perfect version of the story existed. Perhaps this man was set upon the same quest, sent by the same woman, our traveller thought. The newcomer, looking transcendent and at peace, entered the Tower of Babel. For a while our man stood there waiting to be possessed once more, but suddenly he was released from that fate. The arrival of the other man had allowed our traveller to journey on. He had been released. Someone else had taken his place. Glad of his freedom, he left the other stepping to and fro between the arguments of normality and madness till some other poor traveller might come in his turn and relieve him.

Maisie found her husband's eyes upon her.

She stopped reading.

"It must be dreadful," said Sergeant Adams, "to step out into space."

The traveller comes next to a mountain covered here and there with low shrubbery. Overhead stands the lark, fluttering and whistling to the sheepdog, till suddenly she drops loose-winged like a fallen leaf to a place it appeared she had not been guarding. The lark protects by singing above what is not her home. The lark, like a poet, sings not of this place beneath but of over there hidden in the high grasses.

So the story diverged.

The traveller takes the goat's path up the small mountain and arrives to a copse of ash trees and whitethorn. As he penetrates the copse he finds release from the sun and hears the murmur of a stream. In time he comes to a pool dappled with sunlight and leaves. He takes his rest there.

Thinking on his quest he leans forward to drink and sees the sudden flash of the salmon.

Entranced, he watches the pool. Then, in the dark depths, he sees the salmon, the white-bellied pig, turn again. The hero is overcome by a form of sensual melancholia. He realizes the quest that the woman has set him has led back to her. He grows frightened and wrings his hands.

Now I have to face my destiny, he thinks, and this woman may refuse me peace.

Then, what he has to do grows as clear as day. He decides to stay up all night by the pool. But first he must deny himself sleep, for one of the temptations put in the path of knowledge is weariness. So he washes his body in the stream. Next, he must make sure not to catch the reflection of his own face in the pool, else he will lose sight of the fish. So he tells the fish how beautiful she is. Lastly, he must not think of his earlier achievements.

So, he thinks of other things.

Having fought off these three weaknesses, the traveller is filled with hope that here by the pool he will find both the nature of his quest and of this curse that has had him wandering the earth for thirty years, employed in various ventures he must not think upon. For this was the third and final test and the most difficult of all, seeing as he did not know what the test involved or how, being without such knowledge, it might be successfully accomplished.

All he knows is that his soul has been burdened with this quest and that with its completion he may have fulfilled his destiny.

He fed out a dark line of horse hair into the depths. The silver hook shone like an eye. Nervously, he held tight to the eye of the fish, so that whatever form the salmon might change into, the traveller would still have a grasp of its true self, thereby retaining his sense of himself and his sense of the girl, who existed in a further dimension. But, as had so often happened, the traveller was to lose sight of how things stood before. In the pool three silver eyes hung in the dark like stars. Then one eye closed. Suddenly, he found the weight of the salmon on the line. Instinctively, he jerked the hook home and began to draw in. Then, fearing to hurt the mouth of the girl, he slackened off. The fish broke free. With one flick of its tail the salmon changed everything in the nature of itself, so that the traveller, if he must follow on, must also lose his sense of himself.

He was stricken with guilt that he had come so close to completing his quest. And his last thought before the salmon changed back into a woman was: I should have gone by the pool and met her on the far side. I should have hauled in. Now I have no identity and that's how you lose the loved one. Because you leave nothing for them to see except a mirror that distorts them into images of grotesqueness.

It was the traveller that was changing into everything he saw, not they that changed. He realized this as the salmon splashed to the surface of the pool. Then, changing shape, swam towards him.

Feeling wretchedly sad, Jonathan Adams found himself lying next to the ceiling. Below him he heard his daughter continuing with the story. He heard the wind again. The knocking. The feeling returned of being underwater. The journey had drained him. He descended slowly, then went up again. A car turned outside, its wheels churning up rain. For a while he felt like the traveller outside the Tower of Babel, stepping in and out of the consciousness of himself and others. He lay waiting for someone to come and relieve him, that he might continue on. But no one came.

And so Jonathan Adams died after a debilitating cancer of the bowel that he bore with courage. Up till the last the women read to him. Till dawn they read. And whenever they'd stop reading he'd open his eyes immediately and search the room to see why the voice had suddenly ceased.

"You're a good man," said Nurse Eitne.

"Why?" he asked. "Why do you say that?"

She did not know how to answer him.

The marathon reading of Irish mythology continued, night and day, long after he had gone unconscious, for the women knew he was lonely for the sound of their voices. The last time he was coherent was two days before his death. He looked at Catherine's shoes. "Do something about those shoes," he said, "they need polishing." He struggled up and made his way to the toilet. Coming back to bed he saw Maisie and said: "That's it, I won't be doing that again." She read on.

Those last two days there was always a woman's voice in his subconscious. Then at last the voice stopped.

III

THE HARES

17

The Mourners

Jonathan Adams was buried in Fermanagh. Only there, it was finally decided, could his tombstone proclaim that he had been a Sergeant in the Royal Ulster Constabulary. The hearse that took him North was from Belmullet. His family followed behind in a hired car. And behind them in a Fiat rusted by salt from the sea came Joe Love, Bernie Burke and Eitne Noone. Despite Maisie's entreaties the Mullet folk had decided to attend the funeral in the North.

Outside Blacklion, on the Florencecourt Road, when they were safely in the North, the cortege came to a stop.

"Looks like a roadblock," said Bernie Burke, who was driving.

"Well don't do anything hasty," advised Joe Love.

"What's going on?" asked Eitne.

With a sense of disbelief, the Mullet mourners saw another hearse emerge from a side road. Soldiers climbed out from behind a hedge. Three police Saracens cruised up behind.

"Are we going to be kidnapped or what?" asked Bernie.

"Just keep looking ahead," whispered Joe.

A soldier appeared at the window and Bernie wound it down.

"Morning," said Bernie.

"OK," said the soldier, "you with the funeral?"

"Yes."

"OK."

A man in a black bowler and long black coat appeared, and along with him, two men dressed in ill-fitting black suits. The three swiftly tipped Jonathan Adams' coffin into the Northern hearse. His policeman's gloves and cap were placed on it and armfuls of funeral bouquets alongside. The hearse from

Belmullet returned to the South and the new cortege took off into the North. "Jazus," said Bernie, "they're putting the foot down." They went off up back roads, skirting towns till they arrived at the station in the village where the dead man had served his time. All the vehicles slowed to a halt, and stayed there outside the fortress, with their engines running, for a long surreal moment.

Joe Love turned to Bernie: "I told you he was an important man."

All that could be seen of the station was a tall concrete wall, spiked with reams of barbed wire, huge green galavanize gates and a small door, behind sandbags, that opened into the wall. Beyond that were slated roofs covered by green netting and a single watch-tower. The man in the bowler hat stepped out and stood at the front right-hand side of the hearse. He nodded. The Saracens and the two cars took off again at walking pace. Another few mourning cars slipped surreptitiously in behind as the cortege drew towards the church. Then, flanked by two columns of uniformed policemen, who were in turn protected by armed British soldiers, Jonathan Adams' coffin was ferried on the shoulders of four young policemen into the quiet graveyard.

"By jingo," said Joe Love, "he was in the guards."

"The RUC are not the guards," whispered Eitne.

Willy was waiting by the grave. And he chose the same verse to read, from the Gospel according to St Matthew, as the priest had spoken over Matti Bonner: *He is not dead. He sleepeth.*

He is not dead. He sleepeth.

"Imagine," whispered Bernie Burke in awe, "he went to his grave without taking a drink." Maisie, in a black wide-brimmed hat, accepted his cap and gloves and the Union Jack. She shook the hands of the Mullet folk and the police inspector. Then she got into the car. Catherine and Sara stepped forward to the edge of the grave. Justin Ruttle from Rathkeale put his arms around them. The policemen stood to attention for a minute's silence. They seemed to be waiting for a command that never came.

The house, after the funeral, was cold and unwelcoming. The girls moved with trays of sandwiches between the group of policemen in the living room and the few relations who were standing in the hallway and the kitchen. John Lavell, who had driven the Adamses from Mullet, Bernie Burke, Joe Love and Eitne Noone sat together nervously on a sofa, shifting uneasily as if they were only there on false pretences. If anyone spoke to them they answered with unsure smiles. They sat with cups of tea on their knees, each smoking and tapping their ash into a saucer.

"A word in your ear," Bernie whispered to Catherine.

She leaned down.

"Would there be a drop of drink in the house?"

"I think there might be sherry."

"Oh, that'll do nicely."

"You've disgraced yourself again," announced Joe Love, "asking that poor girl for drink."

Isolated from the others, they watched the holstered revolvers, the pictures of masons on the walls, the extract from the scriptures above the fireplace. They in turn were observed – the sea-shined faces, the cracks of dirt in their hands, the tobacco-stained fingers, the old-fashioned blue suits, the quiet repetitive voices.

"So you were friends of Jonathan," said Willy, with a brisk smile.

"I wouldn't say that." Bernie felt the back of his neck and bared his teeth. He looked uneasily at Joe Love.

"I am his brother, you see," continued Willy.

"Ahhh! I've got you."

"You look like him, too," nodded Joe.

"The eyes," said Bernie.

"And the chin."

"He has him round the eyes."

"I was not aware that I looked like Jonathan."

"Oh, but you do," agreed Eitne.

"He was a good soul." Bernie reached up and gratefully took a glass from the tray Catherine held. He downed half the drink in one go. "And he'll be sorely missed."

"And what line of work would you be in?" asked Joe Love.

"I'm in the church."

"Good man, Father."

"Can I get you something?" Catherine asked her uncle.

"No, thank you." Willy gave an abstemious grimace and wandered off. Justin Ruttle accepted a glass and sat in an armchair by the Mullet folk. They talked of the weather and compared the winds in the west with those in the south. A conversation ensued about exactly where the Gulf Stream reached Ireland. They talked land, pigs, cattle and storms. Across the room the policemen talked of the complications of the new witness forms that had to be completed in triplicate; the younger ones listened to their elders fondly reminiscing about conditions in the old stations; they talked of computers, lawnmowers, the Canaries, judges and cars. They remembered Jonathan Adams, a figure from another age.

Maisie, her mind still raddled by the stories she had been reading out loud till first light over the preceding days, moved among the RUC men dispensing cakes and tea, overcome with the feeling that somehow she had betrayed her husband, that he had died not as a sergeant in the police but as something else, something she could not as yet define.

After an appropriate interval, all the policemen left together. She shook each man's hand on the doorstep. "If there's ever anything we can do . . ." "Look after yourselves," she said. They ran down the footpath and into the waiting cars. A bristle of rifles covered their retreat. Then the Mullet folk got up to go.

"We'll see you in the summer," Joe Love said.

"I hope so."

Maisie stood on the road waving till the two cars were out of sight.

"Nothing would stop them but they come," she explained to her father. "I'm sure they found it unsettling being here. You see, we never told them he was in the police. Now everyone will know who we are."

"You should come down with me to Rathkeale for a while."

"And what about the girls?"

"We can look after ourselves," said Catherine.

"Oh yes," she said. "I'm sure you could. I was not much older than you when I married your father."

She did not return to Rathkeale. Although her father thought she should sell the house and leave now that there was nothing to hold her in Fermanagh, she said she'd wait and see. That year Sara would be finishing her A-levels, the year after that Catherine. Then she'd see. And, as she explained, there was always their retreat in Mullet. After her father was gone, she started immediately into the business at hand.

She wrote away to have her husband's pension transferred into her name. She opened a filing cabinet in a drawer and marked it *Jonathan*. Into it went all her correspondence with insurance companies, the Department of Social Security, the Northern Ireland Police Department. Meanwhile she sat out the escalating war in the North and waited for her daughters to finish school. Weeks sometimes passed without anyone calling.

She sold off the geese.

For a period she began regularly attending service with Catherine and Sara in an attempt to meet people again. But everyone, once service was over, withdrew to their houses. The three women were on their own. Then they too stopped going to church. It was not the same thing without Jonathan.

The afternoon Sara finished her last exam, Maisie hired a car to take them all to Belmullet. When they arrived they expected to find the house in chaos. The walls running with damp. Food gone off in the kitchen. The upholstery in the car ripped. Instead, everything had been put in order by Eitne Noone. And Joe Love had come round to light fires. Bernie Burke came down with fish for their tea. The house was just as they'd left it the day they went to the funeral. Now the family cut the grass, aired the house and washed his car that stood outside in the galvanize shed. Somehow, doing all these things gave them the necessary release to mourn.

First Maisie developed asthma and later Catherine went bald. Then both, attended by Sara, stayed on in Mullet to recuperate. It was a great, tall, silent house to be sick in. For a long period of disembodiment and relapse The Dwellings figured in their consciousness as a place perched high on stilts. Added to this was the maddening sound of the crows. The crows were making a battering sound. Hell was outside. The whole day long they feverishly preened themselves on the few small storm-battered sycamores beyond the house, then stopped, looked up suddenly, cawed and began again.

Inside the three women mourned.

As the weeks passed, the girl's mother strode into their consciousness as a single unaligned being. The old relationship was over. Death had put a distance between them. She became a woman who, like them, had been mothered, lived through childhood, experienced adolescence and encouraged courtship. Her womanness shocked them. The secrets Maisie used to tell Jonathan, she now told them. With a cross look in her eye she demanded their attention. Became conspiring and dependent in a flagrant way. Then she'd banish them.

"I miss the birds," she said. "I miss the geese. It's not the same."

It came as a shock to the girls to find that their mother had become cold and withdrawn, even selfish, as she surrendered to the sickness and the identity widowhood had given her.

With the loss of Jonathan Adams they for a while lost Maisie as she struggled with the sentiments expected by the living of those recently bereaved. Neighbouring women they hardly knew called round to offer their condolences. First the Irish language and now death had opened up their house to strangers. The women, who brought warm home-baked bread wrapped in linen, sat by Maisie's bed talking and celebrating death till all hours. They cursed and called on God to protect them. They spoke of their bowels, they described their menfolk with frightening candour. They spoke of their depressions and the visions they'd seen as children. They brought wild flowers and boxes of Cadbury's chocolates. Milk was left at the door. Sheets were ironed. Mass cards, which the girls did not fully comprehend, arrived. A boy was sent round to clean the gutters. A man called to get their orders for groceries. Bernie Burke cleaned the chimneys. The travelling shop called twice a week instead of once. And Maisie revelled in the care, after keeping her distance from the outside world since the day she'd married Jonathan Adams.

She began experiencing the pang of remembering the time before the future was cast. She fetched out of the past aunts from Limerick; characters, young lovers she'd known when she was a girl in Rathkeale; nights step-dancing in Askeaton with the RCs; veiled stories told in her own kitchen of Cromwell who had given their Dutch ancestors the land they owned in Ballingrane; she could see herself walking behind her mother through Adare – her voice suddenly changing into that of a vulgar fifteen-year-old. This talk frightened Catherine. These were the stories their father must have heard of a young girl's first awakening, but hearing them the girls were embarrassed and affronted, for these were seductive tales, stories that had turned into fantasies intended for a man.

Then suddenly would come the change in mood.

"See," said Maisie, and she opened the palm of her hand to show the stones. Immediately she closed her fingers round them and whipped the stones away. She took them everywhere. Even when she slept, Maisie kept a few chips of marble that had been flung on her husband's grave clenched tight in a handkerchief in her fist.

"I notice first," said Maisie Adams, "people's lips." She fell into a doe-eyed reverie. "Maybe that's why I chose him." She laughed. "He was tasty in every way."

"Were you happy with Daddy?" Sara interrupted.

"I married your father," her mother answered vehemently, "and that was that. He was twice my age. And so . . ." she hesitated, "so correct! So intelligent." She laughed unashamedly. "I don't believe he thought he was mortal."

She looked at them.

"I had no ambitions for myself."

Such selflessness angered the girls. But then her voice changed, warning them off. She began to look different, as if she had spent the last twenty-eight years in a different role. Now she seemed intent on picking herself up as she might have been. And the Jonathan Adams they knew had gone missing somehow. She dabbed her lips politely with her handkerchief, then took two long breaths and coughed, her knuckles pressed into her chest.

"I used to climb out of the back window of the kitchen quarters in Brookborough to see him," she said, drawing her knees in. "I always liked a man in a uniform."

Again came the unwholesome lusty laugh.

"Poor Jonathan!" Then she added. "And poor Matti Bonner."

And though their mother was again speaking of their father, this merging of her present life with her younger self threatened the girls. She began to ask them intimate details of their love lives. From upstairs they heard the visiting women burst out into gales of laughter. Maisie Adams had, in a frightening way, returned to grow up alongside her daughters.

She counted across the needle to find her place among the stitches. The heavy breathing started. "I'm not yet fifty." Then she pressed her knuckles to her chest. "I wouldn't let him be," she laughed. She shook her head to indicate it was all beyond her. Her lusts. His lusts. The world's lusts. Then long after the women had gone she would turn on them, the Catholics. How could a man interest himself in them? she'd ask. And so gross! So overweight! Her condescension towards them had a hint of hysteria which she tried to subdue. "Did you ever notice," she'd repeat to the girls, "how tasteless they are? Look at their carpets! How could you – paisley on paisley?" She smirked ungraciously. "Those RCs are sad. They have no idea of patterns. Not an earthly. What I'd like to know is how they sleep in those rooms! And the way they spend money – it's a sin." She shivered, then hesitantly folded her hands and looked towards the sand dunes.

"Still, they're our neighbours." She laughed. "Oh, but your father was a marvel really," and she clapped Sara's knee.

Nothing could be done about the asthma. When Maisie asked the doctor for a cause, he said: "Grief." It fell to Catherine to stay at home and look after her that long summer. Then Catherine woke one morning and all her hair had fallen out.

"If we had been in the North," said Maisie, "this would not

have happened. Somebody must have carried the worms into the house."

It took a while before they could get Catherine to a doctor. One of the consequences of Jonathan Adams' death was that now the Adams family was reliant on public transport because none of the women could drive. And on the peninsula there was no bus. This made Sara, the only woman in the house who was both able-bodied and capable of showing her face, begin taking driving lessons with a fisherman she'd met on the pier. It was the same Leitrim man she'd encountered years ago on the beach.

"Who?" asked Catherine.

"The geranium," said Sara.

He'd given her four turbot the first day, mackerel another, and one day cod. Then, when he heard her circumstances, he offered to teach her to drive. Twice a week he'd walk up to the house, sit into the car and lean on the horn, and then move over to the passenger seat. Sara would run down the path. She'd look back up at the second storey of the house where the two women sat watching her with a mixture of fright and pride.

Then, closing her eyes, she'd turn the key.

"He'll kill her," said Maisie.

As the engine revved into life, Sara would look up again, smiling. With her lower lip pulled in over her bottom teeth, she'd ease out the clutch. She'd cradle the steering wheel. The car jumped and cut out. Immediately, she'd turn the key again. Soon, leaping into the air, the old Ford, with its yellow numberplates and rusty doors, would trundle down the road.

"Who is he?" Catherine asked.

"Jack something."

"Is he, perhaps, not quite articulate?"

"When he condescends to speak."

"And what do you talk about?"

"Well," said Sara, "if you must know, he has a passion for dogs."

"That must be *lovely* for you."

"And films and musicals." She knotted her hands. "Would you like to meet him?"

217

"No, thank you."

Catherine, bald and wide-eyed, stayed indoors, refusing ever to go out till her hair had grown. The days she could have gone to the beach she didn't. The holidays passed as if she were in prison. Sara said it was nerves. The neighbouring women said that alopecia was caused by depression. And Catherine agreed something terrible was happening to her.

But that summer she read many novels. She read *Kidnapped*, *Wuthering Heights* and *Moby Dick*. She read *Jane Eyre*, and started the first of her many diaries with an account of the Irish-speaker, O'Muichin. She wrote down shocking dreams about love-making, and erotic thoughts which were totally self-centred, and sometimes vituperative descriptions of Mayo people and Catholic towns.

As the weeks passed she grew morose and bad tempered, because life was passing her by.

Her mother could not console Catherine. The pills she was given brought spots in front of her eyes. When one spot cleared another greater one began, sometimes obliterating a whole land-scape. She felt that while she slept the spots were spreading across her skin. Her periods lasted for days. She had a sexual disease, she thought. Each morning she checked her breasts, for if spots ever appeared there then life was over. Every few days Catherine shaved her skull with their father's razor to get the hair to grow again. His razor had shaved him after he died and the first time she used it Catherine saw collected in its sharp teeth the few scraps of beard that had sprouted after death. It still smelt coldly and intimately of him.

All of these things became confused in her dreams: her father's razor and her baldness.

When she had to, she went up the road with a scarf wrapped twice round her head. Outside, the summer passed like a room illuminated in another house. She saw the others go down to the sea with their towels. The lads pass by with their rods. The car come for Sara. But she remained indoors. She could not bear anyone to see her.

"You'll get odd," Sara said.

"Show us your head," said Lizzie Summers.

Local girls would collect in her room to talk feverishly about men. When they'd gone, Catherine would look into the mirror. Her high unshapely skull, blue-veined, looked back at her, and for years that image of herself was fixed in her retina and, despite her humiliation, she grew fond of its dark-eyed purity for the absence of hair fixed all expression in the eyes and mouth and nose. Baldness stood for mourning. Her white skull and her mother's terrible breathing were expressions of grief. In time, at twilight, when there were few about, she'd walk the beach hugging Sara's elbow, her head wrapped in towels in the manner of a turban. They'd link each other. Someplace underwater the stones shimmered.

Catherine began wearing black scarves, a habit that would stay with her long after her hair had grown. Her head in a black scarf, she read every minute she could. Sara and Catherine had always spent a lot of time in their rooms. In this they had inherited much of the solitary nature of their father. But that summer a change came about.

Sara began doing things on her own, stopping out late, not telling much of what she did. Before this they had always faced the outside world together. Now Catherine pored over books alone. And it was not just a matter of losing herself – this she could do, but when she'd emerge she would feel transformed. A new dimension had been added to her consciousness. The characters existed more strongly in her mind than real people did. According to their emotions and their standards she measured her life and her worthiness as a woman. The afterglow would make her anxious – anxious enough to read the same book again. Finishing a book was something she never wanted to do. And it was not just being steeped in the character or plot – it was a fright to her that a feeble story could contain a truth that assembled far from the meaning of the actual words.

She moved inside the characters' bodies. She spoke with their voices. When they died or were hurt in love it might as well have happened to her. By reading her father's books she mourned for him. These were the pages he had turned and relished. The print and smell were his. A conjecture in the corner was written in his hand. A small pressed flower that had accompanied him through the pages, now followed her through *Palgrave's Golden Treasury*, nestled at night amid Hardy's poems, or peeped out from *Crime and Punishment*. It sat in the dark of *Huckleberry Finn*. When she lifted any new book in her life ahead it would fall open at that flower. It was the place where her father had lain down to die. Where the voice he had been listening to had stopped. It marked the place where the story was suspended. It marked the place where it would be taken up again.

18

The Greatest Man in Ballyconeely

"I hear it never grows back," said Lizzie Summers. "The doctor told my mother that if it does you'll always have a bald patch."

"Is that so?" asked Catherine curtly. "Do you think, by any chance, that I might grow a new head?"

"That's a dreadful thought," laughed Sara.

She said to Sara that she did not want Lizzie Summers in the house. She barred her from her room.

"Well, of course, you have Mother, haven't you, Cathy?"

"I don't know what you mean."

"I'm envious of how close you and Mother have grown," Sara said thoughtfully.

"You can't be serious."

"Ye are in cahoots."

"You're only imagining things."

Maisie Adams was now completely bedridden. She developed a flu that later in summer led to pneumonia. "Of all things, in summer to be like this," was her cry. Bald-headed, Catherine spent most of her day in her mother's room reading to her. It became hard for her to spend much time away from her mother's side. Maisie Adams was often thrown into fits to get her breath. Her nose shone purple. Her cheeks were clustered with broken veins.

The firm face had cracked down the side.

"I am only a young woman," she complained to her daughter.

In the end, to soothe her mother's sleep, Catherine lay in the bed beside her, with the windows, even on the windiest nights, thrown open.

Then she had to remove all perfumed linen from the room,

clear the dressing table of powders and scent bottles, use only
Simple Soap in washing her mother's face. Any sweet odours
brought on attacks of furious breathing. In time, the entire house
was cleared of perfumes. The girls hid their creams and sham-
poos. Flowerpots were removed, windows closed against hay-
seed and blossoming. The house lost all aspects of femininity.
It became a bare light-keepers' home again. It was a male house
in mourning, and of the chief mourners one was bald, the other
was out of breath, and the third secretly shook perfume down
her breasts when she was a decent distance from home. Sara
did not return till all hours. Catherine would hear the car on
the road tuck in against the gate and come to a stop with quiet
malevolence. In the light of a cigarette being inhaled, she'd see
Sara's head on the stranger's shoulder. She could not look away.
She'd imagine all manner of sordid happenings. The curtain
would shake in Catherine's hand. Later she'd hear the quick tap
of her sister's heels on the steps, then, whistling, Sara would
go noisily by Catherine's door.

"Your driving lessons," announced Catherine sarcastically one
morning, "are practically going on all night".
    "One has to learn how to dip the lights," said Sara as if she
were quoting from some manual. "And reverse, of course," she
added, with shocking irony.
    "Is that so?"
    "You could come if you wanted to," said Sara, without look-
ing up from her breakfast. She curled in round her meal like a
cat.
    "You give promiscuity a bad name."
    "Hark, at the saintliness!"
    "She asked again for you last night," declared Catherine
tearfully.
    "I was in by two," adamant, adamant.
    "She got up. She went to your room."
    "Well, I'm not tied."
    "I'm not worried about you. I'm worried about Mother."
    "Would you like me to bring him home then?" asked Sara
scornfully.

"Why not?" answered Catherine. "At least you'd be here when she calls."

"And where will you hide?"

"You're cruel," snapped Catherine.

A few nights later, with her mother fed and bedded down, Catherine was seated by the fire. She had two mirrors in her hands, one in front to look into the other behind. Then she heard his voice out by the porch, some laughter. He was pleading with Sara, then came further hysterical laughter. Catherine stayed where she was. For no good reason she felt a terrible anxiety. She dropped the mirrors and reached to pull the curtains tightly across, but as she did so, the door opened into the kitchen and Sara entered.

"I've brought him," said Sara. She was still laughing, and she gestured behind her. Whoever it was, he refused to enter. She gestured again.

"C'mon," she said.

"Sara!" screamed Catherine.

As the man entered he took off his cap and with it covered his groin in the attitude of a man at prayer. He nodded at Catherine, whose first reaction was to notice how old he was, then she reached for her scarf.

"Hello, Miss," he said in an unnaturally loud voice, as if he were standing out in the street. "Did you hear the corncrake this evening?"

But Catherine was shivering with rage and despair and staring at her sister.

"Say hallo, Catherine," said Sara, and she looked at her sister, daring her. Near tears, Catherine, in an equally unnatural voice, whispered: "Hallo."

"Now that you two have met," said Sara tipsily, "I'll have to go upstairs to see my Mammy."

"Belmullet is one of the last parts of Ireland you'll find the corncrake," he explained.

"Is that so?"

"It is." He paused. "Sadly. But what can I say that hasn't been said before?" he said.

223

"Our Sara is causing concern."

"Is she?"

"Have you a mother?"

"I always wanted a mother."

He sat down.

"When I was young a little man came out of a chink in the ceiling. It was a ceiling like you have here. Old tongue-and-groove, painted cream, I think. He went along walking upside down. When I think of it I must have took him to be a pleasant fellow because I wasn't in the least afraid. He came to another hole, looked around and went up and in."

"Did you ever see him again?"

"No."

He considered the ceiling.

"And how is Sara getting on with the *lessons*?"

"Oh, she'll make a *dacent* driver."

"Is that so?"

"Inclined perhaps," he nodded, "to wander."

"Especially," replied Catherine, "since she met you."

"I'd say it's in the breeding," he answered cheerfully, and turned his foot.

"Would you." She sniggered. "And where do you go with her?"

"We tour the nightspots of Mayo," he said. "She said she was in need of a chaperone. A'course, I'm only a decoy. That'd be about it. I do the driving." There was the sound of movement upstairs. He looked at her. "Will I go now?"

"Stop where you are," she said sharply.

The man arose, tipped his forehead to Catherine.

"It was very pleasant meeting you."

"Please stay."

"Is there something wrong?"

"Yes, there's something wrong."

"Well then, I'll go."

He lifted the latch and stepped out into the night. Bright-eyed, as if she had been listening all the while on the stairs, Sara breezed into the kitchen, and dragged the heel of a loaf of bread, very ladylike, across the butter.

"Isn't he a dote?" she said.

"He must be nearly thirty."

"Well, you frightened him away anyhow," Sara laughed. She came abruptly to her feet, as was her habit, drew her dress above her knees, and checked the back of her calves for dirt kicked up from the road. "She said to me," and Sara mimicked her mother, "that I was 'to do nothing that Catherine wouldn't do'. I said: 'Ara Mammy, I don't like men.' 'Aye, well,' she said, 'but you can't keep away from them either.' "

"You're perverse," said Catherine.

"Don't think I don't see you at the window looking."

"I do not!"

"Men are right about one thing."

"What's that?"

"It's the quiet ones you have to watch," she said.

A fine bristle soon appeared on Catherine's skull. With delight she watched her hair grow back in blond tufts and wisps. The mixture delighted her. It grew together first at the back of her head. It seemed to take for ever. She sat in a chair in the garden and Sara rubbed ointment into her scalp to hurry it on.

With the return of her hair, she felt ashamed of how much she had withdrawn, but she was not ashamed in the least to discover that she had a woman's vanity. Hair made her feel sane.

And as she returned to normality, she pledged herself to her mother, saying *I've been too long in mourning for my father*, and the thought of the woman upstairs, with the marble chips gripped tight in her clenched fist as she slept, made the daughter flinch with an ache of painful nostalgia and guilt.

Her scalp in this disorder, Catherine bravely answered the door to Jack Ferris. He stood there with a pair of football boots swinging round his neck and a flashlight in his hand.

"She's not here."

"Sara?"

"Who else?"

"You're looking well."

225

"Oh but you have a nerve."

"It's the same with a beard. Every time I shave, the harder it gets." He felt his chin. "Not that I have much anyway. When I was young I shaved my legs. And begod if nothing grew back at all."

He laughed at himself. He had hair that looked as if it had been dyed jet black, and sleepy eyes, mischievous, of a pale sensual grey. They seemed fixed beyond what he was looking at till he took you into view, and he was saying – none of this is true, it's all absurd.

"There's a storm coming," he said.

"Is there?"

"An almighty one. From the northwest."

"I'll bear it in mind."

"Do."

"Why don't you sit down?"

He dusted his knees with his cap and sat down, looked about him and hummed a bar. Could it be him? she wondered.

"Sara is in Belmullet, I think," she said sharply. "As a matter of fact I thought she was with you."

"Ah." He nodded. Continued humming.

"And you are much too old for her."

"Oh," he replied. "Too old for what?"

"You know yourself."

"I get the implication, but you're wrong."

"So that was not you," she answered self-righteously, "sitting outside our house night after night in the car?"

"Not me, unfortunately."

"Are you sure?" she asked incredulously.

"I am," he answered. "I think you have the wrong man."

They sat in silence while she recalled all her perverse imaginings and he laced a shoe that did not need lacing.

"It's extraordinary," she suddenly said.

"The whole thing is a wonder," agreed Jack. He shook his head, brought up his bottom lip and attempted an unexpected, friendly smile. "I hardly know Sara. All I did was teach her to drive."

"Then why do you still call?"

"Because I know so few." He acknowledged the shelf behind her with a nod. "You have a sight of books."

"They were my father's," she replied absent-mindedly.

He looked at her. She gave him the same candid, interested glance. "I was just passing," he explained.

"What do you do anyway?" she asked.

"I do a spot of writing. And I fish here for the summer on the boats."

This made her pause. "Writing," she said disbelievingly. "What sort of writing?"

"Plays, I'm interested in plays."

"What kind?"

"I pen songs of the buck. Billy tunes."

"I'm sorry?"

"Goat songs."

"Is that so?"

"That'd be the height of it."

Catherine looked at him. "That's all very interesting. But I don't know what you're talking about."

"Tragedies. *Tragos* – goat. *Oide* – song. From the Greek."

"I never knew that."

"There you go. Every time you weep in the theatre you're listening to a goat singing."

"You jest."

"Not at all. In the early days the Greek goatherds used to put the bucks on one island and the nannies on another. Then when the nannies were on heat their smell would come on the breeze to the bucks who rose a mournful cry."

"The poor things."

"That's what I thought."

"And why didn't they just jump in the water and swim across, if they were so frustrated?"

"Ah, but that's the crux of the matter," said Jack Ferris. "You see, goats can't swim."

Suddenly, there was a loud crash against the door and a low whine. "Be God," said Jack Ferris. "That's me dog."

"Well, bring him in."

"Are you serious?" He watched her carefully as he ushered

227

in a tangerine shepherd dog, which immediately rushed under the seat Jack sat on and looked out at Catherine through his master's legs.

"I've no luck with dogs. This one is a pup I bought from a home. He's called" – he looked down at the quivering snout of the animal – "he's called, to his great grief, Daisy, aren't you?"

The dog rubbed his back against the underneath of the chair. Jack's touch set Daisy's right rear leg into a state of uncontrollable pleasure. It slapped the cement floor like a drumstick. The dog could not stop himself, went to dart out, withdrew and collapsed.

"Poor Daisy. Daisy," lilted Catherine, "what an unfortunate name for a dog." She returned her gaze to him. "Where do you come from?"

"To my great grief," replied Jack, "I come from Kilty in the County Leitrim."

"The dogs in Roscommon," commenced Jack Ferris as he considered Daisy, "have different-coloured eyes. One brown, one blue. It's hard to credit it. How do you think that happened?"

"I couldn't say," answered Catherine.

"In Leitrim there's a fair few have a twist in the eye, and there's another few albino."

"Is that so?"

"Of course," surmised Jack Ferris, "the shepherd dog as we know him is not the shepherd dog."

"No?"

"Indeed, he's not the collie at all."

"Really?" She felt her cheek. "How interesting."

"I always had a knack with animals," Jack continued, bracing himself, "but never dogs. I always had a fancy towards horses and cattle, right enough," he agreed. "And sheep, maybe. You don't find many instances of the disturbed pupil there." He tapped a fag into the palm of his hand. "The same horse is very scarce where I come from. Do you read the books?"

"No. All I do is look at the pictures."

"Somebody's codding somebody," said Jack, emptying the ash into the fire, "I suppose you were all contrary children."

"I suppose we were."

"And Sara is off to the Abbey Theatre to act, I believe."

"That's right."

"It's all go." He heard her mother cough as she crossed the landing upstairs. "What ails your ma?"

"She has congestion of the lungs. She says it's like someone sitting on her chest."

"Give her goat's milk," he said.

"Goat's milk," repeated Catherine, and immediately she remembered Matti Bonner. "Have you had plays put on?"

"A few," he said.

Silence fell on them. Daisy made his way out, looked around the room, licked the floor with a very tentative, wet tongue and then tried to bury his head in Catherine's groin. "Get down, you cur," said Jack. "He is always saddle-sniffing." The dog climbed back in underneath Jack's chair, then, much to Catherine's distraction, licked at its private parts and, finished with that, began instantly dreaming.

Jack Ferris walked off swinging his boots. He made his way to a low field, partly flooded, dotted with rocks at both sides and patches of heather. There was only one set of goalposts, at the further end, the other posts had crashed to the ground, and through where the goal once stood swans glided. He knelt, pulled his togs up over his trousers, put on the boots, stuffed his trousers into his football socks, then, sitting into a ditch, pulled out a cigarette and waited. Then he began saying to himself in a distracted fashion, altering the rhythms as he chose, changing the emphasis, scattering the feet, a certain phrase he had heard a man from Inishmaan bellow out on Inisheer as he stumbled drunkenly home:

I am the greatest man in Ballyconeely
I am the greatest man in Ballyconeely

and so on, in a traditional self-deprecating way.

The morning after the storm the sky was black. She cycled up to Glenlara. A few villagers were gathered at the cliffs which gave an exaggerated view of the horizon. She walked up the last stretch to join them. Plaid waves broke as far as the eye could see. The salmon boats were speeding out one after the other. A single dull light burned on the horizon. The high tide had scattered debris as far as the road.

The people stood, looking out, in silence. The gaps in the walls shone like mirrors reflecting the blue-black sky. The earth felt dangerous.

To her left, the sea spilled across the small slipway. There was a heart-stopping crack of thunder from the waves. A fall of rain blew in. She felt light-headed and afraid. She stepped into a hollow on the down-wind side of the rocks where the last of the flowering sea-thrift grew in small pink clumps. The weight of the low cliffs was over her head. The land was made of stone, and each stone was neatly packaged away on beds of slate. And on each slate a record of straight lines and broken lines was kept – of distances, of levels, of the sea and its booms, and gravel blown up.

Now the shore was filled with giant rocks that had been blown in by the storm. They rested unsteadily there, waiting to be carried in. She watched them, amazed by the power of the sea.

A guard cycled up and joined the others above. He smoked cigarette after cigarette. More light rain fell. Gulls shrieked. Then suddenly the sun, blazing white, appeared. With great wonder Catherine saw the Glenlara folk fill up with hallu-cinatory light. Over the big shadowy sea the sun worked a chisel through the clouds. It slanted purple, then red, then orange.

A boat broke the water in a pool of sunlight. It lifted on one broad stroke above a bright wave, breathed there a moment, dipped and disappeared. A cheer went up from the crowd. The sight of her plunging on the horizon reassured the onlookers that she was making headway. An old man standing next to Catherine said: "There's nothing more beautiful. To be up at five in the morning, dawn breaking, and nothing else but the tick a'da engine in the background."

"What's happened?" she asked.

"An East German boat was in trouble out there somewhere, but they're safe now," he said. They walked back up the road pushing their bikes. They reached a tall hedge that stood incongruous among the bare windswept fields. "Whisht!" he said. They stood in silence listening. "Can you hear them?" They both listened. "Them's the pigeons of the Coyle brothers. Can you hear them?" He stood on his toes with delight. "They keep hundreds in cages within."

They stood on the road beside a massive shelter of oleria, escallonia, cordyline palms, griselinia, bamboos, New Zealand flax, mimosa, sycamore, and listened to the miraculous sound of pigeons and doves and guinea hens in a countryside where there are no trees.

In compliance with the cure, Maisie began a daily diet of goat's milk and goat's cheese that the two girls bought from some German hippies living on the mainland. Some days later she appeared in the kitchen.

"I think I've passed the badness," Maisie reckoned.

She pronounced herself cured. There was nothing wrong with her at all. There never was. All that summer she had lain in bed, afflicted by nightmares to do with the North. Now she came down in the afternoons, and clucked about the kitchen with such distressing haste that she missed everything she reached for by a fraction. She cooked, some evenings, dishes of extraordinary simplicity: bread-puddings, jam tarts, herring pie. The old Maisie was back.

Time would blow coldly into the room, make Maisie turn, and tip a spoon to her mouth and send her miles away.

She came down eventually, every day, all day, and sewed throughout the mornings, blinked fiercely at her patterns and commenced remembering her years as a cook with Lord Brookborough.

It was true, Maisie did look better.

"Yes," she said, "I've passed the badness. I'm not helpless." She wiped dust off the photographs of the elderly smiling masons grouped confidently in some wooden Tyrone hall. Her husband, spruce and adroit, beamed at the camera from the back row. He looked older, from a different generation, compared to her. She blew on the silver spoons, and handed each sherry glass to Catherine to hold to the light and see if any specks remained.

"I don't know what came over me at all," she said, and shook her head, baffled, disbelieving, and a little pale.

The next time Jack called it was raining, so Catherine ushered him in, and without embarrassment he greeted Mrs Adams, who was sitting in a thick cotton nightdress by the fire.

"I think it's Jack," Catherine said.

"Jack Ferris," he agreed.

"What side of the house are you?" her mother asked.

"Catholic, oh my dear."

"It's not your fault," said Maisie, and she laughed and added: "Once you have your health."

"That's right."

"Sit down, Jack," gestured Catherine.

"That's a bad night," he nodded.

"So, you are the writer," Maisie viewed him, "that's been chasing our Sara."

Jack looked at Catherine uneasily. The large parcel he was carrying he rested on the floor.

"Where's Daisy tonight?" asked Catherine, helpfully.

"He's about."

"I shouldn't bother myself over our Sara if I was you," advised Mrs Adams. "Our Sara has ambitions. She's off to become famous."

"So I heard."

"A Catholic man," explained Maisie to her daughter, "always appears easy going."

"We have our problems, too," he said.

And Maisie replied: "I don't doubt it. I fell for one myself once upon a time."

"Did it not work out?"

"I think he got himself in trouble. One day he wasn't there any more."

"That will happen too."

They laughed scandalously, Catherine realized, like people that had known each other for a long time.

"So I suppose," he enquired smiling, "marriage is out of the question."

"I think you'd be barking up the wrong tree there," said Maisie laughing merrily. "My daughters like to keep their options open."

Maisie leaned a little confidentially towards him. She peered unashamedly at his face. "Look, Cathy, at the lovely curly black hair he has."

"Aye," said Jack, "and eyelashes, I'm told, that a woman would be proud of."

"Hark," said Maisie, "at the modesty of that. A true Irishman."

In reply, Jack moved his parcel again.

"All right," said Catherine, "out with it."

"What?" he spoke gruffly, hoisting an eye in her direction.

"What's in the parcel?"

"Oh, that," the inflexion was casual. "Oh, that's something I brought for the house here."

"Now," chuckled Maisie.

He made Catherine gently lift the parcel onto the table. "Careful," he said. She undid the string that held the newspaper. Then, still in its wrapping, she lifted the unknown object out of the cardboard box. "It's a bit rickety," he advised. She opened the newspaper to display the glass head of an oil lamp decorated with red and blue flowers.

"Well I never," said Maisie. "Of all things."

Her bemusement rocked Jack. From the box he took a brass paraffin dome. He wound a wad of soaked wick into the grill. "Strike the lights," said Jack, as he handed her the glass. Catherine switched off the lights. He lit a match. Catherine screwed the glass down. The wide kitchen filled with a deep rosy glow.

"Why, it's beautiful," said Catherine.

"I found two in an outhouse. I did this one up" – he hesitated – "especially. It's a fine class of a lamp."

He lit a cigarette, and swished the match to and fro unnecessarily before hurling it into the grate.

"You are a dab hand," said Maisie. "It's the very thing. Men have their place in the scheme of things, too."

Jack studied the lamp, then returned his gaze to the fire.

"It's nothing," he said, crossing his legs. An air of uneasiness fell, as if they were finding themselves suddenly complete strangers to each other. The glib foreplay of language flittered out. No one knew what to say. The lamp filled the room with shadows. "Will you have tea?" asked Catherine. But Jack declined. "It's a courting light, that," he said. Just then, Sara came into the kitchen with her coat over her head. She shook the coat into the porch, paused, and looked round.

"What's this?" she said.

"Jack brought it for us," said Catherine. "Isn't it beautiful?"

"Jack? Jack is it, now?" she said.

"I'm going out," said Sara.

"Please yourself," Catherine answered.

"Look, I'm going out for a while, that's all."

"How?"

"Walking."

"Walking where?"

"I don't know."

"Well, I can't stop you."

"Just try."

Sara buttoned up her cardigan. She looked into the mirror on the windowsill, and widened her eyes as she drew her cheeks down with her fingertips. Then she stood by the door, reluctant to leave.

"I find you depressing," Sara said with a tone of bizarre unexpected intimacy.

"Where are you going?"

"I'll be back early," she pleaded, but Catherine continued brooding by the fire.

"Are you going to meet Jack?" she asked, and her upper lip shook.

"It's not your concern who I'm meeting."

"No, it's not."

"If you won't speak civilly to me, then I'm going," Sara said.

Catherine gave her a look of crazy, undefined envy.

"I don't want rancour in the house," Catherine, white-faced, replied.

Catherine talked to herself under her breath. Her face grew ugly when Sara was gone. She cried dispassionately. Waited for the sound of the car starting. She peered out of the curtains but the car remained unlit and untouched. Then, having reached a decision, she stood at the bottom of the stairs and listened. But she could not hear a sound except the constant shifting of the wind, and a hammering from the sea like tent-pegs being banged into the earth. She drew on a coat, pulled the door quietly behind her, and went to the gate.

She looked into the passenger windows of the car.

She stood, self-consciously. It was her first time out by herself at night for ages. She stepped onto the road like a sick person, unsure of her feet, uncertain of her surroundings. Sara was already half-way up the hill. Overhead, four swans, like sheets clapping in the wind, were flying across the evening sky. There was a smell of rain on stones, of coarse unhampered growth from the ditches. Tired valerian was everywhere. She allowed Sara to cross the hill and then flew after her. From the crest, Catherine saw her sister walking very slowly past the beach at Scotchport. Passing the boathouse she became a shadow on the other side of the road. Then, getting by the houses, she ran, one wrist swinging, her other hand held firmly against her stomach, and her head down.

She turned a further corner, and doing so, stole a look behind towards the houses.

Catherine, terrified that she might be seen, hesitated.

But the light was fast fading. Darkness was rolling in from the sea with low, fast-moving clouds. The horizon gave off a thin sheen of electricity. Then, at a given note, all the voices of the birds stopped. Catherine wanted to turn back, hearing the mockery in Sara's voice if she was seen. But she followed on. Three flashes of light from Eagle Island lit up the sky. Breathless, she looked down the straight road that led from the corner, but could see no sign of her sister. With an ache of the groin she thought of Sara holding Jack Ferris in her arms. The distance became a dark spot in front of her eyes till again came the swinging lights. Disappointed, she walked along uneasily. She feared that Sara was hiding from her deliberately, and half-expecting her to jump out at any minute, Catherine stopped, wondering.

There was a lane of white sand to the right that led eventually to the dunes. Catherine, her fists gripped tight in the pockets of her coat, walked down the lane about a hundred yards to where the windswept grass ended and the rising furze of the bog began.

Cold winds from the sea reached her, but there was no sign of Sara. "Sara," she called suddenly, forgetting all her duplicity. "Sara!" she screamed. With a sick feeling of distress she screamed again. It was no use. Soon it would be pitch black. She ran back along the white sand to the road. Finding tar-macadam under her feet, she turned right, she turned left. She didn't know where she was. She turned right and keeping the middle distance of the crest of the hill before her and the single light of O'Malley's to her left, she made for The Dwellings. She rounded Termoncarrach Lough, frightening the lake birds. The high stone wall had a dark human presence. Walking back to Corrloch seemed to take an eternity. The night was filled with the sound of coughing animals, and always, as she ran the last few yards, the impression of someone, stronger and more powerful than herself, gaining on her.

19

Oh No, Don't Stop the Carnival

A few years later, on St John's Eve, fires celebrating the summer solstice of a few days before were burning everywhere through the far west. All along the coast as darkness fell piles of tyres, old furniture, barrels of tar were set alight. On Mullet fires were burning and they were answered by fires on Achill, on Nephin, at Benwee Head, Carrowteige, and Sheskin. Flames leapt up into the darkness as the Adams girls drove towards Barnatra.

Whooshes of sparks rose on every side.

Across the gate that opened into a field a huge banner announced the Folk Festival. The banner plunged in the wind like a parachute behind a seaplane touching down. A string of bulbs had fallen with a spray of light into a corner of the field.

The wind was fierce. The marquee billowed. The girls came up the road through lines of parked cars. A few acres of stony land away was the Atlantic. The girls clung to each other's arms, balancing and laughing against the gusts. The marquee, with sails illuminated, shook like a grounded ship. "The things we do," shouted Sara. "What?" screamed Catherine. The generator hummed and gave off a stench of dark oil. The stewards, laughing to each other, swung bits of twine with a darning needle at the end to pierce tickets. They drank by turn from a bottle and slagged those they knew.

Couples suddenly appeared in restless beams of moonlight, then disappeared as suddenly into the shadows. The members of the festival committee went to and fro, watching for the possibility of sparks reaching the tent. They argued about the cost of certain performers over the coming days, made cynical remarks about the chairman, and blamed each other for what might go wrong. Small tents had been pegged into a nearby field by the *Fleadh*-goers from round the country, and the farmer who owned the field was demanding of the committee that either he be paid a rent or else that they be moved.

"Them lads are all go-boys," he complained, "they'll have my field destroyed."

"We'll see about payment when the event is over," said the secretary.

"You have your shite," replied the farmer.

The local committee humbled by each new onslaught weaved their way smiling through the strange folk people. Each whip of the canvas made their heads turn; nervously they barked orders to the stewards, fidgeted with the cardboard cashbox on a table inside, where the pound notes were clamped down under a tin of nails. The drivers of the cars shouted at the women as they drove by, but Catherine and Sara took no notice. Their Northern solidarity gave them a snobbish and conspiratorial air. Their high heels covered in mud, the women delicately entered the tent. It was like going into a paper bag where you were surprised to find other people gathered and acting natural. The floor was boarded as on an ancient trawler, and gave at the centre to all sides.

Jack Ferris, bright-eyed, passed within a few feet of them. He was smoothing down his tossed hair.

"Hallo," he said.

"It's you," Catherine said.

He commenced some further grooming – patting his pockets, shaking his pants, tying a lace.

"And the girl in the Abbey – is she all right?"

"Fine, Jack, fine," said Sara.

To Catherine he looked a little strange in his flared trousers. To think of her shameful fantasies that had centred round Jack Ferris those few summers ago made her feel weak. "See you later," she said. He walked over to where the men, like something out of another century, went up and down as the boards gave beneath their feet when weight elsewhere shifted.

"Do you see him looking at you?" said Lizzie Summers.

"Who?" asked Sara.

"Your man – Ferris."

238

"Oh him."

Asked Lizzie: "Is it you, Catherine, or Sara or what that he's after?"

"You better ask him," Catherine said.

"Sure, yon fellow," surmised Lizzie Summers, as she shook out her coat, "he only has it for to stir his tay."

Although it was really a folk festival, the committee had decreed that on the opening night there should be entertainment for the locals. So an old-fashioned country-and-western dance and a *céilí* had been arranged before the folk groups started. In a white suit a crooner from the fifties sang Walter Glynn's version of "Where My Caravan Is Resting", then came a local fiddle band who played too fast to dance to, then a long-retired country-and-western showband from Castlebar who looked into each other's eyes as they swept through old popular airs. The band played behind low hardboard screens depicting sunsets, palmtrees and blue morning stars. The elderly singer sang with an American accent and wore a shirt with silver tassels. At the announcement of each new song the folk crowd gave a patronizing, exaggerated cheer. Every so often a priest with a low brimmed hat and billowing coat held a draw in aid of Knock Airport. He was greeted by raucous applause. As the dance proceeded he was out between every tune, sometimes a fraction late, so that, with a backward wave of his hand, the band ended the tune before it had rightly begun.

He saw off crystal vases, cigarettes, a bottle of Black Bush. At one stage he was bartering a tray of Bournville chocolates which he was holding high over his head when someone, it was said, tampered with the generator, one of those fuckers from Dublin it was said, the lights went off and, no way put out, he continued to talk on unseen and unheard while the tent floor buckled as the dancers raced across it. There were aggressive roars of laughter. Shrieks. Screams. The light came back on like the flap of the confessional being suddenly slid back.

The dancers, who were in their thirties and forties, old couples who had come for the nostalgia of the sixties showband tunes, were in each other's arms kissing. Men were on their knees. One man's trousers were down round his shins. The priest shook the chocolates over his head. "Number 242, a red ticket," he roared down the thunderous microphone. The dance continued. The sixties people in their old-fashioned gear went country. The wind charged through the entrance. The stewards drew heartily on their cigarettes. The chairman of the Parish Committee spoke.

And though the Adams girls were asked to dance, they refused.

Sara was wearing a green high-collared blouse, a wide grey skirt and little white high-heels. Catherine was wearing a dowdy, flower-patterned dress that reached her ankles and, as a gesture towards her mother, stout church-going shoes. Her blond hair, tied with a red scarf, was in a ponytail. She had, Jack knew, beautiful legs. The girls had their faces painted. Their nails varnished. Their minds made up. They sat out the *céilí* band and the crooner. Only when the country-and-western started did they dance, and then out of fun. Instead of taking a partner, they took to the floor in each other's arms, slighted the men who asked them out and instead aligned themselves at the foot of the stage with those middle-aged women who danced with each other in a maternal, self-conscious way, with plump elbows held high and shy eyes cast down. Slim and athletic, with a noble head, Catherine danced in a slow shuffle with her sister.

The girls were slumming with the locals.

The lights came and went. The tent rocked unsteadily. At each request for someone from Mullet a cheer arose from the shepherds of Binghamstown. Women were spun away from each other. A stray terrier came in and swinging round on all fours started barking furiously at the band. An odd roar came from someone stopped outside where the long-bearded youngsters were waiting for the real festival to begin. Cigarettes were flicked away into the darkness. Joints passed through various hands. Fires flared along Broadhaven Bay. The outsiders from the east looked at the fires and wondered what they meant. Not knowing increased their euphoria. The sea stood groin to groin against the land. And there was a feeling that the dance music was issuing from a wireless where the hand had not quite found the station; it was a music gone back in time; other timeless conversations kept breaking in – arguments, the mock grunts of men wrestling, women screeching; it was something dangerous, something pagan; winds from the sea blew the tunes around, loudspeakers seemed to pick up one instrument only – and all this sound woven brashly together travelled across to where a small herd of cattle watched ears-up over a ditch.

It reached the old men who stood for a moment outside the houses on the outskirts of Barnatra watching the bonfires the children had lit. It reached a woman making her way home to her daughter's. I remember those tunes, she thought. It was a small insignificant human sound, carried this way, carried that way. Sometimes not heard at all even if you listened keenly for it.

The band was playing a Slim Whitman ballad. Then came another air from the past

And most of all I miss her lips
A shade of eiderdown

and then a brace of Beatles tunes. At one end of the floor, near the entrance, the drunken outsiders clamoured, while further up the locals danced sedately. The girls waltzed across the clattering floor, took bold swings, avoided the middle-aged women who were doing the Twist and Huckle-Buck, and, perspiring, waited during the intervals while the young crowd called out for Planxty. A song by Elvis took the sweating ancient-faced singer, who was encouraged by everyone there, to his knees, while even older men than him, on sax and trombone, pretended it wasn't happening. The different generations roared for more while the stout brass players huddled together and blew wild riffs into a single microphone. Then the guitarist, grey-haired and pot-bellied, turned his back to the dancers and played his solo facing the blustering canvas behind. The air of the tent flickered with static. Jack Ferris danced with all the women who had come by minibus from the peninsula. The girls spied Jack in the arms of a married woman, Annie Burke, whose husband skippered the *Inishglora*, and then with Josie Malley who was beautiful, and Mary Noone who was tall.

When Ladies' Choice was announced a huge cheer of nostalgia and mirth and lust went up.

Jack moved along behind the throng of single men who comported themselves like labourers at a hiring fair. They merrily pushed each other forward. The ones pushed forward kicked backwards. Jack watched over their heads. He never took his eyes off the Adams girls. He was trying to stifle the beat of his heart against his shirt. In the melée, he slipped a hand into his trousers to straighten his penis against his sweating stomach. The palms of his hands slithered. Then Sara flounced over, all confident, and swung him out onto the floor because Catherine wouldn't. She plonked her flat groin against him. "You have to be kind to my sister," she said. The nub of her touched him mischievously, yet she stared unashamedly into his eyes as she danced round to where her sister sat, and much to Catherine's disguised shame handed him on to her. "You're a real ladies' man, aren't you?" said Catherine. The tips of her breasts glanced off his chest. The brief touch of her shoulder in his hands. Then Catherine returned him to Sara, and so for a number of dances he went backwards and forwards between the two women. "I like Catherine a lot," he told Sara. She excused herself with a fey curtsy. He smiled weakly to himself, then turned proud and mellow as Catherine slid into his arms. "This dreadful music must be from your time," she smiled. Her damp forehead dropped onto his shoulder and her left arm encircled his waist. She took the two strands of lace that held the cuffs of her dress and tied her wrists together behind his neck, and so they shuffled in a winding fashion between the two poles that held the tent aloft.

She undid her cuffs, and slid one hand under his jacket onto his shirt.

"Where are you now?" he asked.

"Belfast," she said.

Her other hand cooled his as it lay along his thigh. And all the time her eyes never left his eyes. So the three sets passed.

Catherine let him go. He stood uncertain in the middle of the floor like a man who has just walked out of a cinema.

Jack rejoined the men. And the sisters, much giddier now, as if they knew some awful secret about him – had they felt the slender arch of his cock against his stomach? – began dancing with each other again.

After Ladies' Choice, things were not the same. The tension among the crowd had dropped. The women had spoken. Those left with no one looked round them in dismay. They gazed in desperation at those who like themselves had been overlooked. Pride ran the gauntlet of more refusals. All sat down to wait on the Planxty concert to begin. Some couples stayed in each other's arms like people drowning.

"Oh, dear Jesus," he whispered.

And the girls made no attempt to separate during the last few tunes. Indeed they grew happier, and more indifferent. Jack sat out tangos, twists, jives. He watched the Adams girls. Then the dance ended and the young traditionalists gathered across the floor. In the make-shift toilet he stood along with the other older men and could not piss onto the sodden grass where buckets of sawdust had been thrown. "That was a fucking good night," someone said to him. He marched out into the darkness in a cold sweat, hearing the wind, the quiet lisp of bicycle tyres, the moan of engines, the voices of couples.

Inside, the new generation were screaming for Planxty. The musicians must have come on because a great roar arose. Over the speakers came the bodhran and the mandolin, the bazooki and the Uilleann pipes. Then Andy Irvine began singing "A Blacksmith Courted Me".

The rocking beam of the torch in Catherine's hand skirted the road and Sara laughed.

"Catherine," he shouted.

"Who's that?" she said, startled.

"It's me, Jack."

"How are you going home?"

"I was going in the minibus."

"We can give him a lift home, can't we?" said Catherine.

"Oh, of course we can," said Lizzie Summers.

"Well, he taught me how to drive," said Sara. He climbed into the back of the Adams' car alongside Lizzie and a man. They drove off in silence through the crowds of celebrators making their way up the lane. Lizzie Summers fell across Jack's knee. Gently he lifted her back up onto her boyfriend's shoulder. "Thanks awfully," said Lizzie. "So what are you doing now?" he asked Catherine. "Well, Sara is going to be in a small, low-budget film and I'm working in community theatre and studying at Queens. And you?"

"Salmon fishing," said Jack.

"Will you stop here for a moment?" asked the man. "I have to take a leak."

He stood on the edge of the road.

"We should drive off and leave the fucker there," said Lizzie, "I don't know what came over me to go with yon."

They watched the man from behind, give a little shake, do a bow and draw his buttocks in. Then he turned, and patted his groin.

"Why do men do that?" asked Catherine.

"For pleasure," said Jack.

"To see if it's still there," shrieked Lizzie. She moved over to let her boyfriend in, and slapped a hand on his knee. "You're lucky, Fintan," she said to him, "that I'm here to protect ya. They were going to drive off and leave you."

They drove by glowing fires on the peninsula. Outside Belmullet the three got out of the back of the car into teeming rain, and he was about to make for Annagh Head when Catherine called him. She ran after him. The headlights found her wet cheek. He saw drops of rain glide down her face, stall at the brows, shimmer on her lips, fall from her chin onto her damp gaberdine.

She smiled at him. In the full beam of the headlights Catherine kissed his cheek.

"Well, goodnight," said Jack.

"Goodnight," said Catherine, and she stood there in the rain looking after him.

*   *   *

244

The rain ceased. He was in a land without a horizon. He went on, he came back. He smoked, he cursed himself under his breath, then gave a long wheeze. He stiffened. He barked and sniffed furiously. His armpits grew hollow. Then he spun on his heels, and when he stopped his mind filled with the interior of the chaotic marquee.

"Who's that?" someone shouted out of the shadows. "Who's that?" the man asked again.

"Jack Ferris," Jack whispered.

"I'm Fintan Carmichael," the other answered. "I was with you in the car. The bitch Lizzie Summers showed me the door the minute I dropped the hand." He came closer. "Are you not well?"

"I'm grand, thanks."

"The blondes, they gave you a lesson."

"Do you say so?"

"You have to understand women." His companion clapped him on the back. "You have to stand up to them. Else they'll walk all over you."

"Is that so."

"I know them ladies. The Adamses a' Corrloch." Fintan Carmichael continued in a conspiratorial way. "You have to watch the chicks of the blue hen."

"What do you mean?"

"The father was RUC."

"I know."

"Aye, but who could blame them? There's nothing wrong with having a good time."

The two men stepped on through the night.

"The things I could tell you," said Fintan Carmichael.

"Work away," said Jack.

"Oh, if you only knew all the men those ladies have lain with! Isn't it a terror! The Protestant girls are way ahead of us," Fintan declaimed. A tickle entered his throat. He grew excited. "A man like you," he told Jack, "should watch his p's and q's. Oh Lord, but they're wild women. Certainly," said Fintan. "The Protestant girl," he blew out loudly, "would make you cross the yard."

245

"So that's how it is."

"That's how it is. Women generally," declared Fintan, "have no shame."

They reached the fire on Annagh Head. A crowd were sitting round drinking and singing. Some lay fast asleep a few yards away from the flames. A woman was playing a guitar with four strings. Fintan and Jack sat down. Across the fields came two lads driving before them a tractor wheel. They pushed it into the fire. Sparks flew up. The smell of burning rubber spread.

"Come here a minute," said Fintan.

He unearthed a half-bottle of Paddy whiskey and they stood on a rock and drank it while they looked at the flames.

In a field some distance away they found a goat. Jack stood by the gate while Fintan scoured the field in the wake of the nanny. "Get up, ya boy ya," shouted Fintan. A few minutes later he emerged driving the white nanny in front of him. They tied the animal with the rope that held the gate in place, then led her up the road to Corrloch.

"We'll show them," said Fintan.

Dawn was breaking. The fires had disappeared. The goat kept a steady, reliable pace. The two walked laughing behind her. "If we meet anyone, we're disgraced," said Fintan. When they got to the Adams' house it was in darkness. They listened a while behind the gate-piers.

Then Fintan coaxed the goat forward, while Jack tied the rope that held her to the knocker. They withdrew quietly down the path, hid behind the stone wall, and Fintan called the goat.

"Billy," he whispered.

The creature stood perfectly still, adjusting the coracle-shaped pupils of its eyes. Then she lay down on the step.

"Cynthia," he whispered louder.

The goat did not budge.

Jack threw a handful of gravel and the goat shook herself. She got up and reached forward to pluck at some grass. "Jesus," said Jack. The men, shaking with mirth, waited. The knocker sounded. "Again," said Fintan, with his teeth bared. The goat pulled strongly. The knocker went rat-a-tat. The lights came on. Someone opened the hall door and the rope round the goat went taut. The nanny was pulled inwards as the door opened wider. Catherine was standing there in a man's long white shirt. With her head tilted down in disbelief she stared dumbfounded at the pink ears of the white beast on her doorstep.

When she woke the next morning Catherine was astonished to find the goat was still there eating grass in the garden. She went down and looked into the nanny goat's eye. Its udders shook like bell-ropes. The trim neck was graceful. The gaze ladylike. It was a shock to find the animal staring up at her. The green pupils of its eyes wavered and floated like flakes of snow. The act of seeing seemed to have detached the irises. Her hair was human and white. The gaze ancient.

Beyond the glass eye of the goat Catherine saw a fresh uncivilized place. She watched the startlingly pure, gentle look of the womanly goat.

"And how did you come here, pray?" Catherine asked. She let her out of the gate and watched her stroll off into the sunshine.

20

The Illustrated Sons of Ireland

The summer after she took her degree Catherine came down to the Mullet alone. She took a walk on the beach. Away in the distance she saw another windblown figure approaching her. The figure would stop, bend, go on again. For ages and ages they headed slowly towards each other. Eventually she saw it was a wild-looking man with a plastic refuse sack who was collecting timber from the wrack. At last they reached each other.

He was wearing a duffle-coat and no shirt.

"How are you!" she shouted.

"I'm alive, I think," he yelled. "Where are you from?"

"Belfast."

"Do they have wind up there?"

"Sometimes," she shouted, taken aback.

"I'm sorry to hear that," he yelled, "I thought there might be some place on this godforsaken earth that the wind would leave untouched." And at that he moved on, as did she. At a local pub she enquired where Jack Ferris lived. "He stops above in Thady's," she was told. She touched up her face in the toilet mirror and then looked into her eyes for a while.

She walked through the *gaeltacht* area with the same mixture of feelings that would unnerve her as she'd stride through West Belfast.

Smoke spiralled from the chimneys. The men unashamedly viewed her as she stepped through the small cottages. They turned aside and called out flat, timid greetings, which she answered nervously. She reached the lane that the barman had marked on the map he'd drawn for her. She was met by a blast of wild wind which flew up between the narrow ditches. Fresh cowpats steamed on the grass. A race of warm water ran to her left. She stole curiously down.

A few stunted oleria, whipped inland, announced the low, galvanize-roofed, whitewashed, three-roomed cottage. The first little window she came to she looked in and saw two beds pulled over at angles to a roaring fireplace. Trousers and shirts hung from a cord above the mantel. In the middle room, the remains of a breakfast sat on the kitchen table. Yellow plastic fishing gear was strewn on the floor. Under a window on the far side a bicycle sat upside down on its handlebars and saddle, and beside it, two uncocked rifles rested against the sill. In the third room, lined with books, a huge old-fashioned typewriter, big as a tractor, sat on a green table. She withdrew, knocked and turned away.

"Come in, Josie," a strange voice called.

"It's me, Catherine."

"What?" shouted Jack.

"Catherine Adams," she said.

"Jesus," she heard him say.

She pushed the door in. She walked on towards the far room where Jack was sitting on the side of one of the beds in his underpants.

"Come in, Missus," said Thady, as he looked round the headboard of the other bed. The room was filled with the dry, animal smell of bachelors, the sharp tang of fish and the hissing of wet turf. Jack, white-faced, with a head of uncombed curly black hair, started to pull on a pair of trousers he'd taken down from the line. "Don't," she said, "if they're still wet."

"We got a terrible drenching this morning," Jack said.

"And fuck all for it," said Thady.

"Stop where you are," said Catherine.

She sat to the right of the hearth under a picture of the Jesse James gang, and a copy of Emmet's speech from the dock that had yellowed with age.

"So this is home?" said Catherine.

"That's right," said Jack, "and this is Uncle Thady."

"How do you do?" he said, and she took his hand.

249

On a further wall was a huge framed picture of a group of grey Victorian men standing one behind the other in riding boots and buckled shoes with high heels. Each man wore a bow and wig. The faces looked like they had been added on to the identical bodies afterwards. The picture looked totally out of place on the bare rounded wall.

"Who are these persons?" Catherine asked.

" 'The Illustrated Sons of Ireland' they call themselves," said Thady, "I picked that up in a junk shop in Longford town."

"They look like figures in an old English cartoon."

"That's exactly what they were, Missus," agreed Thady. "Lads in a cartoon. Irishmen abroad."

"And no women," said Catherine.

"No, the women were away that day," laughed Thady.

"Major General Patrick Sarsfield," Catherine read.

"A cannon ball put paid to his skull," said Thady.

"Oliver Plunkett."

"Drawn and quartered."

"John Philpot Curran. Hugh O'Neill."

"The man himself!"

"Oliver Goldsmith, Thomas Moore. Archbishop McHale. Father Matthew."

"The less said the better."

"Wolfe Tone."

"A Presbyterian, wouldn't you know. And a Republican."

"Daniel O'Connell."

"A Catholic."

"Edmund Burke."

"A relation of Conor Cruise O'Brien," said Jack.

"Robert Emmet."

"He should have waited."

"Richard Lawlor Shield. Henry Grattan. Gerald Griffin."

"A clerk."

"William Smith O'Brien."

"A Labour man."

"Reverend Father Burke, O.P. John Mitchell."

"That would be the author of *A Jail Journal*," Thady said. "A mighty man. Did his time in Australia and went straight to the top in America. There you have the whole shebang."

"And you know them all."

"And why wouldn't I? If there'd only been that crew alone, there'd have been no need for the rest of us." He coughed. "When you hear it all in one breath it's hard to take in. And then it means nothing. Nothing at all."

"It's cool," said Thady, sitting up.

"Who's Josie?" asked Catherine.

"Ah, poor Josie Drum," said Thady. "She should be up there too, among 'The Illustrated'. The man above put a fierce cross on Josie – he told her to carry on."

"If I'd known you were coming," said Jack, and he pulled the sheet to his chin.

"But is there a man above at all?" continued Thady.

The two cats on the hearth, with high hips and long hind legs, ran when she attempted to pet them, and skulked together in slow motion at the door.

"You're welcome anyway," Thady told her. He rose a small face filled with mean humour and brown, racy eyes. "You'll find glasses and a cup there behind you." Then he pointed towards the fire. "There's custard there in a pot, too."

She looked at Jack. In his vest he had the thin hooped shoulders of a young boy.

"Why don't you bring me out fishing with you someday?"

"You wouldn't like it," said Jack.

"I won't know till I see for myself."

"Do you see," Thady pointed, "do you see there on the sill there's a bottle." As Thady poured a dram of crystal *poitín* into his cup, Catherine looked at Jack, and Jack looked at her. Catherine was a woman to tie scarves about herself, her shoulders, her neck, her head. Even, at times, round her wrist. The fire whooshed and changed direction.

"The custard," explained Thady, "is for the cats."

He leaned forward to pour a drop of *poitín* into her glass. It smelt sharp and medicinal. He caught her eye with his and gave a grin. "He's not the only man, is Jack, to have a lady come to see him."

"No?"

"No. I have a girlfriend in America got married, had children, don't you know. And now that she's lost her husband she says she'll be back for me." He drank a mouthful, held it awhile, then swallowed it. "And I put a new roof on the house, here, for the very day."

"You should not," said Catherine, with a straight face, "have built a cage before you trapped the bird."

"If I," said Thady, "was a few years younger, this boy here" – and he pointed at his loins – "would be in there" – and he pointed at hers.

This absurd male fantasy made Catherine burst out laughing, and along with her, the men laughed uproariously.

"I'm not supposed to laugh at comments like those," she said.

"Indeed you're not," agreed Thady.

Catherine smelt her glass and tasted the rim. She arched her foot, gave a loose-breasted laugh, and flexed her leg. She drank, then drank again.

"When did you come down?" asked Jack.

"This morning," she said as she read the fire.

"So you're by yourself," he said guardedly.

"Oh, I have plenty of company."

The loose gutter in the east gable pounded, then rain struck the windows and battered the galvanize. Thady lifted his hand to his eyes and yawned. Then, incongruously, farted.

"It's the breakfast," he apologized.

"You should try baby food," said Catherine, and then she added, "and you could administer it to yourself with a spoon."

"Glory be!" said Thady. "Is that the recipe?"

The cats returned and leapt onto the two beds in which the men lay, and nestling, looked across at each other as they stretched stiff paws. There was no sound when the wind died away except the rain hitting the flames and the drip now and then from the steaming clothes. Catherine felt a draught blow round her groin. She drew her kilt tighter about her. The pin flashed. Thady broke into a fit of coughing, spat somewhere and said: "That'll be the size of it."

"I have you now," said Catherine.

"You have what?" asked Jack.

"What you look like," and she laughed. "You look like a vole."

"What's that?"

"It's a sort of a small rodent."

"That," said Thady, "don't you know, would be a class of a rat."

"It must be three years since I've seen you."

"That's right."

"The last time I was here I woke to find a goat tied to our door," said Catherine. Jack chuckled. "You wouldn't know anything about that, would you?"

"The gentleman goat," mused Thady, "is a rascal. He can disgrace himself. He'll tip his head and drink his own urine."

"Is that so?"

"Oh, yes, the blaggard."

She threw some turf on the fire. Thady's black eyebrows rose, and his tongue darted out. "Yes," he said, "keep her going," and he reached out for the bottle. He filled their glasses, then his cup. "I spend my last penny – the bit I have – on this," he said. He drank with a series of dislocated movements of the face and hands, squinted, feinted, then bared his teeth, and finally, with a shake of the head, clapped his lips together again.

Silence returned. The wind shifted.

"You tied that goat to our door," she said.

"I did," said Jack.

"Whatever for?"

"It's the Leitrim twist of mind, Missus," said Thady. "They got scholarship in Leitrim."

"That's lovely," said Catherine.

"We are only passing the time, *tá*," said Thady.

"It often seems to me that I am only indulging myself." Catherine was thinking aloud. She offered her glass. "And I often feel that I couldn't care if I never saw anyone again."

"You should not say that," said Jack.

"A woman can say these things," Thady declared. He refilled

253

her glass. "I think, will you excuse me, that I have to go to the toilet."

He put his bare feet into his shoes, pulled a coat about him and perched for a second, heron-like, at the open door, looked out to sea, then with an exaggerated blink he went to the side of the house.

"This is all very civilized," said Catherine.

"I'm glad to see you," said Jack.

"This," she said looking at her glass, "is wonderful stuff."

Thady returned to the room and stood by the bed again with humorous shakes of the elbow, a small giddiness of the heel, and rose his goat's brows, then his arms jigged the reins. Turning his shoulder blades like the obsolete wheels of a cart, Thady climbed into bed. Catherine stood up and went to the window. She rested her glass on the sill, sat on the further edge of Jack's bed and looked out.

"The islands," said Jack, "are in a different place every day."

She watched the big shadowy sea. Men in oilskins torn at the thigh and the groin were standing on a table of rock against which the waves broke with a death rattle. Her body darkened the room. Silently, to the right, on the beach the water crackled across the sand, then fizzled out. For a long time she looked out till eventually she said, "It seems to me that the islands are leaving."

Jack looked over her shoulder.

It became so clear that things not seen before came into view. Each stone on the beach seemed mere feet away. Cottages suddenly appeared. The sky was windy and blue, the earth white.

"You are right," he said.

The dog began barking.

"That must be Josie, now," said Jack.

Standing up, Catherine had to support herself against the wall.

"I think I'll go," she said.

"Wait," cried Jack, "I'll go with you." And he pulled the bedclothes back.

"No," she said stubbornly, "the fresh air will do me good."

"If you want to go fishing with us," said Thady, "how does tomorrow morning at six strike you?"

"That's an unearthly hour."

"We have to catch the tide," said Jack.

"Take care, Missus," Thady called after her.

When she stepped into the yard she felt her head going round. A small woman was coming down the lane talking to herself. The dog was running between the two women. The woman had a buttered face and ginger-stick eyebrows, huge lips and a tumbling fast stride. She was excusing herself for some misdemeanour.

Then, seeing Catherine, she said: "I beg your pardon."

"Hallo," said Catherine.

"Where did you get the beautiful eyes? And the beautiful hair?" Josie asked. "Some people are blessed." Then, looking at Catherine carefully she added: "Yous have been at the bottle."

"I'm afraid I have."

"Will you be all right, love?"

"Yes," said Catherine, blushing because she felt so tall.

"I'm sure," said Josie, "that you can talk with the best of them," and she trod on by. The moon, like a scooped out melon, was casting a wide ring that would someday soon be full. Bewildered, and breathless, intoxicated, she ran. She stopped on the white shimmering road. Fog from the steaming sea was rushing inland as evening fell. She walked through the fast mist. Birds had collected on their hunkers to the left of the pier. Here, they crouched out of the wind. She could nearly feel the soft breasts of the seagulls in the damp sand. She could feel her own coat, her cold lips, her lust, her cheeks, and the warmth of her armpits.

She touched her eyes and found the lashes wringing wet.

The birds fluttered and moved a fraction at her approach, then, all of a sudden, she was in the middle of the damp mist, and could see neither before her nor behind.

21

At Sea

When they were about a mile out to sea Catherine began to feel ill. She stood alone at the stern thinking the sea air might restore her, but she only got worse. As the boat plunged beyond Inishglora her perspective danced wildly. A cold sweat streamed down her back. The planks buckled underfoot. She climbed down to the cabin where the men were lying on the bunks.

"Are you all right?" asked Jack.

"If you really want to know," said Catherine, "I don't feel well."

"It's the same for all of us at the beginning."

"That's reassuring."

The men smoked in the cramped cabin. Jack introduced her to Hugh. "Hugh is the cook on board," said Jack.

"God bless us," said Thady, "onions in dripping."

"I'd prefer if ye did not talk about food," she asked.

"I know what you mean," said Hugh. "I often feel the same way myself when I have to fry mince."

"Please," she said.

The men drank tea and lemonade, they joked, they slept, waking for a few seconds as the battering gained an extra beat that had not been there the last time. She sat on a bench with her head in her hands. The engine groaned drily, the pistons shook, then the roar tapered off into a low sickening throb.

"You should lie down."

"It's not what you'd call romantic," she said.

She lay on the edge of an upper bunk, very close to falling off, wrapped in a torn sleeping bag and a patchwork blanket covered in fish scales. The smell of oil was everywhere. A few times as the boat lurched Jack nearly jumped up to catch her, but each time she toppled Catherine corrected herself, and cried out: "This is hell!"

"Is this all you do, lie down here and sleep?" she asked.

"Till we get there."

She turned inward and gradually began to roll towards the edge again. He smoked and watched her.

Then the skipper shouted down: "Hi Jack! Wake the boys. We're there."

They let the first salmon buoy out, the rope snapped after it and, flicking off rainwater, the net followed. Catherine, a hand curved round a rail, watched from the cabin door. The men stood either side of the unrolling net, with Jack on the lead line and Thady on the light, each with red plastic gloves on, for fear, as Thady explained, "of losing a digit, don't you know." If the net snagged they hauled frantically till the lines loosened themselves.

When they'd dropped the salmon nets, Hugh began frying breakfast. The smell of liver drove her astray. She stayed on deck till they were finished, then they set off again around the island. They tossed out the first turbot net. When Thady threw the buoy Jack stood with the weight in his hands till the rope had run out far enough.

"Let the fucker go!" shouted Thady.

The minute Jack let the weight go the rope went under with sufficient speed to take a man overboard. He leapt out of the way of the net flying after it. The two men stood watching the net as it ran through their hands until they came to the rope again, then came the second weight, which Jack held till the last moment to straighten the net. The rope rose out of the sea shedding water. He steadied the weight against the prow. He held it till the full force of the taut bristling rope grabbed him.

"Will you let the fucker go!" shouted Thady.

He dropped it into the sea.

"One of these days you'll go with it," said Hugh.

Finally the end buoy, with its black flag toppling wildly, sloughed overboard to mark the drop. The boat revved forward. They pulled away from the shot, and went beyond Inishglora

257

to haul in the turbot nets that they'd lowered to the floor of the ocean the day before. They stood on the bouncing deck without speaking as they searched for sight of the buoys.

"It never ends," said Hugh to Catherine.

She went below but could not sleep. She stood aft and looked into the heaving blue and felt miserable. Each wave turned her stomach a little more. She was shocked to find that a boat at sea is more cramped than an underground tunnel. Although there was that infinite space around, the deck could be crossed in four paces. The bunks below were cramped together in a cabin that was only a few feet wide. If she stood to starboard she inhaled diesel fumes. If she went below the boat was plunging as the net was winched in.

The boat wheeled round the buoy. A mist descended. First the net came through the winch where Thady freed it of fish. Behind him the others drew it into two piles, cleaning it as they went of seaweed and gravel. It came up trailing extraordinary vegetation. A dark green stench from the bed of the ocean filled the boat. Strange shellfish crawled across the deck. Oily blossoms fell away. Jack hauled to starboard on the lead line, Hugh to port. At their feet the net, dripping thick fluids, was piled.

The hauling seemed to go on forever. The turbot, flattened by countless fathoms of seawater, were thrown into boxes. The mist grew dense. Seagulls flew by. The boat slopped in the silence. It seemed they had lost touch with human kind. Then, like a voice from hell, some message crackled across the radio. The silence afterwards was deafening. The brooding skipper leaned out of the window to see where he was. He tacked to port, and they chugged slowly forward. Sometimes through a break in the mist they might see the buoy fluttering away off in the distance, then it would disappear again as the fog closed in around them. The mist moved across the boat in silent wet balls. Catherine climbed onto the foredeck, and tried to hold down the bile in her throat.

From below, the cheerful voices of the fishermen reached her like voices from another dimension. Their normality made each voice discordant. That they seemed familiar with all this ghostly otherworld alarmed her.

"Any sign of the buoy?" asked Hugh.

Hauling steadily, Jack looked out to starboard.

"Any sign?" Hugh called.

"Nothing," he said.

"Will you try and stay with me," Hugh complained.

A few minutes later they were still hauling, hauling.

"Anything yet?" asked Hugh.

Jack did not answer.

"Do you hear me?"

"I hear you," called Jack.

"There's no need to be so fucking short-tempered."

"Stop pulling so fucking quickly."

Their arms worked furiously in short circles as they jabbed out to grab the wet net. The winch screeched. The hauling seemed to go on forever. Falling forward, falling back on their heels with the momentum of the boat. The nets were now waist-high.

"There must be some sign of her now."

"Nothing."

"Look again, will you."

Jack stopped pulling and caught his breath. He straightened. He glanced at Catherine. Then he looked out to sea. The winch kept turning. The net kept coming in. A bird screamed overhead. They were alone in a small clearing in the mist. He searched the sea ahead.

"I can see no sign of the United Ireland," said Jack.

"Oh but you are some bollacks," said Hugh.

Not long after that they pulled the last stretch of net on board. The rope, teeming with wet, came skipping across the water. The buoy came in. Immediately the men sat on the heaped nets with their heads lowered, and smoked. The skipper put the kettle on. He came out to check the loads of fish in the boxes. "Not bad," he said. He drove the gear to forward. The boat headed back over the choppy sea to the salmon grounds.

Over the rail Catherine vomited profusely. Then, when the sea grew heavier, they tied a rope to her so that she would not fall overboard. Around her the men cleaned the insides of the fish.

Out of the skate poured green fluid that smelt dank and heavy like fresh manure.

"How much longer?" she asked sadly.

"I told you," said Jack, "once we go out we can't go in."

"This is the most awful day of my life," she whispered.

"I told you."

"Don't keep saying that," complained Catherine. "I would dearly love to do away with myself."

"Keep looking at the horizon, Missus," advised Thady. "Your brain is receiving the wrong signal, don't you know. Your poor brain thinks you've eaten something wrong. You know and I know you haven't. But your brain does not know that. It thinks you're sick. But you see, you're not sick."

"I am sick."

"No, you're not," said Thady, "your brain only thinks that. The thing to do is to dispute this with your brain. Just look at the horizon. Just keep looking at the horizon. That's the girl."

"Oh God."

Catherine looked at the horizon. While the men worked among the boxes of floundering fish she held the rope that tied her to a metal spar on the foredeck, and looked at the horizon.

They dropped Catherine and the catch off at Blacksod. Jack walked her up the pier. She stood shivering and wet and pale. She had his yellow oilskin jacket on and old woollen gloves belonging to Thady.

"I'm sorry if I shamed you."

"Here," he said, "take these with you," and he handed her a plastic bag of fish.

"What are these?"

"They're monkfish."

"Look," she said, "at their little pudding hands joined over their wobbly breasts. In prayer, I suppose."

"Hence their name."

She looked at him.

"I have to go back out now."

"I don't believe it. Right away?"

"The salmon are running."

260

"You mean you're going to spend all night out there?"

"Aye. If the weather holds. And the next day maybe."

She dropped the bag of fish and took his two hands in hers. "Call and see me when you get ashore."

"I will."

She kissed him.

"I must smell dreadful."

"Not at all."

"Oh dear," said Catherine, kissing him again, "I thought it might come to this."

He went to the end of the pier, waved and loosed the final rope. As he stepped on, the boat was already moving.

From her bed she heard someone passing over the gravel. She waited but no knock came. Then she thought, I've let myself down. Someone went over the gravel again, and even when she knew it made no sense, she listened on.

If the gate stirred in the wind her heart flitted. If the wind blew a can down the road she listened for the silence that would come and bear his step.

In her mind she saw the wall that crept round the yard at the back of Thady's house. She saw the turf in the lean-to. The walls stuffed with old green Guinness bottles. The ass's cock with teats. The ass's teeth on the top of the wall. Then, all the doors of the house blew open. She shot bolt upright in the bed, and ran downstairs.

But there was no one there.

She fell asleep listening to the rain beating warmly on the galvanize sheds out the back. It was her first time in the house in Corrloch alone, and she found it disturbing. The roar of the waves on the curved beach reached the dwellings with the loud moan of trucks going uphill. Catherine afterwards had a dream in which her mother entered this long room and sat at the edge of a small bed – oh, a long distance away from Catherine. Her mother did not look like her real mother, but inside she was still the same. Then her mother lifted up a saucer, tilted her head sideways and rested her cheek in the groove of the dish. At that moment, Catherine had a great longing to be held. She

261

entered a state of pure physical enchantment which was so intense it woke her.

The rain was slipping off the sill.

It was drumming from the gutters into the rain barrel at the side of the house. The door of the house across the street was open, smoke spun to the southwest and Joe Love was seated at the open door, his hands in his lap, one foot dreaming. Chickens were picking through the gravel in front of him. Then it seemed his house lifted off the ground just about one inch. The impression was of gravity slowly losing its hold. Between the walls of the house and the ground there was now this perfect inch of empty space. There was an inch beneath every leg of his tilted chair. Only the chickens remained earthbound. Catherine made her way laboriously back to bed, thinking, What was that dream that I could feel like this?

Later she watched a thrush with richly speckled breast go shopping in the front garden. A girl in bright blue trousers, swinging a bag, came down the gravel road. Catherine accepted her stare, she hers, they merged. She thought, it's two days now. He's got to call. But the days dragged on to three, then four, and still Jack Ferris did not come.

He's out to destroy me, she thought.

She thought of getting the next bus away from the peninsula, of returning to Belfast. And yet she did not move. The house was growing strange. She sat with her back to the window that looked out on the road. Her stomach filled with cramps. With her back to the window she'd hear someone approach, but she must not turn. She'd urge them on, whoever they were, to the door. And then there would be that wonderful moment of hesitation by the gate. The person stopping. She must not turn for fear of having to acknowledge her despair. She'd entice him further on. It was dangerous. Her heart pounded. Only to hear the step pass. And as it would pass then she would turn to see it had been someone else, and begin again.

I would not keep it up for so long, she thought, if someone was waiting for me.

This waiting, it seemed, went on for ever. So that when the person hesitated and the gate opened around six one evening she had already allowed five figures to pass. The steps go on. The despair set in. I've lost him. When Jack knocked on the door she felt she had only imagined it. This human contact was beyond her. It was happening in the past. It could not be reconciled. When the knock was repeated she had to measure each step to the door. The blood filtered from the backs of her hands. And, even when she opened it, his familiar face was like a hallucination. Nor did she know whom he meant when he looked in at her out of the dark and said: "Hallo, Catherine."

Then, dizzy, she led him in, but, strangely enough, hesitated a moment before she closed the door, as if she were expecting some other, as if he had brought someone else along with him.

When the salmon season ended he took her home to Kilty. In a plastic bag he had two large salmon as a gift for his parents. They were on the road for hours hitching from the treeless bogs of the west of Mayo to the watery small fields of North Leitrim. They passed through a storm on the long sounding-board below Ben Bulben. Stood out of the rain under a birch on the road from Buckode to Rossinver. The smell of silage steamed through the bushes.

"I'm sure your parents will banish me," she said.

"Not at all," said Jack. "In fact they're separated – not that they would call it that. He sleeps in the surgery across the street, but comes over home for his dinner."

"That's extraordinarily civilized."

When they got to Jack's village she was too nervous to head ＊ for Ferris' straight away so they went into a pub for hot whiskeys. Soaked and dishevelled they sat in the spirit grocers before colourful biscuit tins, bread in cellophane, bottles of Bull's Blood wine, mail bags, gardening spades and bags of fertilizer seed. Girls, under tweed coats, in dresses of light mustard or yellow and shorn at the calf, passed through to the dark lounge behind. Each called out to Jack.

"I didn't know," said Catherine, "that you were so popular."

"It's a small place."

"I took you to be a shy person."

"Oh, but I am," he laughed.

A small man, poor-featured, manic-eyed, of weak gait, welcomed Jack home with a thump on the shoulder.

"Well, you're the lad," he said, giving Catherine a long unabashed survey.

"This is Catherine," Jack said, introducing her to the woman behind the bar.

"I'm delighted to meet you," she said, dropping Catherine's hand. "Did I meet you before?"

"Not that I can think of."

"Ah, I must be mistaking you for someone else," she said slyly.

"We have salmon here in a bag for the doctor," Jack said for no good reason.

"You were always a good thoughtful fellow," said the barwoman, and then she added with a lascivious smile, "and he was a good court too."

"I see," said Catherine icily.

"You'll give her the wrong impression, Mary."

"He doesn't like to hear it, you know. But you see he was always a man for the women."

"Is that so?"

"That's right," the little man chipped in, "and I haven't the brains to go mad."

"Oh, fair play," laughed Jack.

"And I was foolish enough," whispered Catherine, "to think that you were an innocent."

"You made a bad mistake there."

"How many of these women have you been with?"

"A few."

"It's sordid. And do they always talk like this?"

"Yes."

"Well I don't find it amusing. It's more sordid than amusing."

"You'd be better off keeping out of the courts," interrupted the man, "if you can. The courts are cat. I had to fight through the courts with a neighbour of mine to retain a right-of-way." He moved a salt cellar into the middle of the bar counter. "Do you see that? Let's say that's my place." He shifted an ashtray. "That's the field." A bottle of stout was the neighbour's house and his empty glass was the German's. He flicked a penny on the counter, then moved it into position. "And that's the right-of-way. Now." He reviewed the forces he had collected. Took a long draught from his glass of stout. "I wanted the right-of-way to go down here," he said, lifting the bottle of stout, "as it always used to do till certain parties put their nose in."

"Excuse me," objected Catherine, "that's the neighbour's house you're moving."

"Oh." He studied the bar counter intently. He touched the salt cellar with uncertainty and looked at Catherine. She shook her head. "Hell and damnation!" he exclaimed. He drank again. He lifted the ashtray. "This lad was it?"

"No," replied Catherine. "I do believe that's the field."

"Christ! Where did you get this lady?"

He studied the position, his arms gripped round his chest.

"The penny, is it?" he asked tentatively.

Catherine saw his mother at the uncurtained window as they crossed the street. She was not looking at them. Her arms were folded under her heavy breasts. When they entered the house they could hear a radio playing. Pictures of musicians hung from the walls. There was a piano in the room to the left and next to it a sideboard packed with bizarre trophies. They climbed a small staircase. As they came into the dining room, which had a wall devoted to medals, more trophies and green-fringed certificates, his mother continued to look out onto the street.

"Mother," said Jack, "this is Catherine."

The woman turned.

"I saw you go into the pub across the street hours ago," she said. "And I said to myself, I won't see them again today."

She shook Catherine's hand, then she lowered the radio. She was a tall full woman with a hat wrapped to the back of her head like a clenched fist. There was a white smoothness to her shins. She took Catherine's hand and held it between her breasts. She drew the younger woman's image into her unglazed brown eyes.

"You have lovely skin," Mrs Ferris concluded. "I remember

265

when I was like you." With a sigh she let her go. "Would you like a drink?"

Jack filled the glasses with whiskey. His father appeared at the back of the room followed by a dog. Doc Ferris had priestly, groomed hair and a dark-shaved chin that constantly moved as he chewed on his thoughts. His blue, larkish eyes took in, with quick movements, what was happening each side of Catherine. "Isn't it wonderful," he said.

"Catherine." Still holding her hand, he surveyed Jack. Then, returning to her, he said: "So this is Catherine. You're looking at our display."

"I was just wondering."

"So you're not into the music?"

"When I was young I used to play the trumpet."

"I'm a Comhaltas man myself," he explained and he tapped a certificate on the wall. "I was in on its founding. And these –" he indicated the trophies – "these belong to that boy there."

"Do they?" she said peering down to read the gold scrolls.

"I'm surprised Jack did not tell you that he was once an All-Ireland step-dancer."

"He never mentioned it," she said wide-eyed.

"There you are." He turned courteously to his son. "Oh, Jack was the boy that could dance. We drove together to every *Fleadh* in the country from when he was six years of age."

"They were always on the road, affirmed his wife."

"Listowel, Mullingar, Wexford – we were there."

"It was dancing from morning to night," agreed Mrs Ferris.

"Any place you care to mention. I played and he danced."

"That was it."

"Then he took up the writing. And that was the end of the dancing."

"And the end of the medicine too," said his mother.

Doc Ferris sat down. Catherine and Jack sat down. She was vaguely conscious of the collie dog as he spun by her feet. He dug his snout into the carpet and turned on his back to display his loins. "I know you," she said. "Aye," said Jack, "that's Daisy." Catherine was suddenly embarrassed that the only

266

person in the room she could talk to was the dog. She patted him. He rested his wet snout on her shoe.

"Was there many across in Leyden's?"

"A few," said Jack.

"Has this fellow told you," asked Ma Ferris, "that he was a bit of a playboy?"

"Yes," said Catherine, fretfully.

"He left others," she said. "And if he left others he'll leave you."

"You should not say that to the girl," announced the doctor.

"There was no one could advise him," continued Ma Ferris. "He could have stepped into the practice across the street if he had finished the medicine. But no! Galway destroyed him. And now he's out there in the wilds of Mullet. Fishing! My good God! But what's the use?"

"I saw the salmon in the fridge," said the doctor helpfully.

"Oh, but this is a terrible life, isn't it, daughter?" Ma Ferris pressed the balls of her hands into her flowery thighs and shook her head.

Catherine felt like a big frightened child.

"How is Thady?" asked Doctor Ferris.

"He's fine."

"Another lost cause," said Mrs Ferris. "My brother had everything."

"Back in the old days we had it terrible," announced Doc Ferris. "Now there's a question that never can be answered – why did the people near the coast die of starvation during the Famine and they a stone's throw from the sea?"

"I hadn't thought of that."

"It's simple. You can't fish in winter, and that's six months of the year gone. And you can fish buck-all if you have no boats. And they had no boats. That's the way it was."

"You were not half-fed," agreed Jack. "And that's why you are like you are today. The balance was upset."

"Too much white bread," said Ma Ferris, "that's what's wrong with Ireland."

"Too much white bread," agreed Jack, "and the dog will have fits."

"We are all touched," declared the doctor. "Do you know who the insurance companies in England consider the highest risk in life insurance?" he asked Catherine.

She answered immediately. "RUC men."

"No," he said, "dentists. And why? Because they are always doing away with themselves. For you see looking into someone else's mouth day-after-day drives you demented."

"Then there's laughing gas," said his wife.

"There is. Now a doctor is not under such pressure."

"Can't the bully boy deprecate himself when he wants to," Ma Ferris murmured low.

"Is plenty of money good? I often ask myself," the doctor said, and he moved and sat down beside Catherine. "Is plenty of money good, daughter?" he asked her.

"Why don't you quit driving the poor girl wild with your questions," said Ma Ferris, "and go down to the piano."

The four of them went down the stairs followed by the dog. The doctor put on a wild green jacket with the Comhaltas crest on the top pocket and sat down with his back to them at the piano. He assumed a new personality and struck a chord. The dog fled under the settee. The doctor struck another chord, looked round once and nodded. Watched by the two women, Jack, with his arms perfectly straight down by his side, stood in the centre of the small room. His father found the tune. Jack went up onto his toes.

She hung her clothes in what used to be his room as a child. It was just off the dining room. He stayed outside talking to his mother after the father had returned across the street to his surgery. She looked at the photographs on the wall of him at his first Communion, at his Confirmation, in the arms of some young woman. She looked at photos of him bare-legged as he danced in a kilt and check waistcoat. Late that night he came into the room.

"Come in here beside me," she said fondly. He sat on the edge of the bed. She stroked his shoulder, "I have been warned about men like you." She turned his head in her hands. "And I thought my family were odd."

268

He laughed.

"Did you like them?"

"I do, and I'm afraid of them. This is all new to me, you must understand." She hesitated. "And your mother can be very severe."

"She's disappointed in me."

"And so she should be."

"Will you come for a walk down the village?"

"Wait a minute till I hold you." She reached out to him. "I have a desperate longing for a kiss." She kissed him gently. She kissed him softly. "Will you come to live with me?"

"In Belfast?"

"Yes."

"Why not," he said.

"I like your room. I suppose you had much vigorous exercise here in your day."

"If you start talking like that," laughed Jack, "you'll only disturb yourself."

"I used to fantasize about Engelbert Humperdinck when I was a young girl."

"I don't believe you."

"Yes, and male wrestlers. The bigger the better."

"That's disgraceful."

"I always liked stout people." She blew softly into his ear. "It gives me anxious moments thinking of you as a boy sleeping here."

"Careful," said Jack.

She kissed his ear. "So you were a dancer." She grew playful. "And you have lovely legs. Will you do a little dance in the nude for me?"

"Whisht, Catherine."

"Go on. You're great on your feet."

"She'll hear you. She'll hear you laughing."

"Go on Jack! Just for me. Off with the trousers and dance!"

"Sh!"

"I want to see it swinging round."

"Ca-th-er-ine!"

*   *   *

The earth was steaming. She went out to take her clothes in from the line. A flat expanse of fog was rushing in from the sea across Corrloch. As she took her clothes down she handed them on to him. He saw that nearly all her garments were black. Black tights, black knickers, black skirts. Black blouses, black shawls, black T-shirts. Black.

"And I had a black heart," she said, "till I met you."

Then through the fog a group of hares came bounding down the garden.

"Jack," she whispered.

"I see them," he said softly.

The hares stopped for a long uncertain moment to look at the couple. They were leathery and brown and honey-eyed. With slow thrusts of their hips they moved off, then sat and listened. Then ran away a little, then stooped and squatted again. Their eyes were skilful and wild. Their coats weathered and grim. They loped off.

22

Through the Downhill Tunnel

I've found a red-brick two-storey house with a small garden. It's in the east suburbs, off the Hollywood road. There are two bedrooms with fireplaces, and a sitting room with a huge blue-tiled fireplace and mantelpiece. The walls are a terrible pink, but we could get rid of that. There are beautiful leaded lights to the front of the house.

You can see Belfast Lough from where your study will be. Will I rent it?

I think I should. I know you'll come. I can't wait to see you. The only thing that frightens me is that this is strictly a Protestant area. But no one will know you are there – you'll be safe. I'll hide you away from everyone. Is it possible that we will be happy?

I'm opening in a show at the Guild Hall in Derry in a couple of weeks. It's a big break for me. Get the Derry Express. Come to the show on the last night. We can travel back to Belfast together. I'll have everything ready. A place for your books, a desk. You'll be happy to know that I spied a well-stocked off-licence down the road.

I wake sometimes at night with an awful longing for you. And full of sordid imaginings that you might be with someone else. My carnal desires are dreadful and ludicrous.

I loved last summer. I can't believe that soon we'll be living together. And then we will be faithful to each other, for that's the most important thing of all.

All my love,
Catherine

"Are you waiting on the bus?" an auld fellow asked as he plucked his hat.

"I am," said Jack.

"I came across the eyes bitten out of a sheep," he explained, "just this very morning."

"Could be the golden eagle," another suggested.

"The golden eagle?" the old man gasped, "Oh sacred! Do they get down this far?"

"Or it could be the mink," the second speculated.

To their left Christian Brothers were belting golf balls along the sand dunes. From above came the high, unending call of a lark. Out of a bed-and-breakfast a group of mental patients streamed onto the street chaperoned by two female nurses who the night before had led them in song in a lounge bar. Now everyone was looking sheepishly at the ground. They climbed into a minibus and were spirited away. On the other side of the street the pensioners and Jack stepped on board the Ballina bus. One behind the other, the two buses travelled across West Mayo till they went their separate ways at the crossroads by the power station.

They bounced into Derry station late in the evening to the area marked out for the Lough Swilly buses, and while the driver sat separating sterling from punts, the few passengers alighted. Jack rang the Guild Hall to hear that the play Catherine had been appearing in had in fact finished the night before. By some freak of fate he had missed her. No message had been left. He sat in the station wondering what to do.

He moved to the nearest pub, and rang Catherine's number in Belfast.

"Where are you?" she asked in an excited voice.

"I'm in Derry."

"What happened?"

"I don't know. I must have got the dates mixed up."

"Well look – book yourself in somewhere – then come up on the first train, and I'll meet you. And Jack?"

"Yes."

"Watch yourself."

"I will."

"I don't want to lose you just yet."

He returned to his drink.

"Is there a hotel round here?"

"Not here, fellow," said the barman.

"Could you give me the name of any place I could book into?"

"There's boarding houses. And there's the Blue Tit."

"You see I have a gig in town tonight," Jack explained unnecessarily.

"What are you – some class of a chanter?"

"That's right. A classical musician."

"Classical." He spun a glass in his hand. "Do you play cricket?"

"No."

"I never met a classical musician who didn't play cricket. Cricket is big in Derry."

"Oh."

"We get all kinds of serious clients in here."

"Well look, I'll be seeing you."

"Look after yourself."

By the time he was happily drunk, Jack had risen in rank to be a researcher with the BBC. As a musician again, he lay down to sleep in a lodging house, not far from the station, where all night he heard voices from downstairs that he imagined were discussing him.

I wish, Jack Ferris thought, I was with someone. He moved towards the railway station. Everybody around him looked bitterly sane. The hangover had left a dark gap in his mind. The human spirit was flush against its walls. A distant cramp attacked the calf of his right leg. I could take a drink, he thought. He hurried across a bridge over the Foyle. Rats scurried through the mud below. A shaven-headed chap approached from Waterside like an old man. A policeman looking down at the River Foyle below, dabbed his forehead and sighed. An over-sized gull landed on a rail and turned one bad eye to look at Jack.

Cold sweat dribbled down his forearms.

I feel awful, he said to himself.

He descended the steps. A cold wind blew along his knees. There was a man hauling a case ahead. After him, a raspberry-haired woman, her shoulders sleek as a starling's, flitted forward in short bursts. He saw the train draw up at the makeshift depot. The original cut-stone station, which had been bombed, lay empty. Within a wire mesh on the roadway a JCB was screaming as it tore at stone. Chippings flew like hail. Jesus! A stake was being driven home. Under his feet the station vibrated.

He bought his ticket.

"One way?" asked the booking clerk.

"I suppose so," said Jack.

"Well now, lad, it's you that's travelling." He looked closer at Jack. "Are you the boy I met last night that's on the radio?"

"That's me," said Jack thankfully.

"You were fairly high, son," the clerk laughed, and he peeled off a ticket.

The train pulled away round the swerve of the river. Jack saw smoke rising from the mountains to his left. They were burning something up there. Herons stalked the river, wild duck scouted the edge of the low marshes. A glider came alongside them and then soundlessly pulled away.

Jack was dreaming ahead. When the half-dream stopped, the occupants of the train, the sea, himself, again fell back into place, each thrown together unwittingly and housed in a multi-layered consciousness. He became aware of a man in a grey suit who was watching his every move with a sour look. He was one of those white-haired, rosy-cheeked men with steel-blue eyes that he had seen everywhere throughout the North. Jack looked away, only to find the man's eyes still on him when he returned his gaze seconds later. The stare was making him nervous.

He lit a cigarette. Immediately, his neighbour pounced.

"This carriage is for non-smokers."

"Jesus!" said Jack.

He doused the cigarette, then got up and humped his bags along two carriages till he thought he had put a safe distance between himself and the ominous man in the grey suit. He was sweating profusely. In the final carriage he found a single seat that faced back the way he had come.

*   *   *

On a trolley beside Jack sat tinkling miniatures of whiskey, brandy and gin. Biscuits in cellophane. A coffee urn piped quietly. Plastic cups were piled high. Sitting around him were people drinking. He ordered a coffee, and talked to the woman opposite him. Then he ordered a whiskey to put in the coffee. He praised whiskey in coffee. He praised whiskey. And although the answers he got were without warmth, he persisted. He took off his jacket, and with the driver belling ahead they burst into the tunnel at Downhill, rocked through the darkness, emerged into a brief flash of daylight and the swerving sea, then they were underground again.

As they emerged at Castlerock, he ordered another whiskey.

"He cleans up awful well," the woman said to her friend.

"I was talking tay Alice yesterday."

"I wouldn't be capable of taking on wha' she did."

"He took a fair knock."

The whole carriage shook.

"Whold awne."

"That's nice."

"It's lovely, lovely. It's lovely out be Portstewart."

"Now that he's through he'll blow it all in Israel."

Away from the track the sea spun like a flat disc. There was a sheep down on one knee eating. At Coleraine a crowd of football fans and university professors got on. Beyond Coleraine cattle were searching among the dark-grassed dunes. The train turned away from the coast and headed inland.

"Now that he's through," the woman said with a touch of pride, "at the end of the day, he'll blow it all in Israel."

The floor under Jack shook. "That's nice," he said, imitating her voice. His bladder suddenly eased, and he sought the chain that was not there. He found the foot pedal. The water gushed down the toilet bowl. He felt his way back to his seat and sat down. He looked up and found the same steel-blue eyes fixed upon him. He shifted uncomfortably and smiled.

But the smile was not returned. He suddenly realized that he was looking into the same bad unrelenting eye. He had returned to the seat he had occupied earlier, opposite the man in the carriage for non-smokers.

The man's lower lip curved upward with the disdain of the abstemious.

Jack stood.

"God help us," he said. Deeply embarrassed he returned along the carriages, but now he could not find where he had been. He tried remembering who had been sitting across from him, but his mind was blank. He saw empty seats and any one of them could have been his. He walked along the two carriages searching, but the faces had changed. He could not recognize anybody. Then he saw his bag, and he sat down again opposite the two women. Outside, large fields of potatoes had now appeared. He grew mesmerized by the flowering potato fields. The white flowers, the mounds of earth where the round roots nestled. Soon to be picked, laid in furrows and moved in bags to a market somewhere. In Mullet they'd winter under turf and mould. In Inisheer they'd lie uncovered in a shed. In Cleggan they'd be under sand. After boiling they'd be drained, teemed, and bursting floury out of their steaming skins, they'd be served.

As he watched, the electric wires dipped and rose, then were suddenly halted by a pole. Then they started again, swooping down and off. They'd fling themselves high onto the grips of the trapeze. Take off and, at the next juncture, just as Jack was becoming hypnotized, the wires swung away out of sight from the rails.

He was way ahead of himself. He saw himself alighting from the train. He saw himself searching for his ticket. It'd be in his little pocket. On the crowded ascent to Botanic Avenue he looks around for Catherine. She is standing at the back of the crowd watching his face for his reaction. She is tremendously happy.

I'll arrive, thought Jack, I will.

The train shuttled forward linking his various lives, each in its separate compartment, each swaying gently on. Sometimes he'd find himself in one compartment, sometimes in another. It was painful looking back. Occasionally uproariously funny. A brief patch of Northern light caught his eye as the train hooted. The carriages pulled against one another as if they might sever the chains that linked them. They entered the next tunnel.

"Where's Mammy?" asked a father across the aisle.

"She's a wreck," the child answered, and everyone laughed.

Jack feared that he would carry the present despair of his mind into whatever proceedings lay ahead. His mind, alienated by the journey, was trying to undermine any happiness that was to come when the journey was over. He tried to correct this tendency by dreaming ahead. But his mind continually trapped him in the present. There was nothing after. He tried to think of the carriages ahead. Then he recalled the eye of the man in the grey suit.

I'm exaggerating everything, he thought. Jesus! I'm frightening myself.

He ordered a fourth miniature and gulped half of it down. He might regret this some day, he thought. He did not feel drunk, but empty. What am I worried about? he asked himself. But he could not reason beyond the fact that this was Northern Ireland, people die here. Yet it wasn't that. What was it that was worrying him? And he knew such worry would make him blind to another's feelings.

Then he cheered himself by thinking, Well, on arrival I'll see all my fears were unfounded. So his happiness would be all the greater. But the further now that the train plunged into the late morning the more alien he felt. The veins on the back of his hands began to pulsate.

In the seat behind him there was a sudden outburst of ribald laughter. Only then did his consciousness take in the voice that was speaking. Someone fell against his seat.

"Sorry," said the youth.

"It's all right," said Jack.

"Taig cunt," said the youth.

Immediately, the woman in the seat to his left leaned over and said to Jack that she was on her way for a check-up at the hospital. The ticket collector was flirting with her in the window seat. He winked at Jack. He had a round whiskey face and small eyes. His tie was undone and his mouth was set in a tight bow of short temper. The ticket collector did not want his conversation with the woman interrupted. But as the woman talked away to Jack, the ticket collector became a ticket collector again. He dropped his drunken leer. Jack ordered more drink from the trolley boy.

"Whoopah!" cheered the woman, "you started it, you might as well finish it."

And she ordered a drink for herself.

"The cure is wonderful," Jack said.

Jack moved over and the trolley boy sat down. They began talking of rabbits.

"It's rare that I meet someone employed by the railroad," said Jack, thinking to himself, this lad must be a Taig like me. The conductor is not. The woman may be.

"Don't mind that fucker," said the trolley boy, "that just went through the door." He spoke with a mild trace of self-consciousness, dropping to a whisper because of what they were speaking of.

"Don't say anything," he whispered.

"I better push on," he said loudly and stood. He put a free bottle on the table in front of Jack. A girl student, with blond cropped hair, dropped into the seat beside him. He wondered could she smell the stale sweat from him. She took out a notebook, then a calculator. It struck Jack that there were three or four voices working away in his head simultaneously, though he had no wish to talk to anybody at all. Nor to listen. Stations sped by, Lough Neagh passed like another sea to the right. Time wound down the distance.

The ticket collector appeared again.

"Tickets!" he called. "Tickets! Tickets!"

He disappeared from view.

"I think," said the woman to Jack, "that I know him to see."

"I think he's from Fitzroy," another woman answered. "What's wrong with you anyway?"

"It's my ticker," she explained.

The girl looked up from her book, then down again. Tiredness fell on him. His head bumped against the window. The white plastic cups rocked on the table. He heard the miniatures striking against each other on the returning trolley. The plates linking the carriage buckled. To people on trains this happens, he said to himself.

He wiped away the mist from the window that he might see the city. Plumes of wind-driven black smoke from some house being demolished went by. Then came a graveyard with its back to the road. Each headstone appeared like someone kneeling, head bowed. These were vexed images. He put them out of his mind. Automatically he grabbed his bag by the strap, yet he was determined not to move till the carriage emptied. He held his bag tight against his stomach, then put it down again, for he realized there was a little way to go yet and he did not want to be among those who were already on their feet, hauling bags from overhead, queueing up, as if this furtive preparation might somehow save them a few minutes later on.

He saw the lad who had called him a Taig alight. Then a group of schoolboys harassing each other climbed off. Jack stepped onto the platform, but could see no sign of Catherine. Then she appeared waving at the top of the crowded stairs that led to Botanic Avenue. It was as he had foreseen. She was perplexed and expectant and giddy. He felt immense relief seeing her there.

"Waunker," shouted a schoolboy to another.

The other lad slung his bag onto his shoulder. "Your teacher," he roared back, then seconds passed as he sought the most profane insult he could, "sucks cocks," he turned to go, "in Hell!" The echo of the curse rang through the Belfast station.

23

The Irishman

"This is a nice place," she'd say tenderly. He felt her touch the bottom of his hip. A hollow place in his chest. Places she touched were strange to him. Then his hands wandered over her, marvelling at her soft butt and stiff crotch hair. Her calves. Her breasts.

Then a strange thing would happen. Often Catherine felt him stop breathing. She'd know the tension was leaving him by the way he would grow her full length. Then his breathing would stop. Now she would become frightened. She was being left behind because she was too far outside, just looking in. She'd hold him tightly.

She'd grow inescapably tender towards him.

What he feared most was that everything might become sadly familiar. That his arms would inflate, a fever seek him out, that he'd hear someone say how such-and-such had lost its charm. That Catherine might be the sort of person who would cling steadfastly to her place of residence, wherever it be, and not let go. As her breasts brushed against him, Jack thought of home as a place frozen in the wastes. He was being lifted and transported. He believed in miracles and hated those who did not. He hated those people for whom change was not only unthinkable, but unlucky. He had seen this.

He never really knew whether it was him she was with when he entered her. At first it would appear the perfect lost path to take. Her satisfaction would turn to lust. And then from lust to fantasy. A few seconds later she would open her eyes and look at him. Then he knew that, on that night, he was only one of many.

That he could see so quickly into her intimate deception made him part ways with Catherine. Selfishly he would seek his own pleasure. For now she was not the woman he had gone to bed with some time before. Two other people, strangers, made love in their place, while they themselves voyeuristically looked on, vaguely urging them to passion.

Her affection afterwards would return with a hazy apprehension of defeat. He knew he had adopted a role. It was not the only role he was playing at the time. There was the public persona he adopted when he took to the streets. For the first few weeks he had barely ventured outside the house, and Catherine would bring home what food they needed. Mostly they phoned for Chinese takeaways or pizzas to be delivered. It was her that always answered the door. This life began to make him feel worthless. Mood swings took him from despair to an evangelical wish to be a friend of the unknown people he saw walking the streets below the windows. He soon tired of sitting alone in the house looking for repeats of TV programmes, or sauntering through the small garden where the rhubarb grew. It was not enough to be cooped up watching the strange streets.

The first day he went shopping he was aware of how blatant his Southern accent was. So he portrayed a nonchalant familiar personality, as if to say: I was the man who was here yesterday, and the day before. Surely you can't have forgotten me? But, bleary-eyed and extremely polite, the shopkeepers scrutinized him, or else barely registered his presence. Yet he noted their surprise and their embarrassment when he spoke.

To offset this he became a creature of habit.

At ten-thirty he bought a pack of ten Embassy cigarettes in Seymore's, then wandered into the Pakistani supermarket where he'd stock up with fruit and peas and frozen fish; next he bought lager from the off-licence, then maybe he'd wander through the nicnac shop, and lastly he'd buy a copy of the *Belfast Newsletter* – the proper Unionist paper – at George's newsagents. Only one copy of the Catholic newspaper was ever on sale there. And it sat untouched on the counter throughout the day. It was still there in the afternoon when he came to collect the *Evening News*, which was bought by both religions.

281

"Don't be tempted by it," advised Catherine. "There's not a soul in this area would be seen dead buying the *Irish News*."

"I won't, don't worry."

"It's left there deliberately to trap a body. That's how they'd know who you are. You've got to take care," she said adamantly. "I feel responsible for bringing you here."

"I want to get to know these people," replied Jack. "I'm sharing this island with them."

"But they are not inclined to share it with you," she said coldly. "Remember that."

On her days off she would accompany him on his rounds.

"What are we going in here for?" she asked, as they entered a small hardware shop.

"Nails," he said.

"And what do we want with nails?"

"We want them for normality."

Then he brought her across to the newsagent's. The old lady there and himself had by now, much to Catherine's amazement, grown familiar. She gave him a warm welcome. "Your paper, love," she said and handed him the *Belfast Newsletter*. She picked it out from a bundle of others with the names of those that had ordered them written in pen across the top. On his was written *the Irishman*.

"The Irishman?" said Jack astounded, and he laughed.

"Well, we didn't know your name," she replied, embarrassed at her *faux pas*.

"It's Jack," said Jack.

"Jack," she said. "I'll remember that for again."

His accent had marked him out as *the Irishman*.

"Where are you bringing me now?" asked Catherine. He took her across to a café. Catherine was shocked to find a group of RUC men seated on tall stools at the counter eating sandwiches and sweet cakes. The policemen's rifles were laid across the counter in front of them. They called a greeting to Jack. He tipped his forehead in reply.

"Soon I suppose you'll be on first name terms with them as well," whispered Catherine.

"Give us two Queen cakes and two cups of coffee," said

Jack. They sat down among the building labourers, who sucked homemade soup out of plastic cartons, and local ladies eating homemade scones.

"I feel at home here," he told Catherine.

"Don't tell me about it," she replied, "it only makes me anxious."

In the early evenings, the kitchen and drawing room would be suffused with blues and reds from the stained-glass upper lights in the front windows. Jack placed his typewriter at a clear window facing the back garden. In the distance he had a view of the sea and beyond that, on good days, Carrickfergus. He could hear the ships hooting as they headed into Belfast Lough from Liverpool and the Isle of Man.

The Union Jack, as he sat at his typewriter, fluttered over the roofs of houses each side of him. He began putting words into the mouths of the women he saw, with their breasts muffled in bathrobes, as they stood outside hanging the washing on the lines. Their hoarse voices, as they harangued their children, seemed to emerge from the middle of the head at the point where the inner nostrils entered the skull. The sound was male and phlegmatic. The women were gruff and scolding and full of cheerful morbidity. The men, some thin-faced, others small and stout, sat on deck chairs reading the *Sporting Chronicle* and the *Sun*. They grew vegetables in every available plot and drank tins of Tennants lager. Poorly clad, they shuffled to and fro on the edge of the Empire, waiting to be summoned.

On Sunday mornings, sporting the particular mien of Protestant, Methodist or Presbyterian, the women donned their false mink and fur, and arranged fruit and feathers on their heads; the men wore quiet suits, Russian hats and loud ties; then speaking a broad aristocratic patois they came down the side streets to church. Often from his desk by the open window, Jack would hear their voices raised in song that swelled like a powerful demonstration of defiance against despair, that then became ordinary, and finally sweet.

Their songs had the same exultation he'd heard from churches in the back streets of Brixton, and like the West Indians, the

Belfast church-goers would emerge, gossipy and bantering, and walk the footpaths that ran through the grounds with a busy nonchalance. The children in bright suits and sombre dresses went by in straw hats. A few white-faced males would stand within the gates of the church, whispering to each other like men, who, wary of bankruptcy, had once again survived the uncertain fate of being human.

On weekdays huge trucks drove past, which made the small houses shake.

Then at night would come, in the middle of a dream always, the sound of a single speeding car.

He'd take a bus into town and go shopping at the Chinese supermarkets. Every time he visited the city centre he'd find that a new French or Italian café had sprung up. In them hordes of women in groups ate pasta with their own cheap Italian or Spanish wine which could be brought in at no extra charge. The men filled the bars drinking lager and gin. The light on the streets was the same as that found in north of England cities – cold, industrial, grey. On Sundays, everywhere was closed. The shutters came down over the pubs. Winds charged up side streets. Rain fell, breaking and reassembling the light above the blue roofs. At the end of some streets sat distant mountains. At the end of others were the peace lines – paint-splashed walls constructed from bare concrete blocks.

Sometimes he would meet Catherine after rehearsal in one of these cafés, or in Lavery's or in the Crown. Or sometimes in the Lincoln Inn bar across from the BBC where lawyers and journalists mixed.

If other members of the cast came with her, then he would have to endure long periods of silence as the rest talked with feminist bravado and cynically told each other the real version of what was happening – in politics and in theatre. As he listened to them talking, the distinction between both forms of human activity were constantly blurred. Everything could be told in terms of performance.

Always they referred to the "Hidden Agenda". There was "A Hidden Agenda" in the politics of the theatre, in the politics

284

of the BBC, in the politics of Northern Ireland. It was the secret stimulus that kept the conspirators busy. The "Hidden Agenda" was base camp.

One of the women said she'd seen one of his plays in London. "It didn't seem funny to me," she said.

"Jack is a realist," interrupted Catherine.

"I thought the characters were playing at being peasants."

"They were," agreed Jack.

She hiccupped. "It was way too romantic, and intellectual." She hiccupped again. "All those primates talking philosophy. I didn't understand it."

"Don't worry," said Jack, "the children's version will be out next year."

"How would you know –" and she waited for the hiccup that did not come "– what happens here?"

"Would you like me to slap your back?" asked Jack.

"I asked you how would you know what happens here?" With a particularly gracious yet hostile look she lifted her glass of lager and considered him.

"Who do you work for?" he asked.

"RTE," she snapped. "I've told you that before."

"Oh yes, that's right," he said.

"In fact," she continued, "what are *you* doing here?" She gave a polite yawn. "Don't tell me you're here because of your *art*."

"I came to study you," said Jack, "as you have studied those out there, after your fashion."

"He's with me," said Catherine.

"Oh, I forgot," the woman answered and she smiled triumphantly.

"I think it's time," said Catherine, "we went."

They'd taxi home and light a fire. As she changed her clothes she'd have stories to tell of directors and fellow actors and scripts that went awry. He would recount some of his day, leaving out any stupid things he might have done. Their sense of privacy would return. Since the moment they had decided to live together they had to lean heavily on imagination to see them through. The deliciousness would turn to obsession. Each looked forward with increasing anxiety to these few short hours together, and then, when they would meet, demons would take their place. The hours together seemed too short for them to establish each other's identity again.

She lived in fear that something would happen to him. In total silence they would watch the evening news. At certain items she would snort in derision. Then, having established her fear, and his vulnerability, they went down to the off-licence, skirting the lads who always stood in the doorway drinking cider. They bought gin and wine.

"What do you see out there?" she asked him.

"People stare straight into your eyes here," he said. "Women especially. As if to see which side you're on."

"I do it myself."

"And so do the soldiers. A soldier winked at me the other day. On the Lower Falls."

"And what were you doing up there?"

"Walking about."

"Yes, indiscriminately."

"And then I always go through the barriers a few times."

"Why?"

"I love being searched."

"So that's how you get your thrills." She tapped her cigarette onto the windowsill. "I'm sure your Sinn Fein friends would not be enamoured to hear about your perverse nature. All you Civil Rights marchers are just old hippies, aren't you?"

"That's right," said Jack.

"Did you ever take LSD?" she asked him.

"Oh, once upon a time, for breakfast."

"I thought so," she said, "I couldn't. I don't want to know what is going on inside me," and she shivered and bit her tongue.

Sometimes at work she'd imagine herself arriving back at the house unannounced. She'd come in through the bedroom door and find him in bed with some woman who would be sitting astride him, riding him with passion. She'd grow weak at the thought. She'd ring. "Jack," she'd say, "is that you?"

"I just rang to see if you were OK," she'd bluster.

"I'm fine. How are you?"

"What are you doing right now?" she'd ask.

"Oh, wait till I see . . . What would you like me to be doing?"

"I'd rather not say."

Jealousy was driving her astray.

One evening she came home with a set of new locks. Into the front door they screwed three extra bolts. "I'm afraid for you," she said. "I think you're trying to keep me in," he said. But Jack knew that that was not the way they would come. The kitchen door which led into the yard was made of glass. Steps led up to it from the garden. The garden itself was entered from a lane via a rotten door. That, he thought to himself, is the way they'd come if they ever wanted to.

One morning after she was gone he woke to find himself on the floor. It seemed the wrench of a dream had thrown him out of bed. He climbed back in. And slept till the phone rang.

"Are you all right?" asked Catherine.

"I'm fine," he said.

"Is the house all right?"

"Yes, the house is fine, too."

"Well, you seem to be taking it quite calmly."

"Why wouldn't I?"

"Don't you know?"

"Know what?"

"A car bomb's gone off just down the road from you."

He replaced the phone and looked out the window. The street was cordoned off and policemen and soldiers were strolling to and fro. A UDR man looked up and caught his eye. For what seemed like an eternity they looked at each other.

That night he opened the window in the bathroom and it slammed down on his index finger. Simultaneously he bit his tongue. She held his fingers in her mouth while he spat out blood. He had broken a tooth. The jagged edge continued to open the cut in his tongue. He got a nailfile and began to file the tooth.

"What next?" he asked Catherine.

Jack flaunted himself for her amusement. Wearing his fishing boots he danced a jig in the nude. Catherine could not have

287

enough of his play-acting. Then she touched his maleness. How it mutated. Grew a head all of its own, then drooped, hanging. The flower that hangs its head. *The phalarope*, she called it. Then starting up into that ambiguous hardening in her hand. She studied him, a man laid out in a vest, smoking. Her mouth was ajar like a child's. She held his penis against her cheek. There was white under her eyes from want of sleep. Because of the cold she was wearing long black socks that came over her knees. She watched him. I have not slept since I met this man, she thought. Her knees were spread unceremoniously beneath her father's dressing gown.

She drew his hand to her.

"Feel," she said happily, "how wet I am."

"In time," she said, "I will be as much a part of this as you."

He regretted she had said that.

"And you tell me," she said, as she fondled his head, "that you were never with Sara."

"No."

"I wish I had met you at the very beginning."

"And I wish I had met you then, too."

"The things I used to imagine about you," she said.

"I had a few of my own," answered Jack, "going as well."

"Tell me."

"Now let me see."

It seemed hard to credit that she would ever return from the world of the senses. She held him in a furrow made in her hand. He breathed into her armpit. In the furthest mirror two people were lying wrapped round each other. The sign his penis made. The fozy nest between her thighs. He stopled her. Her hair bedewed. After imagining themselves with all those other selves, they were with each other again. She opened herself to him. It passed all understanding. They slept. And woke to find each other in the cold room. Outside, the silent clock of another Belfast snowstorm.

Jack on one of his solitary walks discovered an old record shop in a side street near where they lived. Here he bought a fairly good 45 of Roy Orbison singing "Pretty Woman". The next time he went he bought an old LP of Cat Stevens.

Each day he walked over there and searched through the cardboard boxes of records.

The man who owned the shop sat in a straw chair in a back room in front of a gas Superser. Through a curtain of lace beads he watched his display of paperback books and records and old Northern lace with the watchful eye of a man minding a pornography kiosk. On the gas fire he always had a can of Fosters lager standing. In his mouth a hand-rolled cigarette. He accepted money for items without a word, so on the day that he first spoke to Jack neither of the two had heard the other's voice before.

"Do you remember Del Shannon?" he asked, without moving.

"Sure," said Jack.

"I have his collected works at home."

"I remember 'Kelly'."

"I got 'Kelly', too."

"Tell us this," said Jack, "do you ever come across an old copy of Graham Greene."

"You won't come across a second-hand Graham Greene in this town," said the man. "The Catholics have him read from cover to cover."

"Are you cockney?"

"Yeah. And you're from Éire."

"That's right."

"Yeah." He ambled over to the light switch. "Do you fancy a pint?"

They walked together across the road to the pub. The shop-owner moved with a slow Londoner's gait, as if he were crossing a desert that might possibly be mined. The interior of the bar was low and dark. Pool balls clashed. Soccer stars were pinned next to the ceiling. A huge Orange flag was tacked to the wall. "How's about you, Chris?" said the barman. Christopher Nolan took on a custodial air. They bought a dozen cans of Fosters, then retired to Nolan's room which was lined with volumes of history on the First and Second World Wars. He had books on the Conquistadors and on the Mexican Revolution. The single room was impeccably tidy. The bed was made like a seaman's. They settled down in the small library of war to listen to Gene Pitney, early Elvis, Buddy Holly, Little Richard and the Crystals, and they drank Australian lager and smoked Golden Virginia.

Finally, Christopher Nolan played Del Shannon as loud as the speakers would take.

He fell asleep, suddenly woke up and saw Jack, and said: "The IRA it was started shooting first in Londonderry."

"Did they?" asked Jack.

"I was there on Bloody Sunday," said Christopher Nolan. "I heard those shots."

He stared at Jack a moment as if trying to remember who he was, then fell off to sleep again. Jack listened to the needle spin. Then he put on Crosby, Stills and Nash. "The Marrakesh Express" played as he leafed through a volume on Ivan the Terrible. He finished his beer and slipped out quietly and made it back through the dusky streets to the house before Catherine came home. "What did you do today?" she asked. "Not much," he said.

The next day he bought an old, withered copy of Somerset Maugham's stories from the shop. A few days later, a book of birds. Each afternoon, he went over to Christopher's shop. When he closed, they'd amble to the pub and then back to the flat. They spoke little, and when Christopher did, the words came out in a disjointed, clipped rush.

"I'm glad you're living here, Jackie," he said. "What are we but a couple of strangers in this town?"

"Either way."

"Yeah." He shuffled to the stereo to change the record. "Were you ever married?" Jack shook his head. "I was," said Chris, "but she took off with some other geezer." His belly swung to and fro. He picked a ball of dust off the needle. Then he filled up two small glasses with the Russian vodka that Jack had brought. "Yeah," he said. "Fuck it," said Jack. "Yeah," Christopher Nolan said and palmed the large stomach under his T-shirt.

*　　*　　*

Catherine was opening in a play downtown at eight and Jack left to get there at three. He started walking, then he jumped on a bus and got off at some place that attracted him. Then he recognized the name of a pub in an area that Catherine had warned him about. He studied the pub's wooden façade, the old plate glass and its silver designs, and the gas lamps that hung outside. A man in electric-blue carpet slippers and a ravaged face crossed the street and opened the door. On a blind impulse Jack followed him into the forbidden bar.

He ordered a double gin and looked preoccupied.

Beside him the man ordered a Carlsberg Special and a Black Bush.

He looked at Jack. "How would you like a thirteen-year-old?"

"I'm all right," said Jack.

"She has a beautiful arse," said the man. "I can get you any wee young thing you want now. Just give me the nod."

"Sure."

"Take a look at these here now," the man said, and he handed Jack a pile of photos in an envelope.

Each was of a young nude girl aged about thirteen or fourteen.

"See the pussies on them?" he said. "They're yours now, boy, whenever you want them."

"Here," said the barman, "put those away."

"It's all right," explained the man with a wink. "I know this lad."

The barman looked Jack in the eye.

"Well that's all right, then," he said, but was not convinced.

"Where are you from?" asked the man when Jack returned the photos.

"I'm from Leitrim."

"Leitrim – it's only natural," he replied. "My mother came up here from the town of Arva in the Free State, if you ever heard of it."

"I know the place," said Jack, and on an impulse he added, "it means 'the place of slaughter'."

"There you are now." He tossed back the Bush. "I would have thought Arva a quiet place, compared to here." He laughed ironically. "My ma was a nurse." Then he brought his face close to Jack's. "You'll be safe coming in here," he whispered. "This place is safe enough, you understand."

"I understand," said Jack.

"Arva – I remember to go down there when I was only a bairn." His voice returned to normal. "I didn't even know it was still standing."

"Oh, it's there," replied Jack.

The man drew close to him. "If you have any trouble here, just give me the nod. My name is Henry Fair." He drew back. "I'll look after you."

"Thanks," said Jack.

"Just ask for me, OK, fellow?" He paddled off in his blue slippers across the tiled floor before Jack had a chance to follow him.

"What time is it?"

"It's six," the barman replied. Then he left down a double gin in front of Jack. "Henry left this for you. All right?"

He had lost his chance to steal away. He was incapable of bringing himself to go – the subterfuge had to continue. He stood alone by the bar drinking very quickly. Someone switched on the TV. A woman in some sunny valley in Antrim was demonstrating the making of wattle baskets. They changed stations. Up came the Conservative Party Conference where Margaret Thatcher was closing her eyes to emphasize the seriousness of her words. They changed again. A black-and-white romantic comedy from the thirties appeared. For a few seconds the barman studied the silent screen so that the figures played across his face.

"Aye," he said as if he were answering some question posed deep within the recesses of his mind.

Jack watched the film. It seemed appropriate that he should be where he was – scared out of his wits and yet turning maudlin and drunk, watching an old melodrama. It seemed somehow appropriate. Words tumbled out of his mouth. He called for a gin.

He wanted to feel the sensation of getting drunk, but somehow he had passed the moment of drunkenness without noticing it. He only knew how bad he was when he realized he was uncertain whether he would be able to lift the glass of gin from the bar.

"What time is it?" he asked loudly.

The barman flicked a button on the cuff of his leather jacket. "Seven-thirty."

Some upright part of his mind carried his body to the door. He hailed a taxi. "It's a bloody great city," he told the driver. "You think so?" answered the driver without conviction. "Well, sometimes," said Jack. "Try living here," the driver replied. Jack entered the small theatre, and ordered a glass of wine. He ordered another because he couldn't taste the first. Suddenly out of the corner of his eye he saw Maisie Adams enter, dolled up in fur. Jesus, he heard himself say. He sat at the back. Later, at a great distance from him, Catherine stepped onto the stage. The lines she'd been practising with him night after night took on a new life of their own.

Onto the record player he put Billie Holiday. Then Van Morrison. He sat on the sofa and looked round, wondering where he had left his cigarettes. Laboriously he searched each room in the house.

At last he found a cigarette. Blatant images and crazy thoughts went through his head. The room was stone cold. When Catherine came home, she found him in the study on the spare bed.

In the typewriter was a sheet of paper filled with gibberish.

She tried waking him.

"You were great, Catherine," he mumbled.

"Why did you not join us?" she asked. "Don't you know my mother was there. We went for a meal. We waited and waited for you."

"I came home."

"Where were you before the show?" she demanded.

At last he answered. "I was drinking in a pub off Our Lady's Road," he said.

"It's not *Our* Lady's Road," she shouted. "It's *My* Lady's Road. It's *My* Lady's Road, Jack. *My* Lady's Road, do you hear?"

"*My* Lady's Road," he repeated.

"What were you doing down there?"

"I went walking," he said. "Walking and walking."

"Oh, Jack," said Catherine.

24

Madame George

"Hey Jack," asked Christopher, "are you a Republican?"

"No."

"It's all right, then."

"I'm just a dancer."

"Yeah, mate. But you have to admit the IRA have got it sussed."

"I wouldn't know."

"They have the hardware. They have the men."

"I don't know anything about those things."

"These UVF blokes here don't have sweet fuck all. They have only the one bleedin' shooter. It's the same bloody gat does all the damage. I don't know. The Provies, they're something else, aren't they, Jackie?"

"Look, Chris, I don't know, right."

"Well, you know I was in the British army."

"It makes no difference to me."

"I did my term, Jackie. And you learn things. You get to know that the Provies know more than you do. Fucking hell. They're fucking technicians, right?" He drank a shot of vodka. "An' you know what we discovered at Ballymena?"

"I haven't a clue."

"A fucking witches' coven."

"What?"

"There were these geezers running around in the nude and young boys laid out on a bleedin' altar."

"Once you keep taking the tablets."

"It's true mate. Bloody right it's true."

"And what did you do?"

"We did *fuckin'* nothing! Now, if we had found the president of your Sinn Fein running round in the buff, that'd be another story. But these were fucking businessmen and farmers. That's why this country is like it is. Your priests and your parsons is all witches. Right?"

"Right."

"It's not on, is it? See, your Provos have it sussed."

"Why are you bringing all this up about the Provos?"

"Because I was asked to, Jackie. Because I was asked. Don't get me wrong. But I said you were all right. I was asked – about you – OK? I said 'Old Jackie's all right.' "

"And so I am."

"Yeah. 'Old Jack's all right,' I said." He shifted his immense bulk and ran a finger across his lips. "I was there on Bloody Sunday, did I tell you that?"

"No."

"Well I was there, mate, and they were shooting at us. Did you know that?"

"I heard it said."

They listened to "Nights in White Satin" as they looked out through the dark curtains on folk going uphill.

The woman who lived next door came knocking on Jack's door one morning. He had fallen asleep on the sofa after Catherine had gone to work and he came to the door with a blanket thrown over him. She was a small cheerful woman of about twenty-two with dark wavy hair and a racy laugh.

"Yes," he said.

"You look like you had a rough night."

"Don't mention it."

"Would you have a tin opener?"

"Yes"

The two of them walked into the kitchen. He began searching in a drawer.

"Excuse me," he said.

Jack walked into the bathroom and steadied himself against the sink. "Christ," he said. He went back to the living room.

"Will you have a drink?" he asked.

"I will, aye."

He took down two fresh glasses and placed them on a tray each side of a bottle of Russian vodka and a carton of orange juice. The bottle looked like the old-style bottle of lemonade. He lifted it to his lips and took a snort. Outside two drums suddenly started to beat. In an archway opposite the house two men in their ordinary working clothes were beating up a storm on a pair of Lambeg drums.

"The marching season will soon be starting," the woman said behind him.

He poured her a vodka and a separate glass of orange. Then he filled a glass with orange and another with vodka for himself. He upended the vodka into his mouth, then swallowed the orange.

"So that's how it's done," she said, and did the same. He prepared the two drinks again.

"Are you a Catholic?" she whispered.

"I'm a Mohammedan," he replied.

"It's a pity the boys didn't get Maggie Thatcher," she suddenly said.

"Sh!" said Jack. "I don't want to hear about that." He waved the palms of his hands in front of his face. He sat down. The vodka made a clear path to his brain.

Then she said confidentially: "Isn't it terrible, living here?"

She had Derry eyes and fine white teeth. She was wearing a blue jump-suit with the zip lowered to her breasts. Her thighs were large. She was laughing.

"You're enjoying that," she said.

She poured out two more.

"What's your name?" he asked.

"My name is Jill. We must be the only two Fenians in this neck of the woods. I know the woman you live with to see."

"Catherine."

"Catherine, yes. She's an actress isn't she?"

"She is."

"Does she like you?"

"I think so."

"Well, that's all right then. That's good. It's less dangerous that way, if the two of ye are happy." She poured out more orange. "You're looking better now."

"I feel a lot better."

"You have a very happy countenance."

"Countenance?" he laughed.

"Yes," she said. "Have I used the wrong word?"

"No," he replied, laughing even more. "It was just kind of unexpected."

"Would you rather I said you had a happy *bake*," she sniggered.

She reached up and kissed him. With her fingers she closed his lips and then held them between hers as she kissed him again.

"It's nice, the kiss, isn't it?" Catherine whispered.

"If you are ever disloyal to me, you'll tell me, won't you?" she asked.

"Yes," he said.

When dawn came, the city appeared like a deserted card table. Rain was thrashing down outside. The people who were setting out to work were wearing the wrong hats and the wrong suits. The first cars sounded like the horn section of jazz band warming up before the jam begins. A cat climbed a tree outside and jumped in the window. It was soaking wet. Its fur could not be distinguished from the colour of the carpet. The jacket of a man's evening suit hung on one wall. Flat blue sea stones from Scotchport sat in a pile on the mantel. On the bedside table sat a collection of poems, *Nights in the Bad Place* by Padraic Fiacc.

"Have you ever worn a sari?" Harry Bunting asked Jack.

"No," said Jack.

"You should get yourself one. They're perfect. I wear one I bought in India about the house. They're beautiful and cool next to the skin."

The other two men grinned. Jack had seated himself by three men in light summer suits when he came into the pub. They were watching an indoor tennis match on television. He was attracted into their company because they had mentioned players from the old days. They talked tennis. Rod Laver. Miss Goolagong. Ille Nastase. And somewhere back there, John Newcombe. They talked of Chinese restaurants, which Belfast proportionate to its population had more of than any other city in Europe. They said that below the counters the owners kept machetes. They talked of the long-distance Ethiopian runners. Then saris again.

"I should buy you all one," said Harry Bunting. "They're nice to cook in."

The others smiled at the thought of Harry baking scones in his sari. The pint of lager Jack was drinking soon became a double gin and tonic bought by Harry. They were joined by another older man, George, who was distant to begin with, and tried to withdraw when he heard Jack's accent.

"Jack's all right," Terence Bellue said. "He's a Southerner." Jack told them he wrote plays. They told him that no policeman was safe walking in Protestant areas.

"Are you not afraid of talking of these things in front of me?" asked Jack.

"If you wanted to leave our company you could have gone long ago," Freddie said.

They were young policemen, healthy, intimate, open featured, with a great relish for vodka. They would not allow Jack buy them a drink. Each shared reminiscences with him. Jack said it would not be believed that Protestants were attacking the RUC.

"Why don't you come out with us one night?" said Harry.

"Could I?" asked Jack.

"It's no problem."

"Then you can write it all down," said Terence, "and tell them in the Free State."

"You just give us a ring at that number," said Freddie, and he wrote it down on the top of Jack's evening paper.

"Then you can see for yourself," said Harry.

"You'll be safe with these lads," nodded George.

"Just call and ask for me – Freddie Wilson."

"I will," said Jack.

On the pretext of going to the toilet Jack managed to order

a round of drinks at the bar. By now he had drunk about five double gins, he was hungry and ready to get away. He sat back down, the drinks arrived. Just then Catherine came in. She stopped at their table. He was about to introduce her when she said coldly: "I'll see you in the lounge."

He said goodbye to the men, who were jovial and understanding, and carried his drink on in.

"Who were those sleazy fuckers you were with?" asked Catherine.

"Tennis fans," he said. "Will you have a drink?"

"I'll have what you're having," she said.

He went to the bar, ordered a double gin, then went to the toilet. When he sat down beside her he knew something was wrong.

"Who do you know at Donegal Pass Police Station?" she asked coldly.

"No one," he replied.

"Then what are you doing with their number?" and she pointed to the top of the newspaper where the young policeman had written it down.

"Oh fuck," he said.

"Jack what are you at? Are you trying to get yourself killed?"

He explained. She got up abruptly and he followed her out into the lane.

"Are you a fool?" she snarled. "You'd be found on some waste dump in the morning."

"I don't believe it."

"I know them," she snapped crossly, and she walked on. He followed her. She stopped and faced him.

"But your father was a policeman."

Her face twisted in scorn. "That's why I know."

"I need to do these things, he said."

"How can you be so stupid?" Then her tone changed. "Promise me you won't go."

"I think I should go."

"If you go with them," she said, "then don't return to the house." Estranged, they walked towards the taxi rank.

*   *   *

Each Tuesday he went to the dole and stood silently in the queue. Then he spent all the cash between the Chinese supermarket and the Pakistani grocer who sold spices and spoke with a strong Belfast accent. He never wanted to find himself owing to Catherine. He had accepted advances from two theatres towards scripts that did not exist. Then, in the guilty throes of a hangover, he prepared an outline for a play, and sent it off to Eddie Brady, who had produced two of his plays.

"What's it about?" she asked him.

"I don't know yet."

She saw no finished texts and yet it was always by the typewriter that Catherine would find him when she came home. "Do you write at all?" she asked him. "Sometimes," he said. Each evening a bottle of wine was opened. He'd try to straighten up and talk sense after his afternoon rambles. Her evening's drinking began. So his day was divided into two drinking bouts, his on his own, and then his with her.

When he was out she looked through the notes on his desk which were often filled with nonsense rhymes or Belfast speech patterns he had written down as he heard them. Notes about Mayo. Descriptions of what people wore. A collection of voices and moods that had no relation to each other. Speech overheard in pubs, on the street, in the back gardens, by the docks.

She found umpteen sheets of paper on which he brought the curtain across in some play that never started. *Curtain opens*, he'd written. Or: *Lights up*. No further words. Nothing else. Jack drew back the curtain on a garden seat. On a café table. The interior of an old antique shop. All unoccupied. He drew back the curtain on a bar in the village. Suddenly nothing. Then one day, when he brought the lights up, she found it was a version of herself she saw standing there, midstage.

He jumped to his feet in the Hatfield Bar.

"Name the fucking thirty-two counties."

"You must be joking."

"I'll give any man here a fiver that can name the thirty-two counties of Ireland," Jack called to the drinkers at the bar.

Immediately the old men and the young punters took out their pens, turned over racing slips brought from the betting shop next door and started to go through the four provinces. Jack strolled round the bar looking over their shoulders. People totted up their score to find that they were four, maybe five, counties short.

"Where are you from?" someone shouted.

"Leitrim," said Jack.

"Nice one," the man replied. "I'd missed that wee county completely."

But still everyone was a few counties short. Louth, the Northerners called Dundalk. Offaly gave problems. Everyone got Laois because one of the main Southern prisons was there. Roscommon was difficult. By some grace of luck they all remembered Carlow. Eventually they had between them reached thirty-one counties, but one remained unfound.

"And yous call yourself Republicans," said Jack.

A young fellow, slightly touched, sat down by Jack and said: "You've set them a mystery."

"I have," said Jack.

"Do you know the answer yourself?"

"No. I've forgotten."

"Well then, we'll just have to wait and see."

"Kildare," someone shouted eventually.

"Kildare it is," said Jack.

"You'll feel better now that you know that," said the young fellow. "You're one nice fellow, but I have to go now."

He got up from his chair and slowly looking back at Jack he went through the door onto the Ormeau Road.

Catherine rang. "Look, I'm going to Dublin to see Sara. She's opening in the Abbey tomorrow night. Do you want to come down?"

"No," he said, "I'll work."

"You sound wretched."

"Catherine, I love you."

"And I love you."

"There's something wrong," he said.

"What do you mean?"

"I can feel it. There's something dreadfully wrong."

"Come in and meet me before I go," she said quickly. "We can eat out."

"OK."

"Jack – are you angry over something."

"I'm angry with myself."

"Don't be."

"I'll see you in half-an-hour."

He lifted the bottle and poured two measures of vodka into two glasses. One after another he drank them down to prepare him for the journey into town. He wrote down the name of the play that he had not yet begun, then stepped onto the street.

Catherine returned on the last train on Saturday night and took a taxi out to the house. He had spent the entire day walking round in one of those exhilarating hangovers that teeter on the edge of despair. Everything he looked at – people, leaves, water – he became engrossed in. Now he was sitting by the fire reading.

"Sit down here," he said.

He lay his head on her breasts.

"How did it go?"

"Sara was good, I have to admit. But she surrounds herself with dreadful people."

"Did you enjoy yourself?"

"I suppose I did. But I missed you."

He heard something wrong in her voice.

"Catherine," he said, "you've been with someone."

She looked shocked, and a little scared, and immediately admitted that, yes, she had. "I didn't intend for this to happen. It will never happen again," she said. But he looked at her in such a way that she felt mortified.

"I knew there was something wrong," he said.

She did not answer him.

"Tell me everything, in great detail, that happened," he demanded.

"Down, I suppose, to the size of his penis?" He did not answer. "Do I have to do this?"

"That way I can get over it."

And slowly she told him, as if in a way she was repeating one of her dreams. The only difference being that in this case he knew he would remember every detail. She was shocked, as he was himself, by how easy he was taking her confession once she had begun. He sought out each salacious moment. He interrogated her until her lovemaking was as familiar to him as if he himself had been there.

"There's no more," she said, "unless you want me to start inventing things?"

"I wish you would," he said hopelessly.

Then at last she said: "How did you know? It's like you've been reading my mind."

"I always suspect you."

First she grew arrogant and high-principled. Then mellow and sad. They began undressing each other.

"I promise you," she said, "it's all over now. I want to love every ounce of you. I don't want remotely to be with anyone else. I'm obsessed with you."

"Did you bring some drink home?"

"Is the vodka gone?"

She opened the wine and began to cry.

"I want us to be happy and safe and free," she said. "Free from all this fighting and estrangement. I know I did wrong. I know the damage I've done." But he just sat there drinking and looking at her. "I couldn't fall in love with anyone else. I am in love with you, Jack. Don't go off with anyone else, please. Please."

"What," he said, "if I already have?"

"You wouldn't put me through all that, and then tell me that you've been unfaithful as well?"

"I might."

She sat nude by the window looking out. He sat on the armchair with his trousers round his shins.

"Can we call it even?" she asked him.

She got up and played "Madame George" by Van Morrison.

It was a long triumphant Belfast lament. Jack tried to concentrate his mind on Catherine. Where had she come from? What had she come home to? What was he doing there? He wanted to say: Look, we have both been unfaithful to each other, but didn't. He didn't do anything. Her disloyalty and guilt drove him to unparalleled lust. They made love in a sweltering panic to someone else's passion. He poured her a glass of wine, then himself another glass.

"Have you another bottle?" he asked.

"Yes," she said sadly.

25

What Did Shamey Coyle Do When He Left Prison?

Left alone in their house in working-class Belfast he often found a sound he could not place running through his head. It was like the static across the trawler's radio at sea. To drown it out he tried talking to himself. But this "talking to himself" implied a mild exchange, an off-hand chat. In fact, what he was at amounted to verbal self-abuse.

In the company of others the rant would stop.

Yet as he stood in the urinal of a pub or sat on a seat in Ormeau Park it would begin again. Till eventually he realized one day in the Hatfield Bar that the sound he was hearing was his own crazy thoughts raging in his ears. A verbal tinnitus followed him across the tiled floor, through the door, over the thin carpet till he took his seat and settled. And still soundlessly it might persist, so loud that Jack felt that whoever was closest to him would hear the echoes from inside his head. He began to dread being alone. After a night of drunkenness he would wake with such overwhelming pangs of guilt that he felt mentally unstable.

His mornings began with unfortunate musings and bullying hallucinations. His romantic self had always rebelled against surreal imaginings but now he found himself stalked by abstractions, ringings, morbid fantasies. He raged to get beyond, to get out. To give up the drink, today! To start today! Now! That evening he'd find himself – with all these promises to himself broken and forgotten – drink in hand, waiting on Catherine to come home. The abuse continued right up to the moment he saw her alight from the bus.

As the front door closed behind her, the silence mysteriously returned. The furies departed.

"There's a community group I know looking for a writer to work with."

"I'd be no good at that."

"Yes, you would."

Through her he established contact with them in West Belfast. They were researching a play about a fictional Republican prisoner who was to be released into the outside world after fifteen years in jail for murdering a policeman. Would Jack be interested? It seemed a way out of the quandary of his everyday life on Belfast Lough. Yes, he said, he'd be interested.

Near St Theresa's private school at Aitnamona Crescent, they rented a room where the Turf Lodge and Andersonstown meet. The first day he walked in there he found himself among a group of people much like himself – outsiders of English or Southern Irish stock; do-gooders who wanted to write meaningful social drama; young writers with a morbid interest in imagining death by violence; women with an axe to grind; people who felt themselves above religious fighting; social workers who had failed to meet the demands of the streets; strident moralists who pretended to liberalism; people with an insane curiosity into why humans kill; and a few Northern Irish who came and went like spirits searching for the bodies they had once inhabited.

Catherine bought a second-hand Lada for £250 with money she earned from two radio plays with the BBC. Each weekend Jack gave her lessons out at Helen's Bay. In first gear they went in circles round the Folk Museum. He taught her how to do a hand-brake start and a three-point turn below Cave Hill. Her concentration and single-mindedness was total. They took with them a half-bottle of whiskey to drink from between lessons.

Each morning she drove to the Arts Centre, with him calling out directions as she went – Hollywood Bypass! Marine Parade! Go handy! One way! Now the Sewage Works. Lights! Lights! Now Belfast Airport. Don't do that! Belfast Harbour. Easy, Catherine! Albert Bridge Road, good woman! Albert Bridge, turn right, turn left, East Bridge Street. Easy! Straight Across! Fuck him! Across Cromac Square. Where are we? Slow now, slower! Shaftesbury Square. Jesus!

He moved into the driving seat. They'd kiss, assuredly and lovingly. And he'd drive from there to Aitnamona. He would scarcely have arrived at his desk when Catherine would phone to see if he was safe.

"I made it," he'd reply.

"The best of luck," she'd say.

The group sat round uneasily in a circle trying to invent someone who would meet their criterion. Their first job was to find a suitable name for the prisoner. At last, after a bewildering argument, Shamey Coyle entered the world of community drama. A street and a suitable family life was found. He had been born in Hatfield Street off the Ormeau Road in 1949. In 1970 he had moved to Gransha Gardens in the Turf Lodge area with his new wife, who was from Thompson Street, off the Mountpolinger Road in the North Strand.

"Would he have married a Protestant?" asked Jack.

"Don't be daft," he was told, "this is a play based on reality."

What does that make me? wondered Jack. The rant began in his head. Oi! Hip! Ya fucker ya! Up the road ya bollacks! Grieving is it? *Mea culpa. Mea culpa.* Through my grievous. *Sacramentum. Conas mara tá?* The fox, the stoat and the bonnie shoals. There is a narrowing constriction at the end of the space. Float through it. It's only whadyacall it . . .

"Do you think so, Jack?"

The question directed at him separated itself from the myriad of other voices.

"Oh definitely," he agreed.

Now the group set off to do their research. Late in the afternoon of his second day Jack drove to the Falls Road. He was directed to wait in Islandbawn Street. He sat in the Lada smoking and planning the order of the interview. Very close to him a British Army convoy passed by. Soldiers on the footpath moved one behind the other. The last soldier ducked down by the wing of the Lada. Various shouts rang up and down the street. The soldier crouched by the window. Playing loudly over his personal stereo came a snatch from Beethoven's *Pastoral Symphony*.

He grunted and ran on down to the next street corner. After the soldiers were gone a knock came to the window. "You the lad that wants to see someone about a play?"

"So, he shoots a policeman," the man said.

"Yes," said Jack, "but I'm beginning to worry about this whole project."

"Why?"

They were sitting in a small, bare living room off Springmartin Road.

"Because I don't know whether it's possible to write about these things."

"I mean why did he shoot the policeman?"

"Because he claims he is part of the occupying forces, I suppose."

"Do you think so?" He lit a cigar.

"It's what I presume."

"I would expect he shot him because he was ordered to do so."

"Well, yes, in the final analysis, yes."

"He's a soldier, isn't he? That's what Shamey Coyle is."

"Yes."

"And if he shot him in Castle Street, what I'd like to know is – did he walk up the street and shoot him at the check-point?"

"That wasn't mentioned."

"For that to happen, the policeman would have to be alone. Do you think a policeman would be standing alone in Castle Street?"

"I wouldn't think so."

"Neither would I."

"But what I wanted to find out about was his life after prison."

"And what I want to know is whether Shamey Coyle shot this peeler? That will tell us what you want to know. And if he did, how he did it. You don't intend having him in jail for a crime he didn't commit?"

"Well, the charges were brought long after he was arrested. He would have been arrested on suspicion."

"Yes, but he's in the RA, isn't he? He's a soldier. If he's a soldier he has already shot someone, or he is about to do so."

"Yes."

"Well then, before you have Shamey Coyle arrested you want to know he killed the man they say he did, and then you want to find out who he killed."

"What do you mean?"

"Who was this policeman he killed?"

"He was just a policeman, that's all," Jack said lamely.

"Well, he has a name, hasn't he?"

"It would be fictitious."

"So is Shamey Coyle, isn't he?"

"Yes."

"Make up a name for him, then. Make him flesh and blood."

"I suppose he could be called Christopher . . . Little."

"OK. I suppose that will do."

"Now what?"

"Who is Christopher Little?"

"He's nineteen. He's Protestant. He's a policeman."

"And he's been shot."

"Yes," said Jack. He thought a minute. "But how?"

"Right. That's the question you should be asking yourself. Yet that's not what you asked me when you came through that door there. You didn't say – look, I'm having trouble finding out how Christopher Little was shot by Shamey Coyle, did you?"

"No."

"It was me put that into your head."

"That's true."

"And you accept its important?"

"I suppose I do."

"And now I hope you realize the value of propaganda."

Jack was startled. He sat there silently looking at the fresh-faced man who stood with his back to the living-room door, a foot raised with the sole flat against one of the panels. For the first time Jack began to see how far he had been led in a certain

310

direction to consider a concept he had not even entertained.

"If you want to write a play about us, you'll have to start from the point of view of propaganda. For instance, do we need your play?"

"You might when it's finished."

"If we liked it, it would be because it suits our point of view."

"So, whatever we do, as far as you're concerned, will only be authentic if it follows your line?"

"Authentic for some people means blood and guts on a side street." He walked over to the window and looked out. "Authentic to me means being true to the Republican cause. If you were writing a play about another class of human being things would take a different course. But here is where we are. People here are either true to their Republican or Loyalist traditions or they are not. This is something Shamey Coyle would have known."

"So what do I do?"

"Well, if I wanted to tell you a story that would suit me as a Republican, I'd have your Shamey Coyle start out as anti-Provo. The Brits shoot his brother and he joins the RA."

"That seems like he joined out of revenge."

"Sometimes it's as simple as that. You're not born with nationalist convictions. People join the RA for simple reasons."

"And what does that make Shamey Coyle?"

"It makes him a true blue. Your problem is you're trying to make him a hero. But that's not the scenario. I'm giving you the true one. You want a Shamey Coyle who has dramatic possibilities. I'd prefer to see a man I could believe in." He put out the cigar and dusted his trousers. "You don't look convinced."

"I'm trying to work it all out."

"He's a complicated man, is Shamey Coyle, right enough. It takes a wee while to invent him. You'd need a few hundred years of history to get him right." He shook Jack's hand. "I wouldn't like your job."

The group met a few days later. They carried on building up a composite figure of Shamey Coyle, a figure who had to

311

represent an IRA man in every particular, and who became, as a consequence, a typical piece of propaganda for them. For him to be otherwise he could not have done what he did, or lasted as long as he would have had to in prison. Soon Shamey Coyle became a source of endless bickering. Each person had their own vision of how a Republican comes into being. They wanted to make him brainless or else highly intelligent; he would be baby-faced, he would be ugly; then came the possibility of him turning from a patriot into an informer.

"Fuck, just leave him in the RA," said one of the Northern Ireland lads. "Leave informing out of it."

"We must be accurate."

"Fuck you. Let him take a bad trip on acid."

"Yes, maybe he turns informer," continued the social-worker. "But what sort of man turns informer?"

"A fucking dick-head, if you ask me."

"Someone who ultimately does not believe in violence?"

"No," corrected Jack, "someone who does not believe in the IRA."

"Are we talking here of a man with high motives?"

"Shit. You have it all wrong," said one ginger-haired lad. "From the beginning Shamey Coyle dreams of getting away from Belfast. If he joins the RA he sees himself as a free man one day walking down the streets of New York."

"It's no wonder," said Jack, "that where we are is called 'the place of the bog'."

"What do you mean?"

"Aitnamona – it means 'the place of the bog'."

"Do you speak the Irish?"

"Yes."

"Well, wee lad, you could be making a few bob just up the road there. I hear they're looking for an Irish teacher in the Mills."

And that's how Jack Ferris, after a few weeks building up a profile of Shamey Coyle, left the group that was trying to put the play together and began teaching Irish in Conway's Mills on the Falls Road. He never actually discovered what Shamey Coyle did when he left prison, but somehow or other he learned to mourn the death of Christopher Little, whose existence he would not have thought of had he not come into being through a conversation with a man who would have killed him.

The teaching of Irish did not bring in much money. His group consisted of two ex-prisoners, a few sons of *Comhaltas* people, two Republican poets, a young short-story writer anxious for fame, and two girls who were actually learning Irish as a foreign language at school.

In the dark winter nights he'd park the Lada in a side street off the Falls outside the door of a friendly couple. He'd walk the rest of the way. Always he would remember those little streets, the few figures waiting smoking in the dark outside the hall, the lighting of the Superser, the coffee break, the strange sensation of hearing the Irish of O'Ríordán the poet spoken by a group of Belfast adults, while outside a British convoy moved down the street, or a helicopter sent a probing light across the Guinness barrels in the yard.

He had never taught before, and did not want to take it on, but it was Catherine that encouraged him.

"You'd make a beautiful DJ," she told him. "If you were on the radio I'd listen to you all the time. And you'd make an even better teacher."

"I'll be too nervous."

"You'll get used to it."

Twice a week he made the trip and then went off with some members of his class to a nearby pub. They told stories of their lives with a harsh fluency in plain English. The young writer wanted to know how he might write a book that'd make a million. See that boy Jeffrey Archer! And what about Barbara Cartland? Ah couldn't be bothered wi' Belfast, who wants ta write about Belfast, said the short story writer, I've had it up ta here.

It was an extraordinary thing for Jack to find that he was a useful member of society again. In the afternoons he drank with disreputable Protestants, then crossed town to engage in the Irish language with puritanical nationalists and would-be commercial novelists. Then, arriving home at twelve, he'd find

Catherine seated by the window of the house waiting for him, a half-bottle of wine standing on top of the fridge and her scripts spread across the living room floor.

"Will you read out that part for me?" she said over dinner.

"Who am I supposed to be tonight?"

"You're a woman who agrees to go undercover for the RUC."

"Oh yeah?" said Jack. "It's getting that I don't know who I am any more."

She had such a generous sense of giving that he felt blessed. In bed he returned to an old habit of his, one she had eased him away from. He started to cry out like a wounded animal as he came. "Sh," she'd say. But still this fearful sound would issue from him. Such helplessness distressed her. And her mind would leap at the thought that she might lose him. "You're unique," she'd say. She held him, saying over and over, "I love you." And, she saw, he was very generous towards her. He seemed to have forgotten her betrayal of him.

Tentatively, she'd kiss him.

She thought how crazy she would have been had the same thing happened to her.

"I love you," she said. "Please let's be happy. I can only think of being happy with you."

But it was also a dangerous time for Catherine. For though she wanted his forgiveness still, privately, her betrayal of him gave her a great deal of satisfaction. Telling him that night of how she had made love to another man had helped put some erotic distance between herself and Jack. It reminded him that she existed in a world other than the one he knew her in. She could go outside of his perspective. She could command his lust at any hour. But now as they seemed to grow closer, she could find no fantasy to sustain her. Always, to retain her identity in a relationship she kept one part of herself free from her lover. This allowed her the possibility of betraying him. But Jack's discovery of her had released her from all duplicity. Never before had she been driven to face up to a lover.

She told him this and held him, and yet wondered privately where it would end.

She began talking of ridiculous plans. When summer came they would leave Belfast. They must leave Belfast, she said. They would go to Europe. They could go anywhere they wanted. "You see," she said, "I can't bear it anymore. I don't want to become a cynic. When we argue I often feel like killing myself. My work suffers when we fight. I suffer, you suffer. But the nightmares are getting worse. Every day I'm full of new grievances. We could go South."

"You think so?"

"I could get a job there with some theatre."

"And what about your work here?"

"What would you know about that? I never see you. You turn up drunk on my opening nights. You're doing things of which I don't approve. I thought you would take care of me. Do you hear me? I thought you would take care of me."

"I hear you."

"There's only so much of this I can take."

"I realize that."

"We could live together somewhere and have children."

"Do you want children?"

She stiffened. "Why," she cried angrily, "what's wrong with that! Do you not want children?"

She let go of him. He lay looking at the ceiling.

"This is a terrible life we are leading, you know that," said Jack.

"Do you think other people go on like we do?"

"If they do," said Jack, "I'm sorry for them."

She did not argue on, for she remembered that it was not so long ago since he could have been indescribably cruel to her if he had wanted to. She lay beside him, deep in a womanly despair that seemed to embrace everything.

"Hugh!" he shouted, "there's water in the engine room."

"Jack," she whispered. "Jack."

He struggled fiercely.

"We have to get out of here." He climbed out and began to

315

drag the bed across the floor. "Jack!" she called. She turned on the light. He stopped immediately.

"Jack," she said, "it's me. Catherine." She approached him fearfully.

"I heard you shouting," he explained. He lay down and went back to sleep.

IV

THE MUSICAL
BRIDGE

26

Flying in Belfast

He was sitting by his empty typewriter with a raging toothache when the telephone rang.

"Ha-ho."

"Eddie."

"I hear you're doing a bit of theatre in West Belfast."

"That has fallen through."

"Oh. Have you got that new play you promised me?"

"Not yet."

"Could I look at what you've done so far?"

"Why?"

"I've been offered to direct a play of my choice, sometime late next year."

"I've done nothing."

"Right. So how do you spend your time up there?"

"In the mornings I'm not well. In the afternoons, while Catherine is off round the province in a minibus doing political plays, I sit in an old record shop listening to music from the sixties. Played," added Jack, "by an ex-British soldier. Then at night I give Irish classes."

"Excellent. OK. Look as soon as you've finished something will you send it on?"

"Sure. I will."

"Ha-ho."

Jack put a fresh sheet of paper in the typewriter and watched the Union Jacks blowing.

He disappeared into his study for three days. She came home each evening to the tap of the typewriter.

The demons that jealousy and drink would unleash were

quietened. The few hours of sobriety made them wise, forgiving and nostalgic. A new beginning seemed possible. They allowed themselves two drinks between eleven and midnight and saluted each other. A mood of religious hilarity would take them.

"Are your characters happy, are they content?"

"They're peaceful."

"I worry about their wellbeing."

"So you ought."

He'd place the pages he had finished before her and watch her face anxiously for her reaction. She'd attempt a few lines, and look at him.

"What do you think?"

"It makes me wonder where you spend your days while I'm away. There's a lot of erotic text here that as woman I have not experienced with you, and that makes me wonder."

Jack laughed. "It's called invention."

"Is it? I find it sexually unnerving."

And it was on one of those nights that Jack partly emptied, for a few seconds, his body of the sex that controlled it.

How he arrived at that state was through a hazardous frisson of the mind. Something had jerked him into a new uncertain state of desire. He had been stretched out beside Catherine. He felt her presence there, long and tall and blond in the bed, a womanly shape sleeping beside him. His full length in every respect. Willing to be abused by him insofar as her turn would come to humiliate him. Then he thought for a second that she was a man in the bed beside him. She, of course, when he told her these things, laughed and was delighted by the thought, because she was glad he was capable of such longings.

For she believed secretly that men only desire men.

For Jack it was a tender moment to be stretched alongside someone laughing.

"Catherine," he said.

It was how he left his body. It was for a minute only. But he felt for a moment that he had become the woman beside him. As she moved around the room in her nightdress, he could feel that he himself was scuttling about in his womanness. He

320

even felt the sensation of breasts. And the soft texture of the things she wore against his skin. What he felt in the night beside him. Was half touched by. For a second he wore round him something shapeless. Still it pleased.

And as he told her of this sensation and saw her pleasure, he knew he had passed some test his mind and body had set him.

The following day he was walking down the road on his own to the newsagent's and again he felt the sensation of his bosom fall. Then came the faint feeling of being possessed. For a second, phantom skirts blew out a little behind him. He stopped briefly and shook his head. It was Catherine who had taken him over. He was grateful when his own identity was restored, for he had not the courage to sustain that rootless feeling a moment longer. He knew what had happened, he had become Catherine, not really Catherine but some other woman possessed him, some ideal shape had taken him along the road for a few steps. It was generous and terrifying when he stepped into that phantom dress on the street, then no more. Yet he proceeded not impoverished by what he had felt and seen, not caring that this was only a fraction of the great void to be crossed.

"How's about ya, Jack?" asked the old lady in the newsagent's as she pressed a tissue to her lips.

"I'm flying," said Jack.

Slowly, his transformation into Catherine took place. Since he could not win her as himself, he would become everything that she loved in herself. Not that he knew that this transformation was taking place. But often he would catch himself rise off a chair as she did, lift a cigarette in the same manner. He felt his back suddenly straighten like hers. It was just these incidental intimations told him that something was happening over which he had no control.

Whenever he wrote formerly, he had always gone sober to keep his concentration for all the insane imaginings that took place. Now, when he sat by the fire with the day's work over, a glass of wine at his feet, a glass of wine at hers, he was amazed at the contentment he felt. It all seemed possible. The play took shape according to her themes, her obsessions, and with all her nuances intact. He wrote about her stubbornness in owning and holding on to what was rightly hers.

"Remember," she said, "that you are not me."

He let a certain amount of time pass. Then he said: "I have just realized that you don't believe in fiction."

"You're wrong," she answered with conviction. "My trouble is I believe it totally, or not at all." She looked at him with mock scorn. "In that, I'm like my father."

They went to a party thrown by Helen, a friend of Catherine's. He stood by Helen's side with a tall cold glass of white wine.

"Are you a feminist, too?" asked Jack.

"I like men too much," she said, "to be a feminist. I need nice male chauvinists to carry my shopping home."

"You're disgraceful!" Catherine laughed.

Helen's room was full of charts of the human body and the human brain.

"Are you by any chance an astrologer?" he asked.

"Not quite," she replied, "I'm a psychiatric nurse, you might say."

"Don't start her," said Catherine. "Talk of the brain only brings bright spots in front of my eyes. At school certain puzzles used to make me feel faint."

"Now it's sex," said Jack.

"Stop," said Catherine, poking him.

Then she turned serious.

"All my life I've feared madness," she said.

"And I wanted to commit suicide," said Helen.

"This is a lovely conversation," said Jack.

"And then," said Catherine, "there's jealousy."

"Oh," agreed Helen.

"For a whole year before I met him I was negligent of sex because all of my affairs provoked in me such wanton acts of jealousy that I was afraid someone might get killed."

"Watch yourself, Jack," said Helen.

"In fact," said Catherine, "once I was alone I thought I could please myself physically more than other people could. When I was lonely I used stroke my own breasts."

Helen nodded: "You can run out of possibilities there in time."

"Yes," said Catherine, and she took Jack's arm.

"I would give anything to be as happy as ye are," said Helen.

"We have our own troubles," said Jack.

Then Helen leaned up and put her arms around him and kissed him. It was a bright sisterly kiss. Then she kissed Catherine. "Ye are lucky to have each other," she said, "and remember, I love you both." Catherine never left Jack's side. Helen sang. Catherine sang. Jack danced. Then, towards dawn, they took a taxi home with a driver that knew them both. When Jack went forward to open the door of the house, the taxi-driver whispered to Catherine as she counted out the fare in the half-light of the car interior: "He is in danger here, ye know."

"What?" she asked, terrified.

"I don't wanna *scar* ye," he said, "but I've heard stories about him swinging in and out of pubs with the wrong people. Like it's none of my business, but you should tell him to be more careful. The whole sectarian thing could start again in the morning."

Catherine sat rooted to the seat of the car.

"This city is evil," she said. "It's evil."

"He's been foolish. He doesn't understand."

She thanked him. She snapped the bolts home on the front door. She pushed the kitchen table against the back door. He was stretched out with an open bottle of wine on the settee listening to an unaccompanied version of "The Lament for James Connolly" sung in a broad Dublin accent. She lifted the needle off the record.

"Why did you do that?"

"Because it's dangerous," she said.

He looked at her. "But it's your record."

"I know that."

When they lay down together she listened to every sound in the street. She lay awake listening for the sound of breaking glass like Jonathan Adams had long before her. She woke out of a nightmare and leaned over his body and looked at his face. For a long time she stared at him and listened to his breathing.

She watched dreams flick across his closed eyes. She fell asleep holding his hand. When she left for work the next morning she asked him not to go out. To stay by the phone.

Later, Catherine rang him. There was no answer. She continued ringing throughout that day, getting more and more frantic. She imagined everything terrible that might befall Jack. She thought of walking into the flat to find a gush of blood still running down the door that led into the living room. She imagined leaning over to look into his face and finding the eyes peacefully closed. Each violent detail was replayed in terror in her imagination. Then in the late afternoon the phone rang. He was in Lavery's pub.

"Oh, Jack, I can't tell you the things that have been going through my head," she said. "Stay there – I'll be right over."

"Look I've met some people I know, we're heading off for a spin to the Glens."

"But I need to see you badly."

"We'll only be away a while."

"Who are these friends?"

"They're from Dublin. Eddie my director is with them. I wanted to show him a version of the play."

"Promise me you'll be back tonight."

"I will."

She smelt him when he came in. Then she perched at the corner of the bed and looked at him as he sat with his back to the wall. He realized she was very drunk. Then she got up and stood by the window.

She came back and sat as before. She lit a cigarette. Her hands were shaking.

"You've been with someone."

"I was with no one."

"Don't you look at me all high and mighty."

"I don't mean to."

"I can see it in you. You think you can do what you like with me."

"That's not true."

"Did you bring some drink back?"

"No. I'll go out and get some."

"Forget it." She tapped the cigarette nervously. "Will we go to Mayo for Christmas?"

"I have to go to Leitrim to see the family."

"To see all the Bleeding Hearts."

"Stop, Catherine."

" 'Stop Catherine,' " she continued, imitating him, "You fucker you."

He looked at her.

"Ah well, don't come back then. Go there and stay there. Don't set a foot inside the door of this house again. Do you hear me!"

"You fascist!" he spat. Suddenly he jumped up.

He grabbed her by the shoulders and pinned her back to him. They fell to the floor and lay there breathing heavily.

"Let me up," she said.

He eased his grip on her neck. She buttoned her coat. She put her feet back into her shoes. "You slept with her, didn't you?"

"Yes," he said simply.

"Did she kiss your arse like I do, you bastard?" she screamed and flailed out with her fists. He caught her again. "Let me go," she screamed. She left. He waited for hours to see would she return. At three in the morning the bell rang. She was at the door, very drunk, moist-eyed and shaking.

He led her in. He climbed back into bed. She climbed in beside him.

Early next morning he found her arm come round and circle him. She turned him over.

"Did I do that?" she said, touching a bruise on his cheek.

He opened his eyes.

"Forgive me, Jack," she said. "I think I am going demented."

"I think I am as well."

"Oh God, I feel terrible." She stood up and tottered. He looked at her long white arms and white shoulders. The fairy hair on her stomach. She looked vulnerable and sorry. She sat where she had sat the night before, at the edge of the bed. Flayed by guilt, he waited for her anger to erupt.

325

Instead she said softly: "I am sorry for hitting you."

"And I'm sorry for hitting you," he replied.

"I suppose you think you have me now. That you think you can do with me what you like."

"No I don't."

"Now you've had your revenge, will you do something for me?"

"Yes."

"Will you swear to be true to me?"

He swore he would be true. She swore she would be true. They swore together. "Now," she said, "you are mine. Remember that." They walked down the early morning streets. Seagulls were chatting in the middle of a roundabout. "Meet me round one," she said and kissed his cheek. He bought a noggin of gin at an early morning pub. Then he sat in a park among the Protestant unemployed drinking it. At eleven he walked back to the house. He halted inside the door. A rolled-up *Irish Press* had arrived from Eddie. A photo of Jack was on an inside page.

"Don't go in there," she said, "we'll have a drink at home."

"Just one," he said, entering a bar.

"I'm going home," she threatened.

"I'll follow you," he said, and left her.

"Please, Jack," she called, "these are bad times."

"Just one," he said.

"We should be together."

"Well then, come with me."

"No."

Alone and disorientated, Catherine headed off into the night.

Immediately Jack broke into a conversation between two men on his right.

"Did you ever do something stupid?" he asked.

"Whadya mean?"

"That's my photo there in the paper," said Jack and he shoved across the *Irish Press* for them to see.

"I don't read that paper," the second man said and he pushed the paper back.

"I wouldn't either," replied Jack, "except you see my photo is in it."

Again he showed the photograph. But without looking at the newspaper the man nearest him said: "What for?"

"I was stupid enough to say I was writing a new play about Belfast, but the truth is I haven't a word written," said Jack. He looked behind him at the people seated round the small tables, their shopping bags at their feet. It was dole day. He wondered what to say. "I know nothing about Belfast" he said.

"Aye," said the first man.

"But we're at home here," said the second.

"Where do you live?" asked the other.

"Up on My Lady's Road," lied Jack.

"Good on ya," the nearest man said, softening. "I'm Bertie."

Both men included Jack in their rounds. They talked of the sports centres in Belfast, of the wave machine in the Shankhill Baths. How Jack loved Belfast a sight better than Dublin. "How long have you been in My Lady's?" they asked him. "A few years," he lied. "Well, you know your way around." They toasted each other. "Do you take any interest in religion?" the nearest man asked.

"No," said Jack.

"Well, you're better off maybe," replied Bertie.

They drank. They would not let him buy. He told them he was from Leitrim.

"You just missed being in Ulster," said Bertie. He turned to the second man, who wore glasses, and shook his head. "We should never have given them back Cavan, either, Willy. The Free State should never have been given Cavan. It was a mistake." He turned back to Jack as Willy went off and joined some others. "Leitrim is a different case entirely," he continued, "there's not many of us left there."

"Why don't you let me get this one?" asked Jack.

"No, wee lad," Bertie replied, "We are all friends here. I'll look after you." He called two balls of Malt Bush.

"I'm feeling high," said Jack.

"Good on ya." They talked of the quality of life in the North.

"And you've been a good few years in My Lady's?" the man asked.

"Aye," said Jack.

"So you'd know your way around?" he repeated ominously.

"I would."

"Who's your local commander there?"

"I wouldn't know about these things."

The man called over to his companion. "Hey, Willy. Come here till I ask ya." The man with the glasses got up. The two turned aside and spoke quietly together a few moments. Jack looked uneasily at the two drinks beside him.

"Are you rightly?" Willy asked Jack as he took the other's place.

"I'm fine," said Jack, "Can I get a drink for us?"

"Sure thing. Go ahead there."

Jack ordered three more Malt Bushes.

"What sort of stuff do you write?"

"Love stories," said Jack.

"What religion are you?" interrupted Bertie from behind.

For a long moment Jack turned the question over in his mind.

"I'm Protestant," Jack answered.

"You're no Prod," Bertie shouted. "You don't fool me!"

Jack saw that people were leaving the bar very fast. Behind his back the tables emptied. The barman was clearing away. The man leaned forward to Jack. "You are probably one fucking Provo. I can see it in your eye." He moved closer to Jack. "I've looked into many a terrorist's eye, in Israel and in Cyprus, and I know one when I see one." Jack protested. "You see this gat?" said Bertie lifting his jacket to show a gun in the back of his trousers. "You see this gat? I'll soon know who you are." But Willy spun his companion round, and the two sat on a seat together, while furtively the barman collected glasses in the now empty lounge.

Willy, tucking his glasses up onto the nub of his nose with his index finger, returned to the bar while Bertie, frustrated and angry, stayed put by a table. Willy called for more drinks.

"We're closing, Willy," said the barman.

"Sure thing, Simmons. Three Bush, right?" He turned to

Jack as if none of the previous exchange had occurred. "So, you're a class of a writer?"

"I'm an idiot," said Jack. "You can see it there in black and white." And he showed him the *Irish Press*.

"I don't read that paper."

"You can find out about me through the *Belfast Newsletter*," said Jack.

"And who do you know down there?"

"They have a piece about a play of mine."

"Who are you living with in My Lady's Road?"

"An aunt of mine," said Jack. The sweat began to roll down his face. "She's getting old now. A Mrs Brooke. She was married to an RUC man."

"I wouldn't know too many round there."

"Good luck," said Jack.

"Aye, good health."

Jack downed the three whiskeys in front of him, leaving just a swallow in the final one. All the time Willy coolly watched him.

"Excuse me," said Jack, "I have to go for a piss."

"Aye."

It was a long walk to the gentlemen's toilet. He felt the eyes of Willy on him in the mirror beyond the bar, the barman's eyes on him as he swept the lounge floor, the eyes of the man who had shown the revolver on him as he sat in a recess by the door. When he entered the bathroom Jack spread both his hands – palm-outwards – across the tiled wall. "Jesus Christ," he said. The tinnitus that he had not heard for so long rose menacingly inside his brain. He could not urinate, nor did he try. He washed his face, then he dried it carefully. He drank from the tap. Then he dried his mouth. He looked for a second at himself in the mirror. "Now," he said. He closed his eyes. He tidied his hair. He stepped back into the lounge like a man without a care in the world. He saw that the barman was standing by the exit with the keys. He walked up beside the man with the glasses and drank the remaining whiskey down.

"I think I'll be off now, Willy," he said, proffering his hand. Willy, out of habit, took it. Jack, smiling madly, turned to go.

On the left he saw his other interrogator had been joined by a young man in blue denims who had just come in. "Hauld on," Jack shouted to the barman by the door.

"Good luck, Bertie," he said to Bertie with a great wave of friendliness. But Bertie looked away to catch Willy's eye. The barman held the door open. His eyes were anxious. At that uncertain moment Jack fled out onto the street. There were two taxis parked outside. He immediately opened the back door and sat into one. "Take me," he said, "to My Lady's Road." "Can't boss. I'm booked," said the driver. "I'm waiting for people inside."

"Oh, sorry." He got out.

"Try Norbert," said the driver. He ran across to the next taxi. "I have ten pound here, Norbert," said Jack, "if you'll take me out the Hollywood road."

"Eight will do."

"Can you take me?"

"I can take ye, surely. Just take your time now."

Jack climbed into the front seat beside him.

The driver looked at him.

"Hollywood, ye said?"

"Aye," said Jack.

"Did you know that Hollywood is the only town in Ireland with a Maypole?" asked the driver pleasantly, as he turned the engine on.

"No. I didn't know that," said Jack trying to stifle his panic.

"There you are now."

The driver eased into first gear, righted the mirror and looked behind him. Is this a fucking set up? thought Jack. In slow motion the driver turned the car round. As they swung out into the traffic Jack took a quick glance behind. No one. They moved slowly through East Belfast.

"You'd be a Free Stater then?" asked Norbert.

"Yes," said Jack.

"And how do you like it up here?"

"Oh, it's grand."

"Once," said Norbert, "you get to know your way around."

They spoke no more. Throughout the entire journey Jack sat

330

there gripping his thighs. He gave a false address. When they arrived he handed the taxi-driver the tenner.

"Eight I said, and eight it'll be," said Norbert. He gave back two pounds change. He watched Jack with a merry smile. Jack thanked him and then he turned casually up a side street. He ran towards a laneway and waited to see if anyone was following him. He went on up another street and waited. By side streets he got home some hours later. A light was on in the house. He ran in and shot all the locks home.

"Jesus Christ!" he said, and sat on the floor. Out of his side pocket the *Irish Press* poked up.

Catherine stood in the door of the bedroom watching him.

"I knew this would happen," she said. "I knew this would happen."

A few evenings later they were walking towards a cinema in the city centre when a man stopped and laughed at Jack, and Jack laughed back, and the man said: "It won't be long now, fella."

They went on walking.

"What was that all about?" asked Catherine.

"That was him. That was Bertie."

"Who?"

"That was the man who threatened me."

"And you laughed at him?"

"What did you expect me to do?"

"I don't know."

"Well, I don't fucking know either."

27

Crossing the Musical Bridge

A few nights later the window of the living room came hurtling in. They heard the noise, and lay petrified in bed.

Jack got up.

"Don't go out there!"

"I can't hear anyone."

They remained perfectly still.

"There's no one there," he said again.

"Yes, there is," she whispered shrilly.

He opened the bedroom door and felt his way along in the darkness. A cold wind was blowing down the corridor. In the living room itself all their papers were hurtling to and fro. As he stepped across the carpet he felt broken glass underfoot. He threw a coat on the floor. He reached the window. He looked out on to the street. There was no one out there.

He moved back and switched on the light. Everything was swirling round in the wind, but there was no sign of a stone.

He shouted in to Catherine: "The wind blew it in."

He took a piece of carpet and nailed it over the place where the pane had given. Catherine stepped into the room.

"My nerves won't take any more," she said. "We'll have to leave."

"Now what will we do?" asked Catherine.

"Move to West Belfast?"

"No," she said.

"I have no money left," said Jack.

"So where?"

"Go to the Mullet, I suppose."

"Is it a dream to think we might get living together peacefully in the South?"

He said: "What I should do is go ahead and find some work on the boats."

"You could stay in our house."

"I'd rather we had a place of our own."

"I don't know where I might get a job." She looked at him. "Are we really moving?"

"Yes."

"And you are going to leave me here."

"I'm broke. I couldn't stay even if I wanted to."

"When are you going?"

"I don't know."

"What about your class? What will they think?" she asked. "Are you going to leave them, too?"

She picked a piece of broken glass out of her cigarette pack.

"Do you think we are suitable people," she said, "to be together?"

"I wish we were."

"We've had terrible times."

"There's worse."

"But we have not experienced it."

She pushed back her hair.

"Do you know that Helen Wynne goes to Mass? I'm beginning to think she's right. We don't believe in anything but we suffer for breaking the rules all the same." Then she looked at him: "What we should do is go off the drink for a while."

"Yes."

"Things are going out of control."

"Yes, they are."

"You *do* accept that."

"Yes, I do."

The first morning of their sobriety Jack received a phone call from Sara asking him to advise Catherine to watch *Glenroe* on RTE the following evening.

"Did she say why?"

"No."

"Can it be possible what I'm thinking?"

"You should ring your mother."

Catherine did, only to find that Sara had already been in touch with Maisie.

"And where," Catherine asked Jack, "are we going to see RTE up here?"

"There's a club I know that has RTE."

"In the Falls?"

"No, actually just a little ways from here."

"A Protestant club?"

"Aye."

"And they have RTE?"

"Yes. To watch the races on Saturday."

On Sunday evening they were seated before two pints of lager in the empty club. A single-bar electric fire was on behind the bar, and to their left, a roaring coal fire. *Songs of Praise* was on the BBC when Jack asked the barman to switch over to RTE.

"Her sister," said Jack, indicating Catherine, "is appearing in an Irish soap."

"You're codding me."

"I'm not."

"Well, fuck." He switched to RTE and sat down beside them. "What's the story?" he asked.

"I don't know. It used to be about sheepfarmers in Wicklow."

"Fuck," said the barman.

Beside them, Catherine sat sober and correct.

"Is that her?" asked the barman when the programme started.

"Not yet," said Jack.

A marital row had broken out in a farmhouse. *She* accused *him* of having an affair. The man went off into the night.

"That's him fucked," said the barman. The estranged husband went into a pub. The other drinkers looked over at him with long knowing glances. "He must be having a bit on the side, all right," the barman concluded.

"That's wonderful," said Catherine.

After the break for advertisements the husband left the pub. Immediately the other drinkers in hostile asides were discussing him and his fancy woman. Much tut-tutting followed. He had been seen leaving a cinema in Dublin holding her hand. Sympathy was expressed towards the wife. Then the bar-room door opened.

"Is that her?" shouted the barman.

"Unfortunately, yes," said Catherine.

"She's a pretty lady," he said, "no more then yourself."

Sara, in a mini-skirt and bright red high heels entered. Her red hair was swept up into a bee-hive. "Oh dear," said Catherine, taking a furious gulp of her drink. With a gleaming smile Sara sat on a high stool at the bar. The shocked pub in *Glenroe* went quiet. "Holy God," said Miley. "That's the hussy," someone hissed. "That's right," laughed the barman. Then with great effrontery, and giving a lopsided grin, she ordered a gin and tonic. All the locals watched malevolently as Sara lifted out a small make-up mirror to study her over-painted face.

"And you'd be?" asked the landlord.

"Bridie Smith," replied Sara. "I'm just visiting."

With an innocent smile, Bridie Smith lifted her hand to shake his. But the landlord did not take it. Her hand stayed there, in the middle-distance, and longingly the camera lingered on it, with its ring and brightly painted fingernails.

"Dear God," said Catherine, and she covered her face.

"Delighted, I'm sure," said Bridie Smith in a broad Northern Irish accent.

"So Bridie's one of us," said the barman as the theme tune played and the credits came up. "That wasn't at all bad."

In those last few weeks Jack was drunk most days. In the Crown Bar he saw Helen sitting with friends. He found his way to her table and swayed lightly to and fro. She got up and took him away to the bar.

"I don't like to see you like this," said Helen Wynne.

"I'm sorry," he told her.

"You're not the real you," she said, "when you're drunk."

"I'm just going out of my mind."

"She loves you."

"That," said Jack, "is unfortunately no help."

"You were happy once, you'll be happy together again."

"I'm sorry to be coming out with all this to you."

"You will just have to sort it out between you," said Helen, "It's up to yourselves."

Helen refocused her eyes.

"You're getting drunk quicker these days," she said carefully.

"Can I join you and your friend?" he asked.

"It'd be better if you didn't. She sees you in black and white, and for the minute you're all black."

"All right," replied Jack angrily.

"It's impossible," she said, "to talk to you when you're like this."

"Fuck it," said Jack. "Fuck it," he said. He took a taxi to Helen's Bay. He climbed into Crawfordsburn Country Park. He lay on his back and looked at the sky. Then, carefully, he climbed over the gate. He took a taxi home. A crowd of young Protestant lads wearing the Loyalist colours were standing, as they always did, up the road from the off-licence. "That's the UVF," Catherine used say, warning him off. Now Jack walked down and joined them.

"Would ye like something stronger than cider?" he asked.

"Why not, Boss."

He went into the off-licence and bought a bottle of Black Bush. "It's Christmas," he said. They stood in a huddle, handing round his bottle.

"What are you doing up here anyway?" one of them asked.

"I'm the man that thought up the Anglo-Irish Treaty," he said. "Do you think will it catch on?"

"Ye're all right, fella. You like your drink, anyway. I see you, whenever I'm out, taking a bottle home," one said.

"It's been a long winter," said Jack.

Jack called down to see Christopher Nolan. He was sitting in the gloomy inner room of the shop by the Superser.

"Jack," he said.

"Chris."

"So what's the story?"

"I'm leaving."

336

"You're getting out?"

"Yeh."

"I don't blame you. Things are getting bad up here again. You can smell it in the air. It's coming into summer. That's always the worst time." He snapped open the lid on a can of lager. "You want to come over to the pad after?"

"Not today. Why don't you come over to our place?"

"Would that be wise? Your old lady might not like it."

"She won't mind."

At six they were sitting in the house drinking vodka and listening to Cat Stevens by the boarded-up window when Catherine came home. She sat down on the sofa and crossed her legs.

"So what's this – a going-away party?"

"Something like that."

"Are you the person from the bookshop?"

"The very same. Christopher. I'll miss old Jackie."

"So will we all, Christopher."

"I thought you said you were coming with me?" said Jack.

"Sara rang to invite me to Dublin."

"And what did you say?"

"I said I'd think about it. I said I was thinking of going down South with you."

"And what did she say to that?"

"She said I was foolish."

"She would."

"She's only thinking of what's best for me." She lifted a cigarette and looked at him. She took a can of lager from the table. "I could have a good life in Dublin."

"I'm sure you could."

"I'm certain I could. And I could find someone there to look after me."

"Well," he said bitterly, "you go to Dublin and I'll go to Belmullet."

"I might," she said. "we'll have to see."

"I'm serious," she said.

"I know."

"Should I make myself scarce?" interrupted Christopher.

"Oh, no," said Catherine. "You pair should just sit there and listen to the music. Meanwhile, can I have a vodka?"

"You certainly can," said Nolan. He levered himself out of the armchair and stood bemused in the middle of the floor. He poured out a small measure and handed it to her. "Cheers!" He rose his drink in the air.

"So you're going," she said.

"I heard from Thady," said Jack. "There's a berth available."

"When are you going?"

"Tomorrow."

"Well, thanks for telling me."

"You can follow me down."

"Are you sure we can be together there?" asked Catherine.

"I can't see why not," he said.

"And you'll find a home for us?"

"I will."

"So that's it then, I suppose," she said sadly. She looked over at Christopher Nolan. "He's deserting me."

When he woke in the morning he found himself on the bathroom floor. The ex-soldier was asleep on the sofa. Catherine was sitting in a chair in the bedroom. She was wide awake and smoking. He leaned down and kissed her. She didn't speak. He took the bus to Enniskillen, and from there to Ballina. It was when he had at last passed the musical bridge at Bellacorrick that he knew he was back in Erris.

When Jack set down his bag in Thady's house and looked out on Mullet it was like he'd just come down the stairs for the first time after a long illness. He spent a few idle days waiting while the boats were re-equipped after the flatfish season ended and before the salmon season began. The first few days of late May he sat on the steps of Thady's house looking out on the dunes, and he was overwhelmed by simple, selfish things.

It was as if Catherine had never existed. He was glad to have escaped. He felt shamefully free. When he opened the pages he had written in Belfast it was like opening the lid of a coffin. Inside a body was putrefying. He put the pages by for again.

He'd take a cup of tea and step outside. Then he'd lie in his bed in Thady's house dreading the moment when Thady would return to tell him the hour that they would be casting off from the pier.

He dreamt up outlandish excuses: I'm sick, I can't, the backs of my legs are fucked, there's no way I'll face a day out there. Thady returned near midnight and said nothing. Jack fell into a deep sleep. Next morning at five he found himself stumbling round the dark house in Thady's wake.

"Keep moving," said the older man.

"I'm moving," replied Jack.

"Good man."

A little while later they walked down the grey pier at Bally-glass which was full of scolding seagulls and silent fishermen. Hugh drove up in a blue Toyota.

The *Blue Cormorant*, a steel forty-footer, worked out of Killalla. Jack brought with him new sea gear, a number of notebooks which he wrapped in cellophane, a pair of boots he'd bought in Lavell's and a pair of new, tough jeans.

The *Blue Cormorant* steamed out from Killalla with the grey, illegal multi-filament salmon nets stored in her hold. As they hauled the first net in beyond Achill Island a shark skidded by below the winch. A salmon that came up with the net was cut perfectly straight across the middle with one clean bite. The skipper ran to stern with his rifle, but the shark had gone.

"Fucking bastard," he said.

Later that day a playful seal rose beside the shore buoy. The skipper shot it straight through the heart.

"Fucking seals," he said.

"If you're going to shoot seals," said Jack, "you can count me out of this crew."

"What are you," roared the skipper, "some kind of environmentalist?"

"He's right," replied a Northerner, who was hauling alongside Jack, "we are out here to fish salmon, not to shoot seals."

"I've got some fucking crew," said Daley, the skipper. "By Jesus, have I got a crew." He replaced the rifle. "Bastards," he said. He drove forward at top revs. "Cunts." He flew along the swirling sheets in a fury. "Fishermen, my arse!" he shouted, and turned in an arc by the buoy and cut the engine. They drifted there, as Hugh turned herrings on a pan, buttered bread and watched the pork chops swimming to and fro in a hot froth of cooking oil. At the wheel skipper Daley stood with his arms folded looking scornfully towards America.

It took over a fortnight before Jack could settle down on board. His hands had softened, the net bit into his palms and his dreams were not dreams at all. His sleep was not sleep. It was one long hallucinogenic recall of an undefinable city, where people harangued and jibed and whinged. Gurning. Then followed lowered voices you might hear from a house in mourning. A house of leaded lights and stained glass perched on the edge of reality, on a street somewhere beyond consciousness.

As he lay on his bunk waiting for sleep, a black-and-white roll call of images would light up on some psychic screen in his mind. Always at sea it began. Blame. Sorrow. Elation. Jack would remember her shoulder blades warm against him. The sweetness would be unbearable. Love smells. Woman smells. The small of her back. The two of them turning in their sleep so that they both faced the same way.

He'd open his eyes to discover he was in darkness at sea in a Force Seven. The sound of the engine was monstrous. Across from him Hugh and Thady were rocking to and fro in their bunks. The quiet Belfastman, Theo De Largey, was sleeping with his mouth open. With each lunge of the boat De Largey fought to keep the engine from intruding into his subconscious. "Daley," he'd shout, "I'll fucking swing for you." Like Jack, he too was trying to enter a landscape that was tranquil. But it was impossible to get the sound of the engine out of your head.

"I had it nearly perfect," De Largey would say.

"Where were you?"

"It's private." He turned to face inwards against the cabin wall. "Maybe I'll tell you some day."

"Yeah, sure." They'd turn away from each other. And start counting down to the moment they could enter sleep again.

Jack would count the revolutions of the engine and seek to enter his dreamworld through a small comfortable gap in the noise. The gap would appear as the trawler perched on one long roll. It felt like they might stay up there for ever. And just as he'd be pouring his consciousness through the break, a new run of thunderous waves would shoot the engine up into a perilous whine. Seven waves later the gap would appear again. As he'd make for it, he'd resurrect Catherine. Then just as he'd reach her the Atlantic would strike the bow, sending the waters flooding into his consciousness. The lurch would send him sliding. He'd hold on to the last image of Catherine in his head while the boat shuddered, and fell down a series of rocky steps.

Somewhere on the descent he'd always lose her. The sense of loss would be painful and bewildering. Then, reaching again a few seconds of promised calm, he'd arrive at a new warm perspective from which to view her. The oily sleeping bag, the coarse wool of the jumper that did as a pillow, became light as air. The floor of the bunk, which was only a few inches away from his face, became a distant ceiling. All receded. He braced his foot against the wall. Her white shoulder would swim into view. Her scandalous shins. His consciousness idled.

"Jesus!" shouted De Largey as the lurch came again. "That fucker Daley."

Searching for Jack in Yeats' County

Catherine moved into a spare room over the Arts Centre. The attic roof sloped over the single bed. At night she was the only human being in the building, and sometimes it scared her, being there alone. She'd hear sounds from the kitchen in the basement. A lamp creaking in the theatre. Footsteps on the stairs that came to a standstill on the landing. And she'd wonder about these faceless men, these violent creatures of her imagination, who were gathering outside her door.

She did stage management. She served behind the coffee bar. She cooked vegetarian meals. She closed the theatre at night, then sat with a bottle of wine reading Anaïs Nin. She read *The Wide Sargasso Sea* and exulted in the erotic details of female conspiracy.

Since he'd left, Catherine had been followed by terrifying memories of the risks they'd taken by living together.

Her dreams were mainland dreams. Dreams of drowning. While the roar of the engine at sea would produce in the fishermen dreams of rare silence as if their consciousness was struggling to rid itself of the mayhem of straining pistons, on land all of the noise from the sea seemed to travel directly into the sleeper's inner ear. Catherine's themes were desertion, betrayal and outrageous sexuality. All of the men she had ever known returned as lesser demons over whom she had complete control.

Wakening was always distressing. To find herself reaching out to Matti Bonner in a scandalous dream. To be tucked away in the spare room beneath the stars and then wake to hear the first of the trendy theatre workers arriving. And sometimes to wake, disorientated, on a settee in a girlfriend's kitchen where a radio was still playing, a cat she didn't know sitting disdainfully on a window ledge, another woman's dress hanging on the back of the door. It seemed an act of treachery that all the things she had collected – her books, her records, her diaries – should end up being stored backstage in view of all the theatre crew.

Some nights she'd find items of her personal belongings used as stage props. Her books sat on a shelf in a one-act play by Sean O'Casey. A woman wore one of her scarves in *The Factory Girls*.

The status her feminist principles had once given her had begun to wear off. She could still draw cruelly on her politics to taunt those men she worked alongside in the theatre, or in the BBC where some afternoons she'd go to record short plays. She walked past rooms in Broadcasting House that contained news items that would never see the light of day. Her cynicism made her many enemies, but her politics kept vigil over her hurt.

"You're using feminism," said a drama producer there, "like those bastards use Royalism. In a few years you'll be ashamed of all this."

"I don't have to answer that," she said.

"As a matter of fact, you're a Romantic."

"It still," she replied, "has a certain allure." Then staring him down she said: "Why can't you give me something to do that I can get my teeth into?"

He pressed the exit sign on his computer.

"See this?" he said, "This is what I do all day. I don't read. I watch. I add up. I edit. I work for the BBC. I drive home. When I wake up at night I look out the window to see if the car is still there. I see my neighbours stretched out on the ground looking under theirs. So I know immediately what they work at. My brother-in-law is pounding at the door. He's a policeman. What's he asking for? Drink. I go to sleep with him sitting downstairs watching videos. He's drinking gin. His sister, my wife, is drinking gin beside him. They're having a party. So you see, you're not the only one. This is your problem, Catherine, and this is my problem. This is what I do. Exit. Enter. OK?"

"I understand," said Catherine.

She walked down a corridor past a window that looked into the radio newsroom. Already the girl had her finger on the switch that a moment later would release a song by Michael Jackson when the last news item from the province had been read, the last denunciation of the latest outrage expressed. Drunk, a news editor passed by oblivious of her, his bow tie soaked in port and hanging askew. Ian Paisley sat in a room waiting to be interviewed on agriculture grants within the EEC. His briefcase, stuffed to overflowing with Euro-speak, sat on the lap of the young economics expert he employed. The accountant looked tiny beside the rangy Reverend. They sat there like two passengers in an aeroplane. Next to them was a room full of Catholic schoolchildren in gymslips and uniforms who suddenly rose to sing an extract from *Annie Get Your Gun*. Catherine, near to tears, stood outside listening.

A porter threw a nut in the air and caught it in his mouth.

He, too, began to sing along with the children.

She took a cup of coffee and stood outside the studio where they were about to record the play she was in. Gangsters and their molls walked up and down rehearsing Mafioso talk with Belfast accents. Others were using the idioms of early rock'n'roll. These were the fantastic metaphors the province's playwrights were reduced to. And she was outraged to find how, in those private moments before she stepped into the studio, what came to her mind was not the poetry she read, nor the moment in a novel that had exhilarated her. Not even one of the lines that she'd soon record. Instead, what she remembered was a series of words that she first took to be some jingle from a book of children's rhymes she'd read as a child. Then the phrase, with a Biblical ring, defined itself clearly – *Seek refuge in the Lord and not in princes*.

"Seek refuge in the Lord and not in princes," she heard herself say.

She'd remember as she sat at the booking-office desk how Jack's grey eyes would go a dangerous violet as he grew excited. She'd think of the dangerous violet in his eyes and look round haughtily in case anyone could detect the soft aura about her body.

Then would come a dark torment, a bitterness, over the waste of time. I'm glad he's gone. There's others, she'd think grimly. She'd look at the queue of Belfast young people in a line before her, chatting, as if they were in any city in the world, and she'd wonder, with malevolence, about their lives. What made them tick? She felt estranged from them, the arts lovers. She was growing away from herself and all the sad conspiracies of the beleaguered city. They said this happened. After a while in Belfast you grew tired. It happened. It was natural. All her fears were shed by the time she'd sit down to write to Jack. When the theatre door shut out the hostile night and the red exit lights glowed in the darkness of the theatre, she'd begin writing in her room above. And though with each letter she felt she was betraying herself, still the minute she started writing, all the arguments ceased. It was as if the act of writing itself negotiated a middle ground. All the ambiguities remained but had somehow softened. The writing down of certain words would strangely enough bring her across the void, as if they contained some power of healing. What she kept hidden, even from herself, poured out. She'd imagine him reading through what she had written. With words she began to seduce him, knowing that each word would travel back to its source in his head.

Of this she was certain. She had never any doubt that he would understand.

Her letters to him were extraordinary displays of trust and tenderness and enchantment. On the table in her small room at the top of the theatre, a bottle of wine opened, a record playing, and the company cat moving about her shins, she wrote effortlessly. She wrote of her day-to-day work, with marvellously destructive set pieces on the new plays that had come to town. On people who might get in her way. Her bitchiness would turn to quirky humour. She'd tell stories of her life. She would grow strident and acrimonious about the false world to which she was contributing. She'd blame him for deserting her. For leaving her stranded.

Then the words would grow laconic and lovely.

345

He'd stand reading her letter in a shelter off the pier at Killalla and feel blessed.

Catherine bought copies of theatre magazines and searched through them to find roles for women in plays in the Republic.

She applied to the Druid theatre in Galway. She had a copy of the *Western People* sent to her from Mayo, she had a copy of the *Sligo Champion* delivered, and in her room she would read through reports of law trials in Castlebar and Grange, sheep markets in Erris, visitations to Knock shrine, fair days in Belmullet, goat fairs in Foxford, and then lie down with a copy of a new script about life in Belfast, which she could not bring herself to read.

She'd wonder was it possible that she could live that sort of a life, out there on Mullet. She read of the neighbours arguing over land, sales in Penney's, *céilí* music in Tubbercurry, prayers for the dead, set-dancing workshops; and she thought: where do I fit into all of this? It was not only that all this had happened a long time ago in another dimension, that it was rural and unsophisticated. Not even that it was Catholic, with pages of newspapers given over to novenas and mindless prayers.

It was foreign, and at peace.

That was what alienated her most of all. And yet she persevered. The replies came. The Druid theatre had no room in its permanent company. The Hawkswell had no company at all. RTE's drama department was not taking on new actors. A number of replies came from various agencies. Then to her disbelief she was offered a part in an advertisement for lager. A note arrived asking her to attend a photo session. A few weeks later she found herself dressed as a cowgirl in a shack out in the Glens of Antrim. A pint of lager arrived on a tray held by a man on horseback. With the cheque for a thousand pounds she bought herself a dress, packed all she could carry into the Lada and left Belfast.

I thought I could never do this, she was saying to herself over and over, as she drove South. In Fermanagh she stopped off to see her mother.

"Stay here," said Maisie, "and continue on tomorrow."

"No," said Catherine. "If I stop now I'll never go on."

As she crossed the border at Blacklion she felt like a deserter, as her father, years before her, must have felt. All that journey west to Belmullet she thought of Jonathan Adams making this same trip away from a reality that must have been tormenting him. She drove through the night without stopping, down small roads that were littered with the corpses of badgers and rabbits, and just after Bellacorrick, a young fox. She stopped the car, got out and lifted the warm body over a white hedge of late may. The body was still warm. Mist was rising.

Catherine arrived that night at ten to the pier on Mullet only to find that the *Blue Cormorant* was working from further up the coast. Killalla they said. She called at Thady's and found the house empty and unlocked. When she opened the huge door of her home place the interior was stone-cold and damp even though it was a warm June evening. It felt strange and unlived in. She wandered the rooms trying to find a place from where she could begin tidying. She found old turf in a shed and a bucket half-filled with coal by Maisie the previous autumn. She lit a fire in the upper bedroom and sat with a blanket round her.

A gale was blowing sand around the peninsula when finally, at three, she climbed beneath sheets and eiderdowns warmed before the low flames. The bed was freezing. At dawn she drove across the isthmus and headed towards Killalla only to find that the *Blue Cormorant* had not docked there that night. She sat in the Lada outside the Bio-Energy clinic and wondered what to do.

A fisherman, who was bad on his feet, passed by.

"When do you think the *Blue Cormorant* might come in?" she asked.

"They could be dropping off their catch anywhere," he said. "There was talk of a great run up toward Sligo. You might try Rosses Point above in the County Sligo," he said, trying to be helpful.

She got into her car again, feeling both bemused and appalled by her circumstances, and drove towards Yeats' county.

She arrived at Rosses Point pier at noon. She was told to look out for a boat skippered by George Gillan, but except for a few small rowing boats there were no trawlers. When she asked around she was told that Gillan's mother lived in the village. She went to Gillan's shop and bought two bars of Bournville chocolate.

"George's been away two days," Mrs Gillan explained, "but he'll be in this evening at five."

"Was there another boat about?" asked Catherine, "called the *Blue Cormorant*?"

The lady couldn't say.

She told Catherine to sit there on the chair in the shop till she rang to see could George be contacted at sea. When she came back she had a cup of coffee for Catherine in her hand. "No," she said, "he knows nothing about the *Blue Cormorant*. The run, he said, is further North." The two women drank coffee and ate buns in the little shop. "It's a terrible life they have," Mrs Gillan said, "but they know nothing else."

Catherine strolled round Elsinore House where the Yeats brothers had been raised. The roof had fallen in and the walls were daubed with names, kisses and obscenities. She walked the first beach, and the second beach, and the third, till across the strand she could see the woods of Lissadell. A red moon rose early in the sky. A stray dog befriended her.

She stood again on the pier, and found that by now she knew every net and lobster pot. She walked down a newly laid scenic path that gave a view of Coney Island. The dog was with her still. Seagulls were perched on the head of the Iron Man, who looked strangely bisexual above the rising tide. When she came back to the pier she was embarrassed to find that the few men there had begun to recognize her.

"If the fish are running," she was told, "you won't see the trawlers back tonight."

She sat in the car and watched the pier. As small boats would arrive she'd get out and watch them tie up, but still there was no sign of the trawlers. She drove to Dead Man's Point and tried to pick out a boat making its way in from the sea. Returning, she cut the engine because she thought she heard the noise of another engine out at sea, but there was nothing. At eight the bay was dotted with the multicoloured sails of small yachts gliding in a perfect V towards the setting sun. And still the trawlers did not come.

The stillness, with Ben Bulben in the distance and Knocknaree across the bay, was unnerving. One by one the lights appeared in the houses in the village, then on the prom all the streetlights came on. But still the salmon boats did not appear. She went into a nearby pub and ordered a hot whiskey.

"It's beautiful here," she said to an old blue-eyed man who was stroking a blond labrador.

"You get used to it," he said.

A small while passed.

"W. B. Yeats lived here," she said.

"So did his mother," replied the old fellow. "God bless us." He looked her up and down. "And what are you doing here?"

"I'm trying to find a fisherman," she replied, "from Mayo."

"You'll have a hard job," he said, "I've never met one myself." He gave an insane peal of laughter without moving his lips, and wrapped the bar. "Service please," he yelled.

"I believe," said Catherine, "that the Spanish landed up the coast."

"We ate them," he replied. "And now they're killing all the rabbits. There's not one rabbit to be had." They drank. He looked at her for ages. "He'll not land here," he eventually said, "whoever told you that was not well."

"No?"

"No," he said emphatically.

"It'll be Killybegs," said the old fellow with relish, "before you'll have him in your arms."

Jack lay on his bunk, the pad resting on his chest and his eyes closed.

He had forgotten. Even as he had observed people he was forgetting their very essence. Except perhaps that there was always the possibility that somewhere in the future the naming might begin. But at that moment in time he doubted it. A face

349

returned perhaps, not a face but an expression, not an expression but perhaps a reading of that expression, not what was in the thing observed but in the observer.

The wrong thing named.

And suddenly he was swept by a terrible fear of years having gone by which were filled with wrong meanings. He had been wrong from the very beginning. He knew nothing of the world. It had passed him by. It had all happened in another room.

"Hi," said De Largey quietly.

"Yeah," said Jack.

"I think we're coming in."

They threw the boxes of salmon onto the pier. Then pushed them on a trolley towards the icehouse. He was surprised to find that the sea had ceased to move beneath him. Thady and Hugh went down to sleep. Himself and De Largey headed towards the nearest pub.

He tasted the pint of Guinness and held it to his mouth, then he took a long swallow. The minute he drank he thought of Catherine.

"You're enjoying that," said De Largey.

"I am," said Jack. The small, quiet euphoria inside him made him bless the nothingness. I have Catherine, he said to himself.

"What's it like above now?" asked De Largey.

"I don't know," said Jack, "what it was like before."

"It was all right, I suppose."

"You'd wonder why the war started if everything was hunky-dory back then."

"I didn't say it was hunky-dory," Theo corrected him.

"Ye are all given to reminiscence in Belfast," said Jack.

"Would you say so?"

"Yes, and of the worst kind."

"I see. Still and all," said De Largey, "something bad may happen to you and then you'll think everything was fine before that."

"Do you ever want to go back?"

He laughed quietly. "No, I don't want ever to go back," said De Largey, "even if I had the choice. Although, to tell you the truth, I went back once. I won't be so stupid the next time."

"I felt bad leaving Belfast, but then it was a relief as well."

De Largey stood as he often did, with his arms folded, taking the rock of the boat as something natural, something that was always underfoot. Even as he moved from the table to the bar it was the walk of a man used to a confined space that was constantly moving. He came back with the pints and put them down very carefully on the mats. His eyes were unflinching, sometimes looking very closely at the darkened window, sometimes looking very closely into Jack's eyes.

"What I reckon happens is a place moulds you," said De Largey. "You grow up knowing nothing else. And one day you wonder when did it all start." They drank. "You're probably guilt-tripping."

"Am I?" said Jack defensively.

"That's up to you," said De Largey. "Do you want to know about guilt-tripping?"

"Yes," said Jack. "It'll make a change from self-pity."

"I'll tell you about guilt-tripping." De Largey moved the glass in front of him to a new position. "It begins in jail."

29

Guilt-tripping

"That's why they have jails. Jail makes all the difference. Prison can break ye, or ye can break out of prison. It depends on your experience of prison and on your experience of family life. I'd a wain but I'd no family life. But when I went inside I started guilt-tripping. From day one I was hung up on my son.

"That's what happens.

"Ye'd expect that I'd be going over what I did to bring me there. It was nothing like that. I'd no guilt over being put away. In fact, I felt safe."

"I once asked a man about that," said Jack.

"And what did he tell ye?"

"He told me about propaganda."

"Propaganda's one thing. It fucks ye up. We've all had to live with that. No one wants it. But it's necessary. Propaganda's one thing. Shootin' someone is something else. They don't tell ye that. In a shootin' there's the passenger and there's the motivator. The passenger might do it easy – the actual shootin'. He's the one who can break in prison. But the motivator is the opposite of that.

"I suppose, that's what I was – a motivator.

"It doesn't matter who pulls the trigger. The deed starts way back, but the responsibility rests with all of ye. Ye cannot get away from that, but in a way there's no one person actually can say: 'I was the man.' Ye can see the actual event in your mind's eye, yes. But it's not the killin' that upsets ye. It's where it leaves your family if ye get caught. And ye could be away, say, seven or eight years. And the lack of a father at home starts ye guilt-tripping.

"When they write about politics they get thon aspect wrong.

In the papers they're always wrong about the domestic life. That's where it begins, and that's where it ends. Let no one tell ye different. The personal life. When ye're inside, your whole personal life assumes enormous proportions. Outside ye were committed. Your personal life didn't exist.

"Inside, all that activity has come to an end.

"So you start guilt-tripping. And the Brits know that. The easier they make it for you, the worse it becomes. You dream of your girlfriend or your woman and children all day long. And you have to offset that. That's why the military life in some way must continue. That's one thing. But something more important emerges. The spiritual life. In the blanket protest you had four to five hundred men cocooned in the one place. They had nothing but themselves, so they had to rely on spiritual strength. Out here there are so many distractions. See here, where I'm sitting, I can look out the window. I can go out and be a part of that – of what's outside. But inside you get to know the value – not of what's out there – but who's in there beside you.

"So demotivation can be compensated for by comradeship. I had trouble with that. I wanted to lie there and guilt-trip. But comradeship increases your beliefs. So the men alongside you become your family. This stops the guilt. And those men represent for you in a spiritual way what ideals you started with. When you started out you knew you might be killed but the date was uncertain. You hoped that your beliefs were in good hands. When you are inside you know – you realize for the first time – what you are fighting for, and you can start to understand in a different way, than before, how you might die.

"Bobby Sands knew he was going to die. The first day he refused food he was setting the date. He came round to thinking he would be the sacrifice. When it came to the turn of the rest they argued. It should have ended with him. Now they knew it was going to be a protracted process, a protracted struggle. I don't think any one of them knew they were going to die.

"And so we began to despair."

"Despair of what?"

"Dying in prison. No one wants to die in prison."

"Do you still despair?"

"I still despair. You begin to think the Brits won't back off. And the widows are left. You get sick of seeing the wrong people killed. Periodically something will spark off that self-doubt. That's how it begins. I met people like me when I was active and they were not. And they'd come to me and say: 'I'm not doing anything now.' They had to say that, because if they did anything in the past they thought when they looked at me: 'He's thinking that I've done nothing.'

"So they had to tell me all they'd done. You see, they were guilt-tripping.

"But when I jacked it in, I offered no apologies. The illusion is that if you disappear off the scene you will not have the strength to continue with your life. That your life will be wrecked afterwards. But look what happened to the Republicans after the Civil War – genuinely active men were released from the Curragh camp, and they went to the States. But it was not into oblivion. They are responsible for the Irish Revival over there.

"Soldiers everywhere wake up and find the war is over. They go back to their jobs. They've done terrible things, but it's over."

"What terrible things?"

"You make mistakes and you regret them. Worse still, soldiers carry out the mistakes other people make. And have to live with it. That's the hard part."

"And you?"

"My war is over. And I stayed on. I answer to no one and yet I keep a foot in with the Provos for some day I might need them. I don't blame the leadership – I've heard enough people doing that. I don't blame the organization. I've given my best. That's what's happened. I've given my best and I've nothing more to give. When you've seen active service it's hard to accommodate other things. That's why I go out on the boats. That's why I'm here with you.

"My struggle now is in 42 Duke Street, Ballina."

* * *

"My wife always played a more important role than me," said De Largey. "She had to make many decisions. Same as an RUC-man's wife. It's always a problem for them. So I owed it to her one day to check out. I had a decision to make. I could have jumped bail, but I didn't. I went through the trial. My sacrifice was going to prison. Then one day they left the back door open. I came south to Sligo in an old ice-cream van.

"I didn't know where I was. I was afraid to go out. I walked round the town of Sligo for four days then I went back to the room they'd got for me. I took an old armchair and placed it against the wall so that I could get the same angle on the sky that I was used to in prison. These guys would come round and they'd try to get me to go out to discos. I thought they were joking.

"I just wanted to stay in the room.

"Then one day I took the Belfast Express from Sligo. I told no one I was leaving, and when I came back no one knew I'd been away. I stepped out into Great Victoria Street from the bus station and for a minute I couldn't get my bearings. So I went straight to St Peters. I used to be an altar boy there."

"Why?"

"This happens. There's nothing you can do about it. You know it's stupid but you do it. It's a sort of a homesickness. For normality. I went to see my mother who had suffered a stroke. Then finally I saw my wife. I met my son. It must have been three years. And in the street where I used to live there was a carnival on. I couldn't believe it. There were five thousand people dancing to a reggae band off the Falls. It was unreal. I had dreamed of returning home there so often I couldn't believe what I saw.

"I contacted no one in the organization. They'd not have been very helpful. I was acting the idiot.

"I was two days in West Belfast and the whole time there was a carnival on. One minute there'd be this silence you can get in a city, the next the music would start up. I found it hard to relate to that – people dancing in the Falls till two or three in the morning.

"Then I went South again. I went back to my room. The

guys called but I couldn't stand their company. All they were looking for was diversion. Up to their eyes in diversion. I was driven demented. I couldn't even bear the box after a while. I had it up to here with the sexual problems of the plain people of Ireland. After a while I began to believe that Gay Byrne was getting a bit like Mr Magoo. One day I went to Dublin. I wanted to straighten things out. I'd arranged to meet someone in Parnell Street. And I imagined I saw a Brit on the street. I stepped into a shop and asked for a packet of fags though I don't smoke."

"How did that happen?"

"Whatever patterns the pedestrians were making on the pavement made me think the Brits were there.

"I stood in the shop unable to walk out until slowly it came back to me that I was in Dublin. That was when I heard the accent of the woman asking me was anything wrong. But still I wasn't sure. I was confused. So I stepped out, ready to make another sacrifice. That's how bad I was. I thought they had come to shoot me. But somehow I knew it was all right. The Brits just became the ordinary people of Dublin walking about doing their business. Then I knew I was finished. It was all over. But it was all right somehow. I started walking among them. By the time I reached the Shakespeare Bar in Parnell Street I must have travelled through my whole life.

" 'I know that I'm not going home,' I told the guy.

"He said I should take it easy, think about it a while longer. But I was adamant. So he said, OK.

" 'I know that I'm not going home,' I told him. 'So I want my family down.'

"Well he looked at me and he said nothing. He knew. So I organized bum passports. We arranged for flights to be booked in a new name they gave my wife and son and me. They had a duty to me. It was in their self-interest to protect their activists. So about a month later I'm standing at Dublin Airport with my wife and son. The De Largey family fly to Athens. De Largey, I liked the name. And we were happy. But at odd moments I was disturbed by the fact that this was not a normal holiday. It came down to that precisely – what was normal and what was not.

"And don't ask me what normal was or what normal is. I didn't want to go to the States. I didn't want to be sitting around gurning in some pub in Manhattan. We could have gone anywhere within reason, but we decided to live in Ireland. She wanted it and so did I. You see, I had been fighting for that. That I might live in Ireland. I knew where, too. In Mayo. Because when I took the name De Largey I began to read up on my roots. Who the fuck were the De Largeys? I wondered. They were a tribe that had been driven out of Mayo by the Cromwellians and taken by boat right round Ulster and forcibly settled in the Glens of Antrim.

"So why shouldn't a De Largey return to Mayo? It was only right. I was coming home.

"There you have it. We booted for Galway. And some months later Mayo. I liked Mayo. Through contacts I set myself up as a house-painter. One of the first jobs I got was painting the cop shop in Tuam. I painted the new government offices in Castlebar. I painted the library. And bit-by-bit time went by. The guys don't think of me and I don't think of them. But I keep in contact. It's in my interest.

"It's history now.

"The guys might see me on the street and they call across and that's it. They don't intrude. That's how I want it. And that's hopefully how it'll stay. I can handle that. But I could not handle the guilt-tripping."

De Largey lifted his pint.

"Once ye don't start guilt-tripping," he said, "you'll be all right."

Daley the skipper came lumbering over from the bar and laid his hand on Jack's shoulder. In his other hand he was holding by the stems three balloon glasses of brandy.

"Is it any harm to ask what you boys are talking about?"

"We're not talking about you anyway."

"That's good," said the skipper, "yous are two nice fellows, believe me. For animal lovers," he added ironically. The three men drank the brandies in silence. "It's all fast cars in Killybegs these days," said Daley after a while. "The boys up here have it made."

Just before closing time Catherine stepped into the bar. She ran across the room into Jack's arms. From the moment she saw him the involuntary happiness that flooded up into her being was impossible to control; it welled up in her like hysteria.

"Are you not introducing us to the lady?" asked Daley.

Catherine, very adroitly, took each of their hands, and then a few moments later, drained by the encounter, she let Jack go. Squeezed him and let him go. She began to speak of her journey. The men got up from the table to leave them together.

She looked at him coolly, judging his response to her sudden appearance and what she was about to say.

"I've come down to live with you," she said.

He startled her by laughing.

"C'mon, say something," she said embarrassed.

"That's great."

"Is that all you can say?"

They knocked up a bed-and-breakfast overlooking the midnight sea and an amusement arcade of expensive trawlers. The landlady seemed not to hear their apologies about the late hour, but led them, in her pink dressing gown and fur-lined booties, to a bedroom saturated with holy pictures, memoirs of Los Angeles and photos of the Niagara Falls. The minute she was gone, Catherine turned the Virgin of Sorrows and Christ in the Garden of Gethsemane to the wall.

"Who was that fellow in the bar?" she asked.

"The skipper?"

"No, the quiet one with the eyes."

"Oh, Theo?"

"Yes, Theo," she said. "He's from Belfast."

"Yes."

"And what's he doing here?"

"Fishing."

"He's dangerous," she said.

"You think so?"

"I do," she replied. "First you leave me with a British soldier lying asleep on a sofa in the house in Belfast, and now I come here to find you tagging along with a Provo."

"He's not a Provo."

"In fact, I think you might be getting out of your league. You don't discriminate."

"He's all right."

"No, he's not all right."

"You're paranoid."

"No," she answered severely. "I'm Protestant."

She slipped off her jeans, tights and knickers in one go and stood in a man's shirt before him in the centre of the room.

"Will you stand back from the window," whispered Jack.

"The only person that could be found out there at night looking in at women as they undress," she answered, "is you."

"Tell me all your dirty stories," asked Jack feverishly.

"They only make you sad, you know," she said, "and then you get these unexplainable white spots on your cheeks. It's not good for you." She held him to her shoulder. "If only you'd hold me and talk to me and kiss my breasts it would be enough."

He smelt of oil, sweat and fish. His face had a travelled, distant look as he lay beside her smoking.

"Did you go off with anyone?" he asked with a beating heart.

"Not consciously."

"What does that mean?"

"It means I didn't."

She cradled his fist in her hands. His breathing matched hers. But already their night together was over. He turned the religious pictures so that they faced into the room again. They descended the stairs in the dark house. On the coat stand he left £20. She walked with him down to the pier. In the darkness men were moving past the lights in the cabins. The radars were already turning, radios were spinning across various frequencies. Food was being passed down by hand. Gas canisters lowered.

No one talked.

The engines began to hum. Then started a deeper throb. The

engine coolers shot out jets of seawater. The pier bristled with light. And before she knew it, the *Blue Cormorant* was casting off its ropes. At the point where he was about to step down onto the boat she said: "Don't go."

"I have to."

"It was very beautiful last night," she said.

"It was," he said.

"When do I see you again?" she called.

"The weekend after next in Belmullet."

"What?"

"Belmullet!" he shouted over the roar of the engines. "In Belmullet!" he roared through cupped hands.

She stood grim-faced as black smoke worked its way through the dampers of the *Blue Cormorant*. The boat seemed to brace itself. The fishermen stood with averted eyes. Water pouring from its sides, the trawler pushed off, the tractor tyres were hauled in. The last thing she heard was Daley screaming something obscene.

30

Corrloch

When they arrived back from the sea, a taxi took Jack and all his belongings from Thady's. The Adams' house in Corrloch was empty. The door was unlocked. The remains of a breakfast were on the kitchen table. He lit fires in all the rooms, set out his work in Jonathan Adams' old study, hung his clothes in a wardrobe in her room, then sat by the kitchen table running the possibilities of certain phrases through his mind. It was here that he looked into a chaos that he had glimpsed before only during the worst hangovers.

He got up immediately and hoovered the rooms. He made her bed. Washed the dishes.

He relit the fire in her room and in the kitchen. The anticipation of her arrival made him giddy, as if he were standing on a great height feeling lightheaded from vertigo. He began to pack scattered turf into a stack at the gable of the house.

He took out the clippers and trimmed the hedge of oleria. Went indoors and stoked the fires. He sat down to dream. Later he took down two pairs of her black shoes from the low ledge in the kitchen and began polishing them. He lifted her clothes that were strewn in a corner of her room. He collected her intimate garments that lay under the bed, and carried them to the kitchen sink and washed them. He hung them out to dry in the Atlantic wind.

He listened, as evening fell, for the sound of her car. He stood outside and searched the peninsula for the sight of the headlights coming.

A furious wind was blowing. Streams, dancing over stones, had turned into torrents. Blue blackness was raging in the heavy, ominous sky. He walked between the low ditches on the white sandy road. Cattle appeared and looked at him as they stood seeking shelter behind the gable of a ruin. The bark of a dog flew by. He turned down an old lane that took him eventually within the spray from the ocean. A smell of burning turf blew past, and then a smell of dung, a handful of bitter salt; a call from a bird he couldn't place; and once a sort of overwhelming non-human presence raced across the dunes.

"I'm tipsy," she said as she came through the door. She kissed him and sat down.

Jack placed her dinner in front of her and she pushed it away.

"I had an audition for a film," she said.

She went out to the car and returned with a few bottles of Rioja. She poured out two glasses of wine.

"How did it go?"

"It was terrible. And I have to go back tomorrow."

"Where to?"

"A disgracefully luxurious house in Pontoon."

They sat in front of the fire silently watching nothing till Catherine suddenly said: "Do you think we should keep up this silly vow of fidelity?"

"It was you who asked me to keep it," he replied sharply.

"Well, I was thinking that we should be loyal without entering into some prehistoric oath," she continued. "We would just have to act responsibly."

"I don't think we are responsible people," said Jack. "You can drop it if you like, but I'm going to keep it."

"Oh, I don't intend to drop it if you don't."

"Neither of us," said Jack, "is strong enough to be able to be true to the other."

"Perhaps you are right," she said tactfully.

They drank till the bottles were gone. Then she stood by the table carefully picking bits of the dinner off the plate.

"Why do you cook bacon and cabbage?" she asked him.

"It's a traditional Irish dish," he replied.

"Not where I come from," she replied, "and certainly not steeped in grease."

"I like it like that."

"Well I don't like it."

"That's the way that it's done."

"It looks revolting."

"Fuck you, Catherine," he said.

The following night she did not come back at all. He phoned the producer's home.

"I would like to speak to Catherine Adams," said Jack to his secretary.

"Is she one of the actresses?"

"Yes."

"I think they are all finished for the day."

"Could you check?"

"Look, I'm certain they've all gone."

"She has not returned home."

"Oh."

"So will you please take a look for her?"

"I think not."

"What do you mean?"

"If Miss Adams is having an audition, I would not like to see her interrupted."

"It will only take a minute to tell her I've called."

"Could I have your name."

"Jack," he said. "Jack Ferris."

When Hugh called to collect him, he did not go. The boat left without him. He stalked the house all day. He tried to imagine who Catherine was with. He went through all manner of vivid recreations of her love-making with another. He loaded the fire with turf and stood at the window. He walked the road over and back through the dunes. He stood in a hollow down from the house and watched through the blowing sands for any oncoming traffic. Every car that appeared, he followed its path along the low peninsula. He watched the headlights coming up the road, and then sweeping by. No car went to the Adams' house. He felt like he might kill her now. He went in and filled a glass.

He walked around under the stars.

363

"God damn you," he said.

He was standing in a field across from the house at four in the morning when the Lada pulled in. He waited where he was, watching. She entered the house running. Jack watched the order in which the lights came on. First the kitchen, then the bathroom, and lastly her room.

He entered the house and stamped involuntarily into the bedroom.

"Where the hell were you?"

"I could ask you the same."

"I rang."

"I heard."

"I was demented."

"I was working till late. I could not get back." She sounded practical and at ease. "They've called me back for a third test in the morning." He said nothing. "The least you could do is congratulate me. They're even sending a car. If I get the third test the part is mine."

"Fucking great, Catherine."

"Jack, if you are going to act like that, I'd prefer if you slept elsewhere."

"You wicked bitch."

"I want to sleep now. And I'd like to remind you that this is my house, do you understand?"

"I understand perfectly."

He started in the bedroom. He moved his clothes into a heap on the floor, then he carried them out to the kitchen. He went back and switched off Catherine's light. Then he went into the study and collected his books. He piled them beside his clothes. Lastly he carried in his typewriter.

He sat down and took a drink. He tried to think of some coherent plan. He lay down on the sofa.

He became aware of her standing in her nightdress watching him.

"Don't go, Jack."

"I should never have come here," said Jack. "This is your house. It's madness, fucking madness."

364

"Please stay," she cried. "Don't leave me. I mean it."

He looked into the fire.

"Please come to bed."

"No." He stood up and faced her. They stayed like that, a long time, in silence.

"I had to stay overnight," said Catherine.

"Why didn't you come home?"

"I was drinking. I was too drunk to drive."

"Who were you drinking with?"

"Oh, just a couple of the crew."

"I thought you couldn't stand the crew. As far as you were concerned a few days ago they were all buffoons."

"I was seeking sympathy from them. The sympathy I can't get from you. At least they're civilized."

"Men or women?"

"A man and a woman, actually," she said guardedly. "They were very supportive."

"I know you were with someone," he said. "I always know. The other day you talk about breaking the vow you'd wanted me to keep. The night before last you don't come home. Now you're out till all hours. I know you were with someone," he said.

"I don't want to talk about it."

"That makes it even worse."

"Nothing happened, Jack. Nothing," she said, growing anxious. "I was only trifling with the implications of having an affair. I am proud of my fidelity to you."

"Did you fuck with him, whoever he was?"

"I was happy to feel that I was not open to a sexual invitation. A man asked me the other night to go to bed with him, but I did not."

"And the next night?"

"Last night I began to entertain a romantic notion of him. It's because of all this uncertainty. I wanted company. We had arranged to meet for drinks. We drank too much. I was trying to skim over the squalor of the situation by flirting with him. I told him I had sworn a vow of fidelity to you. He said that was very old-fashioned."

"Did he now!" he spat.

"He wanted me to go to bed with him. I said it would be on his terms, in that I would keep it a secret from you. Therefore I would only be using him."

"That would not come as something new to you."

"I can see no point in continuing this conversation!" Then she screamed: "And how about that bitch you were with?"

"Jesus Christ, you're not going to start that again."

"Start what!" she hissed. "Start what!"

"Keep your voice down," he said.

"Well then, stop interrogating me. I would have left," said Catherine, "but I couldn't drive back drunk. So I fell asleep there on a mattress on the floor. It was as simple as that. He went to his bed and I fell asleep in mine."

"Yes?"

"Do you have to know?"

"Yes."

"I fell asleep on the floor," said Catherine, "and woke to find him moving against me. We started moving, then we stopped."

"Did you come?" he said in a dry, even voice.

"Stop interrogating me, Jack."

"Did you come with him?"

"Stop it," she called.

She hit him. He kept his face exactly where it was and she hit him again. Then all of a sudden he bounced his forehead lightly off hers. It happened so suddenly that for a moment she did not respond. Then she opened her mouth to scream. He put his hand tightly over her mouth till the scream passed. Her eyes widened in terror. Then the terror passed. Jack went outside and sat on the step of the house. She opened the door and stood behind him.

She said: "There were no orgasms. Nobody came, I swear that. I told him I loved you. That we had made a vow."

She started to move towards him, crying. "You've asked me," she said, "and I've been honest. I've told you everything."

"I need to get out of here," said Jack. "I need to walk."

"Can I go with you?" she asked timidly.

*   *   *

A fog had settled on the shore.

The sea was thunderous. They walked out along the pier. Midway it became dangerous to go any further because the sea every few seconds was breaking across it. They stood watching the seas meeting. Then Jack suddenly, during a lull in the mountainous waves, ran to the far side. He called to her to follow him. But she couldn't hear him. He waved her over. *Come on! Come on!* But she was too afraid to follow him. So he ran back to her. He took her arm. Count three, he said. The waves leapt the pier again. No, she screamed. Then he pulled her across with him. They continued on to the end of the wet pier with the sea breaking behind them, and each side of them. She slipped and fell. Roughly, he picked her up. She held on to him. They could not see anything. The mist was intense and moist. They stood holding the bollards at the farthest point of the pier while the wind tore at them.

She put her hand under his jacket and held him.

"We must stop drinking," she cried to him. "Every time we drink something awful happens."

"I am afraid that if we really start fighting one or other of us could get killed," he shouted.

"No," she shouted, "we'd never go that far."

"It happens."

"No," she shouted. "Something would stop us. Something always does."

"I can't take any more arguments."

"You can fight dirty when you want to."

"I should leave," he roared, "this is all wrong. Something awful might happen."

"Nothing will," said Catherine and she hugged him. "It's over now Jack. We're all right."

They found that the interval between the waves washing the pier had lessened. There hardly seemed time to get through.

"We're stuck," she screamed.

He counted the washes. Then suddenly she ran ahead of him. He followed her. They walked together through the dense fog, taking their steps carefully, hand in hand. The fog stuck to them. Their coats and hair were white.

When they arrived back from the shore they were wearing white coats of mist.

They lit the fire and started drinking again.

"I'm heartbroken," he said.

He started to go rigid. Then he left her there. He fell asleep in the study. Hours later Catherine suddenly appeared like a spectre in the room.

"You bastard," she whispered into his ear.

Jack woke bewildered.

He followed her back out. She had finished all the drink and was sitting by the burnt-out fire. A bruise had risen on her forehead.

"Do you see what you did to me?" she shouted.

"I'm sorry," he said.

"You are a drunk," she said quietly, "do you know that? You are a fucking alcoholic." He returned to the study.

Outside a pig blew on a Venezuelan pipe then, more obscenely, a fight broke out among Joe Love's pigs. He listened to her moving to and fro. Hours seemed to pass. He stared straight ahead at the upside-down trees and flowers on the wallpaper. He heard the clash of Delft. Of running taps.

"Please, Jack, I'm going crazy," she whispered through the door. "Please come and sleep with me."

"Are you going to start shouting again?"

"No, I swear it."

He got up and walked alongside her to her room. Her eyes were fearful. They lay in bed.

He looked at her face. She had wiped some talcum across the bruise. The whites of her eyes were painfully white. She had red lipstick on.

"It was my fault," she whispered softly.

"Oh Christ, Catherine," he said.

They woke at seven. The driver of the car from Pontoon was pounding on the door.

Catherine said: "I can't go in, looking like this."

"The taxi is waiting."

"I feel terrible," she said, "I could not bear to face them."

"What do you want me to do?"

"Let's just stay here. Don't let's go anywhere today."

"What will I tell him?"

"Tell them I'm sick. Send him away. Tell him something. Tell him anything."

Outside the horn blew.

"Oh Jesus, Jack, send him away."

He went and told the driver that Catherine was unable to accompany him.

"Why?"

"She's not well."

"Well she could have rung," he said, "and saved me the goddamn journey." And he reversed and drove away.

"What did he say?" she asked.

He told her.

"Oh God," she said, "I've fucked everything up, haven't I?" She started to laugh. The talcum fell away.

31

The Cuckoo Mocks
the Corncrake

"Get in beside me," she said.

He lay beside her and then when he thought she had fallen asleep again he climbed out of bed and dressed.

"Where are you going?" she asked.

"I've got some business to do."

"Leave it for a while."

"No. I must start.'

He made his way to the table in the study. Later he heard her downstairs moving around. She was whistling.

"You sound happy," he shouted down.

"Yes," she said.

He felt extraordinary relief to hear her singing. She knelt in the garden and wearing Maisie's gardening gloves she began weeding the flowerbeds. The warm winds of July came soothingly over the Atlantic. Hugh arrived at noon. "We're only going out for a few hours," Jack called to her. "OK," she said.

At four o'clock next morning she suddenly started up in the bed fully awake. A ghost she couldn't name was backing off into the corner of the room. She heard him throwing his oilskins aside. She waited and reached out to see if he was there. Jack Ferris, on his back, smoking in the dark. A stranger.

Jack and Catherine lay together in a kind of stupor. When they stepped out, the pale sun was huge on the Atlantic. Closer inland a grey haze enveloped everything. Ravens tossed themselves over the sea. A starling flew up from under a heap of car batteries that sat on the galvanize roof of a shed. Down below, the seaweed was ticking away in the fog. A coot was dabbing along on a small stream that ran down to the sea. Then came a shot. The coot gave a squawk of fear, and without once looking back at the young who were following her, nor her mate who was following her, she dived.

"I had a bad dream," she said.

"What?"

She closed her arms about him.

"It's lovely to feel you here," she said.

"I think there is something wrong with me," said Jack.

He sat up terrified. She found he was soaking. She towelled him down. But the band of burnished heat round his temple would not shift.

"It must have been your sweat I was wading through," she said, "in the dream I had."

Light-headed, she washed his face. The next time she woke he wasn't there. She found him naked on his knees in the bathroom with his forehead placed against the cold tiles on the wall.

"Jack – what are you doing?"

"I'm trying to cool myself down."

She knelt beside him.

"Don't touch me," said Jack.

"No, I won't touch you," she said.

"You promise me?"

"I promise you."

"That's all right then. You can stay there."

"Now you will have to look after me," she said.

"Don't leave me alone in the house," she said. "I dread being alone here these days."

"Why has no one come to visit us?" she'd ask. "The only people we see are fishermen."

"They have their own problems."

"We've driven people away with our arguing," declared Catherine.

"We've made mistakes," agreed Jack.

"We are everything I used hate to see in other couples." She

371

sought out his eye. "Can you imagine a time when we might not be together?"

He thought a while.

"No."

"And yet we should consider it."

"I can't."

"I never realized how vulnerable we were," then she added, "sexually."

Everything was touched by a new grave hysteria. They talked of the possibilities of going sober, of remaining together all their natural lives.

"In Mayo?" asked Catherine.

"Why not?" he replied.

"I'll have to think about it," she said, half indignant, and half joking. "I'm lonely enough as it is. It makes me desperate to think of spending my whole life here."

"Won't I be with you?" he said.

"Will you?" she said.

She heard the key turn in the door and someone came running up the stairs. Sara rushed into her room.

"My God, Cathy," she said, "What happened to your face?"

"I walked into a door."

"You did not."

"I did," said Catherine and she laughed.

When they came down stairs, Sara filled the fridge with parcels of food she'd brought.

"You look terrible," said Sara. "Where's your friend?"

"He's out at sea."

"Did you go to see a doctor?"

"No."

"You could have blinded yourself."

"I'm fine, Sara, it looked worse a few days ago."

Sara had bloomed, and yet she had become strangely diffident. Only in short rushes would she speak, and deliberately avoided all conversation about her recent fame. Her voice when she did speak had taken on a new fluent actorly inflexion.

"Let's go out for a walk."

"I can't."

"Tie a scarf over your forehead," Sara said. "It reminds me of the time you went bald."

Everywhere they went on Mullet people would stop and gather and stare at Sara.

"Are you Bridie from *Glenroe*?" people asked, and when she said she was they were astounded to find her there, walking a beach in a remote part of the west of Ireland.

"I told you it was her," one lady said to her husband. "He said you couldn't be, but I said you were Bridie. Isn't that so?"

Sheepishly, the husband nodded.

"I think you do us great credit," said the woman. "You are the most beautiful looking woman on the television. Isn't she?"

Again the husband nodded.

Sara signed autographs. She stepped into photographs, and herself and Catherine posed for a group of shark fishermen before a sheer fall into the sea at Eachleim.

"Imagine! Bridie Smith here," said one local girl when they went into O'Malley's for a drink. "Imagine that." And she stared at Sara, and shook her head and put out a finger and touched her. "God help you, but they're giving you a dreadful time in *Glenroe*," she said and clasped her thighs, and delighted by the thought of how fiction removes the pain, she shook with laughter and said: "But you're well fit for them."

"So you missed a part in a film, did you?" said Sara, who had her hair cut in a severe parting. She rested her elbow on a wooden ledge to the right of Catherine's arm.

"Yes."

She looked into Sara's eyes seeking there some sympathy, but all she found was ironic detachment.

"You should leave him."

"As a matter of fact I respect what he's doing."

"Oh you do, do you?"

A pale streak of light cut across Sara's cheeks. Her eyes were self-absorbed, and full of feminine contempt, except when periodically they reflected the glitter of the overhead lights. With a new and childish widening of the pupil, Sara delicately looked round the crowded lounge.

"You could have been more discreet," she whispered in a tantalizing way.

"I really didn't want to be disloyal to him."

"None of us do, Cathy."

Catherine did not answer. She reached for her bag, lit a cigarette and held it far from her with her left hand. The heel of her palm pressed against the table. She studied the cigarette as she blew smoke purposefully from her nose. Lights along the wall came on. Sara spoke, and again Catherine noticed the disturbing actorly lilt. Catherine waited for the words to make sense, but they didn't, and while she tried to focus on their meaning other words came too soon for her to follow. She got up and went to the toilet. When she got back Sara had another round of drinks on the table and had gone into a provocative silence.

"We had a few pleasant weeks being sober," said Catherine.

"People who can't hold their drink," said Sara, looking ahead of her, "are a bore."

"I," said Catherine, "am worse than him."

Said Sara distastefully: "Do you seriously think he is ever going to write anything worthwhile?"

"I do."

"Well, you left one job to follow him. You don't want to lose another."

"I don't know what to do."

"Catherine," said Sara calmly, "is he beating you?"

"As a matter of fact we are rarely violent, if ever at all"

"You are being defensive."

"Sad to relate – I'm being honest." Catherine crushed out her cigarette. "You think he did this to me?" and she lowered the black glasses.

"Yes, I do."

"Well, he didn't," and she replaced them.

There was silence a while.

"You," said Sara, "were the one who called herself a feminist. Look at yourself now. Take a good look at yourself, Catherine."

"Did you ever make love to him?" Catherine suddenly asked. Despite herself, her voice wavered and broke into a comical hiss.

"After all these years, now you ask me!"

"Well, did you?"

"I would not call it that," said Sara briskly.

"He has always denied it."

"Has he now?"

"Yes," she said and her heart beat wildly.

"It was not very enjoyable," said Sara. "Trawlers are not romantic places in reality."

"I see. On a trawler, was it?"

"I was only joking. No, we never did."

"Sara! You've just put me through hell."

"You want to get a hold of yourself."

"Are we allowed get drunk?"

"I don't see why not," said Sara. Catherine watched her sister walk through the tables. The men shouted out greetings. At the far end of the lounge the barman turned up his transistor. Joe Dolan began singing "A Westmeath Bachelor", followed by John Lennon singing "Imagine". Then came the news. She got up and rang the house.

"Jack," she said, "come down and join us. Sara is here. I need to see you. OK . . . OK, bring them all down."

Jack, De Largey, Thady and Hugh arrived together.

"Sara," said Jack.

"Jack," she said coolly.

"This is Theo. And Hugh. And my Uncle Thady."

"Delighted," Sara said. "So you are all fishermen?"

"I was until this evening," replied Hugh.

"Hugh's got himself a job in the Erris Hotel," explained Jack. "His fishing days are over."

"Jack," asked Catherine, "can I get you a drink?"

Jack and Catherine walked to the bar together.

"I like the scarf," he said.

"I told her I walked into a door."

He nodded.

"I have never felt so ashamed in my life," he said.

"It's not your fault. It's mine."

"We'll have a few weeks together now. The salmon season is finished."

She kissed his cheek. They rejoined the others. White sunlight was streaming into the lounge and as the sun set a *céilí* band started playing.

"Have we to listen to this?" asked Sara.

"You don't like the music?" asked Theo.

"Not particularly."

Thady spat generously on the floor.

"And how is Catherine?" he asked cheerfully.

"I'm fine, Thady."

"The rain came anyway," he said.

"It came," said Hugh, "it came just in time."

"Did any of you hear the cuckoo this year?" wondered Jack.

"I did," replied Hugh, "and I heard the corncrake."

"And how could you hear the corncrake?" asked Thady. "The corncrake is leaving the Mullet. If he has not already gone."

"Well I heard the corncrake."

"I am disposed towards the corncrake," said Catherine.

"Sure the corncrake is the cuckoo when he's grown old. Isn't that right, Jack?"

"He's the cuckoo with a beard," laughed Catherine, "and there's lots of them about."

"Is this conversation some kind of private ritual or what?" asked Sara.

"Will we go somewhere else?" asked Jack. "What would you like Catherine?"

"I'd like," said Catherine, "to get married and have children."

"Are you listening to that?" smiled Sara.

"I'm listening," he said.

"There's a lot to be said for it," agreed Hugh.

Next morning Sara was leaving. He carried her bags to the car.

"You take good care of our Catherine," Sara said to Jack.

"I will," he said.

As the car pulled away Catherine said: "I can't tell you how envious I am of her. She has everything."

He worked all morning above in the study then brought the text down for her to read.

"When casting for the play takes place," he said, "you should go for the main female role."

"I couldn't," she said.

"Yes, you could."

"I'm too distraught."

"It's months away yet."

"I have other things to think of at present."

"I know."

"Sara thinks I should leave you. She said you were bad for me. But I told her we were bad for each other and that's what made it so enjoyable." She smiled. "Are you sure you want me to appear in a play of yours?"

"It was written for you."

"That doesn't mean I could do it. I don't even know if I approve of this woman you want me to play." She lit a cigarette. "And what would happen if your Eddie person didn't cast me?"

"Of course he will."

"I couldn't bear the disappointment after all that's happened."

"You'll get it."

"If I get it, it would have to be on merit. The difference between you and me is that you don't give a fuck what people think of you but I care what people think of me."

"But you'll go for it?" he asked delighted.

"Yes, I suppose so."

"I'll ring him." He leapt up from the table. "That's great. I'll ring him and tell him."

On the road to Belmullet he met a goat. A black-and-white goat with a long gentlemanly snout started to follow him when he reached the Church of the Holy Family. When he'd stop, the goat would stop. When he went on, the goat would go on. He stopped, the goat looked at him like a shepherd dog. He started forward again, and the goat followed him. "Go long," he shouted, but the goat just moved his yellow shining eyes

377

and stood watching him from the far side of the road. Jack lit a cigarette and dropped his matches. When he went to pick them up, the goat ran off, afraid that the man was about to hurl a stone at him.

"So someone has been ill-treating you, have they?" he said to the goat.

He leaned down again. The goat moved further away and watched him. He reached down one more time and the goat jumped backward.

"Go home!" shouted Jack.

And then as he walked off and the goat stopped where he was, Jack was sorry to lose him. He reached Belmullet town and went into the Erris Hotel and rang Eddie. There were two lassies dressed identically lying alongside a piano, face down, counting dice. Mrs Moloney shouted: "Nessie come here," but the girls didn't move.

"Hallo," they said.

"Hallo, Nessie," called Jack. "Hallo, Trish."

"We saw you with Bridie from *Glenroe*," said Trish, hanging upside down.

"Did you now?"

"Why isn't she with you today?"

"She's gone home."

A man who worked as a gardener at various places on the mainland and on the peninsula was sitting alone drinking pints of Guinness. Hugh was preparing that evening's dinner in a room off the bar. Jack could see him piping meringues onto tinfoil on a tray. The two men were talking to each other about race horses and severed limbs and *The Late Late Show*.

"Give us a brandy, Hugh," called Jack.

"Jazus, Jack," Hugh shouted. "How is life on the mainland? Wait till you hear this job that I've got here." And he brought out from the kitchen a two-wave radio, shot the aerial into the air, pressed a button and spoke to the *Blue Cormorant*. "Ye poor bastard," said Hugh. "Over."

"Did you ever feel the whole thing was a waste of time?" Jack asked in an attempt to ingratiate himself with the gardener.

"If I ever felt like that, I'd change my drink," the man laughed, and inside the other room Hugh laughed.

"I'll have a brandy," said Jack. "and give this man whatever he's having."

"No, thank you," said the gardener, "I'll stop by myself."

"I've just had some good news," announced Jack.

"Is that a fact?" replied the gardener, laughing ironically again. "You wouldn't think it to look at you."

"If that's the case," replied Jack, "it must have been a long time since you heard anything worthwhile."

He brought the corrected pages of the text into a building society office in Belmullet where the woman was editing the disc that contained the play. He gave her the corrected manuscript, let himself out onto the street and walked round the town. I'm raving, he thought. He tried to keep from entering a pub so that his head might be clear if there was any further work to be done. He could not wait to see the text. Each time he called back she was still working on the various corrections. He looked over her head at the computer and saw with relief whole pages being erased. Nights and days of work were disappearing. Characters, lines and moments went off the screen like magic. This gave him a crazy sense of satisfaction.

He would like to have leaned in and pressed the erase button so that the entire play would be wiped from the memory. That would have been the business! Leave nothing, nothing at all!

He watched enthralled as the voices of people he had invented sped by like trains into the night. One press of the button and another whinge disappeared into the void.

32

A Time of Big Seas

The first time it happened Jack was sitting in the council offices that acted as a court house and library. He had been in there sorting through old mariners' maps and local history books. Then he sat back to smoke a cigarette. The window looked out onto a yard with a street beyond. He looked up and let his mind idle. He was thinking of something utterly banal, something nonsensical.

A man walked up and down the street, then another. Their forms passed the window. And though Jack could not make them out he knew they were familiars, they were human beings, he could taste the life-breath of them.

It was early afternoon and over the top of the curtain he could make out a hard blue sky. He was thinking in another language. The eerie language of the half-formed and the unsay-able. He looked round the bare wainscotted walls, feeling with his eyes how the light fell. Then the room seemed to jerk forward in time. All peripheral vision was suddenly obliterated, what he could see was fixed remotely at the end of a long high corridor. He was afraid to look back towards the window lest he might find there evidence of this sudden passage towards evening. That night had mysteriously fallen. But as he looked at the shadowy perpendicular frames of the distant wood-panelling his panic grew. He felt his mouth fall. He was being swept along an indeterminable passage and could not stop himself.

"Oh, God," he said. He gripped the chair so that he might ease the nausea in his throat. Then, slowly, he tried to loosen his grip on the armrests. He could hear each of his breaths distinctly, and as the interval between each seemed to grow, he listened intently in the pauses for the sound of his heart turning round.

He looked up to find the same blue over the curtains, to find that nothing had changed. The same blue was over the curtains, some persons – ordinary, particular – passed again, and his breathing returned to normal.

When he returned to himself it was like it had never happened. What had occurred was something without form or shape. Any words he could conjure up were inadequate to deal with this sudden loss of time and perspective.

It seemed to him, just then, that every person knew this, this loss of self, but it could not be told. It was an opening onto a non-world. He left down the book that was in his hand with extreme care. That, because of the unreality, was necessary. If he did anything too quickly he feared the reverberations that might follow. Yet it was important that he escape. He got into the Lada and sat a moment with the steering wheel in his hands. He was not sure whether he could any longer drive a car. Then he switched the engine on. He drove very slowly to a beach, fearing that any moment his sense of what lay to his left and right would suddenly be removed. He stopped the car on a bed of gravel, and with relief headed towards the breaking surf. There was another walker abroad. Jack fell into step with him. He was wearing a duffle coat and a shirt open to his waist and carried a black refuse sack. He had a genial raving eye, with smiling ducts and generous looks about him that ended in private and imbecilic tittering.

"Are you all right?" asked Jack.

The man stopped to consider the question.

"I suppose I am. I'm getting older"

Now the man was, as many before him were, a stooped creature with a broken wing. Balanced on a stick he dodged through the sands. A young girl in an oilskin coat approached them. Jack saw a seal. He shouted to the young girl who was standing looking out at the Atlantic.

"Look," he shouted, "at the seal."

The girl followed his outstretched arm.

"The seal! The seal!" shouted Jack.

She looked out, but by then the seal had gone. She looked back at Jack and ran away.

"I fear," said the old fellow, "that she thought you were shouting: 'Look at the sea! Look at the sea!' "

"Oh," said Jack.

The two men walked on.

"It'll break before it gets any better."

"Are you expecting a storm?" asked Jack in a neighbourly way.

The man stopped and swung his arm in a curve. "I carted this beach most of my youth. Do you see the stones? There were no stones." He moved on. "There were no stones then. Only sand. We took away layers of sand for building purposes. That's how the stones got there. That's stopped now. The authorities put a stop to that."

He halted. His black shoes sank into the sand.

"Only for I was pensioned off I wouldn't be here. They don't want you here. It's the Famine mentality. If you are feeling bad they'd make you feel worse. In these parts the cuckoo mocks the corncrake." He spat. "Once you start thinking for yourself there's something wrong with you."

"Where were you?"

"Down Clydebank for twenty-five years. I'd prefer to be there now. I should be in Scotland. Scotland has the best health service in the world. If you fall sick you'd get the same treatment as Prince Charlie. I know no one here now. But they know me." He spat to the left. The wind blew across his bare red chest. "Neighbours of the presumptuous propensities!" He spat again to the left. "But I don't know them."

The old fellow laughed. Some specks of wet sand had blown about his trouser legs. He studied them with the tip of his stick. He laughed again and slung the bag on his back.

They took leave of each other in a slow fashion: waving and looking back and going on again.

A few minutes later, as Jack was crossing the field behind the beach, it happened a second time. Just when he had forgotten, the same mental gap opened again. But this time the wrench was longer and more frightening, for now all natural things – grass, birdsong and sea air – were becoming objects of horror. He went back to the beach and lay down on his back. His heart was beating furiously. It began to drizzle. Then followed a series of highs and lows – he would feel exhilarated to be a part of the world, then would come the low pitiful sound of his own breathing.

The walk to the car which was only a few hundred yards away seemed like miles. His wrists became itchy. He rubbed them fiercely. A knuckle on his spine started to throb. He started the car. Every mile or so it cut out. The people he saw on the road home he imagined nude, squatting over a bowl to shit. This is normal, he said, there is nothing wrong in seeing that. It happens. He saw them again and again, people sitting upright with innocent looks while under them their waste accumulated. He drove fiercely by them in the Russian car.

"I'm losing my senses," said Jack.

"Are you all right?"

"Lie beside me," he whispered, "I don't feel well."

But even as she lay beside him, he could not bring himself to touch her.

She had broken their love-vow. With terrible regret he felt the love-feeling leave his body and return deadened. If a hair of her head touched his ear, it felt like electricity. He tied back his hair with a ribbon of Catherine's and listened to her aggrieved, disturbing breathing.

"Do you mind if I ask you something?" she said.

He did not reply.

"Will you be there when rehearsals start? If you are there, I'll be too self-conscious."

"I don't know."

"You see, it's painful for me reading these lines."

"Catherine, I just don't want to talk about it right now. Just leave it for now, all right?"

She pulled away. Don't move, he thought. Just stay perfectly still. Don't move, Catherine.

* * *

She caught him on the hill. She flung her arms around him.

"I'm sorry about everything," she said. "Please forgive me."

In the spitting rain they turned back to the house. She would not let him go. He was in a cold sweat. He sat on the step of the house and looked at the mountains on Achill Island and wondered: Where does it reside – the will to go on? They walked towards Scotchport. The sun pooled on a cluster of whins. Seagulls changed to ravenous crows. A seal, with a porter face, surfaced for a look around the bay. Fish jumped in ecstasy. The seawater glimmered like saved hay. And he was sorry that he had made Catherine's simple needs into fantastic demands.

"Take a taste of this," he said, picking some wild leaves. They both walked on chewing .

"My God," shouted Catherine, "is this stuff poisonous?"

Suddenly he realized that his mouth was red hot. They stopped and started spitting furiously.

"I thought," he said, "they would taste of lemon."

"Sometimes, you know," she said, "I despair of you."

It was a time of big seas.

At night they spoke of Scotland in the bar.

He did not, on wakening, put out a hand to touch her.

Through his mind raced all the bad things. The light of the morning reached into the room full of a wicked shining truth. They were bodies in a pure stupor. If she touched him, he would freeze. For he felt his body to be shamelessly packed with sweat, urine and excrement. Catherine sat up, gripped her knees and looked towards the window. Then she looked at him a second. He wanted to disappear and come back in another shape to please her. But she misunderstood this fear and self-loathing. She leaned over, nevertheless, and kissed him. But then turned tetchy at his lack of response.

She got out of bed, went to the toilet, then sat looking out of her window. Eventually she went about her business of half-dressing.

She began to test him, seeing how far she could go saying wild things, then wilder things, things that once used to unsettle him, make him dizzy. In her melancholia she looked dated and a little odd. She talked indecently of all his friends, and her lovers, and the village folk. He, not to be outdone, continued the same comical, slanderous talk. His hands joined between his knees like an embarrassed schoolboy, he told her that he often took her erotic asides as somehow a slight on himself.

"Can we go somewhere together for a holiday – somewhere foreign?" she asked.

"Like where?"

"Anywhere. Majorca. Cyprus – places where normal people go on holidays."

"You really want to go?"

"It will be good for us. Cheap wine, swimming, sunshine and no wind."

"OK," he said.

"But where?" she asked.

"Some place" said Jack, "with a bar."

"Can we afford it?"

"I'll have a few bob from the fishing. And there'll be an advance."

The next day she booked them into Majorca through a travel agency that was based in a draper's shop on the Moy.

The night before they were to leave they walked up the town of Castlebar. While she went shopping he sat in the car. She stepped out of a boutique holding a new dress before her for his opinion. He nodded. She leaned out of a shop with a scarf round her head.

As she walked happily up the street towards him holding her new clothes he was overcome with sentiment. She kissed his eyes. In a bar in Crossmolina they had their first drink in a few days. She put her arm over his shoulders.

"I'd love it," she said, "if we were always as happy as we are now."

"We will be," he said.

She stood. "I'll go and get some groceries. It'll only take a few minutes."

"Meet me here", he said, ordering another pint.

"Stay sober for me," she said and kissed him. "I can't wait to get home."

"Please be here," she said.

Half an hour passed, then an hour. He stood at the door and looked up and down the street, but she could not be seen. He walked the town, returned and sat there in the empty bar. The panic attack came again. She had deserted him. He was overcome with nausea. He tried to see himself reaching the bar but felt it was an impossible task. Though he was going forwards some irreversible backward pull was gaining on him. His body felt like a worm, bloated below the neck. He heard the hard snip of an insect buzzing round his ear. He tried to detect the insect but just as he thought he had trapped the sound it began somewhere else. He scratched his wrists. He followed the hopper for ages because its sound felt like a stitch in the heart.

He sat on drinking by himself waiting for her to appear. The waiting seemed to go forever. His thoughts seemed loud as screams. Then he went to the other end of the town and found her sitting drinking in the small hotel with men he didn't know.

"I've been waiting for you," he hissed.

"Oh God," she said, "I forgot all about the time."

"I've been waiting for hours."

"I got held up here."

"You got held up drinking. Why didn't you just lift the phone and ring?" he persisted angrily.

"I didn't think of it."

"Who is this?" asked one of the men.

"This," said Catherine biting her lip, "is my friend."

"Oh." He looked at Jack and smiled sarcastically. "So this is him."

"Who is this bollacks?" asked Jack.

"Could you leave her alone?" said the man.

"Jack, this is the director of that film. Peter. I was just explaining to him what happened to me."

"C'mon, let's go," muttered Jack.

"In a minute," said Catherine with charm, "this is the man who wrote the play I told you about."

"Congratulations," Peter said.

She introduced him to the others. Which one of them is the fucker? he thought.

"Can we go?" he asked her again.

"Jack, please!"

"This is the exact moment," he said, "when we should be elsewhere."

"In a few minutes, all right?"

"I'll have a brandy," he demanded, and sat apart from them.

He watched her, talking, laughing, being coy, enjoying herself. He tried to catch her eye but she deliberately avoided him. She came back with a third brandy and set it on the table in front of him, and was about to move away when he grabbed her hand.

"Let's get away from here," he pleaded with her.

"I'd rather stay for a while," she said. "Just give me a little longer."

"Suit yourself," he said.

"If you want to go, why don't you go on?"

He did not reply.

"Look, if it's going to be a problem I'll go now."

"Suit yourself," he shouted.

"Hi, pal! There's no call for that."

"Look," decided Catherine, stepping down gracefully off the stool, "I'd better go with him. I have an early start tomorrow anyway."

"Enjoy your holiday, Catherine," the director said.

"Thank you," she said, giggling nervously.

"Jonathan," a woman cried, "don't be running."

"Some day," Jack said, "I'll see the funny side of this."

The minute they were outside the hotel Catherine suddenly ran away from him. He ran after her. Then he stopped. He went back to the bar of the hotel. The men deliberately tried to avoid him when he appeared. They looked behind him at the swinging door, waiting for Catherine's return. Then, astonished and uncomfortable, they threw him wary glances as they tried to turn back to their conversation. He stood unconcerned, silently drinking beside them, as if they were not there.

Looking away they talked knowingly of the film world. They joked disparagingly about famous actors. Just then, Catherine returned. She was so shocked to see Jack still there that she stood uncertain for a moment with the door ajar. He smiled across at her. "Catherine," called one of the men but, abashed, she closed the door. Jack ordered another pint. He began a loud conversation about the nature of the salmon's radar system with the barman.

Then, from out of nowhere, Hugh appeared.

"Is that you, Jack?" he said.

"Can I have a lift home with you?"

"Sure thing. Can I get you something to drink?"

"I'll have a brandy."

Hugh came back with a brandy and crème-de-menthe for Jack and an orange for himself. He waited a few moments and said: "How are things?"

"So-so."

"Well, just remember you are not alone."

"I'll remember that."

They drove back through the black night. He fell asleep in the front of the car and swayed gently in the safety belt. At Corrloch Hugh woke him.

He got out and rapped the top of the car.

"Here," said Hugh, and he handed him Catherine's shopping bags. "Will you be all right?"

"Yes, I will. Thanks."

He sat by the light of a fire he lit in the kitchen. Sometime later two cars pulled up outside. "There's no one here, thankfully," he heard Catherine say as she entered the house. Then she saw the fire. She stood a moment on the threshold in the dark. She switched on the light.

"I thought as much," she said.

Two of the men were with her. They put their takeaways on the table.

"I've brought some friends home," she said.

"I can see that."

"If you are going to start an argument I'd be grateful if you'd leave us alone."

"Why certainly," said Jack, imitating Stan Laurel. And he stood and tickled the scalp of his head with a bunch of fingers.

"Do you want a can?" asked one of the men contritely.

"No, thank you," said Jack.

He climbed to the study. In a little while he heard Van Morrison singing. The next time he woke there were voices laughing.

"Fuck off!" he screamed down the stairs.

The voices stopped, and then there were whispers.

"Will you fuck off!" shouted Jack.

"You better go," Catherine said to them downstairs. "I thought this might happen."

"Will you be all right?" they asked.

"Yes."

They withdrew reluctantly. He heard her apologizing to them outside. He switched the light off again and climbed into bed. He heard her moving through the house. Eventually she came into the study and switched the light on.

"Turn the light off," he said, keeping his back to her.

"Let me in beside you," she demanded.

"No."

"Jack, can I go to bed now?"

"No!" he said savagely.

"I'm going to bed now," she said. He could feel her coming closer. "I must sleep," she pleaded.

"I'm not stopping you," he said coldly.

"I just felt I owed them an explanation."

"I don't want to know," he said.

"It's my career, Jack. They just wanted to be friendly."

She reached an arm round his neck.

"No!" he screamed.

"Please Jack, let's not fight. We are going away together tomorrow."

"You're going on your own," he said. "I'll not be going with you."

The light went off. She ran downstairs cursing him.

*　　*　　*

389

In the morning he woke to find her standing startlingly nude by his bed in the study. Her sunny bush sat high and transparent on her long legs, her small breasts were white and cold. There were red weals across her stomach and shoulders from where she'd lain in sleep awkwardly across some unmade bed. He turned his back on her nakedness.

She laid a hand on his shoulder.

"Jack," she said, "I'm freezing. Let me in beside you."

"No," he said.

She cursed him and went back to her room. Sometime later she was back.

"Jack," she said, "I'm really sorry, I really am. Please talk to me."

"No," he said, "I can't take any more."

"You disgraced me last night, do you know that?"

"Just fuck off, Catherine, and don't come back."

She went away again. The next time she came to his room she was partly dressed and smelt of male bodyspray. She laid a hand on his forehead. "Please, Jack, forgive me. Please let me lie beside you."

"No."

"What am I to do with the other ticket?"

"Bring Helen, bring anyone you want."

"Jack. Jack. I can't go away without your blessing," she said.

He remained quiet. She moved round the bedrooms as she packed her bag. Then she sat on the bed again.

"Jack, please." She was crying.

But he would not look at her. She stood at the door of the study.

"You'll be sorry," she said.

He turned and looked at her.

"I know I'll be sorry," he said.

33

Popular Songs

Now Jack, on certain nights, would find the sexual scent of Catherine on the breeze. But he could not reach her. She was off on another island, and he was trapped on his. The more she stayed away from him, the stronger she would get. A note arrived a few weeks later telling him to send her mail to Dublin. Then another note came to say she was coming to collect her belongings. He stayed out of the house for four days so that she could do that without him being there.

On the fourth day she arrived with her mother. She stepped out of the Lada. She looked brown and beautiful and not his. Though she was still in her fifties, Maisie's hair had gone totally grey. Little worry lines had etched themselves in folds beneath her eyes. She looked at Catherine in consternation when Jack appeared.

"I thought you might like a hand to move your stuff," he said.

"No, thank you," said Catherine. "We can manage fine."

"Hallo, Mrs Adams," he said.

"Hallo," she replied and stepped inside.

"Catherine," said Jack.

"I'd be grateful if you'd leave this house as soon as you can," she said. "I am sure you are aware that none of my family can stay here while you remain."

She put her head down like a goose and sped by.

In her absence, life became one grey hallucination. He was waiting for his body and his brain to return to normal. He phoned the theatre and spoke to Eddie. "Things are going well," Eddie said. "We have found the money, we should go into rehearsal in a few months."

"Will you be using Catherine?"

"I think we will, Jack."

A few sober days passed. Some self-respect would return. They asked him to return to the boat, but he said, "I can't, I'm working." He made plans to leave, and yet there seemed no place to go. And her smell was on the breeze, the fresh smell a body brings in from the outside world. A ripe, perfumed presence would slip through the room. A teasing whiff of her frustration. Then he could actually feel her bed down at night beside him.

As he lay in bed her body-presence would float past. Warm. Protestant. Seductive. He kissed the place where her face would have been. Now at last apart, whatever the hurt, at least they were themselves.

Now that she was gone, he did not move as one person through the day. Walking the street of Belmullet he would hear a laugh he'd think was hers. Then would start the search. He'd go from pub to pub – shifty, transparent, bad company, nervous – searching for her. His jaunty conversation would become deadly earnest. Have you seen her? Oh yeah, she had been in town. Collecting her things. Oh, she was happy, they said.

She said she was happy?

She did.

If he turned a corner he expected to see Catherine. Some days he'd stay out of the house and stop with Thady. He imagined that if he stayed away she might return. While the boat went to sea without him, panic-stricken, he watched the house from the dunes. The rain would blow. He'd get drenched. She'd not come. Then one day she did.

He saw the light go on in the house. He ran back.

She was walking down the path to the Lada carrying some clothes she'd left behind. As they approached each other his heart and her heart beat furiously.

They recognized each other, not with a start but with a fatalistic shudder, for that meeting was not by chance. The meeting had occurred in the mind over and over. It had happened long before it had taken place. And as they walked by each other they were already preparing for the next encounter.

She did not speak. He called her name.

He put his hand on her arm. She shook it off.

"Catherine, please."

"No," she said. She pulled away.

For her, it was necessary to show no affection. If he was suffering, then that was good. She wanted him to suffer. His suffering lightened hers. He sat in the house dreaming of making a new beginning while, estranged and angry, she drove back to Dublin. He waited on the phone to ring. She stood remote at the furthest point of his consciousness, at the end of a long tall corridor which had no sides.

For days he searched the peninsula looking for a house to rent. He stood under thatched roofs, galvanize roofs, and despaired at the thought of starting a new home. It seemed an impossibility.

"Move back in here, can't you?" said Thady.

"No, I must have my own place."

"And you should come back out with us."

"When I get myself sorted out."

He stood in the house of the postmistresses waiting on the sergeant to arrive with the dole. The homely unemployed sat round *céilidhing* before a roaring fire. He'd take down directions to cottages and the names of owners who were selling. Then one night Bernie Burke, the old fisherman, took him up to the last cottage at Aghadoon. It sat on a green hump of land above a steep fall into the sea. They walked through the three rooms by candlelight.

"I'll take it," said Jack. "How much is the rent?"

"I don't want to rent it. I want to sell it."

"Well I'll buy it."

"Have you the cash?"

"In a few days."

"Four thousand and it's yours."

"Done."

393

"You'll see your time out here," Bernie Burke said, as he closed the door and handed Jack the key.

Then he returned to the Adams' house and began the nightmare of constructing their next meeting. He packed his things. Bought blankets and sheets and a tilley-lamp in Belmullet. Phoned Eddie and asked for the advance to be sent on. He moved down to the cottage in a gale and set a row of oleria cuttings round the garden.

He lay on a thin mattress on the rusted iron bed of the previous owner. Under it were yellow piles of *Irish Independent*s from the fifties sitting on the damp cobbled floor. With candles burning on an upturned tea chest, he read the old newspapers. Vigils to Knock, Mr De Valera, Lyon's Tea. There was a drawer with letters from Scotland and the States. In the dark the storm pressed home. Unclean wings slapped on the galvanize roof. The furies took their seat upon the midnight pillow. He was afflicted. He let his beard grow. He felt the peninsula was going through a spell of speaking evil of him. Everything felt evil to his senses. What was once candescent burnt not at all.

He was the deer with the beard, the tragelaph, whining each night for the return of his beloved who he himself had sent away. On certain nights the breeze would carry the heat-smell of the lady he loved to his bed. The house smelt of goat piss. He lolloped about, only waiting for the day to end. Then, at night, Catherine slipped under the sheets. A goatsucker, she milked him. The sound of the tilley went up into a whine. The time spirits sent dreams to confuse him. He'd wake to find that red whorls, itching like mad, had appeared on his thighs.

A new day began. Stationary above the green sea, a wisp of cloud hung below the level of the house. Boats stirred beyond. He walked down the white road that was fenced and wired on each side. Sheep sheltered in a dyke from the wind. The road turned yellow and creamy. Suds flew up over the cliffs from the Seagull's Rock. Rain fell, beating a left–right dance rhythm on the surface. The cloud dispersed into thin air.

Seaweed glided past.

Rain went by the window in waves. He cleaned each room to find his way to the front room again. A great fondness went through him for the dozen or so pictures – the Madonnas, the Rose of Mystica, the Child of Prague, Our Mother of Perpetual Succour, the Crucifixion – that lined the walls. A farmer dropped off twenty plastic bags of turf. Then, that weekend, Thady appeared with cement and sand on a tractor. Jack and Thady started to break up the damp, cracked floors with a sledge hammer. By the light of a tilley-lamp Jack stood in the evenings mixing concrete with a spade from sea sand and gravel. The line of mountains on the mainland hardened into a deep evening blue. The mountains went perfectly still. The air filled with last birds. Then, in his new home, her smell came on the breeze again.

Thady rode off into the dark.

He began to imagine that they would meet on a certain street in Dublin. He planned the encounter meticulously. He could see the street in his mind's eye – the parked cars, the green canopies over the two Italian cafés, the windows of the various clothing manufacturers filled with curtains and fabrics for dresses, the mannequins wearing orange and blue, the antique shop below the level of the street, the iron railings, the newspaper seller under his canvas, the sandwich bar, the wet pavement. She would have just come out of the pub he was walking towards. They would be taken unawares. They would look at each other as they had the day he'd stepped off the train in Belfast.

Then, as he began to imagine her smile, the vision faded.

For he did not know what would happen then. His stomach was giddy as he saw her falter.

One day he walked the road from Aghadoon, past the thatched cottages, the wreck of a car sitting snug in a small quarry, the Church of the Holy Family, the mobile homes behind brick walls, and slipped on to the Ballina bus. As they drove east his conviction grew that he would meet Catherine at the corner of South William Street in Dublin. As he sat in the train, snippets of their life together went through his mind. The most outrageous things and the most banal.

When he alighted in Connolly Station he had no doubt that she would be there as he imagined her.

But first he had a gin and tonic in the Plough bar alongside a group of Abbey technicians. Then a gin and tonic in Mulligan's among the dockers and journalists. He coughed up the white phlegm that now attended all his drinking, shoved a finger into his hip and drank a third in a pub he didn't know. The afternoon news came on the TV. He recognized the area of Belfast that was being shown.

"I used to live there," he said to the drinker beside him.

"You'd want your head examined," the man replied.

The last drink he took he could not swallow. He retched violently on the street. He crossed over at Trinity, sweating heavily. A pigeon swung out of Wicklow Street and, turning to the right, flew low up Grafton Street over the heads of the advancing, retreating pedestrians. He walked up Wicklow Street, then turned left. Everything was as he visualized it, except perhaps for the pedestrians about their business. He looked into each face as you'd look at the names of stations flying past from a train.

The railings came to an end on his left. Now was the moment. He walked like a man with a fine sense of purpose. He was about some urgent business. He lit a cigarette and looked at the sky. He asked someone the time. I have an arrangement, he said. But she did not appear. Yet he had so convinced himself she would be there that he traversed the street countless times.

He walked into a bar he knew she used.

"Where's Catherine?" the barman repeated his question. "I saw her here – when was it? – oh, yesterday."

Jack nodded. He understood. He was a day too late. This was how it would be from now on, he knew. They would arrive at a place where they thought they would meet. But they would arrive a day early, or a day too late. Soon it would be a year too early, or a year too late. But what length of time it was made no difference. He would imagine a place and go there to find she had just been, or hear, in the future, that she had just stepped through the door after he was gone.

He sponged smooth the wet cement floors. Threw bucketfuls of sea gravel on the path. And took a dead crow down out of the chimney.

And now came the turn of popular songs. In his cottage by the sea he would listen to the radio with great attention. He'd prop a transistor on the bedside table and search till he found music from the sixties and country-and-western songs. A rush of sentiment would go to his head. He'd feel a great benign sadness. If he turned the radio off, in came the sound of the September ocean growing towards the full. He knew that somewhere inland she'd have her record player going. Her songs would be intelligent and sophisticated, while his were belligerent and sentimental.

At five in the morning the radio was a cache of memories.

There came a time when he thought she had slipped away. He could not know what she was doing at all.

Some thin psychic line between them had snapped.

Now came the sound of a quarrel from the past. He saw Catherine's face switch from hurt to sadness. He heard the static of raised voices. The torch of hatred from an eye. But mostly the awful sound of his voice pleading his case. The malignant cries of blame, and then nothing, absolutely nothing, except a radio tuned to popular songs until the dawn brought short newsflashes that became extended news bulletins, then there was talk of traffic congestion; advertisements shrieked through his brain, the radio studio became smaller and smaller, he felt the wary consciousness of the early-morning announcers as they slipped a new day on to the turntable, and began, at short intervals, reading out the time.

When he turned the radio off for a second there would be a thunderous echo through the room. Then, after a while, a timid silence. It was like he and the radio had travelled out on a boat. They had made a night-crossing together. They had survived. Despite the moments he had suddenly switched the radio off

397

because he thought someone was at the door, when he had lowered the sound because of someone at the window, or because he had heard someone in the other room, they had landed.

He bought a gas oven and had it delivered, but had not as yet taken a gas canister home. He cooked on the open fire with a frying pan, but mostly lived off toast. Toast and gin and bread buttered with black layers of Marmite. Then he'd walk the fields down to Corrloch and stand guard on the dunes waiting on the lights that would signal her return.

He knew she wasn't coming, and it didn't matter that she wasn't coming. This, too, had to be gone through. He woke up in the chair beside the dead fire in the kitchen of the cottage and saw the bottle of vodka on the table. Where it came from he could not answer. He saw a leaf pinned neatly to the window like a musical note. From somewhere inland it had been blown against the pane during a storm, and stuck there.

He filled a glass and sat. A blast of cold damp air hit the back of his upper arms. The leaf stayed pinned to the window, marking the highest note the storm had reached. At the thought of the loneliness ahead he'd grow dizzy and euphoric. There'd be lumbering and dissolving. The closed door. The damp carpet. Sootfall.

Walls running with condensation. Then, for a moment, the memory of corncrakes. Then one day no corncrakes.

34

Happiness

He painted the gables of the house with lime and cement, and scraped the weeping walls in the bedroom down to the original stone. Early October light came crashing across the silent sea towards the door. His cottage seemed from a distance to be riding the waves. The air was like champagne in the north wind. He installed a bucket for a toilet in one of the abandoned sheds in the back garden.

He came down one morning and discovered a rat sitting in the embers of the fire. The rat flew up the chimney. In the warm ashes he found two potatoes, well chewed, that the rat had carried over from the vegetable box.

When he opened the door, a wild cat was lying on her back, dusting herself.

"That's right," he said to the cat.

He travelled back to Leitrim for a weekend. Dr Ferris and Ma Ferris and himself ate Sunday dinner in a hotel in Bundoran. From across the street came the sound of a bingo announcer calling out numbers, while at the other end of the dining room a bunch of Ireland soccer fans were singing.

"You're not drinking," said his mother.

"No."

"That's good. It will do you good."

"How is that girl Catherine?"

"She's fine."

With his father hunched over the wheel and his mother perched precariously in the passenger seat, they drove him back dangerously and slowly to Belmullet in the roaring Volkswagen. Cassettes slid along the floor. An accordion in the boot wheezed as they took long corners. The moment they arrived, Daisy leapt out of the car and sat at the gable end of the cottage. The cat came over and perched beside him.

"I'll keep the dog," Jack said.

His mother peered into the house.

"They have terrible lives in Mayo, glory be to God," she said sadly. "No light and no electricity. It makes a body think Leitrim is not so bad. And how is poor Thady?"

"Fine mother."

"Aye," she said, "the poor soul."

Without going beyond the front door, she sat back into the car, disdainful and perplexed.

"I don't know what took you out here," she said.

"When the weather gets good we'll come and see you," the doctor said. His mother gave her son a polite nod as the Volkswagen, with a blast of its exhaust, pulled away into the cloudy evening.

It was raining. Daisy, who was now slightly arthritic, had grown a wizened grey beard. He perched and tried to scratch himself. He lifted a back paw awkwardly to a downcast ear, shook uncontrollably and fell on his rump. He howled lonesomely.

With Daisy by his side, Jack walked up to the forts on the cliffs above Aghadoon.

The sea had risen wide and high. The moon came and went behind clouds that dotted the blue sky like bruises. He missed the landscape even as he walked through it, as much as he had missed her while she was with him. All the weight of the responsibility had somehow shifted to him.

The spiritual numbness was entire. He had handed his entire being over to the care of another. He should not have done it. The centre had shifted. The islands were leaving.

Each morning he woke early, tried to stifle his panic, then walked out the back for a while, set the fire, fed the dog, breakfasted, washed in a bucket of warm water, and read in front of the fire.

At the sound of the post van coming up through the valley he was on his feet. He had already written to Catherine. He had written a very businesslike letter saying he would light a fire once a week in her house. He told her where he had left her key. He described the cottage he'd bought. He wished her well in the forthcoming play. *I'll not intrude*, he wrote to reassure her.

And I'm sober, he wrote. *Let's grow old and sober together.*

But no post from her came. The van would swing away well before it reached the road that led to his house.

A dead seagull fell at the back window. A crate containing two rotten dogfish was left at the back door. What were these signs? Each night he masturbated, and thought of her masturbating; he imagined her fingers flicking her groin at a giddy tempo till he came with a low moan that made the old dog on the mat before the fire start to howl.

"Aisy, Daisy," he shouted from the bedroom.

Meanwhile he waited for word. But nothing came. Once under a stone at the pier of the gate he found a subscription request from a missionary group in Africa addressed to the previous owner of the cottage. That was all.

In the afternoon he walked the three miles to Corrloch to O'Malley's bar and drank coffee that disorientated him. He sat there one afternoon before a gas fire and listened. He ordered a Smithwicks beer. It had no head. No bubbles. The froth was flat and yellow-covered. He drank more coffee.

He began to piss every few minutes. He walked past the Adams house to see was there any sign of life. But the house was cold and dark. He stood by the window and peered in. He was startled to see the wild reflection of his face. He stepped back frightened.

He walked the white road through the night. Unable to sleep, he'd go out for a piss and watch the lights of the few cottages that lay beyond him in Aghadoon.

"Eddie," he said.

"Ha-ho."

"Eddie," he said again. "Have you cast the play?"

"I have."

"Is she in it?"

"She is."

"Well I don't fucking want her in it."

"It was you asked me to arrange it, for Christ's sake."

"Well, I've changed my mind."

"Are you drunk or what?"

"What's that to do with it?"

"Well it's too late now. She's in it and that's that."

"Fuck you, Eddie," he said. "You can't have the play. Do you hear me?"

"I hear you and I think you're fucking crazy."

"I don't want her in it, do you hear?" he shouted, and slapped down the phone. He stood in the hallway of the hotel and glared at the gardener. The moment he most dreaded had come. "What the fuck are you looking at?" he shouted at the gardener in the Erris Hotel. Then he called for more whiskey.

He woke at one o'clock.

He walked to the kitchen opening all the windows of the cottage as he went. He boiled the kettle. Then the hangover struck. Suddenly he felt a burning pain in his lower back. "Good Jesus," he said. The first bottle he found he drank from. Each move he made re-echoed in his mind. He drank the last of the *poitín*. He made toast. He went down the garden to the toilet. All the grass and the small shed stank of piss. He vomited once, two, three times. In the kitchen he rinsed his mouth. He found an old glass of whiskey and drank it. Then he rinsed his mouth again.

I've fucked everything up, haven't I, he thought, as he set off for Belmullet. Every few yards he stopped to puke. It took him hours to walk to town in the driving wind. Immediately he entered the bar he ordered a double gin.

"Will you have one?" he asked the gardener.

The gardener stood up and left.

"What's wrong with him?" he asked Hugh.

The emptiness struck again. It seemed, as he stood in the cold back room of the bar, all the props that had been used to preserve the illusion had been withdrawn. The emptiness seemed per-petual. Yet he felt something would give, something would break the cycle and allow them to be their natural selves again. Even if that self was diminished.

He wanted to beg forgiveness but did not know how. He must wait for her letter to arrive. He sat down. He got up and phoned Eddie. "Look," he said, "forget all about what I said."

"I will."

"You didn't tell her?"

"No."

"Sorry about that, Eddie."

He thought some form of death was approaching, one that he would survive, and after that he would know his limitations. Whatever he expressed now would be visited on him later in some recess of his mind. He stood and looked at his hands. They were pulsating again. He smelled the damp from his clothes. The corridor was forming.

The next day he woke to a land with no horizon. He found that the whole house and landscape was reduced to a mere dot in time. He did not think he could survive one minute. Then he survived the minute only to find that the clock had begun another. And then he knew, with a sense of furi-ous sadness, that this would be followed by another minute, and another, and throughout each one he would be like he was now, only worse, for each second would – though the same in the mathematical sense – have increased in psychical length.

He was trapped within ever-increasing particles of time that were the same in shape and distance and size, and yet their interior was endless. His despair became greater than ever his passion had been. His mind was making each second into an eternity.

He was gripped by single hallucinations.

A dog, his dog, vomited a wad of fat on the doorstep of the house. It lay there steaming.

* * *

He wrote to Catherine. *Please come back to me. I want you. I am sober*, he wrote.

He dropped the letter off in Corrloch and went into O'Malley's bar and bought a bottle of vodka. He walked across the fields with the dog and lay down on the old bed.

He woke to find a mirror-image of himself seated in a chair at the other end of the room. The other fellow did not look wise. Jack rose disheartened, only to find that he kept meeting after-images of himself in the small rooms of the cottage. When he suddenly turned he got a sense of himself where he had stood before. When he raised a hand to his face the action continued long after it had finished. He could feel the back of a chair pressed tight against his spine minutes beyond the moment he had risen from it. Though he stood, he could still feel the chair beneath him. He saw himself seated in the chair. Then from the chair he looked across at his own standing figure. He could see himself sitting there, scared, heavy-limbed, weighed down white-faced, shivering, because that person, too, was recalling where he had been a moment before.

Was this death, he wondered, when the time came that he did not know in which of the images his consciousness rested? Which was him he did not know.

Scattered round the room were representations of himself, and each viewed the other with trepidation. To go anywhere was to assemble a train of disparate images and fragmentary moments that moved along with him. First he'd wait on the image to catch up with him. In triplicate he moved from the chair to the middle of the floor, to the door. Each self looked at the other to see who was at the fore. Habitual movements, that were once natural, now appeared strange and distorted. Any movement increased his anxiety, and yet to remain still was even more terrifying for then the waiting made the horror in each image climax in his mind. The one mind was shattered into pieces. The pieces were stored in these ghosts that hovered round.

He waited, they waited behind him, the door closed twice, his feet came down the steps many times. Breathing furiously, he walked. Then, he waited on the others to catch up with him.

This series of deep-breathing ghosts moved down the white road.

Objects took on other presences. For a certain amount of time the objects remained what they were – chairs, stones, shadows, a holy picture, a bend in the bed, a bottle – then there would be a slight alien encroachment, a vague déjà-vu, but before they could entirely become something else, the hint of change receded.

There was a tilt, a moment of horror. Then the irrefutable presence of the object took over again. A chair soon had a gagging, stifling presence like a clamp.

Then it began to change, to merge with its background. For a minute he thought he had moved forward, but the next reflection in his mind's eye showed he had stayed still. The same image remained. He had felt the urge to go, but he had not moved. And though he looked the same, he was not the same. The chair was in a different space. He was in a different space. This was the difference. Then he realized that space was provided by thought. So he tried to fill that space with comforting things. But sometimes the exact same retinue of resentment and nothingness would present itself. Then came a grand spasm of panic.

What was worse, he had no pity for himself. Some cold part of Jack Ferris viewed his disorientation and his collapse without compassion. As he sat in his shirt by the fire in late autumn, with cold knees and thighs, and a mind obliged to consider itself, some cold ghost turned aside.

It was this ghost that took him outside. A whiff of turf smoke told him that there were others about. When he saw a trail of turf smoke going up from a neighbour's house he knew that at the foot of it was another soul warming itself by the hearth, in britches or frock, easeful.

As he stood out on the moist grass watching his cottage, his head grew enormous, and the parts of his body under his shirt became moist and wavery, then they too became enormous. The sky went back and forth. He dragged the bags of bottles along the front wall. Then he dragged them across the garden and put them round the back. He looked up. There was no smoke coming from his cottage. That meant there was no soul in his house. All of a sudden he realized that the consciousness he inhabited was of a mean, limited kind.

The skipper met him on the road as he was setting off for Corrloch.

"Jack," he said, "have you finished with the writing?"

"I think so."

"Good. I need you out on the *Blue*."

"When?"

"Tomorrow. We could get in a couple of weeks before the storms. The forecast is good."

He would have refused but could not. De Largey came for him in a car. They drove down the valley in silence. They went to sea for two weeks after the flatfish – plaice, turbot, white sole. It was a sober, spiritual time. He was standing one morning by the skipper in the wheelhouse looking towards the Skegs. On the radio various voices of other fishermen were cajoling, complaining, cursing, talking of the forthcoming storms. Their voices were always in the background, and sometimes the sound of the radio would drown the sound of the sea. Then suddenly, as he and Thady were cutting slices of white bread, Jack heard Catherine's voice.

"Calling the *Blue Cormorant*."

The strange feeling of her personality at the other end of the radio unnerved him. Each nuance was hers, and yet not hers. She was present in the small engine room in a disembodied way, full of tact, irony and sounding genteel.

"That's for you, I'd warrant," said the skipper.

"That's Catherine," said Jack, disbelievingly.

"The Adams girl?"

"Aye."

"You have to cherish the ladies," said the skipper, and he cut the engine.

Theo De Largey and the other fishermen looked in to see what was wrong. The skipper held his finger to his lips. They all moved out of the wheelhouse.

"Jack," she said, "are you there?"

"Jack Ferris here. Over."

"When will you be coming in?"

"Friday at eight. Over."

"Oh. That's a pity. Did you get my letters?"

Jack looked round and whispered into the mike: "No. Over."

"That's strange. You should have had them by now."

"They haven't arrived, Catherine. Over."

"You don't sound like yourself."

"Neither do you. Over."

"Have you been drinking?"

"No," he lied. "Over."

"Well, that's wonderful. You sound very businesslike. Over."

"Under the circumstances, so would you. Over."

"Am I embarrassing you?"

Her voice, filled with static, cut through the quiet, while the boat drifted in a calm east wind on a sea that was suddenly without landmarks, on a day that could have belonged to any of the seasons, in a sea that could have been any sea, until the Skegs drifted into sight again. The men smiled at his embarrassment. The feeling he got when he heard her voice was of pride and closeness. That the skipper should cut the engine that Jack might listen seemed a comradely thing to do.

"I've made my mind up what to do. I'm sure you'll be glad to know."

"You have? Tell me. Over."

"It's all in the letters I wrote."

"But I haven't received them. Over."

The radio gave a hoarse crackle. A whistle blew. A sound like a strimmer went through the airwaves.

"What did you say? Can you please repeat the message, Catherine? Over."

"I can't hear you properly. I'm going now."

"When will I see you? Over."

"I'll be down next weekend. I'll leave a letter in the house."

"See you, then. Over."

"Goodbye, Jack. Over."

"Goodbye, Catherine. Over."

When her call ended, the skipper started the engine up again.

They went on. She was never mentioned. It was as if a fantastic sea-animal had been sighted. They had circled it. Then it dived. Then they went on.

He lifted the key out from under the stone and threw open the door of the old light-keepers' house. He stepped into the hallway and found the letter for which he had prepared himself waiting inside the hall door. It had slipped off the hall stand onto the ground. With the envelope in his hand, he stepped into the kitchen. Unwashed dishes from an unfinished meal sat on the table. A black jumper belonging to Catherine was thrown over a chair. He touched the dark wool. He marvelled at its familiarity and warmth. He lifted the envelope. When he saw how she formed her letters, her presence came very slowly to him. He stood for a split-second with a marvelling look on his face.

Then his heart began its furious beat. He kissed the damp envelope and tore it open. *It was good to hear your voice. I hope you remember your promise to me. We must stay sober. And I have to admit I'm also fighting off wretched imaginings that someone else will be enjoying you in my place – but I'm trusting you, treading thin ice in the hope that some day we'll be skating along without fear.*

I love you.

He was possessed by a terrible sensation that he was deluding himself. He could not believe it. He searched round in his mind for the signs of insanity, but there were none. He was in the kitchen of the old light-keepers' house on Mullet peninsula. It was blowing sand. His world had been magically restored. The nightmare was over.

Jack, she had written, *I love you and want to be with you. We have a break this weekend and I'll be down to see you. There are other people and we could be with them. But we know we want to be with each other. Let's grow old and sober together.*

He saw himself waiting on the new bridge the following afternoon. He saw her alight from the car and begin running towards him. Overcome with happiness he sat there in the December dusk. He hung the cloth out to dry on the line. The bark of a dog flew by.